WHERE LIGHT IS A PLACE

WHERE LIGHT IS A PLACE

A NOVEL

Beverly Conner

Adams Street Press
Tacoma, WA
2013

This book is a work of fiction, and any resemblance to persons living or dead is purely coincidental. Manhattan Beach and its Pier are real.

A portion of this book appeared in slightly altered form in *Nine by Three: Stories* by Beverly Conner, Hans Ostrom, and Ann Putnam, published by Collins Press, University of Puget Sound, 2011.

Adams Street Press
Tacoma, WA

ISBN 978-1480233997

To Terry,
who embraces light

WHERE LIGHT IS A PLACE

Nineteen forty-eight. If you were young and understood your world from newsreels, it could seem as if everything important (like the War) had already happened. How could you guess the Soviet Union would soon test its first A-bomb? Or that McCarthy would tell Truman the State Department was riddled with communists? True, W.H. Auden had won the Pulitzer Prize in poetry for The Age of Anxiety, *but poets, the newscaster chirped from the black-and-white movie screen, were seldom larky fellows. Even grown-ups sat in the dark, not imagining loyalty oaths or a swelling Hollywood blacklist. And Korea was still oceans away in most minds. So the present moment held people like the hesitation between breaths, the trough between waves. Like latency before adolescence, it was a time of treading water.*

Prologue

ONLY A MONTH AFTER SEVENTH GRADE had started at Las Olitas Junior High, Palmer McNeil lay stomach-down, baking on the sultry autumn sand of Manhattan Beach, a white-sun town bordered by the green Pacific. On one side lay her seven-year-old sister Maggie and on the other the tanned blond boy who lately turned Palmer's pulse to flutter kicks—three California-born babies on three well-washed towels.

By summer's end even Palmer, with her freckles and fair skin, had tanned to a slight glow, her dark hair, like Maggie's, sun-bleached at its tips. As the Saturday afternoon dozed past three thirty, other kids, some of them also trailing younger sisters or brothers, headed for home, but Palmer wanted to stay as long as JJ was bedded down in the hot sand beside her.

For nearly a week Maggie had been pestering Palmer to take her out into water over her head. Palmer had put her off, for no particular reason beyond the fact that five years lay between them, so she could. Besides, Maggie was still pretty young to take into deep water, even if she was a sturdy dog-paddler.

Palmer felt the scatter of fine sand across her calves. Maggie was restless, and Palmer wanted to head off her sister from asking yet another time. Anyway, JJ seemed ready to leave, his chin propped now on a forearm, one hand idly sifting sand, the mica glistening and blowing slightly as a late-afternoon breeze came up.

Palmer rolled onto her side and lazily pushed herself up. Maggie was burying her sister's feet in a desultory way. "Well, do you want to go in or not?" Palmer asked her. She jerked her head toward the surf and briskly brushed off her legs. "I guess this is as good a time as any."

All the little kids begged for this adventure, since they were forbidden to venture past their waists and not even that far if the undertow was strong. Maggie often dreamed of undertows, especially after a long day at the beach when her little brown body, sunburned and waterlogged, replayed at night the rhythms of waves pulling at her legs. She'd long known the difference between an everyday sort of undertow—the kind that was fun, trotting you back into the surf—and the bad ones on rough-water days when the beach slanted steep and dangerous, and your first step into the surf was already too deep.

Palmer noted the full tide with the surf running high, but the undertow still seemed mild. Teenage boys were bodysurfing. Few had the cash to buy the heavy, redwood surfboards they coveted, let alone a car to transport six-foot boards between home and water, one end poking pridefully out a car window.

Some days the surf was rough enough to keep the little kids digging moats and building castles above the waterline. But as twelve-year-olds, Palmer and her friends skipped going to the water only on the darkest days when the ocean turned to slate and the waves rose high enough to spray fishermen on the Pier—waves that held their crests as they moved toward shore, then peaked before pounding into a backbreaking froth that could catch a swimmer and beat her into the sea bottom. More than once, Palmer had her bathing cap ripped off her head. Girls joked about losing the tops of their swimsuits in a wild surf.

One boy had his neck broken in fifth grade when a wave carried him high into shore and dumped him headfirst into shallow water. He'd worn a neck brace the rest of the summer and half the school year. But by now kids Palmer's age were good at gauging weather and surf, their instincts telling them what could be risked. It was a point of pride: only tourists got in trouble.

Palmer stuffed her hair into her bathing cap, holding the white rubber away from each ear to make room, snapping the strap beneath her chin. Maggie's hair was a mop of saltwater tangles. Palmer had started wearing a cap at the beach only this year, along with her first two-piece suit that shimmered now in the sun like a pale peach shell.

Except it wasn't quite her first, though she tried to forget the trouble over the original suit back in late May; "one more brouhaha," Daddy had called it. Mother had taken Palmer to *Jean's Apparel*, and Palmer had picked out a two-piece, navy-blue Catalina in the newest latex stretch fabric, really more than they could afford, but Mother said it was time for a grown-up bathing suit.

The first time Palmer wore the suit to the beach, she carefully rinsed it out afterwards and hung it on the line to dry. Before the sun had set, the suit turned a mottled purple, like a bruise against the sky. Palmer had actually cried. She couldn't wear such an ugly, faded thing; she'd rather go back to her old one-piece. In fact, the old suit had looked better. Mother hugged her and promised they'd take care of it, but she had that nervous look on her face, and her blue eyes had seemed to go pale. Palmer wiped her tears away quickly.

Mother had started drinking first thing the next morning, and by the time they walked into the store with the bathing suit, she was bristling with outrage.

"May I help you?" The saleswoman was about Mother's age, but very tan. She wore a navy skirt with a white blouse, a blue silk scarf knotted at her neck. Gold earrings dotted her ears. The woman's nails gleamed with a dark red that matched her lipstick. Mother's lipstick, a pink shade, was crooked, and Palmer swallowed against the small panicked birds that seemed to flutter in her stomach.

"I need to speak to the manager," Mother said, her feet planted slightly apart for balance, making her look ready for war.

The saleswoman's eyes narrowed. "I'm the only one here right now. What seems to be the problem?"

Mother was pulling the faded suit from a paper grocery bag.

Palmer wished they'd kept the cream-colored bag that had *Jean's Apparel* printed in dark-green letters. Half the suit fell onto the carpeted floor, and Palmer scooped it up. Mother snatched it away and thrust the suit at the woman. "Look at this!"

"Yes?"

"*Yes?* That's all you can say about shoddy merchandise that fades the first time it's worn?"

The saleswoman ran one blood-tipped nail over the fabric. "Our bathing suits are not guaranteed to be 100% colorfast. Naturally, the darker colors—"

"Well, why the hell didn't somebody mention that when we bought the damn thing?" Mother was leaning toward the woman, who was trying to stand her ground.

"Did you dry it out of the sun? It should be hung in the shade for best—"

"In the *shade*? This is a *bathing* suit! My daughter wears it in and out of the water all day long. How is it going to dry out of the sun unless she strips it off and walks around naked? Or is that also what you recommend?"

Palmer touched her mother's forearm. The old, sweetish smell steamed off Claudia in the warm shop.

"Do you have your sales slip?" The saleswoman had raised her chin slightly.

Mother took a step toward the woman, who quickly began to examine the suit again. "We bought this two days ago. The suit fit fine, and my daughter liked it. Why would we keep the receipt?" Mother shifted her pocketbook to her other arm and threw back her shoulders. "Naturally, we assume that *Jean's* stands behind its goddamn merchandise."

The saleswoman sighed. Heaven only knew what her boss was going to say. She looked at Palmer. "Would your daughter like to choose another suit in exchange?"

"Thank you," Mother said with dignity. She wobbled only slightly. Palmer's face felt stiff, even though they'd won—hadn't they?

Now Maggie scrambled up and raced for the water, sand flying behind her.

"Maybe I'll hang around for a while," said JJ when Palmer stood up. She nodded at him before starting after Maggie, who had already waded up to her knees. Together the girls splashed into the waves and quickly ducked their shoulders under to put that first cold-water shock behind them. Palmer grabbed Maggie's hand.

It was fun jumping combers together, Palmer throwing her body side-first into each wave, one arm raised high to cut a swathe so that she took the surf's force, holding tight to Maggie's hand behind her. When the water deepened, Palmer struck out in a crawl with her sister hanging onto her shoulders. Before any time at all, they were safely beyond the breakers. Even with more whitecaps than Palmer had noticed from shore, these dark-green swells were a smooth payoff for battling through the surf.

Maggie was giggling, her hand hooked in one of Palmer's pale shoulder straps, her body streaming out behind as she kicked to help propel them along. A few years back, there'd been no one to take Palmer over her head when she was Maggie's age. Daddy was frank about his distaste for the beach. But Mother? Palmer didn't know why her mother seldom left the house except to walk that small radius down Manhattan Avenue, past the library and beauty parlor, doing errands at the post office and drugstore, Wahlberg's Market, maybe Weber's Bakery, and finally the dime store before turning back towards home. It was little more than a six-block journey, round-trip. Even her AA meetings were only a few blocks away at the Community Church.

So with friends or by herself, Palmer had inched her way into deep water, first in swimming pools where she'd learned to swim with Girl Scout lessons, then in the ocean, where she practiced jumping waves and ducking her head under them.

Today Palmer was glad the waves were not so big that they'd had to duck under. It could be hard to hold onto Maggie if a wave gave them a good tumble. Before long, her sister would learn the waves, first bobbing under smaller ones and opening her eyes to look upward into the green-white bubbles, that swirl of diamonds as a wave churned overhead, to feel its pull and power so that in the calm she would know the wave had passed and it would be safe to come up.

Some kids held their noses when they ducked under, but Palmer would teach Maggie to close her nasal passages far back, like a mouth breather, to hold her breath as long as she needed and then blow out like a young whale as she surfaced. You learned to crouch or lie on your stomach, hands and forearms gripping the bottom sand that was swept smooth of shell in these southern waters. Most of the time Palmer just dove deeply, her belly skimming bottom, to let the wave roll on over her. Even so, now and then a pounder reached down to churn up sand and swimmer alike.

"Okay," Palmer said, "I'm treading water now, see? It's just like dog-paddling, except you stay straight up and down and don't go anywhere. Work your legs like a bicycle."

Maggie gulped a shot of salt water and coughed. "Let me just dog-paddle."

"Okay, but go around me in a circle so you stay close."

And like a little dolphin, her wet head jerking with the rhythm of her arms and legs, Maggie paddled fiercely in water many times deeper than she was tall. Her eyes were wide with the enormity of the sea. Palmer never took her own eyes off her sister, feeling the responsibility for where they'd traveled grow heavier. Except for the scream of a tern high above them, there was no sound out here except the ceaseless wind and water.

And Palmer suddenly saw how her parents might view this ocean adventure.

She glanced toward shore, and her stomach lurched. How could they have drifted this far out? People on the beach looked tiny, and some of them seemed to be waving. One figure detached itself, and Palmer thought she saw the Kelly green of JJ's swim trunks.

She looked back at Maggie. The water around them was roiled in an odd way, different from the usual chop. Another whitecap smacked Maggie in the face, throwing off the rhythm of her dog paddle. Palmer was beside her in two strokes.

"Grab onto my shoulders," she said. "It's time to go back." Palmer strained to make her voice sound calm, but the truth was that she'd finally snapped to their situation. How long, she wondered, had they been in this *riptide*? She was furious she hadn't noticed the river of foam that was right now sweeping them out to sea.

She peered back at the beach, hoping the lifeguard wasn't swimming toward them that very moment, his buoy streaming behind him. It would be humiliating, and besides, she was sure they could make it in on their own. Didn't the guards have to call your folks when they made a rescue? Mother would lay down a beach ban on both of them, for sure.

"Why aren't we swimming in?" Maggie yelled.

"We're in a rip." Palmer made her voice calm. "But I know what to do. Just don't let go!"

She felt her sister's fingers bite into her shoulders, but Maggie didn't make another sound. Palmer put all her energy into her crawl, breathing with every other arm pull. She was moving them parallel to the shore, as if they were swimming across a river. She could see why swimmers panicked at finding themselves so far out to sea. The ocean looked vast from here, and Palmer had a prickly sense of creature-filled depths beneath their white, kicking limbs. She'd often thought Maggie's little seal head was cute, but now she imagined the view from below—the two of them on the surface of the water, how they genuinely looked like seals. And seals were shark food.

Stay calm, she told herself, stay calm. Great Whites were so rare in these waters that the newspaper reported every shark attack, and there weren't many. Everyone knew the *real* danger, especially to tourists, was fatigue or cramps from trying to swim straight to shore against the riptide that was sweeping them toward the horizon.

Once she and Maggie could swim across and out of the rip, the swells would push them toward shore; the trick was to stay afloat. If she didn't get too tired and could keep swimming, all the better. Even so, Palmer felt the growing temptation to turn directly toward shore, like the pull of a magnet she knew she had to resist.

But in the next moment, the texture of the water turned silky. Palmer looked back at the riffled channel that was so hard to spot if you were already in it and wondered about the chances of a rip's widening, casting a net to capture them once more. She realized for the first time that gaps in ocean lore could cost lives, the realization like a wave breaking over her head.

Still she resisted the siren's lure of the shore and kept swimming parallel to the beach. Her arms felt heavy, but when she looked behind her again, the rip seemed far away. Safely out of the treacherous current, they just had the swim into shore to worry about. While they'd been swimming out of the riptide, they'd been swept even farther from the safety of the beach. Palmer longed to feel sand beneath her feet.

Glancing toward the Pier, she could see they were nearly even with the end of it, and she shivered slightly. She'd never been out this deep alone, though lots of times, she and JJ and other kids had swum as a group as far out as the Roundhouse, then turned and ridden the swells in. She was sure she could manage it alone, but she'd never before had her little sister hanging onto her back.

"We're outta the rip, Mags—headed in now."

"Okay," her sister said, teeth chattering from cold or fright or both.

Palmer knew she had to take it easy, not muscle her way through the swim. She used the slight momentum of the swells. Any other time she was so buoyant in the salt water she could tread water just by using her legs, her hands raised high above the surface—a show-off trick. But now Maggie's body hung like a bedraggled anchor behind her.

On the beach more people seemed to be gathering and waving, and Palmer thought she saw the red-suited lifeguard wading out into the shallow water. Adrenaline surged into her stroke. She kept checking her distance by looking across the water at the

Pier. They were making progress, opposite the bait house now.

The swim out had been easy and lighthearted, but now Palmer was breathing hard. Her legs felt cold, while her arms burned. The strap of her bathing cap cut into her neck. But they *were* inching toward the line of breakers, and at last Palmer felt the first strong swell lift and push them forward, then another, until she heard the first wave break behind them, and suddenly they were in the midst of them. She caught Maggie's hand and yelled, "Hold your breath!" The wave tumbled them forward, where another swell rose up, blinding them for a second to everything except high, green water. They slipped over the top before it broke. Another wave rolled them into its crest, and when they slid down the other side, Palmer was startled and grateful as hard sand brushed her toes.

Suddenly a man rose up in front of them, shaking the water from his hair. They were face-to-face with the lifeguard, and he didn't look happy.

"Didn't you kids see that rip?" he yelled. "You had no business out that far!" The guard's face was red, and he made no move to help Palmer as she pulled Maggie the last yards to where they could walk through the waves. Instead, he reeled in the torpedo buoy that streamed behind his chest harness.

"Sorry," Palmer said. She was shaking now. Cold, relief, embarrassment—one feeling after another smacked her in the face like the whitecaps only minutes before. Why did it have to be the redheaded guard, the one they called Terry? He was even cuter up close. Ever since fifth grade, Palmer had had a crush on him, always checking the lifeguard tower to see if he was the one on duty.

He scowled at her, his eyebrows one furious line above his green eyes. "You knew you were in a rip out there?"

Palmer nodded. People around them laughed and began to walk away. They'd lined up to see a rescue that had petered out. Only the little kids were hanging around to watch the lifeguard bawl these two out. The guard secured the buoy line and tucked it under his arm. He looked at Maggie, who was shivering like a little rat, then back at Palmer. His face softened to a mere frown.

"I've seen you around here, kid." It sounded to her like a warning. "You swim okay; otherwise I'd 'a been out there," he said, gesturing toward the horizon. Freckles fine as sand sprayed across his face and shoulders. "And *then* it would have been an official rescue." He didn't smile. "Don't swim out that far," he ordered Palmer, "and don't *ever* take *her* out there again."

He turned to Maggie, whose thin arms crossed her chest, clutching her elbows. "Don't go in over your head until you can swim the distance. Got that?" She nodded miserably. "Keep your feet on the bottom," he added, as if she still didn't understand. She nodded again. He shifted his stare to Palmer, then turned abruptly and marched out of the water toward the tower.

For a second Palmer was too mortified to move. The kids around them giggled until she shot them a dark look. She unsnapped her cap and pulled it off. "C'mon, let's get warm."

Someone splashed up behind them. "You okay?" JJ stood knee-deep in the water. He'd heard every embarrassing word.

"Oh, yeah," Palmer said, rolling her eyes at him. She took a deep breath and rubbed her arms, trying to relax so she'd stop shaking. "It was dumb, but I knew we were okay."

"Sure. I was watching, too. Almost swam out myself," he added.

"Thanks, but we were okay."

"Sure," he said, walking beside them, up and across the beach. When they reached their towels, Maggie dropped like a rag doll and burrowed directly into the hot sand. "Sorry," she mumbled, probably not even sure what for.

Palmer toweled off quickly, spread the towel and lay beside her. JJ threw himself down next to Palmer. "It wasn't your fault," she said to Maggie. "Just don't tell Mother, or we'll never see the beach again as long as we live, and I'm not kidding!"

Maggie nodded and wriggled deeper, her cheek against the sand. Palmer turned her head toward JJ. He reached over and squeezed her hand, his palm hot around her chilled fingers. The sun beat down on them, and Palmer closed her eyes, trying to still her trembling and shutting out the waves behind her and the deep currents in her head that still held Great White shadows, swimming like bad dreams. The onshore breeze whispered across her outstretched legs.

Gradually the screen behind her eyelids, where this drama of her own making still played out, darkened softly to violet, the way she liked to imagine the deepest parts of the ocean. Today, so far out in the water, nothing had seemed soft, but now, with her hand curled warm in JJ's, her breathing slowed and her body drifted on sun-spotted swells of approaching sleep.

Immigrant Parents

Whiskey and Los Angeles melted
blizzards out of their young,
unforgiving bones.
Loving the beach from a distance,
he hated sand beneath his fingernails
and dreamed against the pier's railing,
casting his line far
from barnacled pilings,
the one menace
he thought he could control.
While she pulled down parchment shades
like mummies' skins
to keep the long-day sun
out of the kitchen's smoky twilight
and made up stories of her life.

California Snowstorm

In January of 1949 the gods of strange weather surprised Southern California. Sometime during the night, against all climatic odds it began to snow. Mother and Daddy awakened Palmer, sleeping in the top bunk, Maggie below her.

"Look outside," Daddy whispered. "You won't believe what you see." He slid open the window in its peeling wood frame just a foot from their beds in the cramped sunroom where the girls slept in the tiny beach house.

"The Shack" they had christened it, knowing they were lucky to rent any place at all. They had spent nine months in Portland, Oregon, then moved back to California after the war had ended. "For opportunity's sake," Daddy said. "Because he lost his job," said Mother.

Now, just outside their bedroom window, snow swirled through the blackness as far as they could see, and all the while just a block and a half away, the constant rush of the surf sounded through the night air.

Palmer struggled to slide out of her bunk onto the cold linoleum floor. "What time is it?"

"About four in the morning," Daddy said, smiling up into the dark sky. Mother stood behind him, watching over his shoulder.

Maggie crawled from bed to put her arm out the window. She turned her palm up to catch the flakes and brought them like frosted lace to her tongue, eyes alight. Palmer stood transfixed beside her. The salt air smelled sweetly icy.

"I'll put on some coffee," Mother said, backing away from the open window.

Neither of the girls had ever seen snow. And though the parents had fled the storms of Ohio and Washington state years before, even they seemed stunned. The coastal snowfall that year—snow that for one night and day drifted over the beaches as if millions of seagulls had shed frozen feathers—was a California miracle.

Half an hour later, bundled into layers of clothing, they were driving through the still-dark morning to the hills of Palos Verdes to play in snowdrifts. The steam from Mother's coffee mug dimmed the inside of the windshield, and Daddy wiped at it with his bare hand, snorting impatiently and glancing pointedly at Mother's cup. Palmer could feel old ghosts rise up in the darkened car.

Before they'd left the house, each wearing two pairs of socks, their feet in rubber galoshes, the girls drank hot, sweetened coffee-milk, dunking buttered toast into their mugs.

Mother poured herself a second cup while Daddy warmed up the Plymouth. She disappeared into their bedroom, pulling the floral curtain closed behind her. Only the bathroom and the house's front entry, which both opened right into the kitchen, boasted real doors. Like many of the cottages hastily built near the beach, it was no more than a small kitchen and living room, a bedroom alcove, and a bath. The narrow sunporch that served as the girls' bedroom was the only room that faced the ocean, but the new apartment house next door—only feet away, really—blocked any view and most of the light, so that by two in the afternoon the house was dim even on the brightest summer day.

Palmer heard her mother's dresser drawer slide open. A half-minute passed, the drawer slid shut, and then Mother appeared through the curtain, her face already softened, the mug in her hand.

"C'mon, sleepyheads, stop gathering wool. Your father's waiting!"

And now, as Daddy drove slowly toward Palos Verdes, familiar landmarks turned wondrous, draped in strange, snowy shawls. He drove past the sandstone public library, past Stephen's

Bootery and Jean's Apparel for Women and the Rexall Drug, all the while muttering under his breath—"Jesus S. Christ!"—and shifting gears roughly. Mother gazed serenely through the windshield, but the set of her shoulders had squared, as if she were braced for battle.

"Don't spoil this, Daniel." She drained her mug and set it carefully by her feet.

"It's not me who needs the warning."

Palmer leaned over the front seat between them. The cadence of her father's voice signaled danger. It felt to her as if the air in the car were being swallowed up, and she took a deep breath. "Are we almost there? How far now, Daddy?"

"You getting wheezy, princess?" He glanced at Mother, blame smoldering in his eyes.

"Of course she's not! Or if she is, it's because you dragged her out of bed in this freezing—"

"Judas Priest, Claudia, here we go—"

"No," Palmer said, sweating now in her jacket and two sweaters. An asthma attack would turn them home. "I'm okay. Honest. Why don't we just stop *here* and play in the snow? This looks like a good place!"

"Here," echoed Maggie, "and I have to go to the bathroom, too."

Daddy glanced in his rearview mirror at his younger daughter, gauging her need. "In a minute, Magpie. Let's see if somebody has opened early." He swiped again at the windshield. "Okay, up there ahead."

He made a left turn into the Texaco station, and Maggie was out the door almost before he stopped. "Whoa, kiddo. Palmer, you go with your sister."

"But I don't need to!" Palmer's voice was a nervous whine. She didn't want to leave her parents alone together just now.

"I said—"

"Oh, for heaven's sake, I'll go!" But Mother had trouble opening the passenger-side door. Daddy didn't reach across to help her. Finally she shoved it hard with her shoulder. The momentum nearly toppled her out of the car, but she straightened, swung her slender legs to the side, and stood up shakily.

"It sure doesn't take much anymore," Daddy said.

Mother ignored him and followed Maggie to the restroom, her head high with wounded dignity. She called over her shoulder, "You want cigarettes?" but Daddy shook his head. She pressed her hand protectively against the bulge in her pocket. Palmer imagined she could hear the half-pint gurgle.

Daddy leaned back against the seat, and Palmer reached over to pat his shoulder, but he didn't move. Now the car seemed cold, even though Daddy kept the engine running, and Palmer could see her breath, like a warning spirit that had been there as far back as she could remember.

When they were all in the car again, Daddy drove in silence. Finally he whispered, "You've had yourself quite a snootful!" But the fight had gone out of Mother, and she slumped in the front seat, head thrown back, her hair a dark halo. Soon her mouth fell open, and she began to snore lightly.

Still, they did play in their first-ever snow until the girls' toes began to burn with cold. The snow-covered fields of Palos Verdes gleamed above the ocean, smooth as a ghostly airstrip, and below them green phosphorescence flickered in the waves that swept toward the cliffs. Daddy stood near the edge, looking through the falling snow at the surf below, until Palmer and Maggie tugged at him to come play.

Mother slept through their snowball fights, their whoops and snow angels and miniature snowmen, slept all the way home in the car, where Daddy threatened to leave her all night even if she did freeze her ass off—"Pardon me, girls"—but he finally shook her roughly and then half carried, half dragged her inside, through the kitchen and the curtained doorway of their bedroom, where Palmer saw him throw her down on the bed.

Palmer followed behind and began to take off her mother's shoes.

"I'll take care of it, princess," Daddy said and sent them off to their bunks in the pale early-morning light. They were both so cold that Palmer crawled in next to Maggie's sturdy little body, and they pressed their feet against one another's legs, squealing, until Daddy yelled for them to pipe down.

At last they warmed up and settled in for a few more hours of sleep. Everyone overslept, and Daddy left for work late, without breakfast. Mother was cross and sat in her chenille robe over coffee at the kitchen table, smoking one Camel after another. The girls stayed home from school but were glad to escape the house. Dressed warmly, they ran down to the beach to play in the snow that still carpeted the sand.

Sometime before lunch, the sun broke through the high overcast, misty at first, then brighter and brighter. And for just a few moments before the few inches of snow melted into the sand, the beach gleamed, sunstruck and blinding, a silver-white ribbon that rimmed the deep blue of the Pacific as far north and south as they could see. Like that albino snake at school, Palmer told her mother, when it had slipped out of its old skin and looked so clean and new.

Because her mother was afraid the old movie house was going to tumble into the Pacific Ocean, Palmer was no longer allowed to go to Saturday matinees at the Redondo Theater. With the way the McNeil luck ran, her mother said, the place would probably topple over on the very afternoon her daughter was sitting there in the dark, watching Joel McCrea kiss Barbara Stanwyck. Besides, there were other theaters in the beach towns strung along that half-moon of water they called the South Bay. Yes, thought Palmer, but the Redondo was the most *precarious*, a delicious word from her seventh-grade spelling list.

Restricted now to the La Mar Theater just blocks from home in Manhattan Beach, she at least escaped her parents' endless stories of the notorious Redondo, how the WPA had built that retaining wall clear back in the thirties. Probably safe enough in its time, but a double-story theater standing up to winter storms year after year? That kind of battering takes its toll, they said. Besides, you didn't have to be an engineer to see how the breakwater had changed the tide's flow. Erosion problems ever since.

Even Palmer had to admit that the white stucco building with its red roof and inlaid Mexican tiles of cobalt and yellow seemed to lean with a suicidal bent for the surf-drenched rocks below. But that irresistible element of risk was precisely why all the kids had wanted to go to the Redondo. No matter how engrossed you might be in the action on the movie screen, from time to time you'd feel the building shudder when an enormous breaker smashed against the foundation.

Sometimes, piling one imagined disaster upon another, Palmer could hardly contain her glee—though this was not something she mentioned to her mother—at the possibility of being in that darkened theater when an earthquake hit, wrenching and rolling the building and even the breakwater itself. If that wouldn't shake the old girl loose (the theater, not her mother), nothing would.

At twelve, Palmer had enough sense to realize she herself could be in some danger, but she was still child enough and brave enough to believe that somehow she could ride out the bucking of a quake, even if the building did topple over. Her mother just imagined too many catastrophes. Wasn't she also worried her husband or daughters might be out on the Manhattan Beach Pier just when an earthquake sent it crashing into the ocean, even though that concrete pier had stood up to storms and quakes for years?

Besides, Palmer had already been through a quake, and she'd been inside a movie house, too, though it had been the smaller La Mar. All she'd felt then was a little queasy—one too many Clark Bars, she figured. She hadn't known it was an earthquake until she went home. Mother and Daddy had heard about it on the radio—no injuries, the newscaster said, little damage. But Maggie looked scared and held tightly to her cat.

"The hand of glory," her grandmother Sydney had called it when she phoned from Seattle to make sure they'd all survived.

Perched on a hillside three blocks up from the ocean, the La Mar was in no danger unless an earthquake shook the whole

California coast into the ocean. Few besides her mother worried about that possibility.

These days newsreels showed the country filled with veterans who had returned to families forced to do without them during the War. In the shimmering sunlight of Southern California, husbands, sons, and fathers still looked for jobs in an overwhelmed labor market, signed up for classes at UCLA and USC on the GI Bill, and ran head-on, just like the McNeils, into the long postwar housing shortage.

Bedtime

Tired child falls around sleep's edge,
down drains, between waves of family
arguments—white jaws that chase
the night's ocean, dark
shouts and deep-current shame.
Her small hands spread like stars
against blame and restless sheets.
Weeping palms, her pillow alive
with mother-taunts, father-lies,
words that swarm the Sandman,
like biting ants that wander
far beach roads.

Spring 1949

As THE WEEKS MARCHED BY, KIDS prayed for another snowfall, but January would stand in the record books. Spring arrived early with budding hibiscus and oleander and weekend tennis. Between his job at Wahlberg's Market, his hours fishing off the Pier, and his recently begun love affair, Daniel McNeil already had little time for family life, though he swore the sun rose and set on his daughters. At night he'd drag himself home from work, and if Claudia was sober, she'd have coffee perking, and he could smell it as soon as he neared the door.

Every Saturday morning he washed the blue and gray Plymouth he called "Nellie" and took the whisk broom to the upholstery before he left for the City Hall tennis courts. He was ranked an A player on the city ladder, where he vied for the number-one spot with men both younger and bigger. Tennis suited him, from his tennis whites that Claudia kept pristine with trips to the washing machine in the basement of the apartment house next door, somehow sweet-talking the manager into letting her use it, to the symmetry of the courts glaring white under the California sun.

Lean and quick, he played mostly singles, though he could occasionally be pressed into mixed doubles, especially if the women were attractive. "Gorgeous Gussie" Moran, as the sportscasters nicknamed her, was his favorite of the national women players, the audacity of her lace-trimmed tennis panties tickling him as much as her athletic ability. Soon he would come to admire the twin Panchos—sturdy Segura and the powerhouse

Gonzales. Years later Palmer would think of her father whenever she saw the Australian Ken Rosewall—graceful and dark-haired, his shots deadly with precision.

Before Maggie was born, Claudia would come to watch some of Daniel's matches, but one afternoon Palmer, then only three, had crawled under the green wooden bench where her mother sat. A Scottie dog, already unhappy to be leashed to the leg of the bench, had snapped so close to the child's eye that Claudia decided it was safer and easier to stay at home during the long weekend hours. Besides, she never did get the hang of scoring tennis. What was the point of love equaling zero, she'd complain—a heartless system, probably thought up by some jilted man—and anyway it was just too hard to keep Palmer corralled on the court, Scottie or no.

From then on if she did happen to go along, Claudia usually gathered up her pocketbook and the straw carryall with the extra underpants and juice, and strolled beyond the wire fences and iron gates of the courts, letting Palmer play on the City Hall lawn, where the child rolled down the grassy slopes until she was half hysterical with dizziness and laughter. The ocean was two blocks down the hill, so Claudia could sit on the grass, keeping an eye on her daughter, and still gaze at the spangled water and hard-edged horizon.

When Maggie was born, Palmer was five, and probably to pacify Claudia, Daniel sometimes took his older daughter along when he played. Now he was using the newer courts at Live Oak Park, built on sand dunes north of the City Hall, the park nestled in a hollow. Long concrete stairways and landings led up from the park to a summit where city streets crested, beginning their downhill march to the ocean. On those stairs Palmer invented fairy tales and movie-star games involving royalty and dramatic entrances into foyers and ballrooms, scenes she'd seen in movies like *Gone with the Wind*.

So long as she didn't pester her father during his matches, he'd come to the stairs when he finished and act out stories with her, usually playing the courtly prince. Daniel soon christened her "princess," a name she couldn't guess was given to an untold number of daughters everywhere.

About the queen mother who now stayed back at the castle, Daniel guessed that Claudia felt jealous of the tanned, white-skirted players. Because, she would point out whenever she was hitting the bottle, he found them so "fucking fetching" he could hardly keep his "goddamned prick" in his pants. He sighed. Claudia was not a happy drunk.

But she'd been lovable when he met her over thirteen years ago now at that Hollywood party: sexy and smart-mouthed and damned good-looking. He'd been divorced for over a year, the sting nearly gone from having come home one night to an empty house: no Pauline, no furniture, no appliances or dishes or towels, not even a can of soup left in the cupboard. She'd cleaned out everything but his clothes and hadn't even left a note. She served him papers, asking for no alimony. (Judas Priest, she'd already taken everything he owned except his beat-up car.) He never saw her again. And he never did understand what had happened. Probably, he finally figured, there'd been another guy.

So when he'd seen Claudia at that party—pretty well liquored up, he realized later, but not as snarly then—he was eager to be-friend the lonely widow. When he asked about the gal with the great legs, someone told him her husband had been killed in a plane crash, one of those accidents that was never supposed to happen. Rising young artists for 20th Century Fox, he and his buddy, who owned a small biplane, had just been offered a con-tract for art direction, and with hopes soaring they went flying to celebrate.

Both men had served in the U.S. Army Air Service in WWI, cocky young pilots who came home without a scratch, but that day, in the bluest sky imaginable, with no enemy artillery to give them trouble, something had gone wrong, and they'd plum-meted into the waters off San Pedro Harbor. Claudia claimed she heard it on the news before they'd released the names, before next of kin had been notified, said she'd known it was Philip right away, even though he'd promised never to go up without telling her first.

When Claudia phoned her mother in Seattle, the operator announcing "long distance"—the code for tragedy or celebration, because such calls were too expensive for chatting—Sydney claimed to have dreamed about the crash the night before it happened.

As far as Daniel was concerned, Sydney was always coming up with these psychic predictions a day late and a dollar short. What good was foreknowledge if you couldn't warn the poor sap? In all honesty, though, he was probably prejudiced against this woman who had not liked him from the beginning and had not bothered to hide it.

"Tea leaves," she had said with a sniff. Said she'd seen Daniel's coming in tea leaves, but one time when he asked her to predict something about his job prospects, soon after he'd been laid off by Alpine Milk during the Depression, she claimed to have sworn off tea leaves. Or was it fortune-telling with cards—right after a reading where the ace of spades kept coming up and some poor schmuck had died on the spot?

Well, yes, Daniel said when she told him why she'd quit the cards, he could see how that kind of power might be unsettling, but privately he thought she was a fake and a meddler, a widow herself after Claudia's dad died young, a woman whose major contribution, from Daniel's point of view, had been the slender legs she'd passed on to her daughter. He had to admit, though, that she had her moments as a *grandmother*—his daughters seemed to think she walked on water—but for his part he was just as glad she mostly stayed put up in Washington state.

For now, he tried to ease Sydney and Claudia and even the girls out of his mind. He'd played well today, winning all three sets, though the last one had gone into a tiebreaker because he'd lost his concentration. Probably tired, he thought, though secretly he was afraid that at forty-three his legs were beginning to go. Hadn't his own dad been old by forty-five, the years of railroading taking their toll, his face scarred from cancers cut from his lip and ear?

Daniel shook off thoughts of aging and eased the car into the curb in front of Lars and Alice Norquist's apartment. He was looking forward to a hot shower and a beer before he headed home, though the image of Allie's blonde hair in its theatrical upsweep was an added treat. The Norquists lived near the courts, and while the beefy city policeman wasn't a tennis player himself, Lars often parked his squad car nearby to watch matches. That was how he and Daniel had met and soon after become drinking buddies.

Lars understood that a man liked his shower after sports, and because Daniel had once mentioned that he and Claudia had only the bathtub—more as an idle, macho comment than a real complaint—Lars had offered Daniel the amenities of his modern apartment-house shower. The beer they shared afterward usually turned into four or five—a man deserved to relax on the weekend—and by the time Daniel got home, his tennis might have stretched into an eight- or nine-hour absence.

Claudia had never liked the Norquists. A Manhattan Beach policeman didn't make a fortune, but it was a job that had paid well right through the war, offered a pension, and now in the postwar economy was paying decent money. Allie worked as a secretary at a casualty insurance office. Without children, the Norquists, unlike the McNeils, had plenty of time and money to enjoy themselves. Claudia said they didn't have anything in common, but more likely it was Allie's scarlet lips and nails, her bleached hair and thick mascara, that set Claudia off. Or maybe it was the way Claudia could smell perfume on Daniel when he came home after those long days.

Daniel rapped on the Norquists' bright-blue front door. California poppies grew in a wild border, their heads flashing against the white stucco of the apartment house. The Norquists' place seemed closer to the California life he'd imagined for himself back in Ohio after the divorce, and very unlike his and Claudia's dilapidated—well, you couldn't even rightly call it a bungalow, just a place he considered himself lucky to have rented in the first place, despite its peeling yellow paint. Even beach shacks were scarce as hen's teeth these days.

He loved the peace of the Norquists' newer and more expensive apartment—no toys scattered around, the kitchen cupboards a cool, white metal above the ceramic-tile counters, so unlike the scratched linoleum drainboards in The Shack. (Even *he* had started calling it by the nickname that hurt his pride, though none of them knew that because he joined in the joke, a joke that showed his three girls were brave about—he heard Sydney's voice—"coming down in the world.")

Suddenly Allie pulled open the front door, startling him. She smiled and framed herself for his view, seeming to have fash-ioned herself after a Technicolor Lana Turner, everything tight or bright. Today she wore red shorts over a white one-piece bathing suit, her latex-sheathed breasts pointing aggressively toward him.

Daniel grinned at her, and his cock stirred. They were nearly the same height, but where he was all sinewy cord and muscle, Allie was soft and voluptuous, probably softer than was good for her, but Daniel wasn't complaining. They'd been attracted to each other from their first meeting down at the Knothole, when the two couples had gotten together for drinks. Claudia smelled their chemistry right away, but Lars seemed oblivious—either that or he was proud of his glamorous wife and used to men falling all over her. Maybe wearing a holstered gun at work had something to do with his confidence.

For his part, though, Daniel wasn't about to fall for Allie. She wasn't his type, too much a chippie, and besides she was his buddy's wife. Today he walked in before she could invite him, brushing her shoulder lightly with his own.

"Where's Lars?" he asked. "I didn't see his car outside."

Allie shrugged. "He got a call on his radio. Something's always going on." She sounded aggrieved and shut the door. It took Daniel a moment to adjust to the dim light of the apartment after the ferocious sun outside. Allie's perfume hung in the air. "Beer?" she asked.

Daniel nodded and followed her into the kitchen. She opened the refrigerator and her studied languor as she bent to get a couple of bottles told him she was intentionally presenting yet another view to be admired. When she turned to hand him the cold Schlitz, she smiled slowly, her lips glistening. A tinge of lipstick, like blood on a toothbrush, stained her teeth.

Daniel was just reaching into his shirt pocket for a cigarette when the back door banged open and Lars walked in, filling the kitchen with his bulk.

"Hey, buddy," he roared, "how'd you do today?" Allie handed her husband the second beer, and he kissed her cheek with the practiced air of a man avoiding makeup.

"Took three sets," said Daniel. "Can't complain."

"Hell, no. Did you play that fart Henderson?"

"He's in a different draw."

"Sure, that's right." Lars liked the action of the game but didn't really understand the mechanics of tournament play.

"How 'bout you?" asked Daniel. "What's up?"

"Domestic shit. Some couple mixin' it up good enough for the neighbors to call us. Told the guy to shape up, but until he really clobbers her, there's not much to do."

Daniel nodded. Allie had disappeared, probably to put on a blouse. In front of Lars, she still flirted but toned it down some. She walked back in holding a towel and washcloth, a sleeveless blouse, half buttoned, over her bathing suit. Lars wrapped a proprietary arm around his wife. "Clean yourself up, man, and get back out here."

Allie handed him the linens. "Plenty of hot water, as usual. Enjoy yourself."

Much as Daniel did enjoy himself around Allie, he suspected she promised more than she'd ever deliver. Besides, he didn't have room in his life for another woman. He already had Loretta, and she was as much as he could possibly want, or handle.

Their affair had begun some months back when Sydney had totaled her car speeding along Highway 99 during a rainstorm that was fierce even for the Pacific Northwest. At first it looked like her head injury might result in a tumor on her optic nerve, so Claudia took Maggie out of school and the two of them rode the Greyhound bus up the coastal length of California and Oregon clear to Seattle.

To economize, they bought only one ticket, so for two days and nights, Maggie sat on her mother's lap except when an empty seat opened up. When Claudia came back five weeks later, still holding Maggie most of the way, her chest, just below her collarbone, was black and blue from Maggie's head jostling there mile after long mile.

Sydney had recovered after time in the hospital and a lot of home nursing from Claudia. One night when Claudia called home, Sydney got on the phone to tell Daniel about being trapped in the car, how her gift of "second sight" improved after the head injury—something about a "third eye," whatever th' hell that meant—and how she'd met her long-dead husband halfway over on "the other side."

"Burl just said to me, 'Sydney, love,' he said, 'you can't come over yet,' but I said, 'Burl, I'm not going back without you,' and he said, 'That's foolish talk, because we're in different dimensions'—that's what he said: 'different dimensions.' And, of course, he was right, but I wasn't afraid for one minute—"

"Aren't you a little old for him by now?" Daniel had asked.

"What—?"

"Or has he been aging there at the same rate as you here on *this* side?"

Sydney grew quiet.

Claudia, listening in, took back the phone. "Cut it out, Daniel."

But on the night of the accident, when the phone call had come from the hospital—that terrifying long-distance buzz—and they'd decided Claudia and Maggie would make the trip, the McNeils needed a place for Palmer to stay because Daniel was working long days at the market. The mother of Palmer's best friend, Bonnie, offered to take Palmer, and if Claudia hadn't been so desperate and sick with worry, she'd never have said yes, because there was no love lost between the hefty Elinor Stafford and her, especially after Elinor had the nerve some months before to ask if she and her husband could *adopt* Palmer.

After a string of miscarriages (a wonder, Claudia said, the woman had ever conceived in the first place, with her husband gone all the time), Elinor was unable to have the brother or sister she'd wanted Bonnie to have. Ford Stafford, a mining engineer, worked the better part of each year in South America. So for over eight months of every year, Elinor and Bonnie lived alone in one of the largest houses in Manhattan Beach, a house located right on The Strand, about a block north of the Pier, with a 180-degree view of the ocean, and that's where Palmer stayed the weeks that her mother was gone.

Not long before that, Elinor's cousin, Loretta Sprague, had moved down from north of San Francisco to take up residence in the apartment built at the back of the Staffords' home. A newspaperwoman hired by *The Daily Breeze*, the paper that served the South Bay area, Loretta was two years older than Daniel, slender and elegant, with silver-blonde hair drawn back in a chignon. She was one of the few professional women Daniel had ever known, and the combination of her journalism training, her sophistication, and her trim-fitting periwinkle and cobalt suits made her the most exotic creature he'd ever met.

During those five weeks when half his family was in Seattle, he was invited nearly every night to dinner by Elinor, ostensibly to be with his daughter, but of course after Palmer and Bonnie went to bed, Daniel and Loretta were free to "get acquainted," as Elinor so encouragingly put it, waving the two of them off. Most nights they would stop in at Ercole's Fine Dining and Bar for martinis, or Daniel might take her to the La Mar for the latest Cary Grant movie. Elinor couldn't have been more pleased with the developing situation. In one fell swoop, she might be rid of that McNeil woman *and* get Palmer into her home as a companion for Bonnie.

By the time Claudia got back to town with Maggie, Daniel

had spent many a night in Loretta's apartment, leaving early in the morning, before the girls were awake, to swing by home to change clothes before work. But Loretta proved to be an oddity. Single by choice, she had no designs on Daniel as a husband, and God knew, she didn't want to be anyone's stepmother.

For their part, Palmer and Bonnie adored Loretta. She was unlike anyone's mother and dazzled them both. Each morning she left for the newspaper office dressed in one of her colorful suits, hose, and heels. She wore earrings and a necklace or a pin every day, and rings on both hands. Palmer memorized her jewelry: the lavender jade earrings, the antique garnet necklace, the Victorian amethyst broach, and the gold lavaliere watch that hung from a braided gold chain. Loretta had shown the girls how it held a picture of her mother on one side and her father on the other.

At night Loretta and Daniel would come into the girls' bedroom on the second floor to read them a bedtime story, *The Secret Garden* or *The Little Princess*. The grown-ups took turns, Loretta in her precise English, Daniel with his cadence, the two of them exchanging such pleased looks over the book that the children nestled down delighted in the attention from these good-humored adults. At those moments, so unexpected in their pleasure, Palmer hardly missed her mother.

The night that Claudia returned from Seattle, Daniel picked her and Maggie up from the bus station, dropped them off at home, and then drove the Plymouth to get Palmer, even though the Staffords' home was only blocks away. Elinor wanted to be sure that Palmer's clothes were sent home in good order, because they certainly hadn't been received that way. Oh, they'd been clean enough and ironed, but the McNeil woman hadn't done any mending in heaven knew how long. Underarm rips needed sewing up, and sashes needed to be attached to dresses where they'd been held in place by safety pins. Elinor felt pleasantly vindicated when she sent the clothes back.

Maybe Claudia would think twice about drinking the day

away in the future, though Elinor doubted it. With a man like Daniel, you'd think she'd have more sense, if not self-respect. It would serve her right if he left her for Loretta. The only fly in Elinor's self-satisfied ointment was the continual absence of her own husband.

That his traveling was no burden on himself, she'd known for a long time, though Ford would always bring back stuffed animals at Christmas and jewelry made our of gold from the mine he'd named the "Bonnie Rose" after his daughter.

Each summer the Staffords would plan a long motor trip to Las Vegas or to Oregon to see relatives. One year they had gone on to Winnemucca and Walla Walla and Wenatchee, trying to see how many cities whose names began with *W* they could hit along the way.

That was the year they'd taken Palmer along. She'd been nine then, and she came back with tales of a life as unlike the McNeils' as any of them could imagine: a couch made out of swans' down that had to be plumped daily, water goblets beside each plate at dinner, Mrs. Stafford's success at breaking Palmer's habit of finishing her mashed potatoes before she started on her peas and finishing *them* before eating her lamb chop. Claudia had been depressed for days after her daughter returned.

But Elinor was often depressed, too, though neither woman ever knew that about the other. When Ford flew back to South America, and he always did, she knew she'd hear nothing from him but the occasional letter; he'd be home at Christmas, then off again until late spring when he came back for the summer.

Any woman who had a husband at home, especially one as charming as Daniel McNeil, was duty-bound to take care of him. Elinor didn't like to think about the care Ford might be receiving during those long months away from her and Bonnie. She filled her days as a Brownie troop leader, secretary-treasurer of the PTA, room mother, and president of the Sandpipers women's club, and her nights with bedtime snacks of peanut butter-and-mayonnaise sandwiches, sitting alone in her large kitchen, the windows clean and dark, listening to the radio long after Bonnie had fallen asleep.

Claudia returned home worn out from caring for her mother. She slept ten hours the first night and woke up realizing she hadn't had a drink in nearly six weeks. She'd been too busy, she supposed, just like those early days after each girl was born: nursing the baby every few hours, dead on her feet from getting too little sleep and washing endless diapers, undershirts, and kimonos—all with the need to be alert, because who ever knew what might go wrong with an infant, what terrible, unforeseen tragedy that only the mother—it would always turn out to be the mother—might have prevented?

This time with her own mother had been the same—her sight coming back only gradually, the complicated regimen of pills and compresses, driving back and forth to the doctor's office with Maggie in the back seat. Everything depended on Claudia. Maybe it always had or maybe she only felt that way, but the burden of responsibility was a familiar haunt. And no matter how good a job she did, she always knew that next time it probably wouldn't be enough, that she wasn't really up to it, whatever ghost *it* was going to turn out to be.

If she hadn't been preoccupied with cleaning the house—it looked like Daniel hadn't dusted or swept once, though to give him credit, the kitchen wasn't very messy—and with trying *not* to walk the five blocks to the liquor store, she might have noticed Daniel's preoccupation—an air more absent than usual. But whatever she noticed she put down to their coming together after the only separation of their marriage.

On the day after her return, Claudia stepped outside the kitchen door. Soft morning air warmed her face, and the surf sang its familiar song. Even in spring Seattle had been a cold-hearted city, and edgy or not, she was glad to be home.

Easter Vacation Dangers

ALONG WITH BEING SPOOKED ABOUT THE Redondo Theater, Mother was also terrified of polio, especially when the quarantine signs went up. Even after construction of the Hyperion—a treatment plant north of Manhattan Beach that piped treated sewage out to sea—water quality experts would still find contamination along the shore. Daddy said the plant was better than nothing, but Bonnie's father didn't believe in the Hyperion's engineering. "A pipeline of shit," he called it.

So each spring began with the dictum that neither girl was going swimming in that dirty ocean because they were sure to catch polio, though Mother always referred to it as "infantile paralysis," since that sounded more serious. And they'd better stay out of swimming pools, too, just to be on the safe side. The Biltmore Plunge in Hermosa Beach was off-limits, as was Clyde Henderson's pool, opened by the city councilman on Saturday afternoons to the neighborhood kids.

But it was an edict born to be broken. Four days was Mother's record, and so with the warm days of vacation spreading before them, the girls began their campaign.

"Please-please-please," begged Palmer. "Everyone's going to the beach!"

"And I suppose if everyone were jumping off a—"

"Oh, Mother."

"Please-pretty-please, with French fries and artichokes," wheedled Maggie.

"The answer is no. I'm not having you girls exposed to infantile paralysis." She was dicing cheddar for macaroni and cheese and paused with her knife in midair. She turned to Palmer. "If this is about seeing JJ, you can invite him over here after dinner."

Well, it *was* about JJ Wilson, at least partly, because Palmer's boyfriend was always at the beach along with a bunch of other seventh-graders and the little brothers and sisters, like Maggie, they were assigned to watch. By the time kids were allowed to go to the beach on their own, they'd staked out territory. Palmer's bunch claimed a spot south of the Pier, midway between the waterline and the high schoolers who crowded the slanted retaining wall by the stairs that led up to the parking lot.

Sometimes Palmer caught JJ eyeing that wall, where the high school girls spread their beach towels half on the sand and half against the warmed, sloping concrete. They leaned back, their faces and shoulders gleaming with plummy-scented Johnson's Baby Oil, their breasts in the two-piece suits aimed at the sun. Palmer watched the high school boys race out of the surf to throw themselves down in the hot sand at the girls' feet, raising their heads from time to time to survey the length of golden legs stretched toward them from pink-tipped toe to latex crotch, half hidden by the straight cut of the suit's modesty apron.

But as much as Palmer admired these golden girls holding court, she also scorned them. Somewhere along the line they'd given up *swimming*. It was the rare high school girl who pulled on a bathing cap and fought her way out through the breakers to swim the smooth swells that rose and fell beyond the surf toward the end of the Pier and beyond that, toward open sea.

They rose gracefully in pairs, brushing invisible sand from their smooth hips, lifting long hair from their necks as they nonchalantly walked to the water's edge, acting as if every boy's eye were not on them. They were lightly splashed by the older boys, who suddenly, impetuously decided to go for long swims, but not before they made the girls jump and squeal at the cold water. The most adventurous girls waded into the surf to mid-thigh, bending over gentle, ruffled waves, bathing-suit tops dipping to reveal delicious hollows, so that even the younger boys liked to surf the small waves toward them. The girls cupped water in their hands to spill over lithe arms—a cool-off rather than a swim—and Palmer hated them, especially when JJ gazed toward their ice-cream bottoms that were raised just high enough above the water to stay dry.

And so, after the quarantine signs were posted, it took several tries to convince Mother to let them go to the beach, where she and JJ could lie side by side on the hot sand, their towels touching, half asleep, though not really, in the drowse of the afternoon's heat. Sometimes there'd be half a dozen kids, sunning or maybe shivering from an exhausting race past the breakers.

Eventually the afternoon came when Mother took one of her naps, and Palmer waited until she fell asleep, then nudged her gently.

"Mother? Can Maggie and I please go to the beach?"

"Hmm?" Her hair was tousled on the pillow, one cheek creased by the wrinkled linen.

"Okay if we go to the beach?"

"Girls, don't bother Mother." She waved them off with limp fingers.

"Can we go, then?"

"Yes, yes, go," she said wearily, pulling the sheet up around the shoulders of her sleeveless blouse, some part of her knowing that consistency was just too much work. Palmer backed away from her sweetish smell and the coffee cup with no coffee stains, sitting on the floor beside the bed. She felt guilty, taking advantage this way, but she did it, anyhow. Besides, no one they knew had come down with infantile paralysis yet.

Daddy rarely took Mother to the movies because, he said, the La Mar had fleas and he always came home with a line of bites beneath his belt. Palmer doubted he much wanted to go in the first place, since he was the only person she knew who ever got a fleabite at the La Mar. He even claimed the fleas were thicker in the loges, but Palmer also knew he didn't like to pay the extra money for the plush seats at the back of the theater where the floor rose to give better viewing. Still, he was always willing to shell out fourteen cents apiece any Saturday or Sunday for her and Maggie to go to matinees.

After the opening newsreel from Warner-Pathé and before the double feature, these matinees offered cartoons, Previews of Coming Attractions, and one episode of a serial like *Flash Gordon,* starring Buster Crabbe, along with the villainous Ming, who made Maggie shiver. For some reason her father called the previews "trailers," which never made sense to Palmer because previews came before the double feature. Everyone knew that trailers were towed behind and came after.

Inside the La Mar, nude women of the classical tradition graced the walls that sloped toward the screen. Impossibly long tresses streamed behind them, tangled in stylized waves. A few strands floated magically over the fronts of their shoulders to hide the strategic points of their breasts, while their full thighs met rounded bellies in a discreet and undifferentiated *V.* They rode open seashells, like muses come down from Mount Helicon to have a holiday on surfboards made of clamshells.

And in front of these sirens, wavelets curled toward the screen, which was hidden by heavy gold draperies and bathed in spotlights. When the newsreel music signaled the parting of the drapes, golden sheers were revealed, a translucent cloud as layer after layer was swept back finally to reveal the movie screen itself. It was a ritual that silenced even the noisiest children, a moment when magic was about to transfigure them all. And no one worried about being indoors during spring vacation or on the weekend, since the California sun was always waiting.

Palmer and Maggie had been waiting impatiently to go see *The Secret Garden,* and at last the film opened at the La Mar, just in time for Easter vacation. On Saturday afternoon, they got in line early, finding seats just down from the middle in a row that was still practically empty. With a bag of popcorn between them, they settled in to wait for the crowd to file in and for the lights to dim. A big blond guy came in, passed up all the empty seats, and climbed over both girls to sit next to Palmer.

He was loaded with treats, and every once in a while he leaned over, pressing his shoulder into Palmer's, to offer Necco Wafers or Junior Mints. He even offered her a whole box of Cracker Jacks. Palmer shook her head. The previews had begun, and she was more annoyed at his interrupting than anything else, though she had been raised never to accept candy from a stranger. He seemed to settle back after the movie itself began, and Palmer relaxed.

Then, just when Margaret O'Brien and the little crippled boy found each other in the garden, the man started snickering and nudging Palmer's arm with his elbow. She wanted to be polite, but he was ruining the movie. Suddenly he tapped her hard on the shoulder. She turned and found his face only inches away. He ran his thumb under her chin. Palmer's head jerked back.

"After the movie," he whispered, "I'll buy you a root beer soda. Your little sister, too." He leaned in front of Palmer, nodding at Maggie and blocking the screen. Maggie ignored him, and he sat back.

Suddenly the movie screen blurred, just the slightest shift out of focus, and Palmer felt that touch of motion sickness, the vertigo she'd learned in that last small earthquake, the roll rather than the jolt. Her muscles tensed; she was ready to grab Maggie and run for the nearest doorway to stand under its crossbeam in case the theater collapsed. She was a girl schooled in earthquakes by lectures at home and drills in the classroom. But even so, right then her bravado at the Redondo Theater was the farthest thing from her mind.

Like a dark shadow, the man used that moment to lean in front of Palmer, his silhouette between her startled eyes and the still-fuzzy screen. With thumb and forefinger, he flicked her small nipple, its rise barely visible through her seersucker shirt.

Palmer straight-armed him in the chest, catching him off guard. She grabbed Maggie and hauled her out of her seat, shoving her sister ahead of her toward the aisle, but not before his hand brushed hard at the back of Palmer's shorts.

"Hey!" Maggie tried to shake Palmer off.

"It's an earthquake!" Palmer hissed. Her sister didn't need to know more. They ran to the top of the aisle, where Palmer paused before the draped doorway and looked back, but he was already gone.

"I don't feel anything," Maggie whispered. And it was true; the mild earthquake was past. Everyone else was still watching the movie.

He probably ran out through the curtained hallway, thought Palmer. It lay just beneath the exit sign, whose neon letters glowed green as the X-ray machine at Stephen's Bootery, with its invisible radiation. As Palmer sneaked herself and Maggie into the loges to be near the ushers, she knew the stranger would have to stay her secret, because if she told anyone, then the La Mar itself might go on her mother's list, right up there with infantile paralysis and the Redondo Theater.

The Manhattan Beach Pier, a mammoth structure of concrete and reinforced steel, anchored the beach town, drew it to sea level from the backcountry east of Sepulveda Boulevard all the way down the Center Street Hill. Like a roller coaster diving toward the sunset, Center Street plunged across the railroad tracks, past the Metlox Pottery plant, the La Mar Theater, and its next-door neighbor the Sweet Shoppe, through the business district, then two final steep blocks to the smoky Knothole on one side and the greasy-spoon White Stop Cafe on the other. As if relieved to at last find the shore, the street leveled out to cross The Strand—a double-wide concrete walk that stretched for miles, from the Con Edison plant at one end to the oil fields of El Segundo at the other.

The Roundhouse sat at the circular end of the Pier—its design swelling like the bulb of a giant thermometer poised to take the temperature of coastal currents. At the Pier's entrance, a life-guard tower stood watch with its ladder hanging over the side of the railing, straight down to the sand where the guards kept their wooden dinghy and torpedo buoys. Just past the tower, two large and identical white signs hung from the Pier's railing, their black printing faded and cracked from sun and storms.

NO JUMPING OR DIVING
FROM PIER
CITY ORDINANCE #34219

North of the Pier rose fifteen-foot bluffs with concrete stairs leading down to the sand. Ice plant thick with flowering threads of violet silk hung from the cliffs. In a variation on their mud ball fights, boys pulled up chunks of ice plant to hurl at one another, but the plant proved tough. Its succulent spikes seemed to grow as fast as they were torn away.

To the south the cliffs began to level out, and The Strand came even with the beach. Families had an easier time getting kids and towels and beach balls from car to water's edge.

Onshore winds swept sand over the walkway to pyramid against porches and fences, waiting for Santa Ana winds to hurl it back to the beach.

The Pier itself just marched across the beach and into the sea, prompting another of their mother's prohibitions. "Don't *ever* play under the Pier. No one can *see* you, and it's filthy dirty. Bums sleep there at night. They get drunk and bury broken bottles. You could cut off your toes!"

"Now, Claudia—," Daddy began.

"Well, they could, and what's more—"

So Palmer and Maggie didn't explore under the Pier too often, and when they did, they watched where they put their feet. It was a smelly place with too many cigarette butts, but even so, their mother had managed to give the Pier's underbelly a lurid fascination.

But far worse than broken glass, to Palmer's way of thinking, were the soft-shelled sand crabs no bigger than her thumb that periodically lurked by the hundreds of thousands just beneath the sand in the shallow water. They were harmless, pale creatures, harvested by fishermen for bait, the men hefting homemade wooden strainers into waters just beyond the surf's edge. With their backs to the beach, they'd let the weight of the harvester sink a few inches into the silky bottom sand and wait for a strong wave to wash past them and then recede, riffling crabs into the wire mesh. The fishermen hauled the bait traps to shore and dumped their glistening catch into buckets.

Sand crabs didn't bite, but Palmer could hardly stand the feel of their prickly little bodies poking her bare feet as she raced into the surf. There in the shallows, the sand crabs wriggled in a wide band she had to cross to reach water deep enough—a couple of feet would do it—to throw herself into a dog paddle, her feet kicking above their writhings.

Palmer never knew whether the crabs were seasonal or tidal, but from time to time there they'd be. "Lotta crabs today!" someone would yell, and the boys would laugh. Sometimes JJ walked into the surf and twisted his body back and forth, working his feet deep into the crabs. To Palmer, it was like standing in a field of spiders.

By Tuesday of Easter vacation, Mother had given up the battle to keep them from the beach. The morning was unusually hot, with a blustery onshore wind. Palmer had already opened all the windows in The Shack. She was thinking how the surf would likely be high. But only fishermen consulted tide tables. To swimmers, the tide was either coming in or going out, and you adjusted accordingly. To kids on the beach, it meant simply keeping your towel above the tide's mark, that wavery line of kelp, broken shells, Japanese floats (if you were lucky), and other debris the ocean spat up. It was a daily treasure hunt at the water's highest reach.

Palmer and Maggie were getting ready to go to the beach, which usually meant simply changing into their bathing suits and grabbing towels and a few beach toys for Maggie. Palmer was moving especially fast because Mother had started on a zinc oxide crusade, and Palmer wanted to get out of the house before Mother got back and swathed their noses in white salve. Maggie didn't mind looking like a clown, but Palmer wiped off the crème with her towel as soon as they were out of sight. When they got back home at the end of the day, she would claim the water had worn it off her blistered nose, though the whole point of zinc oxide was that it was waterproof.

Palmer also resisted her mother's efforts to get her to wear a shirt to the beach. "I'll look like a tourist," she complained. That was a fate worse than the sunburns she suffered each summer until she built up the meager protection of a slight tan. Despite her dark hair from both parents, those McNeil genes had left her with her father's freckles. She dreamed they might merge into one glowing California tan, a color that lived in Palmer's fantasy, fueled by the tans of the high school girls who religiously applied their homemade lotion of baby oil and iodine, a concoction that offered no protection from the sun and no inducement to tanning beyond the slight stain of the iodine. So Mother forbade it. Daddy favored the loathsome-smelling Skol. It was the *Rexall Drug Store's* oldest and cheapest brand, and no kid would think of wearing it.

To beach kids, nothing was more repulsive than the blue-white skin of the tourists in their Hawaiian shirts and cloppy sandals as they struggled down the concrete stairs to the beach, loaded with umbrellas, beach chairs, picnic baskets, and worst of all—hats! "Whale bellies," the kids called the tourists. So Palmer endured her sunburns, dumping vinegar into hot baths at day's end on the faulty but popular theory that as she eased her lobster-red body into the tub, the terrible stinging she stoically accepted was "taking the burn out."

Many nights she'd go to bed with taut and fiery skin. Sometimes by morning she'd be unable to straighten her legs because the skin behind her knees had contracted. She'd slather her sunburned body with cool Noxzema. (Decades would have to pass before any of them learned about actinic keratoses, basal cell carcinoma, or malignant melanoma.)

Still, a few days after the sunburn, the miracle would always blossom briefly, and Palmer would stand before the mirror in her shorts and sleeveless blouse and admire the ruddy gold of her arms and legs. But it was a glory short-lived. Tiny blisters would flower, and then the itching would begin. Before long she could peel off strips of sloughing skin, like a burnished snake shedding down to its pink skin, so baby-tender that it was destined to be burned again and again.

With the luck of the genes, Maggie took after Mother, who tanned easily, or would have if she ever lay in the sun, but neither parent much liked the beach. On weekends, Daddy fished from the Pier that stretched a quarter mile out into the ocean. He wore wash pants and long-sleeved shirts and the greasy Skol on his face and neck. Sometimes after fishing he'd meet Mother in the tiny Knothole. Palmer and Maggie weren't allowed in there, so Palmer knew it wasn't really a cafe but a bar. Occasionally, to beg for snack money, the girls would venture into the cool darkness, the smell of beer as rank as the cigarette smoke that hung inside like a fog bank. It was grown-up territory, where people spent long weekend hours hiding from the light. Mother loved the one-armed bandits, and she collected quarters at home in a mayonnaise jar that would usually be empty after a Knothole afternoon. Now and then, it would magically overflow.

Sometimes the girls would sit on the concrete curb of The Strand, damp towels wrapped around their shoulders, waiting in the evening breeze. And sometimes, when Mother and Daddy came outside laughing, he had his arm around her. Other times he walked out quickly and strode angrily down The Strand toward home. Mother would walk less steadily, and the distance between them would lengthen as Maggie ran ahead to catch her father's hand and Palmer hung back with a vague sense of guarding her mother.

But on this vacation day of spring when their bodies were still pale, the girls pulled their dry suits from the porch railing, with Mother off grocery shopping at Wahlberg's Market, where Daddy had been hired on as produce manager. Maggie held her bathing suit, an old navy-blue wool inherited from Palmer, at arm's length. The suit had gotten to be a problem, and Maggie would need a new one come summer. At the beach it was the rare child, naturally enough, who trudged up from the water, clear across the hot sand, then up the stairs to the damp restrooms. Even Palmer occasionally peed in the ocean, especially when she'd swum beyond the breakers and wasn't near ready to come in. So the crotch of the old wool suit, perhaps reaching some saturation point, had taken on a smell not unlike a toilet stall.

Now Maggie wasn't going to put it on, and if Maggie didn't go to the beach, Palmer couldn't go, either, because her sister was her responsibility whenever her mother wasn't around.

"C'mon, Maggie, as soon as it's wet, you won't even notice!"

"It'll be worse," Maggie whined. She thrust the suit at Palmer, who quickly backed away but still caught a whiff.

"Look, we'll wash it good with some Ivory Snow tonight, okay? 'For all your fine washables,' remember?" But Maggie was settling in to be stubborn; Palmer knew the signs and could feel her own impatience heating up. "I said *c'mon*! Before Mother gets back!"

But Maggie stood in her underpants, little legs planted, and shook her head. It seemed to Palmer no time ago that her sister had played in the sand wearing no more than her panties, and now she was making a big deal over a bathing suit. Still, it did smell like a dead sheep.

"I've got an idea," she said, taking the suit from Maggie, careful to grab it by the shoulder straps. She led the way into her parents' bedroom, and there on the mahogany-veneer vanity that Mother had bought at the Episcopal Church's rummage sale stood her mother's perfumes: a blue and silver bottle of *Evening in Paris*, and the tawny *Tabu*, all sophistication in its orange and black stripes.

Palmer thought her brainstorm gave *eau de toilette* a whole new meaning, but she just said, "Take your suit and stretch out the crotch. Now—which bottle do you like best?" Wide-eyed, Maggie pointed to the cobalt bottle. "Okay, but you can't tell, understand?" Palmer doused the crotch of the swimsuit and nodded at her sister. "Now you'll smell pretty, so put it on and let's go!"

Maggie hesitated. "It's wet."

Palmer groaned, but her sister had a point. Nothing was worse than pulling on a wet bathing suit, whether it was yesterday's salt water or today's perfume. "I know, let's put it in the oven—perfume dries really fast." She turned on the gas, waited for the blue flames, and then set the oven knob at 425 degrees. "Just put it in there on the rack and get your other stuff. I'm going to change."

Soon they were out the door, Maggie in warm, dry wool, padding barefoot down the street toward the beach. By some small miracle they had *not* set the house on fire. And the girls moved happily into their beach day unaware that Maggie, carrying her brightly painted tin shovel and pail, smelled like a very short streetwalker. Behind them in the kitchen, wafting throughout the overheated house, an aroma awaited Mother that she later described to Daddy as a combination of wet wool, cheap perfume, and a diaper. He asked if she'd been drinking, and by another small miracle, she laughed.

Stench aside, the real problem with the wool bathing suit was that it always stretched alarmingly as soon as it was soaked, so that Maggie would emerge droopy-crotched from the water, her suit sagging nearly to her knees. But now as they walked across the hot sand to where the group lay, JJ waved at them and then grinned up evilly at Palmer.

"Crabs are bad today, Palm!"

Palmer rolled her eyes, tried to look exasperated rather than afraid as she mentally braced herself for the race through the surf. But that could wait a little, she thought, spreading her towel next to JJ's darkly tanned body that didn't seem fair with his blond hair.

Maggie threw down her stuff and took off for the water, but not before JJ caught her scent and raised his eyebrows. "Girls," he was probably thinking, but Palmer knew he had a soft spot for her sister, partly because Maggie was a busy kid at the beach and didn't spend too much time pestering them. She had her repertoire of beach games: playing cowgirl with kelp whips, building sand castles, drawing pictures in the hard-packed wet sand, or just wading for hours near the shore.

Maggie had been schooled not to go beyond thigh level in the surf, especially after the riptide fiasco last autumn. Palmer was in charge and lifeguards were on duty, but it was her own job to pay attention and not go out too far. Besides, by the time the water was over her knees, she could throw herself down and splash around, walking on her hands with her legs kicking behind, looking as if she were swimming. Few kids actually learned to stroke until they were nine or ten, so most of the younger ones spent much of their time building elaborate drip castles with turrets and moats.

Building close to the surf, kids scooped up a slurry of mud to dribble layer after layer, like candle wax dripping down a wine bottle, creating a fairy-tale effect. "Medieval," their grandmother called it. Because they were so close to the water, the race was to get the castle built before the tide demolished it. Some evenings after everyone had gone home, the high tide left behind lumps of dark sand like primitive huts, up and down the beach, a miniature civilization razed by the sea.

But today Maggie headed directly for her favorite game of just being buffeted by the waves, half invitation, half battle. She plunked herself down in the shallows, her legs pointing with determination toward the surf, and waited until a large wave broke and played out its power, sending its lift of water rushing toward shore. She braced her arms behind her, trying not to be budged, but the rough waves tumbled one after another into shore, nothing dangerous, but rushing between her legs, into her face, drenching her hair and toppling her over backwards 'til she flopped like a little perch. Her shrieks and laughter carried up the beach to her sister.

Palmer was lying on her towel next to JJ, putting off her swim as long as possible because she hoped he might move his hand closer to hers, which lay between them in a sort of neutral zone. Suddenly her sister screamed, the timbre edging toward panic.

Palmer rolled over and sat up quickly. The midday sun on the water was blinding. Maggie was running towards her from the water, her legs splayed in an awkward straddle, the crotch of the blue suit slapping comically against her little thighs.

"Palmer!" she yelled, and her fingers stiffened into claws as if she needed to scratch at herself. Just as quickly her hands flew away from her body, and she made little mewing sounds.

"What's the matter? Did you get hurt?"

Maggie pointed between her legs, and for a second Palmer thought she might be chafed, or that the perfume had irritated her because of the alcohol or something, but she looked too scared for a patch of sore skin, and how could that happen so fast? Wouldn't water dilute perfume, anyhow?

"Something is—" Maggie sobbed outright, her hands rigid in front of her thighs. "Something's sticking me."

Palmer grabbed Maggie's hand and scooped up both their towels. "Got to check this out," she said to JJ, shrugging as if to say, "*Little sisters.*" She hustled Maggie toward the shadows that hid the deserted, damp underside of the Pier.

Palmer spread one towel on the sand. "Get down here on your back and let me take a look. Here, pull up your knees." She draped the second towel around her own shoulders so that as she bent over Maggie, it formed a kind of tent. Her sister might have no qualms about peeing in the ocean, but she'd recently come into her own sense of modesty.

Bending over Maggie, Palmer thought of the times when Mother had let her help change the new baby's diapers, and here was this same pale bottom, cold as a tadpole, a little bigger, but still a baby bottom, risen from the ocean like the rump of a seal pup. She pushed aside the soggy crotch of the suit. "Keep your knees like that, Mags." Not a sign of rash. And then, trying not to gasp, she saw the problem: the wriggling hind end of a soft-shell sand crab lodged at the tiny opening to Maggie's vagina.

Palmer could see it all suddenly: her sister sitting at the edge of the surf, her legs wide, the water rushing toward her. And somewhere in that wave a little crab had been tossed, a crab that had poked its head too far above the sand in which it was supposed to stay safely buried. Its prickly body had been aimed against all odds like a tiny torpedo, and Maggie's droopy crotch had washed to one side.

"It's okay. We can fix this." Palmer tried not to shudder. "Does it hurt?"

Maggie had stopped crying. "Just—stickery, sort of."

Palmer clenched her teeth as she lifted a corner of the towel on which Maggie lay, just a pinch of fabric to grasp the sand crab. Anger washed over Palmer, like being blindsided by a wave. How dare they—? She couldn't even finish the thought, not knowing, exactly, what it meant, but as the adrenaline cleared her mind, she knew she'd have to be calm, to pull slowly, because if she tore the crab in half, then what would happen? Her knowledge of female anatomy grew vague here. She knew where babies came from—Mother was good about answering questions—but just how high this dark tunnel ran, she wasn't sure. The idea of the creature scrabbling inside the private parts of Maggie's little body was unendurable. Palmer took hold of the sand crab, concentration sinking both fear and fury like a deep-water anchor.

"This is gonna feel icky, Mags, but try to hold still." She reached up and patted her sister's stomach to comfort them both as she felt the crab's legs scratching through the fabric of the towel. Slowly, now. Pull and twist. And then she had it free, and whole. She dropped the crab out of the towel, disgust nearly swamping her, and in one motion scooped a handful of hard, wet sand over it.

Palmer was shivering. The temperature was probably fifteen degrees colder under the Pier, and it felt as if she and Maggie had been there all afternoon. She saw no trace of blood and pulled the floppy crotch back to cover Maggie, who'd barely moved. "Better?" she asked. The little girl scrambled up and fell into Palmer's arms.

"What was it?" she wailed.

"Some ocean speck that got stuck, lost maybe. It's gone. Don't be scared—you're okay. Tonight we'll just tell Mother you really need a new suit."

And as she sat and hugged her sister, Palmer remembered herself at seven, that summer when she had played on the front porch of a nicer beach house, back before the move to Portland, a porch shaded from the sun by oleander and bougainvillea. She'd picked hibiscus leaves, the curled undersides serving as hospital beds.

Into this hothouse infirmary she'd brought her patients: small black ants she had carefully maimed with a shard of abalone shell. Not killed, no; she had judiciously crushed legs and occasionally burst a thorax—though it was her father who'd used that term, later, after Mother discovered what she was doing—the ants' blood the merest pinprick of yellow fluid. With no sense of her own cruelty, she'd *nursed* the few ants that somehow lived through their ordeal, tenderly scooping them up with leaves to deposit each on its own hibiscus bed. She'd been squeamish about touching them, though later, after they died, which they always did except for the few who staggered piteously off, she flicked the dead ones unceremoniously off the ledge, out of her hospital forever.

She remembered how in third or fourth grade, when she was old enough to feel guilty about her nursing experiments, she read in her *Weekly Reader* that ants will follow a trail made by other ants, but if one accidentally starts going in a circle, they may all walk that endless trail until they fall dead. Another way to be precarious, she'd guessed. And now, as much as she hated sand crabs, especially this one, some small, pitying part of her was oddly glad she hadn't killed it—a tiny, independent danger that even Mother couldn't have imagined.

Pirates and Penitents

As SPRING PASSED INTO SUMMER, EARTHQUAKES and candy-toting strangers faded from thought at the La Mar. *What's playing?* was all that mattered, and on this particular Saturday in July, Gene Kelly and Judy Garland were starring in *The Pirate.* The matinee was a rare single feature, Technicolor to boot, but what with the *Flash Gordon* serial, four cartoons, the newsreel, and Previews of Coming Attractions, Palmer and Bonnie didn't get out of the movie until close to 4:00 p.m. A summer storm was brewing, and the sky looked bruised as Palmer's knees after roller-skating.

A satire of movie musicals, *The Pirate* was also a parody of adventure-film excess, with black tights and high boots, crimson sashes, swords that slashed more air than flesh, blousy shirts open at the chest, and black capes lined with purple satin. Gene Kelly swung from balconies to rooftops and swaggered with such style and bravado that only a dancer could have pulled off such moves.

But the send-up was lost on Palmer and Bonnie. Their pulses raced with the story's melodrama. They pressed cold hands against hot cheeks and sighed with *twitterpation,* a word they'd learned from *Bambi.*

"Imagine being forced to marry Walter Slezak," Bonnie said with a shudder, and Palmer agreed. Later she heard Daddy tell Mother that *The Pirate* gave the Hays Office no end of trouble, parody or no. Mother wondered if it was a good movie for children to see. By then it was too late.

But at the moment, Palmer, who had been interested in boys since first grade, knew only that she hated to leave romance behind in the dimmed theater. At home waited her little sister, cranky with a cold. And chores. Not even the promise of dinner, pot roast simmering when she'd left—potatoes, carrots, and onions caramelizing in the cast-iron Dutch oven—was enough to lure her from the turquoise of the Caribbean and the dashing Gene Kelly.

Bonnie rattled on, but Palmer listened absently. She was remembering the last time she'd felt like this, her chest warm and tingly—or was it her stomach? In a movie a few weeks back, a doctor had been summoned to treat the barely conscious Linda Darnell. Her dark hair fanned across the pillow. The doctor untied her negligee and opened it to reveal a clinging nightgown. With professional fingers he placed his stethoscope where her breast swelled from the gown. Palmer felt the blood rush to her face then, too. The doctor, businesslike, his gaze fastened on the wall, slowly lifted the stethoscope to press it snugly beneath each rising and falling breast.

Then he wrenched the scope from his ears, leaned over, and pressed one ear into the deep shadows playing on her chest. Palmer had been ashamed at her reaction to a *medical* scene, but for days after, she thought about that stethoscope. As for the two small swellings on her own chest, Palmer alternated between scorn and despair.

Now, as she and Bonnie walked down the hill and out onto the Pier, she felt that same sort of restlessness, an emotional stirring that she called romantic but that agitated her in odd ways. The girls decided they'd walk around the end of the Pier before the lights of home could mute their delicious feelings.

"So did you hate the mustache on Gene Kelly?" Palmer asked. Bonnie's favorite actor was Roy Rogers, and Palmer knew her friend disliked mustaches and beards. Personally, Palmer thought a little cowboy goodness went a long way. She favored the more dangerous Tyrone Power. His *Zorro* had made her *swoon*, a word she'd taken up from the screaming bobby-soxers in newsreels who fainted at Frank Sinatra performances. Just the other night, Daddy had looked long and hard at her and said, "Don't imagine we're going to have any *teenage* behavior in *this* house, young lady."

"I liked his dark eyes," Bonnie said.

"And the very first time she sees the ocean, right then she meets him. It was—I don't know, like the two most important moments in her life came together."

They pulled their jackets close against the wind. The Pier was crowded with people fishing, mostly men and older boys, some of them fishing for subsistence. When her father wasn't playing tennis, he was often on the Pier. "Recreational fishing," he called it, with a tone that implied a definite class difference. The only difference Palmer could see was that he gave away any tomcod, which were considered "garbage fish" to those who didn't count on them for dinner. Her father said tomcod had worms. She couldn't tell if he was kidding.

Daniel checked tide tables and listened to the old-timers in the Knothole. He would rarely pass up an after-dinner stint fishing if smelt were running—or mackerel, bonito, sculpin or croaker. But halibut was king. Occasionally he'd snag a hammerhead shark or a barracuda, and then everyone would gather round to watch the creature flop until Daniel cracked it over the head with a fish bopper and threw it back for the gulls and pelicans.

Palmer didn't fish. Hardly any girls did, and only a few older women—those mostly for food. But she liked to go along with her father and lean against the pitted metal railing, daydreaming to the rhythm of the swells, gazing out at the coin-speckled water. She liked the way old fish scales glistened like mica on the concrete deck of the Pier, the salty-bait smells. Pier fishing had its own dance, punctuated with drama like a shark catch or the arrival of the live-bait boat.

She'd lean over the rail to watch that dilapidated boat motor up beside the Pier. Whoever was working the bait shop would lower the bait bucket, really just a big net rather than an actual bucket, and someone on the boat would dip it into the hull, then swing it up into the shop's tank, the gulls raucous for any fish that slopped over. Bait ran five for a nickel, usually anchovies, and Palmer knew how her father hooked them right behind the gill on his three-foot leader that flashed with the large halibut hook. A snelled hook, he told her—many barbs. And finally, on the end of the leader hung the four-ounce pyramid sinker.

Casting was the trick, the art of fishing, he said. He used a Penn reel with a Star drag loosened to let the fish run, especially halibut, which dove straight to the bottom. A tight line usually became a broken line, and with every leader that was lost, some fisherman cut loose with a volley of swearwords, most of which Palmer understood in a general way. Once the fish took your line, you let him dive, tiring himself out. *Let the sonofabitch run!* Then began the task of working him back in, and at the end trying to keep him from diving again. *Watch out! Don't let the bastard have his head!* The swells made it trickier yet, and the fisherman would yell for the net if he glimpsed a good-sized halibut on his line—often a fourteen- to twenty-pounder.

Daniel cleaned his fish at the rust-stained porcelain sink flanked by wooden drainboards. Fish guts sloshed down the drain into the ocean or were scooped out and thrown over the side. Either way the seagulls went crazy, screaming and fighting to get every scrap. Palmer loved the show.

Her father used to say that piers were built to let man walk on water, but woe to any man who thought himself a god above Fishing Law. Signs were posted everywhere: NO OVERHEAD CASTING ALLOWED. Still, every year some *damned tourist* would think he was all by himself on some *godforsaken mountain stream* and would let fly with a cast way back over his head. He'd snag a guy fishing behind him or, worse yet, some kid riding by on his bike or scooter. All her life, Palmer had heard tales of eyes being ripped out or lips torn away, so she had learned to pay attention.

It was a beautiful sight: her father leaning out over the rail, pointing his pole toward the swells, thumbing the reel, then letting out just enough line to get a swing going beneath the

Pier. At the right moment on the forward swing, he'd let the line whistle out to hit water like the single puff of a distant locomotive: *chuu*. Palmer was proud of the distance he could cast.

But as well as she knew the technique herself, she never asked to try, and he never offered. While he didn't lament not having a son, girls just didn't fish. So if she wasn't watching or daydreaming, Palmer spent her time at the snack counter in the Roundhouse on the end of the Pier. Like movie money, her father never minded shelling out change for Palmer to run off and entertain herself.

Unlike Grandmother Sydney with her special powers, Daddy took pride in claiming to be average, not that he believed a whit of it, of course. "Just a working Joe," he'd say. After missing both wars because of his age not falling right for either, what he probably wanted to say was, "Just a *GI* Joe." But if there was anything out of the ordinary that Mother or sometimes even his daughters wanted to do, he'd get this mild look on his face, a bit put-upon. He'd shrug with palms up, saying, "Look, I'm just a working stiff," or he'd roll his eyes and mutter, "Holy simoleons!" Either way they'd feel ashamed for having asked for more than he could provide.

They knew he took a salt-of-the-earth pride in being in management, even if it was just in produce. In fact, he made *produce* sound like a vast, exciting world of commerce, confidently discussing the lettuce fields in the San Joaquin Valley or the smudge pots in the Coachella orange and lemon groves. During the snowstorm, he'd worried right along with the growers over the citrus crop that was pretty much wiped out for the year. He talked about shipments of fragrant coffee beans from South America and often told his artichoke story with a stubborn pride. After all, he'd come from railroading stock, had turned down a scholarship to Oberlin to go to work with his father and brother in the railroad yards of Ohio, before one too many blizzards and a failed marriage had sent him across the country to California.

Before he met Claudia, one of his girlfriends worked as a governess in Beverly Hills. Her employers were out of town, so she invited him to have dinner with her and her little charge in the family's pale coral mansion. They were seated at a gleaming Spanish table in the dining room, Daniel, the girlfriend, and this "starched little twit of a boy." Cloth napkins, real silver—the works. Then the maid served them each an artichoke with Hollandaise sauce, and Daniel didn't know what'n the Sam Hill the prickly vegetable was and had no more idea than a spook how to eat it. He waited to see how his girlfriend would attack the thing, but the kid caught on and laughed, calling him an "Okie."

Daniel excused himself, pushed back his chair, left the dining room, the house, and the manicured grounds. He never saw the girl again. At that point in telling the story, he'd often give a snort as if he sure showed that snotty kid, but his daughters always wondered how the girlfriend felt. Palmer was glad he'd gone on to meet her mother, but the story always struck her as sad.

As far as the artichoke was concerned, it was Palmer's favorite vegetable. Somewhere Daddy had figured out how to eat them, and Mother fixed them often. Dipping the curled leaves into melted garlic butter, Palmer thought they looked like little hooded cobras. An artichoke was to be respected, a *fierce* vegetable with thorn-tipped petals whose prick could easily draw blood. She loved to scrape the tender flesh with her bottom teeth and felt only a little silly to be *proud* it was her favorite.

So Daddy's philosophy was that if the family couldn't swing something by their *bootstraps*, then it just wasn't for them. When she entered eighth grade, Palmer would have to make a choice for high school: college prep or the commercial course. She knew which direction her father would favor. After all, returning soldiers were going to college on the GI Bill. Kids these days just had to figure out how to pay their way. Secretarial work was plentiful, and as for teaching, which Palmer had wanted to do since fifth grade, well, really, he'd sniff, teaching paid so little that it was hardly worth the investment of a college education.

Palmer knew her family didn't have money for tuition, but her grades were good, and she was hoping for a scholarship, though she didn't quite know how you went about getting one. Anyway, whenever she started fretting, she'd remind herself it was too soon to worry about college.

Now, after the movie, as she and Bonnie approached the Roundhouse, Palmer could smell hot dogs and grilled cheese sandwiches. She'd already spent her snack money on popcorn, but she was too filled up with the movie to feel hungry anyway. The wind at the end of the Pier was fierce, and she turned her face toward the Roundhouse. Its peeling wood siding served as a kiosk for notices about every event in town. Brand-new posters in royal blue and metallic gold had been stapled everywhere like heavenly flags:

ARE YOU SAVED?
YOUR REDEEMER LIVETH!
YOUTH FOR CHRIST RALLY
7 P.M., SATURDAY, JULY 23, 1949
THE HOLY SPIRIT CAN CHANGE LIVES!

That was the only warning Palmer had before JJ called that night and asked her to go with him the following Saturday to the YFC Rally. Mostly the event appealed to her because of its novelty, offering something different from Saturday evenings at JJ's house or even the occasional party.

As for religion and the McNeils, Daniel seldom went to church, saying he could get a better handle on God when he grabbed hold of a fishing rod and felt that tug on the end of the line. Occasionally Mother took Palmer and Maggie to the Manhattan Beach Community Church. She said *that* minister had some sense in his head. Palmer noticed only that he quoted from Shakespeare as much as from the Bible. As for Grandmother Sydney, her metaphysics were more intense and more varied. "*To put it mildly*," her father said.

In addition to her psychic interests, Grandmother Sydney was also an Elder in her Seattle Presbyterian Church. She was president of her women's Bible circle, worked on the committee for a new sanctuary, and helped serve communion in her three-piece black knit suit, edged with satin piping. It was an outfit she loved, old as the hills—"scandalously expensive," she always told anyone who complimented her.

Before settling on the Presbyterians, she'd sampled other denominations. For a short time in 1919—the year after Granddaddy Burl had died of influenza when Claudia was only thirteen—Grandmother Sydney had tried Christian Science. Palmer listened raptly when her grandmother told the awful stories about the flu epidemic, stories of undiscovered corpses and whole families dying. Maybe that had been the start of her mother's fear of germs and other dangers that could strike as you sat in a crowded movie or turned a city corner—dangers that could shatter your world like a lost father or a husband's plane spiraling out of the bluest sky.

Grandmother Sydney loved telling Palmer the common gossip about Mary Baker Eddy, Aimee Semple McPherson, and Billy Sunday—evangelists whose theology was rivaled only by their sense of the dramatic. Her own problem, as her grandmother saw it, was that none of these religions understood Sydney's distinct sense of being *special*, a psychic awareness she'd had since she was a child. The Presbyterians, she said, just got in her way less often than the others.

JJ belonged to the more conservative Orthodox Presbyterians, who had split off from the regular Presbyterians because the regulars, he said, were too "modernist," which meant they allowed dancing, playing cards, going to the beach on Sunday, wearing makeup, and drinking—none of which the Orthodox folks at Prairie Presbyterian cottoned to. Even wine with dinner was considered a sin.

Palmer didn't have to wonder what they'd think of the bottle stashed in her mother's underwear drawer, or the one tucked behind the sack of Gold Medal flour high in the kitchen cupboard. When Mother was out of the house, Palmer often made the rounds, checking the usual hiding spots, like the folded sheets on a shelf at the back of her parents' bedroom closet. She'd caught hell once for emptying a bottle down the sink, and since her guerilla tactics didn't stop her mother's drinking anyway, she left the bottles where she found them. Sometimes just knowing where they were seemed to help, though each bout of drinking still caught her by surprise.

At the rally, JJ's youth group from Prairie Pres would be in charge of ushering. To Palmer, who was used to movie ushers and usherettes, busy with their flashlights and shushing people or making sure no kids sneaked into the loges, it didn't seem like such an important job. Sometimes ushers didn't even get to see much of the movie, sweeping spilled popcorn in the lobby into little dustpans with long handles. But JJ was clearly excited about his responsibilities and assured Palmer that as soon as the program started, he would come sit with her. After that he'd have to get up only once, to take the offering.

The day of the rally, Daddy gave her a quarter for the collection. "Don't get carried away with this Holy Roller stuff, princess. It's pretty much a sideshow. In town for a night and then off to Peoria."

Palmer had never heard of a Holy Roller and couldn't pinpoint Peoria, but she got her father's drift. Still, something about the overly casual way he spoke made her figure she might see more on the Pier that night than in a week's worth of fishing.

She dressed carefully in her angora sweater and the almost-new poodle skirt her mother had picked up for fifty cents at a rummage sale. Since JJ had given up movies and school dances last Christmas for the sake of his Religious Convictions—"to put the 'Christ' back in Christmas"—they'd found fewer things to do together on the weekends. Even their phone calls were limited by her folks to fifteen minutes apiece, and it usually took them that long to warm up and get around to something interesting.

The first time JJ kissed her had been last year in the fall when he walked her home from a matinee. The sunset sky had seemed molten. They stopped under a eucalyptus tree while he worked up his nerve. Palmer had a pretty good idea what he was going to do and helped in whatever way she could think of, short of kissing him herself, which she knew from movies you just didn't do.

Under the tree, she stood closer than usual and kept her chin raised so that he wouldn't have to search for her mouth. Really, all he had to do was point and lean, but it had taken him nearly twenty-five minutes to summon his courage, while growing darkness wrapped them together. The eucalyptus had smelled like bay leaves her mother put in spaghetti sauce and homemade soup.

When the moment finally arrived, her neck was stiff, she was late for dinner, and she had to pee so badly she could hardly stand up straight. Still, if not an earth-shattering experience, it had been worth the wait. JJ was a couple of inches taller, and he'd leaned down and brushed her mouth with lips as cool as her mother's shell-pink satin blouse.

For a heartbeat she even forgot she had to go to the bathroom as her mouth pressed his back. This response seemed to surprise him, their lips springing apart as he stumbled sideways against the tree. They laughed with embarrassment. But each remembered the brief part in the middle where for a second or two they floated softly in the tree's dark leaves.

After that first try, they got it right most of the time, though they hadn't tried French kissing yet. Patty Lantz was the one who explained it. She was called "fast" because she was said to have let Mike Buchanan go all the way. Patty never said so, of course, but Mike said so to anybody who would listen. Mostly, Palmer thought, Patty just needed to make some different grooming choices. The tight sweaters and pierced ears didn't do her reputation any good. But the boys noticed her all right, and Patty seemed to think that would get her what she thought she wanted.

Maybe, thought Palmer, a girl like Patty who had filled out a sweater by the end of third grade just naturally came in for a lot of pressure from boys—and not the flattering kind that came to the popular girls. Palmer had never seen Patty on the beach, but the girl was often out by the Roundhouse. Rumor had it that sometimes the janitor forgot to lock up, and the old leather couches inside were great for making out.

Palmer wondered if she spent too much time thinking about sex. They called boys who talked about sex and told certain kinds of jokes "dirty-minded." Was that what her daydreams made her?

But really, couldn't you *think* whatever you wanted? Gene Kelly's athletic swing through the air and Zorro's wicked smile made her stomach tighten in such an interesting and pleasant way. Those thoughts that swooped into the mind like gulls diving after silver fish—weren't they at least your very own?

Sin, Salvation, and Ceilings

And though the last lights off the black West went
 Oh, morning, at the brown brink eastward, springs—
Because the Holy Ghost over the bent
 World broods with warm breast and with ah! bright wings.

—"God's Grandeur"
Gerard Manley Hopkins

As Palmer and JJ walked out toward the Roundhouse on Saturday night for the Youth for Christ Rally, half a dozen pelicans flew over the Pier. The birds were close enough to see their gray-brown feathers, their throat pouches beneath dark bills. They flew in formation, passed the Pier, and then dipped low over the gleaming water. One scooped up a fish, water streaming from its pouch before it swallowed its catch. Palmer knew they did everything in flocks: "from breeding to feeding," her father always said.

The sun was blinding just above the horizon so that they couldn't look directly at it, but shortly, once it had slipped below that knife-edge of the world, its reflected glow would light the sky in fuchsia and gold.

"Hey," said JJ, waving toward the sun. "Look at that! It must be God's searchlight. This rally is gonna *serenade the spheres!*"

Palmer studied the tops of her black ballerina flats and kept on walking. When he talked like that, she felt embarrassed, as if she'd walked into a movie that seemed too showy, though she couldn't always say why. She knew JJ was sincere; maybe he was just talking like his minister.

"The weather *is* neat," she said. "There'll be a big crowd, and you guys will be so busy with all your ushering." His shoulders straightened at that. By then they had reached the double doors, the Roundhouse thrown open that night with a huge blue and gold banner pinned above that read, "*Youth for Christ.*"

Inside, the auditorium was transformed. The moldy make-out couches had disappeared, and a stage had been erected. On each end loomed a basket of white carnations tied with royal-blue ribbon. In the center perched a podium like some gold-painted bird, holding its wings in tight to its body, waiting for a signal to fly. Metal folding chairs marched in rows like uniformed soldiers, and lights shaped like frosted-glass torches were mounted on the walls. It was so splendid that Palmer half regretted her mean thoughts about JJ's description of the rally. It *was* a kind of heavenly gathering.

Girls were lighting candelabra on the stage, but the atmosphere was as much pep rally as church. An upright piano stood to one side, and already a handsome man was playing spirited hymns as the volunteers finished up and groups of people, mostly teenagers, started arriving.

> *Stand up, stand up for Jesus, ye soldiers of the cross*
> *Lift high your royal banner, it must not suffer loss—*

JJ steered Palmer to an aisle seat seven rows from the front. "Seven," he whispered. "The perfect number." Perfect for what? Palmer wondered. He handed her a program. "Save me a seat, and I'll be back after things get started." At least he was unusually gallant, steering her by her elbow. That was a new touch she didn't mind, but when he left and headed toward the door to hand out programs, she felt self-conscious and awkward sitting alone. She swung her feet back and forth.

The floor was sprinkled with sawdust, and she thought it

would be a great place for a dance. Years ago, when the Pier had been new, they held dances in the Roundhouse with live music and liquor, but her folks told her fights broke out and too many men got knocked over the railing, which meant some guy would have to jump in with a rope tied around his chest to make a rescue. That was nobody's idea of a good time. On a rough night the swells could knock any swimmer, rope or no, against the huge pilings with their crust of razor-sharp barnacles. And while few man-eating sharks prowled these waters, it could be unsettling for even a brave man to know he was trailing blood into deep water.

> Rock of Ages, cleft for me
> Let me hide myself in Thee
> Let the water and the blood
> From Thy wounded side which flowed—

Even from where she was sitting, Palmer could see the pianist sweating. Young singers in blue satin choir robes filed out onto the stage and began to hum along with the piano. She opened her program and read that Pastor T. Randall McManus, nationally acclaimed evangelist from Trenton, New Jersey, had given up a *dissolute* life to follow the Lord and to worship him with music and song.

Palmer tried to spy JJ in the crowd that was surging into the room, people already standing several deep across the back. It was probably against the fire code, but Palmer doubted the fire department would do much enforcing, though she had glimpsed a couple of Manhattan Beach policemen, probably hired just for the event; one of them even looked like her father's friend Sergeant Norquist. Finally she saw JJ, flushed and smiling, his hand on the elbow of a pretty blonde who looked old enough to be in high school. Palmer wished she were ushering, too, wearing a carnation pinned to her chest, though all the ushers seemed to be boys. She wished she were doing something other than just sitting—"like a bump on a log," her grandmother would say—

but just at that moment the pianist switched to a less peppy hymn, one with deepening drama.

A Mighty Fortress is our God
A bulwark never fa-a-ai-ling—

The crowd settled down, anticipating, and onto the stage stepped an enormous red-haired, red-faced man in a powder-blue suit. He reminded Palmer of the setting sun, rays almost emanating from his huge head. He held his arms aloft as if there were balcony upon balcony of them and roared out a welcome.

"In the name of the Almighty who gave his only begotten Son, we welcome you to the first annual meeting in Manhattan Beach, California, of Youth for Christ International!"

The crowd clapped wildly. "We're here to do the Lord's work, to save sinners who repent to be born again in the name of Jesus Christ." His eyes swept the room as he stepped out from behind the podium and leaned toward the crowd. "Are you glad to be here? Let me hear it!"

"Yes!" they yelled back.

"That sounded mighty pathetic to me! I said, ARE YOU GLAD—"

"YES!" the crowd roared.

"—TO BE HERE?"

"YEESSS!"

"That's more like it!" He already sounded out of breath. "And to get things rolling, folks, we have a surprise—the prettiest little group of sweethearts for the Lord that you ever saw. Come on out here, girls, and tell us what you're gonna sing for the folks."

Palmer's program listed them as the King's Garden Trio—three teenage girls dressed in blue taffeta dresses with matching headbands. They sang a cappella in three-point harmony, pageboys swaying in rhythm:

What a friend we have in Jesus, all our sins and griefs to bear!
What a privilege to carry everything to Him in prayer!

Before they quite finished spinning out their last note, Pastor McManus snatched up a gleaming brass saxophone and delivered his rendition of the song, while the trio swayed and cast worshipful glances at him. His face turned even redder as he blew into his horn. Someone started clapping in rhythm, and soon the Roundhouse was vibrating with handclaps and foot stomps, until Palmer had a vision of the whole place crumbling in on itself like an earthquake of human making, crashing like the Redondo Theater into the ocean—pilings and concrete, stage, choir, the pageboy-wearing trio, and saxophone—all sinking toward the sandy bottom. It was an idea that had seemed more exciting in the past than it did tonight.

At last the torchlights dimmed and a spotlight lit the stage. A free-will offering had been collected and dedicated to God's glory. The choir sang throughout, their voices masking the clink of coins and whisper of bills, and now the choir and trio were seated in front-row seats reserved for them. Pastor McManus prayed for God to touch the hearts of those present, especially those who were seeking the Higher Way.

To begin his talk (the program called it a *message*, not a *sermon*), he gave his personal testimony and confessed to having committed Unspeakable Acts while gripped by the Demons of Hell that resided, Ladies and Gentlemen, Boys and Girls, in the amber glass of a whiskey bottle. Palmer wished he would tell about some of the Unspeakable Acts, but he said only that he had not treated his sisters of the world with the respect that God demands.

"Oh, yes," he said, "jokes have been made about Demon Rum, but I am here to tell you that liquor grips the soul with a vise like steel, but not as strong"—he paused, open hand aloft in benediction, and his words rushed over them like a wave cresting— "not as strong, I tell you, as *prayer*!"

His voice dropped to an intimate tone. "For liquor has *never* been as powerful as a mother's prayers." He pressed his hand against his mouth, as if damming up an unvoiced cry. "And that, friends, is what I had going for me in my corner—" He did a sudden dance like a boxer in the ring. "I had the prayers of a mother made whole and clean by His love." He jabbed the air with his right fist, guarding with his left, his face growing redder as he bobbed around the stage until Palmer half believed she saw the devil himself counterpunching. "Prayers that made me a winner"—he raised one fist high over his head—"against Satan!"

As Pastor McManus paced, shouted, and cajoled, Palmer thought of her own mother, who was surely in the grip of a drug stronger than herself, and she wondered if Grandmother Sydney ever prayed for Claudia. Years ago, when Palmer herself had been just a baby and nearly died of a mysterious sickness, her father and mother had prayed for her in a Mexican chapel.

The preacher's voice pulled something tight in Palmer's chest, the way she sometimes felt in movies when people got hurt. That stretched feeling reminded her that her own mother was no stranger to drama, either. How many deathbed scenes had there been now? As Pastor McManus wiped the sweat from his face with a snowy handkerchief, Palmer recalled the first one, before she'd understood that her mother was not really dying.

It was also a Saturday, and Mother was agitated, taking quick sips of coffee and smoking one cigarette after another. Daddy had left early for the tennis courts. Finally Mother disappeared into her bedroom. A minute or so later she came out, drinking deeply from her coffee mug. Maggie escaped to play outdoors, but something had kept Palmer rooted inside, drawing with the set of pastels she'd gotten for her birthday.

Before the afternoon was over, Mother was half passed out on the living room couch, calling loudly for "Paaa-mer" to come kneel beside her. Maybe Claudia herself had attended a few revival meetings, because there was something ministerial in the way her hand fell heavily on Palmer's shoulder.

"Promise me—," she slurred.

Palmer was frightened. She'd never seen her mother act like this before. "Do you want me to call the doctor? Should I go find Daddy?"

Mother looked annoyed. "No, no, just promise—" Her voice

trailed off.

"What?"

"Promise that after I'm gone—"

"Oh, Mama, don't—"

"You have to promise—"

Mother's features had somehow blurred, as if her makeup had run together, her eyelids heavy, her lips swollen. It was easy to believe she was dying. Palmer began to cry.

Clumsily, Claudia patted her head. She seemed pleased, as if Palmer finally understood the gravity of the moment. "Promise me you'll never be separated from your sister. Even if I die." She frowned and amended the last sentence. "I *am* dying."

"Oh, no, Mama. Let me get help." Claudia scowled her back into place. "I promise," said Palmer, "really and truly."

"Say it! Say it all."

Palmer was puzzled. She'd thought she *had* said it all.

"Say you'll never, ever be separated from Maggie."

"I'll never, ever be separated from Maggie."

Satisfied, Claudia rolled over to face the back of the couch. "Pull th'afghan over me," she commanded. And fearfully, tenderly, Palmer lifted the crocheted afghan her grandmother Sydney had made for Palmer when Claudia was pregnant, and drew it gently over her mother's shoulders. And during the hours before her father came home, whenever Mother stopped snoring, Palmer would hold her dime-store mirror before the sleeping woman's mouth, looking for the faint fog of breath to make sure her mother were still alive.

That night her folks had another of their fights, her mother screaming and cursing, until Daddy had left the house and slept over at the Norquists'. Since then, Palmer had lost count of deathbed scenes, had stopped taking them at face value. During a recent one she asked her mother if she could have her *Alexander Wright* ring after she died. Claudia looked startled, then puzzled, but quickly she waved her hand airily and said, "Take the alexandrite! Who gives a goddamn, anyway?"

And now Pastor McManus half-crouched on the stage. "Who,"

he asked, "is praying for *your* soul at this moment?"

Palmer couldn't think of anyone unless it might be JJ beside her, whose hands were clasped so tightly his knuckles shone like white bones. "How can you hope to intercede for your loved ones unless you yourself have been reconciled to God? Unless you have been saved from the fires of Hell, you have no hope for yourself and no hope of bringing the Word to those most dear to you!"

Palmer felt a tremor in her stomach. Was she going to Hell? Was her mother? Hell wasn't spoken of much at the Community Church, but then that church didn't even know about the awful thing she'd done to their ceiling, either.

"Friends, God is on this Pier tonight. I can feel a wind blowing as He rends the strongholds of evil. *The Bible* tells us, 'You will receive power when the Holy Spirit has come upon you, and you will be my witnesses.'" Pastor McManus stormed to the other side of the stage, wiping his forehead again. "Let Christ bring you into the Fold, Christ who has made the Church His holy Bride—"

Bride? Palmer suddenly saw how even the Community Church's ceiling belonged to Christ, the drywall crashing to the ground, white plaster dust rising like an unholy veil. Since then she had barely tried to make amends, though she did put her savings of $1.75 in the collection plate the next time she went to Sunday School, causing Bonnie to raise her eyebrows and nod, but she'd certainly never confessed to God, let alone to her folks or the minister.

She heard herself gulp, almost a sob, just loudly enough for JJ to look inquiringly at her while she tried to settle the feelings rising like dusty ghosts around her. She was so hot, and she longed for just one sweet, sliding breath of ocean air. Couldn't someone at least open the doors? Oh, please, she thought in a half-prayer, don't let the asthma start.

Now the piano was playing gently, and yearningly.

Just as I am, without one plea ...

The choir sang softly, achingly, and Palmer almost made the noise in her throat again.

"I can hear that one troubled young soul out there," Pastor McManus called urgently, "who longs to know the security of resting in the safe, strong arms of Jesus. Dear young man or woman, don't deny your God any longer. Accept Christ as your personal Savior and become a force for redemption in your school and home. Remember that as God moves, so you must move with God!"

Palmer was crying now. JJ placed one arm gently around her shoulders; he'd never done that in public before, but he probably meant it in a religious way.

"Right now I'm going to ask you to come forward and stand before me here. Listen to the urgings of your heart and soul, and make this commitment. We stand here upon the Pacific Ocean, remembering how Peter once walked on the Sea of Galilee, so great was his faith in the Lord Jesus. If Peter could walk upon the waves, you can summon the courage to take these few steps forward to stand before your God."

Palmer wished she could throw herself on JJ's chest, feel both his arms around her, but she knew this was a moment between her and her God, a God she thought she knew. But she saw now that never before had she made a *public commitment*, never had she been *totally assured* of her place at God's right hand. Never had she been *saved*.

Out of the corner of her eye, she saw a man stepping over the feet of others, making his way to the aisle; he walked forward and stood before the stage, his head bowed.

"'Where two or more are gathered in His name, there the Lord will be, also.' Who else has heard the voice of God in the still, quiet places of the heart? Who else will come forward and join this man before the Lord?"

Was that what was bursting in her chest? Was it the voice of God speaking inside her? Suddenly she saw the blonde high school girl, tears streaming down her face, eyes riveted on Pastor McManus as she walked between the folding chairs. He beamed down at her and opened his arms as she approached the stage. "The very road to glory! Others of you, come be with your sister, as we sing one more verse."

Just as I am, and waiting not
To rid my soul of one dark blot—

Palmer could hardly breathe. Others were going forward, men and women, even some of the kids from JJ's church that Palmer would have thought were already born again. "And those of you who *are* saved, consider coming forward to rededicate your lives to God." She thought she felt JJ stir. "Be consecrated for all time in the Lord."

The pastor paused, his eyes squeezed shut in prayer as the choir kept singing, over and over, "O Lamb of God, I come! I come!"

"I hear you, young person, *you* who are afraid to take this step. The Lord hears your silent cry, and He is waiting for you to come forward. Don't leave this temple with your soul in immortal danger. What if you should *die tonight* without Christ in your heart? Our God is a loving God, but He also has righteous *wrath*. There is a time when it is too late, my friends." His voice softened. "Remember that they nailed *His feet* to the cross. Surely you can walk down here now."

Sobbing, Palmer turned away from JJ's comforting arm. What good was a boyfriend if you were burning in Eternal Fire worse than the most horrible sunburn when you couldn't even stand the touch of your softest undershirt against your blistered skin? It would be worse than stepping barefoot on a lighted cigarette, and the hurting would go on *forever*.

Eternity, she had heard, was more than all the grains of sand on all the beaches in all the world! Wiping her eyes on the cuff of her sweater, she stepped in front of JJ and made her way forward to stand with the dozen or so others who had come forward, though later she would not remember the walk to the altar, only the wrenching in her chest and the soft voices of the choir.

"We have Christian workers who will step beside each of these newborn souls in Christ. And those that you came with will wait for you, I promise."

But just before a pale young woman appeared at Palmer's side, guiding her to a place beside the stage and embarrassing her by suggesting they kneel there and pray together, before she received her literature describing this "once-in-a-lifetime step" she had taken, how "once saved was always saved," before all that happened, Palmer glanced up and saw Lars Norquist in his uniform, his police badge shining like a searchlight in that crowded room, his gun quiet in its leather holster, standing by the double doors, his eyes on her.

But he couldn't know about the church ceiling, or if he did, he couldn't know she had had anything to do with its crashing headlong into the church sanctuary.

And the choir sang on:

> *Just as I am,*
> *O Lamb of God, I come! I come!*

After the rally, just as Pastor McManus had promised, JJ waited for Palmer, the crowd already thinned. Walking away from the Roundhouse, they didn't talk much, holding hands and stopping to peer over the railing into the dark water spangled by the Pier's lights. Palmer felt that old urge to jump. She imagined it would be like falling into stars. JJ figured someone looking down from an airplane might think the Pier an amusement ride, bigger than anything at Ocean Park. In some way she couldn't explain, being *saved* made everything vivid, brought her closer to JJ. The night air was salty, and when they reached her house, his lips tasted faintly like popcorn as he kissed her, a kiss too tender somehow, like a benediction.

Now Palmer lay sweating and restless in her top bunk. Away from the crowd and the blue and gold and the music beating like wings against her eyes, and most of all, away from the drumbeat of Pastor McManus's voice, Palmer thought that even the night breeze slipping past her window seemed more real than forgiveness. Guilt congealed like lard in her stomach, as cold as if she'd never been saved, as cold as the attic of a church or the eyes of a policeman searching out a criminal. Had there been clues after all?

Always the *good girl.* How *could* she have sneaked up through the trapdoor of the choir room into the unfinished rafters above the sanctuary? Sneaked up there not just with Bonnie but also with Lincoln Pease, a freckle-faced boy who kept them laughing with Kilroy jokes and the one who discovered the attic in the first place.

And it hadn't been just the one time. For half the summer now they had stashed candles and matches, oranges and comics and Tootsie Rolls in that loft they visited on weekday afternoons when the unlocked church was vacant. In their defense, they never did anything wrong, if you didn't count illegal entry. They only wanted to whisper and giggle and read, suck on oranges, eat candy, and play with fire.

But two weeks ago when they left the attic, following a complicated route that involved swinging from high rafters to low ones, Palmer's foot had slipped, plunging through the ceiling's Sheetrock. A four-foot section had collapsed into the sanctuary with a terrible crash.

Palmer had read about churches being defiled, about acts of desecration. She was glad Lincoln hadn't been there that day; it was bad enough that afterward he'd had to forfeit his Batman comics because none of them was ever going back. As for *Bonnie's* conscience, her best friend quite accurately pointed out that it had, after all, been *Palmer's* foot that had done the damage, not hers.

As a rule, Palmer's code was pretty much to confess any crime as soon as possible. It usually struck adults as honorable, but mostly it got the guilt off her back. She couldn't bear waiting to be found out. There had been the time she'd lost her mother's yellow silk scarf, the time she ate the strawberries that had been set aside for Maggie. But never had she gone this far. Destroying church property was probably a felony. That made her a juvenile delinquent. Why else would Lars Norquist have his eye on her?

Worse yet, what about her folks? Aside from their shame, wouldn't they have to *pay* for a new ceiling? And how could they, when she'd already heard Daddy tell Mother that if things didn't get better, they might have to go on County Relief and take *handouts,* and then everyone would know he *couldn't cut the mustard*. Palmer wasn't supposed to know he'd been laid off by Wahlberg's, but she learned a lot lying in her bunk at night in the dark sunroom that had a doorway with no door.

Returning GIs were getting all the jobs, her father whispered harshly, young guys who would work for peanuts. Her mother was quiet. Palmer understood more than she was given credit by grown-ups like Bonnie's mother, who'd muttered that Claudia shouldn't put on airs, given her "weakness."

But when Palmer had finally worked up the nerve to go back to church again, the damage had been repaired, everything cleaned, swept spotless. Not even a crack showed where the hole had once gaped. Tonight, Pastor McManus had talked about the Broom of the Lord that swept away the unjust. She supposed that since she'd just been saved, she probably should—more than ever—confess her ceiling sin, but she just couldn't tell her folks, not right before Bonnie's beach party. Not only would they make her stay home, but they wouldn't go *themselves*. And wonder of wonders, Mrs. Stafford had asked them to chaperone.

Though Palmer lived much of her life on the sand, *beach party* meant something else entirely: bonfires against the black sky, with weenie roasts and marshmallows. The beach at *night* was more romantic than on the sunny, athletic afternoons. In those hazy years after WWII, freed at last from blackouts, people built fires all over the beach in shallow holes they dug in the sand. They left behind their charcoal litter to be swept clean and carried away with the next tide. They trusted the sea to do their housekeeping with the same tides that might later wash in a load of tar.

JJ would be there, of course, but Palmer was nearly beside herself that her own parents had been invited. Surprised, too, because Mrs. Stafford didn't like Mother. Still, Bonnie's mother needed *somebody's* father along, with Mr. Stafford out of the country as usual, and Mrs. Stafford did like *Daddy*, of that Palmer was very sure, so, of course, *both* parents had to be asked. And they'd said *yes*.

But lying in bed now, the sheets feeling sticky, Palmer kicked the covers off altogether. She could hear Maggie's soft sleep breath beneath her. What had Pastor McManus said? It had seemed comforting at the time. You had to *believe* that Christ cleansed you of sin. It all came down to *simple faith*. But staring up at the ceiling, her hands pressed against the ache in her stomach, Palmer couldn't see anything simple about anything in her life, much less faith.

On the morning of the beach party, Palmer washed her red pedal pushers and white sweater and hung them out to dry. She shampooed her hair in the kitchen sink with a vinegar rinse to make it soft and shiny. She started the chicken that Mother would fry for the party, scooping Crisco out of the silvery can and setting the big cast-iron skillet on the gas burner. She rinsed the chicken, patted it dry, then dumped it into a brown paper bag filled with flour, salt, pepper, and paprika. When Mother came into the kitchen, Palmer was holding the bag above her head, one end squeezed shut, shaking it to the rhythm of Tennessee Ernie Ford's rendition of "Mule Train" on the Philco.

Mother smiled. "Lose hold of that bag, and you'll have white hair before your time."

Palmer handed the chicken over to her mother, trying not to be obvious as she scrutinized her. No telltale signs of drinking, particularly that strange shift in Mother's eyes, as if Claudia herself were the one a little out of focus. Relief made Palmer almost giddy.

"The grease is hot!" she sang out.

"My, aren't we in a good mood! Let's have a beach party every night!" Claudia said, but she leaned over to kiss Palmer's hair. "Mmm, smells good. Good enough to keep you out of the water tonight?" She nestled the chicken piece by piece in the sizzling pan.

"Never!" Palmer imagined swimming in the dark, the green phosphorescence curling like Christmas ribbon through waves, the water softer than air, JJ swimming near, reaching out to wrestle with her in the surf—

"If you don't get your head out of the clouds, this chicken won't ever get fried! Such a daydreamer."

Palmer rummaged in the silverware drawer for the long-handled fork. She needed to keep her mother busy, happy, *whatever* it took, so she'd stay sober for the party. But she also had to be careful. Palmer had a sixth-sense kind of feeling that if she made too big a deal out of tonight, her mother would feel some kind of pressure, and that could lead to disaster, though Palmer had never figured out with any certainty what got her mother drinking one day and not the next.

Late that afternoon, Palmer went on ahead with Bonnie and Mrs. Stafford to lay down blankets and lug the grocery bags full of potato chips, wieners and buns, marshmallows, graham crackers and Hershey bars, ice for the cooler, bottles of pop, fresh cherries and oranges, and a huge bowl of potato salad. Once the other kids started arriving, everyone scrambled to find firewood, because the wide white beaches were often swept clear of driftwood.

Palmer had gathered a small armload when she glanced up toward The Strand. Her parents were walking across the sand, and they were holding hands. Palmer hugged her armful of twigs to her chest and took a deep breath of salty air so pure and fine that her feet felt buoyant enough to fly—or "levitate," as her grandmother would have said.

Mother and Daddy actually looked like a couple. Her trim father wore a clean pair of wash pants and his red, white, and blue tennis sweater. Palmer couldn't remember ever seeing him at the beach—not down on the sand, anyway. He was too restless for sunbathing and complained of sunburn, though the burns he received on the tennis courts or the Pier never seemed to bother him. He said he hated sand underneath his fingernails, and he *was* a fastidious man. Palmer used to watch him clean his nails carefully and methodically with his pocketknife.

But it was her mother who made Palmer's heart want to burst right through her chest. Claudia was beautiful, her hand pulling a strand of dark hair out of her eyes. More than a couple, even, they were a family, like JJ's, like Bonnie's when Mr. Stafford was home. Then Palmer saw Maggie galloping along behind them and felt just a twinge of dismay. No one else's little sister was going to be at the party, but who *would* take care of Maggie, since Palmer herself was at the party? Then she felt mean. Besides, she decided quickly, Maggie just added to this perfect family snapshot.

As it turned out, Claudia didn't let Palmer down. She sat close beside Daniel at the fire and talked in a mostly friendly way to Mrs. Stafford. She let Palmer eat hot dogs and potato chips and s'mores and said not a word when the kids rushed into the water fifteen minutes before the required hour was up. She watched Palmer swim in the dark, riding white-crested waves into shore, shouting in the night air, and she casually tossed out a beach towel when Palmer at last ran, shivering, from the water. Whatever fear Claudia felt trying to keep track of Palmer's moonlit face flashing amid the whitecaps, that night she hid it. She even saved any mothering touches that might have embarrassed Palmer and lavished them on Maggie, who finally curled up with her head in Claudia's lap and her feet in Daniel's.

The night was like one of those postcards on the circular rack at the Rexall Drug Store where the picture of the Pier was even more beautiful than it really was, with palm trees and flowers that didn't actually grow there. Palmer wondered why God would give her such a night after she'd sinned. When at last she climbed into bed and lay quietly, her body still pulled by the undertow and the lift and drop of the swells—"waterlogged," they called it, like having sea legs on land—she thought how good and evil, reward and punishment, sin and salvation, were even more complicated than she already knew.

Claudia heard Daniel's light snore. She pushed gently against his shoulder, and he rolled onto his side and was quiet. How long had it been since they'd made love? Of course, it didn't help that their bedroom door was nothing more than a curtain, the girls sleeping only a few yards away.

Still, the beach party had been fun, though she could sense he'd been ill at ease with his arm around her. Maybe because Elinor had sat there alone? Daniel just seemed different lately, even though she'd stopped drinking since her trip to Seattle. Pray God this time it would hold, that she could stop for good.

And speaking of *good*, Palmer was setting records this week, ever since that youth rally on the Pier. Helpful, polite—not that she wasn't usually, but every now and then her mood reminded Claudia, God save them, of those teen years approaching.

But right now Claudia was more concerned about whether Palmer were going off the deep end over this religion business. She'd asked Claudia if she ever prayed for her. Nothing wrong with that, of course, but she didn't want her to get fanatical or anything.

Why hadn't she asked Daniel? Or maybe she had. He was the one who never went to church, not even when they asked him. Still, Claudia would never forget how he had prayed for Palmer that time they'd thought they'd lost her. More than a decade ago. It made Claudia feel old to add up the years.

Palmer had been about twenty months old, talking like a mynah bird, though not everyone could understand her. Together at the beach they sat on a blanket and shared a picnic lunch. Claudia hoped her daughter might take a nap, a gauzy diaper draped to shield her from the sun, but the child was wide awake, toddling back and forth, filling her tin beach bucket with sand that she dumped mostly on their blanket.

That night, when Claudia had given Palmer her bath, she'd noticed a red spot on the back of her neck. She kept an eye on it, afraid it might be a sign of impetigo. By the time two days had passed, it had grown larger than a half-dollar, so Claudia took Palmer to the doctor who treated it with mercury lights and sent

Claudia home with mercury ointment to rub on the spreading rash.

The next day it was worse, seeming to spread by the hour. Claudia kept smoothing on the salve. When Palmer's skin had suddenly peeled away, her undershirt and diaper already stuck to raw spots oozing with lymph, Claudia rushed Palmer back to the doctor. He took one look, wrapped the child in a dampened, sterile sheet, and packed her off to the hospital.

Then the terror had deepened. Once each day, Claudia and Daniel were allowed five minutes to see Palmer through a glass window. She was kept swaddled in wet sheets. It was like standing outside the nursery those months before, looking at their newborn, except this baby couldn't be touched because no skin remained on her body. Even her scalp, under the baby-fine hair, was raw. But they talked to her through the glass and sang her favorite nursery rhymes in those few precious moments before the nurses wheeled her crib away.

Claudia never knew how much Palmer had cried for them, how much she hurt, or what other symptoms she developed. The doctors said they'd never seen anything like it, were treating it as best they could. One day Claudia overheard some nurses talking about mercury poisoning, about leg cramps and rapid heartbeat. One nurse said she hoped there wouldn't be retardation. When Claudia asked if they were talking about her baby, the nurses' faces closed up, and one said they weren't allowed to discuss patients' conditions.

Daniel had nearly gone crazy. He even visited a Mexican chapel on Olvera Street, lighting a candle each day for his daughter. In the darkened sanctuary with its vivid, brooding icons, the air heavy with mysterious scents, rows of candles flickered in red glass holders. He wondered how many of them were lighted for sick babies. Hot shadows danced on the walls and over his face, like healers from some primitive tribe. It seemed better than doing nothing.

Weeks later, they brought Palmer home, a pale baby with fragile skin who could not be bathed for weeks. Even when the diminished risk of infection had at last let them dip her in tepid water, they wrapped her afterwards in soft flannel that Claudia had cut from dime store yardage and washed twice by hand on a washboard to remove all trace of fuzz. They wrapped her loosely and let her skin dry naturally.

Going outside was forbidden, and they even kept her out of the indoor sun that splashed across every room of that house (before Portland) like water spilled from rivers.

Claudia tried feeding her everything from mashed banana and applesauce to soft-boiled eggs, but the baby had no appetite. In the afternoons, small bowls of vanilla ice cream melted with barely a taste.

Not only had Palmer grown thin in the hospital, but she had also ceased speaking. The silent baby sat in her bed, sifting lethargically through a basket of red, white, and blue poker chips, as if she were listening for the sound of rain.

Each night in the living room, Daniel rocked Palmer wrapped in a flannel square after her bath. She looked into his face with eyes that seemed both wise and sad, neither fussing nor smiling. One night, he felt her squirm. She freed one arm and reached a hand into his breast pocket to tug at the ever-present pack of Camels. Looking at the golden animal, the pyramids and palm trees, she said her first word since the hospital had swallowed her up over a month before.

"Pretty," she said and let the pack slide back into her father's pocket. She lay quietly, watching as he rubbed his shirtsleeve across his eyes.

Palmer herself didn't remember any of it, but she had heard the story many times. Mostly she was unhappy that Claudia insisted her scrapes and cuts be treated with iodine, which stung, rather than the painless Mercurochrome that most of her friends got to use. Every year on her school forms under "Allergies," Claudia carefully wrote, "Medications containing mercury."

No one figured out what the *original* rash had been, but for years after, Claudia wouldn't set foot on the beach, and it hadn't been until well after Maggie had been born that she'd even let

Palmer go with friends and their mothers to that sunny, danger-ous place.

"I've never trusted it," thought Claudia, drifting at last towards sleep.

Even tonight, as nice as the beach party had been, she kept remembering Daniel's restlessness, submerged like an ocean current in his lean body. There just weren't a lot of places she dared put her faith.

September 1949

"You don't like bright colors, do you?" Miss Sittern, the eighth-grade art teacher, leaned over Palmer's crayon drawing of a dancer in a delicate pink tutu, tying her toe shoes.

The teacher had shown them pictures of famous paintings, and Palmer had loved the sturdy ballerinas of the artist named Degas, taking note of how Miss Sittern pronounced his name. Ever since Palmer had embarrassed herself in fourth grade by pronouncing the name of their national park *Yos-might* during a read-aloud session, she'd been alert to tricky words. "What you don't know won't hurt you," her grandmother was fond of saying, but Palmer wasn't so sure. Seemed to her that what you didn't know could barrel out of the darkness like the delivery trucks that parked behind Wahlberg's Market.

She studied her dancer and considered the teacher's question. Palmer had never thought about *not* liking *any* color.

"See how every shade is pale? You do nice work, but I wonder what makes you so fond of pastels." The teacher fixed her with an oddly intense gaze. "Are you *afraid* of intense hues?"

When Palmer couldn't think of any way to answer that question, Miss Sittern moved on to the next student, but by then Palmer's ballerina had turned pasty as uncooked biscuit dough. She *thought* she liked bright colors. In fact, yellow was her all-time favorite, and she'd always liked the reds, which could be as varied as the inside of a hibiscus blossom. She didn't know how you could be afraid of *colors*, but as Palmer leafed through her pad of art paper, all the pictures looked wan, every color laid down carefully and very evenly.

Maybe *that* was the point—not a matter of preferring pastel shades so much as the desire to keep the colors even. She remembered bearing down so hard once on Red-Orange that the crayon had lifted the waxy color right back off the page, as if reclaiming a small extravagance. Palmer made a terrible mess of that sunset and never did get it right.

Anyway, pressing hard on a crayon dulled the point and usually broke it. Then you had to peel away the colored paper, making the crayon look old and messy. A light pressure made the crayon glide across the paper, right up to the outlined edge. Palmer didn't like going beyond the edges, even when she sat side by side with Maggie at the kitchen table and they colored opposite pages in her sister's *Snow White* or *Brenda Starr* coloring book.

In fact, Palmer didn't like edges of any sort. She had a recurring dream of crouching beside Maggie in the back seat of Nellie, both parents in the front. Daddy was driving a mountain road too fast, headed for the San Bernardino Mountains and somewhere they'd never been before, like Lake Arrowhead, and as he took each squealing turn, Palmer looked out her window straight down a mountainside that seemed to fall away beneath the car's wheels. Live oak and manzanita grew out of the cliff like clawing fingers, and far down the deep ravine, she could make out stunted pine trees struggling to grow among dark boulders.

Palmer always woke up before the car could go into that final, terrifying skid, heading broadside toward the cliff's edge, the four of them teetering there. She'd heard someone say once that most people weren't really afraid of heights so much as edges, and she thought that might be true.

Yet on sunny days when lifeguards were busy elsewhere, she often climbed outside the railing of the Manhattan Beach Pier, leaning far out, her hands behind her holding lightly to the rail, her feet barely braced against the concrete, or maybe standing even a few inches lower on that pipe that ran the length of the Pier, a yearning in her heart to take that brave leap, to fly on no wings at all. Wasn't *that* beyond the edge?

Then, oddly, she thought how pressing hard on crayons and all that vivid, messy color were somehow like Mother when she was drinking: unpredictable, veering off in unexpected directions as she marched down the street to the liquor store, purchasing one bottle at a time, never sneaking the cash for more. The truth was, Palmer liked shades as deep as her mother's plum-colored lipstick, colors that seemed to explode on the back of her tongue like sourballs. Trouble was, such colors weren't dependable.

She sighed at how complicated even crayons had suddenly become. Now the idea of being a professional artist, a secret and early ambition, made her feel tired, and she put her supplies away early. She walked down the corridor to the girls' lavatory to wash the stain of crayons from her hands, pink and lavender swirling together as if the sink were swallowing her ballerinas.

But later, the longer she thought about it, the more Palmer decided her art teacher's comments were off base. She'd go ahead and breathe in the whole damned (*forgive me, Jesus*) color wheel if she wanted. That liberating decision seemed linked to Grandmother Sydney's coming for another visit. Both seemed to beckon in Technicolor.

Daniel made little attempt to disguise his annoyance that Sydney would crowd herself into a house that was already too small for the four of them.

"I don't see what difference it'll make," Claudia said. "You'll be off playing tennis or fishing all weekend, anyway. Seems to me it's good news she's well enough to come see her granddaughters."

"Mooching is more like it."

"Oh, Daniel. You think I'm going to be out buying Porterhouse steaks? Another bowl of stew, more oatmeal in the pot—that's going to be more than we can afford? She'll just be here a week. All she's asking from you is a ride from the Greyhound station."

Palmer sensed he was shamed by appearing cheap, so of course he was irritable and ready to bolt out the door. "I'm going to pick up a paper," he said brusquely. Palmer was pleased she had predicted what he would do next and wondered if that was how Grandmother Sydney had begun her psychic ways. Perhaps in some small way, it foretold powers for Palmer. More likely it was a lucky guess.

Sydney arrived Friday night. Maggie slept on the lumpy sofa and gave her grandmother the bottom bunk out of deference to her continuing recovery. Daniel was dressed in his tennis whites by seven the next morning, his racket under his arm, but when he stepped through the bedroom curtains into the bright kitchen, Sydney was standing at the sink, about to fill the pot for coffee.

They stared hard at each other for a moment before Daniel grabbed a couple of oranges. "See you later," he muttered and headed out the door. He'd get coffee at the drugstore. Sometimes it was hard to beat the old bat at any game.

Palmer wondered about the tension that flashed between her grandmother and her father. Other kids had plump grandmas in aprons, as different from her auburn-haired grandmother as pelicans were from swans. "A henna job," her father said, but Palmer didn't see what was wrong with that. Wasn't henna some kind of natural root?

Sydney's collar-length hair waved softly off her face to show the opal earrings she always wore—a gift long ago from Grandpa Burl. Palmer could see her mother's looks, the high cheekbones and long legs, the graceful hands and narrow waist, though Grandmother Sydney sometimes pressed at her tummy with long fingers, as if impatient that it was slightly rounded now, unlike in her younger days.

She'd worn nothing but black ever since her husband died all those years ago, but Claudia said it was less a matter of mourning than a trademark, and economical as well. For jewelry, she had her wedding ring and the opals. Palmer asked her grandmother why she never wore a pin or necklace or even other earrings.

"Pins are for old ladies," she sniffed, "and if you already wear rainbows in your ears, anything else would be too *busy*."

That evening after meatloaf and baked potatoes, Mother put the food away, and Palmer washed and dried the dishes. Maggie got out a coloring book. Drinking a fresh cup of coffee, Grandmother Sydney sat at the kitchen table, gossiping about the feud between sisters Joan Fontaine and Olivia de Havilland. The rest of the family used mugs, but Claudia kept a china cup and saucer in the highest cupboard for her mother. Daniel took off to the living room for his easy chair and paper.

When Claudia went next door to gather the laundry, Palmer pulled up a chair to the table. "Tell us a story, Grandma."

"What do you want to hear?"

"About the boat," Maggie said quickly. Palmer nodded. The stories never came out the same way twice, and the girls always hoped for a touch of magic or romance, or in Maggie's case, something about an animal.

Sydney seemed to stretch without moving a limb. "Ah, yes, the belle of Puget Sound," she said at last. "You know that *Kalakala* means 'flying bird' in Chinook?"

Palmer nodded. Yes, flying bird. She'd heard this story before.

"Just a beautiful pewter fish flashing between Bremerton and Seattle." Sydney paused, as if staring across miles and years, remembering ferries that flew. "Oh, she had her detractors, all right, those who called her the *Kalunka* because she did pitch and roll a bit, and she was, apparently, more than a little difficult to steer, bashing into other boats—but only a few—demolishing docks, that sort of thing."

She waved her hand dismissively at invisible and disgruntled boat owners and smiled. "More than once she bumped another ferry so hard she crunched a few cars. But why wouldn't she, built of solid steel like that."

Palmer knew her grandmother would take her own sweet time with the telling. When you *read* a story to yourself, you could jump to the dialogue where the action happened. With storytellers, you waited on their pace, but that usually suited Palmer and Maggie just fine.

"Yes, solid steel, a massive ferry. But bumpy—the *Kalakala*'s restaurant would only sell half-full cups of coffee so passengers didn't get a scalding. It had a horseshoe-shaped counter with an edge to keep spoons and whatnot from rattling right off onto the floor."

Sydney adjusted her black-framed eyeglasses. Palmer thought they looked like glasses Katharine Hepburn might wear in one of her career-girl movies. Her grandmother claimed their real purpose was to deepen her second sight.

"That boat gave a marvelous foot massage. The vibrations tingled clear up your legs. One of the first streamlined ferries—very modern." She sipped her coffee, and Palmer wondered if those earlier half cups had anything to do with her grandmother's always wanting her cup filled to the brim. If Daddy were pouring, he'd roll his eyes.

"They had moonlight cruises aboard that ferry, and the vibrating felt wonderful to danced-out feet when you came on deck with your date to cool off." She twirled one slender ankle. "You girls understand in those days we couldn't just waltz into some department store and buy a new party dress." Palmer didn't think there was much of that going on these days, either.

"But I could sew like a dream. Make myself a party dress in a day, if I had to."

Maggie suddenly upended her box of crayons, startling Grandmother Sydney.

"Darling, can't you just take them out one by one?"

Maggie held up the crayon she'd been searching for, a rust color that Palmer could see was just right for Brenda Starr's hair.

Sydney smiled herself back into memory. "The first date I had with your Granddaddy Burl was a moonlight cruise on the *Kalakala*."

Around the corner, Palmer's father rustled his paper, impatiently, it seemed.

Sydney looked at her granddaughters. "Well, I suppose you'll want to know that he kissed me that night." Maggie slid her eyes sideways, grinning. "Yes, on our first date. I was only seventeen years old, and I *let* him, too. It wasn't any *stolen* kiss. From then on, I knew he was the one. My, he was gorgeous in those days, like a matinee idol, and don't think a few others didn't bat their eyes at him, either."

"How old were you when you and Granddaddy got married?"

"Palmer, you already know I was no more than eighteen."

"Oh, yeah, that's right." She'd really just been prompting her grandmother.

"Say *yes*."

"What?" Palmer frowned, and Maggie looked up, a yellow crayon poised in her fingers.

Her grandmother's lips were pursed, as if she'd poured salt in her coffee. "*Yeah* is not a ladylike word."

"Oh." You could never tell when Grandmother Sydney was going to get finicky about manners. "Okay."

"Not that word, either, Darling. Just say 'all right' or 'yes.' You must understand that your vocabulary brands you. More than your clothes or the house you grow up in." The girls' eyes darted around The Shack, and the newspaper crackled again in the living room.

Sydney hurried on. "Of course, not everything on board that ferry was romantic. Below deck it could get very dark and even claustrophobic for those so inclined. And when it rained, which being Seattle was generally, the roof tended to leak and the dance floor got a little damp, but we just put up with it."

She glanced at Maggie. "And if people walked their little *dogs* around the cars, you had to be extra careful where you stepped."

Maggie giggled. "Poop?"

"Oh, my, let's just say not all the dampness was rainwater."

Maggie looked gleeful.

"What finally happened to the boat?" Palmer asked.

"Can you imagine, they turned that beautiful ferry into a cannery. It nearly broke our hearts, but change is the way of the world, girls. And a good thing, too. If you don't change, Palmer-child, you get brittle, and things that are brittle are too easily broken."

They sat together for a moment, Palmer trying to sort out this bit of wisdom. There was no sound from her father. Finally, Grandmother broke the spell by elbowing Palmer and laughing, "Like peanut brittle! Now somebody bring me my pocketbook."

Peanut brittle was Sydney's favorite candy, and she always brought some in her purse and then rationed it out to everyone, herself included. She was more than a little vain about her figure, especially her legs, which were so trim she could cross her knees and then wrap her top ankle around the bottom one. She watched what she ate but didn't like to be caught doing it, insisting *gardening* kept her thin, that and an occasional flare-up of diverticulitis. When the hot pain appeared in her lower abdomen, her first line of defense was to go on a liquid diet with no caffeine. The *worst* of deprivations, she said.

If the liquid diet didn't work, the next line of defense was penicillin, but that always gave her a yeast infection. Sydney kept few secrets about her health, though Palmer didn't know exactly what a yeast infection was, only that when she asked, her grandmother would look heavenward and say, "Pray to God, child, you never have to find out."

Aging was "no piece of cake," according to Grandmother Sydney. But it was her magic and her stories that endeared her to her granddaughters. With each retelling, the *Kalakala*—that beautiful flying bird—glinted and shimmered a bit more, and now the romance between Burl and Sydney had taken on a luster like the shining opals.

Palmer liked thinking that her imagination had been passed down to her from this colorful woman. "Just make sure you tell things straight," her father would warn her. But sometimes Palmer wondered whether *facts* alone always pierced the shadows around truth, the way afternoon sunlight didn't reach every part of the Pier's underbelly.

She thought of *Bible* stories she'd read, of the *New Testament* parables. She remembered Greek, Roman, and Norse tales from the library, the *Aesop's Fables* her father had read to her. Perhaps stories and myths could shine some truth into the shade of the future.

Of course, as JJ told her frequently, *every single word* of scripture—every *a, an,* and *the*—had been dictated by God exactly as it appeared on the pages of the King James Version of the *Bible.* Hearing this, Palmer felt wistful, as if mystical men like Jeremiah and Ezekiel, Isaiah and Solomon—even Matthew, Mark, Luke, and John—were no more than sacred stenographers. Maybe the prophets were part of God's vast secretarial pool. Maybe all writers were taking cosmic dictation.

Working on school assignments, even she found that words could spring out of nowhere: *insidious* or *harpy, mesmerize* or *solemnity,* words she didn't know she knew. Her grandmother spoke of something called "automatic writing" in which you cleared your head and listened for an inner voice or sometimes an otherworldly one, and language just poured right out of your pen.

Anyway, what exactly made a story *straight,* as her father put it? What about suspense and yearning and mystery? That scratchy-voiced Walter Winchell on the radio: "Good evening, Mr. and Mrs. North and South America and all the ships at sea!" Did *he* tell things straight?

And hadn't she seen her father get misty-eyed over a favorite book? Maybe facts alone told only parts of the truth—an illusion in itself.

By the time Claudia came back with her basket of laundry, story time was over. Grandmother Sydney helped Mother fold clothes on the kitchen table, while Palmer made up the sofa for Maggie's bed and her sister went looking for Floozy. Ever since Maggie had dragged the skinny, abandoned kitten home one afternoon, the two had slept together.

Palmer remembered how they'd all stood around in the kitchen of the Portland house to examine the orphan's oversized, six-toed paws, how Daddy started snapping his fingers, singing, "Flat-foot floozy with the floy, floy." Mother joined in, the two of them doing a quick swing step around Maggie and the bedraggled cat who by this time was drinking milk from a saucer at Maggie's feet.

"Floozy," Maggie said, "that's what I'll call her."

Mother tried to talk her into calling the cat Mittens, or even Floy, not sure that Floozy was as suitable a name for her daughter's kitten as she would have liked, but Floozy she remained.

Palmer finished tucking in the blankets on the couch and glanced at her father. He was still immersed in his paper, his face grim. She knew he liked to read every editorial from start to finish, but tonight he looked cross. She want to make it better for him, not really sure what *it* was exactly. Palmer the Peacekeeper, her grandmother called her.

Determined not to act like a teenager, which never failed to annoy Daddy, she aimed for entertaining instead and leaned against the arm of his easy chair. She bided her time, and when he finally glanced up at her with a look that resembled something almost friendly, she launched into her grandmother's courtship story—keeping it short 'n' sweet, as he often urged, the very opposite of taking your own sweet time.

Her father raised his shoulders as if to shake her off and rustled the editorial page angrily. He didn't even try to keep his voice low. "What kind of bilge is she feeding you now?" The voices in the kitchen stilled. "That ferry wasn't even launched until 1935. Not likely they courted on that tub, when Burl had already managed to drink himself into the ground years before!"

Palmer's face blazed, and she turned away quickly, walking into the sunroom as if she needed to smooth her grandmother's bed in the lower bunk, a bed her grandmother had made with perfectly square corners that morning before either girl was awake.

Maybe wishing he could reel in those last words, the fish too small for such cruel tackle, her father cleared his throat sharply, the only sound in the little house. But he didn't call Palmer back.

October 1949

IT WAS ONE OF THE GLORY days of fall. The high overcast burned off by noon, and as Palmer and Bonnie walked home from school under the blue crown of sky, they tied the arms of their jackets around their waists and swung their arms like small Amazons, pretending to be Wonder Woman, their magic bracelets flashing gold in the sun, invulnerable to the bullets of the world.

Bonnie suddenly broke stride and scuttled crab-like beside Palmer.

"What are you doing?"

"I'm scraping my shoes on the sidewalk, dummy." Palmer eyed her friend's handsome penny loafers, their sides now a chalky gray from the concrete. Bonnie alternated feet, dragging the side of each shoe in turn. "Once they look bad enough, Mom buys me a new pair. I'm just speeding things up. Go on, try it!"

Palmer didn't even need to look down at her own shoes; she knew the laced-up oxfords from County Relief looked huge and cheap, as if her feet belonged to some clumsy and overgrown toddler. Tentatively, she dragged the inside of one brown shoe against the gritty sidewalk.

"That's it," Bonnie said. "Wow, what a trail of leather *you* left!"

Palmer looked down at the sidewalk and felt a little sick. Much as she hated these shoes, she felt as if she'd just shredded an elbow across the concrete. What would her father *do* if these shoes wore out? Ask the County for another pair, drawing that flat outline of her bare foot as she pressed it against the white paper he held still on the kitchen floor? Could you even do that, ask for a second pair so soon? And wouldn't they look just as bad as these clunky shoes that embarrassed her at school? Like the twin cotton dresses they'd sent her and Maggie, the flowered print too pink, the fabric so stiff and coarse that the skirts stuck straight out. And wouldn't Daddy feel even more awful than he already did about being on County Relief? "A guy on the dole," she'd heard him say scornfully to Mother.

What if they subtracted the new shoes from the McNeils' food allowance? Mother had already cut back on the cheddar in her macaroni and cheese. Even with all her folks' troubles, when the last day of September had rolled around, they'd given her a new drawing book for her thirteenth birthday, and Mother baked an applesauce cake with caramel frosting.

Palmer pressed her hands against her stomach, her fingers spread like Grandmother Sydney's before she'd gone back home to Seattle, to ease a kind of gnawing inside like hunger pangs. Except she wasn't hungry.

"What's the matter?" Bonnie yelled. She had walked on ahead.

"I need to go home," said Palmer.

"How come? I thought we were going to my house."

"I just do."

Minutes later, when she walked in and found no one home, Palmer pulled the shoebox out from under the kitchen sink where Daddy kept his shoe-buffing brushes and the tins of colored wax that opened with a twist of a tiny lever shaped like a butterfly. Using an old toothbrush, she spread coat after coat of dark-brown paste over the shoes that even her grandmother had called "Clem Kadiddlehoppers," and then she hid them in the back of her closet. She hoped the thick polish would eventually dry into one even color, but the next morning, her right shoe bore a brown scar where its thin leather had been scraped away and then polished over. The shoes were no less ugly. One foot just seemed to have stepped into a dark and muddy shadow.

At night, October clouds smothered the stars, and by day the silver slant of light bleached the ocean pale as a nickel in a child's fist. Mother wasn't drinking. Yet sometimes the anger in the air of that little house pressed against Palmer until she could hardly breathe, like that old wives' tale (though Grandmother Sydney always swore this one was God's own truth) about cats sucking the air right out of the mouths of sleeping babies.

Palmer and Maggie had been in bed for nearly an hour. Palmer was still awake, listening to *The Mysterious Traveler* on a single tiny earphone. From her right ear, its pink cord trailed like a baby rat's tail down to the radio on their bedside table. At least that's what they called the orange crate Daddy had lugged home from Wahlberg's and set on end beside Maggie's bunk.

Mother had run twine through a hem of yellow-checked cotton and tied the fabric around the crate, leaving the shelf side open. Maggie filled the bottom and the middle shelf with animal books and crayons and two miniature plastic horses that she played with under her covers. The radio sat on top.

At the other end of the little bedroom, just opposite the doorway, stood a makeshift closet with a rod and a couple of shelves for storing shoes. A matching yellow-checked valance was thumbtacked around the top of the closet.

Mother had looked at her sunny handiwork, hands on hips. "Well, it's not the Taj Mahal, but at least you can tell *girls* sleep in here"—she jerked her head toward their metal bunks—"rather than a couple of sailors."

Listening to the radio in the dark was one of Palmer's *privileges* as big sister, along with her fifty cents-a-week allowance that towered over Maggie's quarter. But now she stopped listening, aware suddenly that Mother and Daddy were buzzing like wasps in the kitchen, probably thinking both girls were asleep. She pulled the earplug out and tucked it under her pillow.

"Why in heaven's name would I make it up, Daniel?"

"Because you don't want the ol' man out here—more work for you—though anytime Syd wants to come, it seems to be okay. Anyhow, you're still pissed because last time he emptied your booze down the sink."

"No longer a problem, in case you hadn't noticed," Mother said stiffly. "I just don't want him grabbing my breasts."

"Jesus—"

"'Ah, daughter,' he said to me, 'it's so good to feel a woman again.'"

"Shut your face!" Daniel forgot to whisper. "What a dirty—"

Palmer peered between the curtains and tasted that bitter thing at the back of her throat like choking on salt water. Daddy started toward Mother, but at the last minute he grabbed up his keys and slammed out the door into the dark. Mother sat down slowly at the kitchen table, smoke from her cigarette rising like a spirit toward the naked bulb in the center of the ceiling.

Watching that smoke spiral upward, Palmer thought of the Holy Ghost, except instead of being filled with the Spirit, she was struggling to draw breath. She climbed out of bed and padded into the kitchen. "I'm getting asthma," she said. The ghost in the house was gobbling up all the air.

Mother didn't look surprised. "I'll find the adrenaline. Go on back to bed."

Palmer wanted to ask about their fight, about her grandfather, but didn't dare, couldn't even think how to find such words to speak aloud to her mother.

"Go on." Claudia's voice was weary. If she suspected Palmer had heard the argument, it didn't show on her face.

Minutes later Palmer lay in her bunk with her thoughts racing and that feeling in her stomach like being scared, except she knew it was mostly from the medicine. She often had trouble getting to sleep after Mother used the medicine dropper to place those amber beads on her tongue. Her mother didn't like to use the adrenaline very often, worried it might be hard on the heart. Lots of things were, it seemed.

Sometimes Mother would skip the medicine and just take Palmer into bed, talking softly to her. They would lay curled together while Daddy slept, and Mother would whisper about magic gardens where fairies danced on wild lilies, where elves counted out pennies to reward good children.

Palmer was really too old now for such stories, but they still relaxed her. Often while Mother was talking, Palmer fell asleep without the medicine, her breath sliding easily, her heart beating a solid measure in her chest.

"Christian Science," Mother called it.

When Palmer had read every collection in the library from Andersen to Grimm to the Scandinavian myths, she'd given up fairy tales, though she still liked them. They were a lot like movies: things *worked out* in the world of make-believe. Pretend people got what was coming to them, good or bad.

Before Maggie was born, Mother often sent Palmer out into their yard at the old house on Center Street. "Magic time," she'd called it.

"Go out and tell stories to the brownies," she'd say. "Sing them all the songs you know, and during the night they'll come back to thank you with pennies."

And sure enough the next morning, out in the early sun with a milkshake glass full of hot Cream of Wheat mixed with milk and brown sugar, and an iced-tea spoon to keep the cereal from settling, Palmer would find two or three pennies lying wherever she'd sat the day before, entertaining these little folk.

Then the next time that Mother wanted to lie down in the afternoon with a magazine, or sometimes with that sweetish smell upon her, she'd say, "Palmer, I think I hear the brownies outdoors—or maybe it's the fairies." And Palmer would run outside to sit under the oleander or the jacaranda with its lacy leaves and delicate purple flowers to tell stories like "The Lion and the Mouse" or "The Tortoise and the Hare." She'd recite endless nursery rhymes. And while she loved finding the pennies, which she'd spend for candy down at the Sweet Shoppe, mostly she hoped that one day a sprite would trust her enough to flutter from its hiding place. She was greedier for enchantment than penny-candy.

"They are very shy," Mother would say when Palmer turned wistful. "But keep trying." And so she had, for a very long time.

Palmer saw now it had been a convenient way for her mother

to keep her entertained and out of the house. Not a bad lie, really—a lot like Santa Claus or the Easter Bunny.

But sometimes, it was hard to tell when to believe. If Mother was drinking, she'd launch into tales about things Palmer herself had seen or heard, and Palmer would know how Mother exaggerated the story in the telling. The funny things were funnier, the sad things sadder. Of course, Palmer did that herself sometimes without even meaning to. The story just popped out with a better shape than the way it really happened. Daddy claimed Grandmother Sydney invented half of everything and three-quarters of the rest.

But Mother made up things that ached like a chip of ice lodged in the throat. One time Mother said that Daddy hit her so hard her eyeball had popped clear out of its socket and was hanging down her cheek. It had taken a doctor to put it back in, she said.. A wonder she kept her sight.

Palmer squeezed her own eyes shut, trying to erase the gruesome image. She didn't *really* think it had happened that way, wasn't sure such a thing was even possible, though her mother *had* nursed a fierce shiner. But would Palmer have missed a doctor's coming to the house at night or her parents going off to a hospital, leaving her and Maggie alone together?

Sometimes Palmer tended not to believe things her mother said that were probably true. And it was odd how her mother's storytelling seemed to give Palmer permission to side with her father. The decision as to who was right and who was wrong was always murky at best, like sand-filled surf. But because of the lies, Palmer felt at liberty to harbor a certain righteous anger toward her mother.

But the judgment didn't sit easily with her, because how could she ever excuse her father for *hitting*? Both lying and hitting were forbidden to her and Maggie—and which one was worse, anyway? Seemed like hitting would always be worse than words, no matter how false they were, except that Palmer didn't *see* the hitting, the way she did the lying—Mother's face up close, loud and boozy. And because Palmer had been brought up not to talk back, she couldn't do much when her mother started in.

Drinking lay behind the lying, of course, behind everything that made Mother act so … *different* from other mothers. Palmer didn't know how to describe it. She knew only that she felt ashamed for feeling shamed by her mother. And because Palmer loved her mother, she would have died rather than show anyone how she felt. That pleasant face she put on for the world often took some doing.

So what about this business now with Granddad? Mother was cold sober. It was probably the truth, and Daddy just didn't want to believe something so ugly about his own father. Maybe he was ashamed, too. Grandma Sydney had made it clear she didn't like Granddad, either. Maybe this was why.

When Palmer thought of JJ's fingers brushing the top button of her shirt as if he might actually unbutton it, her stomach softened with excitement. But when she imagined Granddad's touching Mother with his brown-spotted old-man hands, she felt queasy. She wondered which was worse for Mother: Granddad's touching her or Daddy's not believing her.

Monday afternoon the sky turned dull as old tin—weather that pecked at Palmer like a cold beak to the bone. The high overcast was neither fog nor rain—the rain often seeming cozy to California kids. Invariably, the high cloud cover darkened Palmer's mood. Its white-sky glare revealed storefronts and houses that needed paint and repair. Even pretty faces looked flawed in the chilly light, and actresses wrapped gauzy scarves around hair and necks, donning dark glasses as much to protect themselves from the eyes of others as from the sky's stare.

Daddy always said the weather *he* hated most was fog because it was treacherous stuff for ships and cars. "Here comes another *damned* fog bank," he'd say in disgust, then quickly add his "pardon me, girls," as the mass crept toward shore from the horizon. Driving around familiar streets turned dangerous. Every stop sign, pedestrian, and auto loomed as a surprise. Drivers lost their sense of direction, center lines disappeared, and cars wandered out of their proper lanes.

To Palmer, the real distinction between high cloud cover and a billowing fog bank was perfectly obvious. Fog had drama. Playing outside or walking to school, she loved the mystery of fog, putting her face right into it, turning around to watch it swirl shut behind her, as if hiding secrets. She loved the way it transformed the town into an unknown world, without even the pitying presence of shadow. She wondered if being blind might be something like walking in fog, with the world dark as those snapshots that sometimes for no reason came out blank.

Mother complained that fog straightened her hair, but when they awoke to the sound of bell buoys guiding ships, Palmer just braided her own hair into one thick pigtail that hung down her back. Water condensed on her eyelashes like invisible mascara, making her feel pretty and mysterious, the air heavy in her chest, like a swallowed sponge. She liked the muffled sounds of fog's breath, as if they shared an easy kind of asthma.

So today, without a sign of fog but with the high overcast already dispiriting and her mother sure to be home feeling depressed or worse, Palmer couldn't think of any reason for her and Bonnie *not* to go exploring after school in the deserted army bunkers.

Every kid knew the history. During the War years Manhattan Beach had feared an attack by the Japanese, so sixteen-inch guns had ridden flatcars down the railroad tracks to bunkers the army dug into the hillside. Those guns were long gone, but kids still played soldier or hide-and-seek in the bunkers.

Not surprisingly, Mother had forbidden Palmer and Maggie ever to set foot in one. At any moment there could be a cave-in, she said, and they'd be buried alive with no one to hear their cries, if they were even conscious after the crossbeams and tons of dirt piled down on them. Her mother was always graphic about the results of disobedience.

As Palmer and Bonnie walked home, Palmer pulled her red wool jacket close around her. Mrs. Stafford had made the girls matching jackets, boxy and unlined. Palmer wore hers every day, but Bonnie had four or five coats to choose from. Today she wore a fuzzy gray one, darker by several shades than the sky.

"We're not supposed to," Bonnie said, but not as if she didn't want to.

"How's anybody going to know?"

"What if it caves in?"

"C'mon, Bonnie, the bunkers have been here for years, practically since Pearl Harbor. You think one is going to collapse the very minute we're inside?" That was, of course, exactly what her mother thought. "We won't dig around or kick timbers. We're just explorers." Bonnie didn't look convinced. "You know, don't you," Palmer added, "that high school kids go in there to make out?"

Bonnie hesitated. "I'm not supposed to play in this coat."

"How can you get dirty if we don't touch anything? Anyway, we can drape our coats out here over a bush or something. We won't be inside long enough to get cold!"

The bunkers were dug into hard-packed dunes. Ice plant and scrubby wax myrtle had sprung up around them, a tooth-edged barrier. But kids always found ways to get inside.

"Watch out you don't snag your coat along here," Palmer said, as they threaded their way over the narrow path worn by other young explorers.

"What about this one?" Bonnie asked, standing before a dark hole framed by timbers. A couple of warped pieces of plywood hung askew in the opening, remnants from after the war when the dugouts had been boarded up for safety.

"Sure, okay," Palmer said. "Wish we had a flashlight." She took off her jacket. "Let's spread our stuff on the ice plant. It doesn't stain."

They set down their books and carefully laid their coats over the dense ground cover. Bonnie peered into the bunker. "I don't know."

Now that they were this close, Palmer didn't think the place looked nearly as interesting as she'd imagined. Still, it was dirty and dark and definitely creepy; it at least had that much going for it.

"Look," Palmer said, trying to work up some enthusiasm, "we haven't had a fort since the church attic." Bonnie scrunched up her shoulders as if she were ducking a blow, and Palmer wished she'd picked a different example. "How do we know," Palmer wheedled, "that this bunker might not be perfect?"

Bonnie looked skeptical but a little curious, too. The girls inched around the broken plywood and walked carefully inside. The top timber was low enough that soldiers probably had to duck their heads. "It's like a doorway for tall trolls," Palmer said, hoping to sound playful.

The dirt floor was littered with candy wrappers, broken beer bottles, and cigarette butts, the air dank. They stood a few feet inside, letting their eyes get used to the darkness.

"There's nothing here," Bonnie whispered. "It's just a hole in the side of a hill."

"It's a *cave*." Palmer gave the word as much awe as she could muster. "They hid guns in here. My dad was an air-raid warden."

"I know all that."

But Bonnie was right; there wasn't much of anything inside. Kids had carved graffiti into the hard-packed dirt of the back wall, as well as on the timbers that supported the ceiling and sides, some of them crooked, as if they might really fall down at any time. A broken apple crate was half buried in the sand. It smelled faintly like Floozy's litter box.

"This is dumb," Bonnie said, "and I'm cold."

Palmer had to admit it wasn't much of an adventure. One corner of the bunker looked as if it had already collapsed. Her mother would have a fit if she could see them now. She might even be right about this being a dangerous place.

Palmer turned to follow Bonnie outside, but before they could leave, the entrance darkened. A man stepped inside, his bulk blocking the opening. Bonnie shrieked, and Palmer's heart squeezed into her ears. With the light behind him, he loomed like a faceless shadow, holding a sack in one hand. Every terrifying story that Palmer had heard about the Lindbergh kidnapping flashed through her mind, especially the images she'd tried to forget. Mother said they propped the dead baby's eyelids open with toothpicks to make him look alive.

"You kids got no business in here."

Palmer's knees went weak with relief. It was Lars Norquist.

"What're you up to, anyway?" His voice bounced against the dirt walls, and Palmer saw that he was holding not a sack, but her red jacket. A pinprick of light bounced off his badge. Bonnie let out a whimper, probably thinking she was going to jail, and darted past him out of the bunker, her shoes thudding on metal as she ran down the railroad tracks, leaving Palmer behind.

"Hello, Sergeant Norquist," Palmer said politely as she sidled toward the opening, her back almost against the dirt. He was looking at her with a funny kind of smile, and Palmer prayed that he didn't know about the church ceiling. In movies, there were always clues left behind that tripped up the criminals.

"My, my, Palmer McNeil playing house in the dark." He looked around. "Or maybe playing doctor? I'll bet your folks would be mighty interested in this little clubhouse of yours."

Palmer smiled her peacemaking smile, the one Maggie hated because she said it looked more scared than polite. Did this mean he wasn't after her because of the church? Could they possibly be in the clear? Or—the back of her neck prickled—was it something else that made him study her so keenly?

"We just wanted to see inside a bunker"—she licked her suddenly dry lips—"on our way home from school." Palmer couldn't even imagine how much trouble she would be in if Lars told her father, who would be sure to tell her mother. "We didn't touch anything."

She started toward the bunker's opening.

"Don't forget this," he said, holding out her jacket. Palmer reached for it, murmured "Thank you," but as she took her coat from him, his fingers followed it to brush her arm and across her chest. "Looks like you kept your clothes on, anyway."

She wanted to believe the touch was accidental, wanted to give him the benefit of the doubt, and maybe she would have, but he came a half step closer and traced the underside of her small breast, his thumb hard. "Developing nicely, aren't we, princess." It wasn't a question. His brass buttons glittered in front of her face.

Shock claimed a second's pause before it propelled her to duck under his arm. Just as Bonnie had fled moments before, she flew out of the bunker, past his squad car, over the tracks, and headed down the hill. Why hadn't they heard him drive up or slam his car door? Had he meant to sneak up on them, or had they just not been paying attention? She felt like throwing up. Had he *let* her go, or had he believed she was frozen against that bunker wall, tangled in her own fear? For a few seconds she had felt helpless as a snagged fish.

Bonnie and her precious coat were gone, and why should Palmer feel so furious at her friend, anyway? Because the stupid coats were how he'd spotted them in the first place, her own red jacket like a tumbled-over stop sign.

Palmer ran hard, scrambling through the mesquite until she reached an alley. How could this have happened? Her father's best friend. A policeman, even. Her breath was ragged. What if he chased her in his squad car? What if he *caught* her? She couldn't breathe. "At least you kept your clothes on," he had said. And she hated his using the pet name that only her father called her. The image of Lars felt pasted on her eyeballs, no matter how hard she blinked. And suddenly she realized she'd left her schoolbooks behind.

Bonnie stepped out from behind a garage, swaddled in her gray coat. "Hey! You okay?"

Palmer nearly stumbled. "Geez, you scared me to death!" She looked back again. No sign of Lars.

"I've been waiting for you here. Did he bawl you out?"

Palmer opened her mouth to tell, but some deep current of intuition bubbled up to warn her that keeping a secret—especially one dark as a cave, dark as that place hidden inside her body—meant keeping it from everyone. It felt like a reminder of something she'd known for a long time.

"What do you *think*?" Palmer gasped, figuring it wasn't a real lie if Bonnie *assumed* the policeman had read her the riot act.

Because if Bonnie knew more, she'd probably tell Mrs. Stafford, who was sure to tell Mother, and Palmer could hear the blame in Mrs. Stafford's voice for Mother having failed again, this time to protect her own daughter. And Mother would get so furious at Mrs. Stafford and especially at Lars, she might start drinking again. She might even attack the policeman. Her mother could go to jail, and for a horrifying moment, Palmer saw her lying unconscious on a prison cot with Lars looming over her.

"Is he going to tell on us?"

"I don't know." Palmer braced her hands on both knees to catch her breath, coming now in labored wheezes. "I don't think so." And neither would she. What would be the point? The word of a girl—a disobedient girl at that—against a policeman's?

Besides, if Daddy didn't believe Granddad had touched Mother's breasts, why would he believe Palmer now about his own best friend?

A Morning Cup of Tea

With some cool and rational part of his brain, Daniel knew that Loretta's cocksure attitude not only had attracted him to her in the first place but was also the key to making their affair work. She was independent, and she didn't require a lot of time. The puzzle was why an affair, with its lies and complications, was just so much *easier* than reaching out for Claudia. His wife was even prettier.

But these days he was just so pissed off at her, or Claudia was mad at him—one or the other, and sometimes both.

They'd be lying in bed reading, and he'd start down that road in his mind, imagining something easy like just stroking the palm of her hand, not really committing himself. But even if they hadn't been arguing, he'd feel that tension in her wrist before she'd gently draw her hand back as if she needed just then to turn the page of her book. And that would be enough to finish him right there, without his having moved a muscle. Why couldn't he even picture one of those other nights—Lord, how long ago now?—when Claudia would turn to him?

If she was drinking, of course, forget it. She'd be passed out cold, and there was nothing he needed that badly. But more often than not, it just took too much energy to get past—well, past everything and all of it. Maybe for her, too, and he wondered how much she might suspect these days—and what had come before *what*, anyway?

Easier to read themselves sleepy one more night after one more night.

Ever since Claudia returned from the Seattle trip, the only way he and Loretta could see each other was by his claiming to have an early-morning tennis date, and that's just what he did most Saturdays. Claudia no longer came to the courts, and the girls liked to sleep in at least until eight, when their radio programs started. His tennis hardly suffered at all, what with Saturday afternoons and all day Sunday to work his matches in.

And while his landing the sales job with Smart & Final Foods wasn't ideal—commission income a damned tough way to make a living, though traveling a territory appealed to him, especially the nights he stayed over at little motels along the coast in Ventura or Santa Barbara—at least the job was strictly Monday through Friday, unlike Wahlberg's.

So come Saturday he'd wake about six thirty, shave and pull on his tennis clothes, down a cup of coffee, and leave the pot on the stove for Claudia. He'd walk up the hill, just as if he were off to the City Hall courts. Out of sight, he'd double back towards the big house on The Strand, climb the side stairs that led to Loretta's apartment, and tap on the glass pane of her door.

They were taking chances, especially in a town as small as Manhattan Beach, but he was counting on most folks still being asleep. With Loretta's working afternoons and evenings at the paper, there really was no other time for them. If he'd tried to go out alone late at night, Claudia would have asked where he was going, and if he'd offered up Ercole's or the Knothole as an excuse, she would have said she'd come, too.

He wanted to see Loretta every moment, but he also knew *not* seeing her kept things hot. Still, he worried that she'd find a guy who could take her nice places. Their "dating," such as it was those nights when Palmer was staying at Elinor's, had stopped once Claudia came back to town.

But this morning, as on every other Saturday when Loretta opened the door to him, he forgot his worries. She was wearing that blue satin nightgown with the sheer negligee, a regular Jean Harlow outfit. He knew she favored high-heeled slippers, but they made too much noise on the wide-planked hardwood floors of the apartment, so she'd bought a pair of satin slides just to wear on Saturdays. That way, she said, she wouldn't wake Bonnie by clomping around, though Daniel couldn't imagine her *clomping* anywhere. As usual, she had made a pot of tea for them. Daniel hated tea.

But he loved that first kiss, sliding his hand around the warm satin of her waist, pulling her close, catching the scent of cream and sugar and English Breakfast tea. She always had some little *biscuits*—cookies to him—and they'd sit at her small kitchen table with the morning sun streaming in, Loretta's unbound hair a platinum halo. It was catch-up time, conversation as foreplay, until she decided to push her chair back from the table. Loretta always picked the moment, and that suited him fine. She'd reach for his hand, pull him down the tiny hall, then around the corner into her bedroom with its sun-darkening window shades behind sheer curtains.

Then, as he'd taught her, it would be his turn to lead by standing motionless. He'd watch her eyes as she slipped the negligee and gown from her shoulders, letting them fall in a silky puddle. Something appealed to him about her being naked while he was still wearing tennis whites, as if he might bound off to some mythical courtside, some urgent, manly competition, and leave her begging. What a joke. As if that would ever happen. But she would look small and vulnerable, with no trace of the high-powered newspaperwoman. It was a ritual that sustained him through their tangled, sunlit mornings.

But today as they sat at the table, she looked at him with what he could only call regret, and his stomach clenched. The damned tea tasted like boiled kelp.

"Daniel—" Loretta pushed at crumbs with a polished nail.

"What is it?" he asked levelly.

"I don't like having to tell you this—"

Jesus, another guy after all, but why not? Why wouldn't she want a good time? Jesus. Still, she'd never complained, had said more than once he was her best.

He tried for a breezy tone. "Go ahead, gorgeous, spill th'beans."

"I've been offered another job," she said. "A paper in San Francisco."

He hadn't figured on this. "You haven't been *here* all that long—"

"It works that way sometimes. I guess 'assistant editor' looked good on my résumé, even if *The Breeze* is just a local paper—"

"You *applied* for this job?" He felt as if a backhand volley had caught him south of the belly.

"It's where my home is, Daniel, my family and—other friends."

She meant another guy. Wasn't this always the way, and wasn't a poor chump like him the last to figure it out?

"So who is he?"

"Pardon?"

"Who's the old friend you have such a hankering to see?"

Loretta shook her head. "It's more money and a bigger paper. I can't pass it by. No more than you would. Wasn't that why you moved your whole family to Portland, to get ahead?"

He didn't want to talk about Portland, about that asshole of a boss, about losing everything they'd owned in the storage fiasco.

"How do you know it'll work out?" But he really wanted to ask how she could leave him, how she could possibly bear to throw him overboard after these months together.

"Everything's taking a chance in some way, Daniel." She reached over and touched his wrist with warm fingers. "Look at us." He nodded grudgingly. "But you have your family to fall back on." Ignoring his snort, she pressed on. "I have to take care of myself; you can see that."

But he didn't have to like it, even if the situation did call for him to be generous. Gracious would be better, heroic in a way, but he couldn't manage all that quite yet.

He nudged the cup and saucer with his thumb. "Even if Claudia stays sober, which I very much doubt, we're not—that is, maybe you and I could think about—" He stopped, seeing a flatness in those eyes that usually reminded him of violets.

She looked away. "I told you from the first that I've never wanted to be married. And never wanted to be a mother, let alone stepmother. That wasn't some ruse to put you at ease."

The tea was long cold, but he took a swallow, anyway, to give himself a moment. "When are you going?"

"In four weeks. I want to give the paper plenty of time to replace me."

He wished she'd said, "Because I can't bear to leave you any sooner."

"You know I'll miss you dreadfully," she said, her voice softening, but by then the *missing* part had come too late. He was already second fiddle. Face it, the whole deal was about her and her damned career. He wanted to storm out, knock over chairs—do anything but sit there and be so fucking civil! Though to be fair—and he did not *want* to be fair—*he* was the married one, not Loretta. Yet marriage wasn't even the issue, was it? Damn it to hell. He needed this woman, but he couldn't think of any way to keep her—not with sex, not with marriage, and certainly not, he thought bitterly, with the money he was fresh out of and didn't seem to have a chance in hell of getting anytime in the future.

"Loretta—," he said with far more control than he felt, not really knowing what he would say next.

But she heard it as an invitation, and with something more like relief than desire shining from her face, she pushed back her chair and stretched out her hands to him.

Daniel didn't hesitate, but as she pulled him to the bedroom, his limbs felt bruised, as tired and heavy as if he'd played too many sets of singles in the hot morning and lost every last one.

Thanksgiving Leftovers and New Storms

It seemed to Palmer that so much of life happened in the afternoons. After school there was the dash home to change clothes and grab a snack before biking or roller-skating on The Strand. She always saved homework for after dinner. Eighth grade wasn't turning out to be all that hard. And on weekends year-round, double features at the La Mar filled both Saturday and Sunday afternoons with suspense: men came home from the war with mechanical hooks where hands should have been; cattlemen fought range wars with sheepherders over grazing rights; spunky Jeanne Crain helped her GI husband turn from soldier into college student; and Olivia de Havilland fought for her sanity in *The Snake Pit*.

Drama could lurk at home, as well as at the movies. If Mother started drinking in the morning, then by mid-afternoon she might be passed out on the couch, lost to herself and to her girls as well. Palmer tried to predict these times that flew at her like scavenging gulls, but since Claudia herself didn't seem to know what set off a drinking bout, there wasn't much hope for anyone to guess right.

Palmer mostly tried not to let her thoughts wander home. Recently, Mother had slipped a couple of times back into drinking—especially after Daddy had begun traveling with his new job.

But on this windswept Monday after the Thanksgiving holiday, when Palmer dashed in from school, Mother was humming in the steamy kitchen making homemade noodles. Palmer could smell the soup stock before she even opened the door. On the back of the stove, the leftover turkey carcass simmered gently, along with carrots and celery, onions, cloves, and bay leaves. Mother turned to kiss Palmer. A broom lay across the backs of two kitchen chairs, its handle draped with clean tea towels. One by one Mother hung homemade noodles to dry from this carefully balanced rack.

The onshore winds had been blowing hard since before Thanksgiving, when there'd been an actual sandstorm, keeping everyone indoors. Each day had been cold and sunny, with the wind screaming around the beach houses. Silt piled up inside on windowsills, even when windows were kept locked. Sand blew into people's hair, crunched between their teeth, and irritated eyes already red from the previous day's blow. Housewives went crazy, trying to keep floors swept up. They covered food and even swiped at clean dishes when the table was set. Children were scolded for not putting lids back on butter dishes or sugar bowls.

Every afternoon Claudia gave the girls damp rags to dust with, the cloths making dark swathes across the furniture. Maggie whined at night when Claudia cleaned her ears of grit, and Daniel complained the sand was going to blast the paint right off his car. Even light from the sun in a cloud-scoured sky had been diffused by blowing sand, like a movie star's close-up shot through layers of gauze.

Secretly, Palmer enjoyed the storm. It had somehow shuttered Thanksgiving so that it more closely resembled those cozy scenes on Christmas cards that bore no resemblance to Yuletide in California. And besides, she didn't care if her parents grumbled good-naturedly about winds that howled in from the ocean and over the beach, scooping up sand to hurl at the town.

It was the edginess in those other winds that sent Palmer scurrying home after school to check on her mother.

Santanas, her father called them, using the old Spanish term.

Devil winds. But the newscasters called them Santa Anas—powerful winds out of the east that swept down from the mountains, skimming arid deserts, to arrive hot and dry, frazzling nerves and fraying tempers. Winds that always seemed to find a spark somewhere, usually from a cigarette thrown out of a car or a campfire carelessly smothered, to fan into firestorms that destroyed acres of forest and chaparral, and sometimes homes. Coyotes, cougars, jackrabbits—all fled the infernos. Nests and young were consumed. Maggie hugged Floozy close when the radio reported wildlife loss.

Claudia hated the devil winds. Daniel said it had to do with ions in the air. Claudia said she didn't care what it had to do with, they made her jumpy as hell. And all too often, when the Santa Anas began to blow, Claudia started to drink.

Then Palmer would scurry home, sometimes running downhill the last quarter mile from school with those winds howling at her back, to find Mother passed out on the living room couch. Palmer would wash up the breakfast dishes sitting crusted in the sink and sweep out the kitchen. It wasn't that she cared anything about housekeeping, but she hoped that if she made the house look *normal,* her father would overlook her mother's drinking, and Palmer could hold their arguments at bay for another night.

She'd scrub potatoes and put them in the oven to bake, though Claudia would make only a pretense of eating if she even came in to dinner. Usually before Palmer finished these chores, her mother would rouse herself to walk with extraordinary care into the kitchen, her feet planted too far apart.

"Tell your father," she'd say, "that'm not well." If the bed was made (you never knew how far she'd get with chores), she might order Palmer to turn down the bedclothes. Claudia would sink onto the sheets and waggle a high-arched foot in the air to have her shoes pulled off. She'd fumble with the waistband of her skirt. "Help me wi' this goddamn zipper." When she was drinking, Claudia smelled like persimmons set too long to ripen on top of the icebox.

But today was a safe day. With Mother busy and the buttery

scent of noodle soup filling the house, Palmer knew she could flop down and read until it was time to set the table. Maybe Mother would even forget about the dusting for one afternoon. Palmer headed for her father's easy chair—the one in which he read each evening's *Herald-Express*. Lately he'd refused to buy *The Daily Breeze*. "Nothing but a rag," he called it.

Most evenings before bed, he still read aloud to Palmer and Maggie. They perched on the broad arms of the chair, leaning into his warm shoulders. But sometimes he shook them off. "C'mon, girls, give your ol' man some breathing room!"

They'd straighten up, and he'd go back to fiddling with the wooden match he always picked up in the kitchen before reading aloud, sliding his thumb and index finger up and down in the steady rhythm that Palmer found comforting. The one time she tried it, she ran a splinter into her thumb.

Claudia said he picked books too adult for the girls, especially for Maggie, like *Treasure Island* and *Huckleberry Finn*, but he said if he didn't enjoy the book himself, he'd just nod off. Besides, he wasn't so sure the books were too old for *smart* kids. Lately he was reading them *Tom Sawyer*. The girls liked Tom even better than Huck.

Before kids turned twelve, they were restricted to the children's section of the Manhattan Beach Library. So in years past, like a cartoon character scooting from tree to rock to bush, Palmer had practiced sneaking into the adult stacks. Furtively she devoured the lean cowboys and sassy women of Zane Grey. She'd read all of Sinclair Lewis, and had pored with special attentiveness over an illustrated anatomy text.

She learned to digest whole portions of books before a librarian could swoop down and march her back to the children's section. Besides improving her reading speed, she also learned *subterfuge* (another word on her spelling list). To herself she called it *illicit reading*.

Once she realized that escaping detection lay primarily in keeping still, she managed to start and finish *The Red Pony* all in one afternoon behind a pillar. She also learned that people in charge weren't right about everything and she didn't *always* have to obey. Mostly she came to trust her imagination to ease her through the pangs of daily reality.

For their part, her parents seemed neither impressed nor un-impressed with her reading. It was something they all did, including Maggie, who was racing through Albert Payson Terhune and slept with *Misty of Chincoteague* under her pillow. Library books formed the bulk of their entertainment, along with radio and the girls' matinees.

Friday nights after dinner Daniel made his special popcorn—butter, salt, and a dash of sugar. On Saturday mornings, Palmer and Maggie loved the butter-soggy popcorn more than Wheaties, and they'd polish the leftovers off while listening to their favorite radio program, *Let's Pretend.* One thing about fairy tales—books or broadcast—no matter how many witches, ogres, giants, or trolls loomed in dark forests, every Saturday morning the prince married the princess. And in the end, children were always safe.

Mouths stuffed with popcorn, the girls sang along softly with the commercial that opened the show, where even the ads were upbeat and wholesome: "Cream of Wheat is so good to eat that we eat it every day!"

They listened to *Lux Radio Theater* and thrilled to the dramas of *Grand Central Station.* Once, Daddy caught the opening and pronounced it all "a bit overwrought." Palmer wondered if he resented "the glitter and swank of Park Avenue." For her part, these imagined lives on the radio, in books and in movies, buoyed her spirit. It was the undertows of everyday life that knocked your feet out from under you.

Winds or not, Mother stayed sober over Thanksgiving weekend, sweeping out the constant sand, cooking, and trying as best she could to get ready for Christmas. Her holiday decorations collected over the years had been lost in last year's "storage fiasco," as Grandmother Sydney always called it. No more shining balls or glittering stars. But Mother was determined.

She brought home a two-foot artificial tree from the dime store, so pathetic and raggedy that she'd been able to talk the price down. Palmer and Maggie tried to be good sports.

Mother set it on the black bookshelf in front of the living room windows, dripping tinsel over its small, arthritic branches. She glued tinfoil—the wartime habit of peeling foil off gum wrappers hard to break—on both sides of a cardboard star that Palmer fastened to the top of the tree. She cut cardboard circles and let Maggie glue them front and back with more foil.

It was a valiant effort, but in her mind Palmer kept seeing the Staffords' tree, a seven-foot Douglas fir drenched in lights and glass ornaments that Bonnie said had been hand-made in Norway, the first to be imported since the War. Though they'd set it up only yesterday (they always decorated the Sunday after Thanksgiving), the Staffords' tree was already circled with presents wrapped in gold paper with green ribbon—the "color scheme," Bonnie said, her mother had chosen this year.

So on this Monday afternoon, with Thanksgiving over, Palmer settled down to read for a couple of hours until Mother called her to slice cantaloupe for dinner. When Daddy breezed in from work, his cheeks ruddy from the wind, Mother had biscuits baking to go with the turkey soup. Maggie read at the kitchen table.

"Mmm, smells good in here," he said, kissing each one. "Let me just write up my paperwork—move over there, Magpie— then we can dive in."

"Everything's all ready," Claudia said mildly, taking the biscuits out of the oven.

"Can't relax until I'm done, not with leaving tomorrow."

"Leaving?"

Daniel smacked himself in the forehead. "I didn't mention it? Smitty's sending me up to Santa Barbara for the rest of the week. Back Friday, as usual."

"But I've made enough soup for an army—"

He swung his sample case onto a chair. "I just found out myself the other day."

"If you'd told me, I wouldn't have gone to all this work." She slid the biscuits onto a plate.

"Look, I'm sorry, but sometimes until I actually have to pack, even I don't remember my schedule." He studied her face. "C'mon, Claudia, just be glad I'm working. You and the girls will gobble this soup up."

Palmer figured they'd eat it every night all week long, which was okay with her. She loved her mother's soup. But Mother didn't look happy.

"I *am* glad you're working," she said quietly.

Daddy looked at her sharply, but Mother had turned to the stove and was stirring the soup.

This time Palmer guessed right though she couldn't see what practical good it did. Daddy left early the next morning, and by the time school let out, Mother was *drunk as a skunk.* As bad as Palmer had ever seen her. Wednesday and Thursday, too. The girls ate soup every night, the two of them quiet at the kitchen table, Mother passed out on the other side of the bedroom curtain. They listened to their radio programs and read library books. Palmer did her homework while Maggie colored, and they put themselves to bed. Nothing they hadn't done before.

The wind blew all that week, the December sun piteously thin. Late Friday afternoon Palmer crept into the house. She'd stayed at Bonnie's after school for as long as she could. Maggie was probably still playing with toy horses at her girlfriend Nancy's house.

But Mother was up, alert and sober. She called out from her bedroom, "I'm straightening up in here, Palmer. Your father will be home tonight, so you can help me later with spaghetti." She sounded on edge—not unusual when she quit drinking abruptly. "Set the hamburger out."

Almost giddy with relief, Palmer opened the icebox and pulled out the butcher-paper bundle of ground beef. By now, even *she* was tired of turkey soup. But more wonderful than spaghetti, *Daddy would be soon be home, and Mother had already stopped drinking*—probably on a dime that morning, sobering up fast, the way she sometimes did. Maybe Palmer wouldn't have to pay so much *attention* for a while.

Because she had other worries, too. At Bonnie's, they'd been playing with her friend's collection of porcelain Storybook Dolls that Palmer believed had been deliberately set in her path as a spiritual test. Just four inches tall and beautifully frocked to represent fairy-tale characters, these dolls swept Palmer with a fierce envy. Or was it covetousness? She should probably check the dictionary. Now that she was saved, keeping the Commandments seemed trickier than ever.

This envy had lately spread beyond even dolls and Christmas decorations to include clothes and shoes, not just Bonnie's but what other girls at school were wearing, too. As if this Commandment weren't hard enough to keep, there was also the one about not lying. Nearly every day, it seemed, Mrs. Stafford asked how her mother was doing, as if she knew something about what went on in that little house, and maybe she did. And every day, no matter what her mother's state, Palmer answered, "Just fine," even managing to embroider a smile on her face when Mrs. Stafford peered at her closely.

On these occasions of sin, she was at least grateful not to be much given to murder and adultery. Perhaps God kept a running average on Commandments.

But now with the promise of spaghetti, with her mother sober and tidying up, the kitchen already clean, Palmer had not so much sin as a story on her mind. She was about three chapters from the end of *Ramona* by Helen Hunt Jackson, and she and Bonnie were racing to see who could finish first. Bonnie, who rarely had chores to do, would be settling in for a head start. Trying not to look at the pathetic Christmas tree, Palmer grabbed an apple and threw herself into her father's chair. She swept away the light dusting of grit from the book's cover and rubbed the apple clean against her blouse.

With Mother bustling about in the bedroom, the strain of the past few days began to leak out of Palmer's bones; she felt relaxed and even a little sleepy, as if she'd spent the afternoon swimming against a winter surf.

Sobering up after a three-day binge, and a bad one at that, Mother would naturally be irritable. It was an old pattern: hard drinking for a few days, especially when Daddy went on the road for a selling trip, then the abrupt stop—"going on the wagon," they called it—a tense time for everybody, but far better than the drinking. With their father's new job and Mother's lapses, the girls sometimes felt as if both parents had set off on separate journeys away from home.

Palmer had learned the term *drying out* from her father and Lars one day as the men had come out of the Knothole, talking about Claudia before they'd seen Palmer waiting there with her bike.

Sobering up, Claudia would take a hard look around the house and see how things had gotten out of hand while she'd been sleeping it off. If Daniel were out of town, dishes would be piled on the drain boards, clothes thrown over furniture, and Maggie's toys strewn around the living room. With her father gone, Palmer herself had no interest in making things look *normal*.

One time when their father was on the road, the girls ran out of food. Because Palmer always knew where her mother hid her pocketbook, it wasn't a real emergency. She was used to helping herself to grocery money. That particular time, feeling lazy and knowing better, she walked down to Wahlberg's and bought two Cokes and a large bag of potato chips. Maggie was tickled with their dinner. During the night, the unrinsed Coke bottle and a few stray chips attracted the tiny brown grease ants that everyone at the beach guarded against. They wove a path like a ribbon from the trash container, up the front of the silverware drawer, and onto the drain board. In the morning a sobered-up Claudia had given Palmer a good bawling-out for that one, though Palmer wasn't sure if her mother were angrier about the ants or the pop-and-chips dinner.

When her mother *came back* (that was how Palmer thought of it), it was often one more time to be on guard. "Don't bother Mother, she's nervous today" was how Claudia herself put it, smoking one cigarette after another, her hands unsteady, the tips of her first two fingers stained amber as the camel on the front of the pack.

But today, knowing her father was due home and lulled by Mother's brisk voice, Palmer missed signs that she was normally good at reading. Certain other afternoons when she walked in the door, the very air—too still in some way—told her all she needed to know. Those times the clues were obvious from the breakfast clutter or knickknacks tipped over as her mother had wandered the small rooms, alone and drinking through that day's long, muted sunlight.

Drowsy now with safety, Palmer bit into the tart green apple. Even its color said go right ahead, unlike the dangerous red of Snow White's poisonous fruit. Palmer sank deeper into the chair, into the Sierra Madres of times past, where a love like Ramona's could only be troubled by a changing world she couldn't control. Palmer turned pages quickly.

A crash from the bedroom startled her, sounding like a perfume bottle flung against the wall. Before Palmer could jump from her chair, Mother burst through the curtains, her face white as apple's flesh, eyes stretched in terror, screaming at Palmer to get down on the floor "right now!" For a second Palmer was disoriented, as though she were riding in a car as sunlit buildings flashed by. The apple tumbled off her lap.

At the same moment, Maggie banged into the house.

"Get down!" Claudia screamed. "Stay away from the window! Those curtains are open!" Palmer dashed into the kitchen as Mother half tackled Maggie, the two of them falling onto the kitchen floor. Claudia pulled Maggie across the linoleum toward the table.

"What's wrong?" Maggie cried.

"Under the table—now!" Claudia whispered frantically, scrabbling on her knees, clutching at Maggie. She flung the kitchen chairs out of her way, one toppling backwards. "Get under here!" Her teeth were gritted. "They'll see you!" She made a grab for Palmer's skirt as she shoved Maggie ahead of her under the table.

Palmer squatted down, and Maggie whimpered.

"Who are you talking about?" Palmer tried to sound calm.

Panting, Claudia reached out and caught her by a handful of hair. Palmer lost her balance and fell; the three of them knotted together under the table. She gasped with pain.

"Shhh!" Claudia spit at them. "Don't you think they can hear you? It's a wonder they let Maggie in the house!"

Palmer pried her mother's fingers out of her hair and rubbed her scalp. "Mother, *who*—?"

"Those men out there!"

Maggie started to wail, and Claudia clapped her hand over her daughter's mouth.

"Where?" Palmer whispered, tremors now in her own chest.

Anger edged the panic in Claudia's voice. "For God's sake, they're standing right across the alley." She pointed. "By the telephone pole!"

Even from under the table, Palmer could peer outside over the window's low sill. No one stood by the telephone pole.

Trying to shelter both girls with her body, Claudia was keening, "Stay down, stay down, stay down!"

But Palmer raised her head again to look past her mother. She could see the empty alley, but someone *must* be out there. Men who were menacing the three of them as they crouched, helpless, inside the flimsy house with its one and only door unlocked. Then like a Saturday cartoon, the sudden image of the Three Little Pigs cornered by the Big Bad Wolf ballooned in her mind, and Palmer let out an hysterical giggle.

Just that fast, her mother's hand snaked out and slapped her hard across the back of the head. Her mother, who never even spanked them, hit Palmer hard enough to knock her over, hands flailing to keep her balance, catching the hem of the kitchen curtain and pulling it all—curtain and rod—clattering onto the floor, revealing the street to be empty from end to terrifying end.

"See?" said her mother. "Right there!"

Bent over Maggie—who was staring out at the empty alley, her tears stifled by astonishment—Claudia cradled her baby daughter. Palmer turned back to them. She understood the terrible truth now. Pity strong as an undertow washed over her, and she wrapped her arms around them both, trying to shush her mother, to comfort her bewildered sister, rocking them all back and forth in some tidal rhythm, herself crying now, silent tears for her beloved mother, who had clearly gone insane.

And that was where Daniel found them, in the near-dark, after he'd parked Nellie and lugged his sample case into the house. Maggie had wet her pants, and the little kitchen, closed up tight against the endlessly blowing sand, was humid with pee and tears, wheezing and terror. Daniel switched on the overhead light.

Claudia was still babbling, wondering how Daniel had made it in to rescue them. He tried to take hold of her, but she was too frightened of dark strangers to be comforted. The curtains and rod were twisted around each other on the floor. On the drainboard, watery blood dripped from the package of warm hamburger.

Daniel forced her to swallow four Empirin tablets with a glass of water, and he sent Palmer and Maggie off to take a hot bath. Through the closed door, they could hear him murmuring to Claudia in the kitchen. Their parents' voices rose and fell and then moved to the bedroom, her mother occasionally shrill, her father more and more exasperated.

The sudden silence was both a relief and a worry. Palmer and Maggie looked at each other over their comic books across the length of the bathtub until Palmer said, "Turn on more hot," and Maggie wriggled to the middle of the tub to get out of the way of the steaming rush from the old, pitted faucet.

When the girls finally emerged, pink and sweet-smelling in their nighties, the hot water exhausted, Claudia seemed to be asleep. On one side of her face a shadow darkened a swollen cheek. Their father was talking to Lars on the telephone.

"My God," he said, "*DTs!* Can you believe it?" Palmer listened closely. "Late afternoon, near as I can figure. Look, I gotta go; the girls are out of the tub. I have to tell them *something*."

But as Palmer heated up the very last of the turkey soup, all three seemed to be listening hard to the silence from the other side of the curtain. Maggie, who usually saved her noodles for the end, left half her soup uneaten. Daddy tossed out the spoiled ground beef and wiped up the mess. He rinsed out their three bowls. Like the Three Bears, Palmer thought, with Goldilocks asleep in one bed.

"Leave these," he said to her. "And the pan, too."

Maggie's eyes looked dull as old agates. Daddy dried his hands, then hugged and kissed them.

"Your mother is sure to be better tomorrow. Go on to bed now."

In the sunroom, Palmer crawled after Maggie into the narrow bottom bunk. They put Floozy near the wall farthest from Palmer, even though Palmer's breathing was clear, the asthma as unpredictable as everything else.

Palmer held Maggie and Maggie held onto her cat, the three of them spoon-style. They were exhausted, but sleep seemed anchored out of reach in the dark. For a long time they lay quiet and listened to the sound of sand caught up in the wind's harsh breath.

Movietone News and Real Life

FROM THE LA MAR, PALMER WOULD always remember the war in Europe as black on white: swastikas and armbands; Nazi flags and burned-out trees; silhouettes of buildings blown in half, their rooms open to the sky like jagged dollhouses waiting for a giant hand to straighten a kitchen table or right an overturned bed, furniture that against all odds had survived.

Sometimes she thought she learned more about the world from newsreels than from social studies and geography put together. *Pathé News* with its crowing rooster had led her through the maze of the War: kamikaze planes and amphibious beach landings, PT boats and soldiers in trenches, jokes about K rations and "Kilroy was here," movie stars at USO dances, Bob Hope in fatigues at overseas Christmas shows.

She had cheered V-J and V-E Day in the boisterous theater, then weeks later watched in silence, like everyone around her, unable even to whisper, as skeletal survivors of concentration camps had flickered across the stunned faces of the audience. Claudia had worried over the children's viewing such horror, but Daniel asked how else they would know, how else they would remember. He'd worried about what might be coming down the pike next that they'd all want to forget.

As for the newspapers her father bought at the corner Rexall, Palmer wasn't much interested in them except for the funnies. On the radio, she thought Drew Pearson and Walter Winchell were boring men with scratchy voices that she tolerated because her father liked to keep up with the day's news. When she was assigned to do something on current events at school, she clipped articles from the *Weekly Reader* or wrote up something from the newsreels.

She remembered when President Roosevelt had died, her father wet-eyed and her mother subdued. She saw the huge funeral in the newsreel, watched Harry Truman with his thick glasses being sworn in. Another day, when the Dalai Lama and his pilgrims wound through steep mountain passes in Tibet, she cried without knowing why.

On the screen, she watched California manufacturers of wartime material return to private industry. Wives and mothers had joined assembly lines for the Duration, their hair caught up in scarves against cogs and gears. They had called these women by a single name: Rosie the Riveter. When peace was declared, they sent them home to free up jobs for returning men. Some women wanted to keep on working, but many people said the natural order of things was finally being set to rights.

After the War ended, Palmer watched Japanese families leaving their makeshift camps in the deserts and mountains to piece together shattered lives. Her mother said Tule Lake had been no better than a prison, and the girls were *not* to call them *Japs*.

Palmer didn't remember the terms *internment camps* or *relocation*. She had been five when the war started, used to riding in the back seat when her mother would drive uphill away from the beach, across Sepulveda to fly along an undulating two-lane road bordered with shaggy eucalyptus—the backcountry, they called it. Her mother would stop at open-air Japanese markets, picking out the best tomatoes, lettuce, avocados, beets, and spinach.

But during the early years of the war, those trips had stopped. The fields had lain fallow or been farmed by families not considered a threat to security. Mother said she didn't see how the backbreaking work of farming would have left Japanese farmers much time for spying. But from then on strawberries, blueberries, string beans, and cantaloupe—all produce, in fact—had been sold from grocery stores.

Wahlberg's Market lay open to the day's weather, its heavy

wooden doors, metal-hinged like an accordion, folded up against one another. It was as close to an open-air market as a building could be. People didn't speak of the *store's* closing, only the *doors'* closing as stock boys pulled them shut, the doors ratcheting along runners where hardwood floor met concrete sidewalk. But Mother said it could never be the same as those shining green fields.

Newsreels and a popular song of the day taught Palmer that California swelled as veterans, migrant workers from Mexico, and Okies from the Dust Bowl all tried to "make the San Fernando Valley my home." Never mind that the Valley was already stuffed to the gills. One announcer called population growth "the greatest transformation since the Gold Rush."

But most people blamed it for the worst housing shortage in the nation's history. Families rented converted army barracks and Quonset huts. One enterprising veteran who had returned to grammar-school teaching slept in his classroom on a folding cot, cooking over a hot plate, until the principal kicked him out. Palmer knew her family was lucky to have The Shack.

As much as she loved school, it seemed that what she learned through newsreels was more—oh, relevant, somehow. Look how the War had already made obsolete what she'd learned about biplanes in first grade. When she thought of airplanes now, she remembered black-and-white fleets of U.S. warplanes streaming across the glistening movie screen, like the P-51 Mustang that Daddy said probably won the War for them. She could recognize Corsairs, with their folded wings, the planes lined up on the decks of carriers like giant insects; and the Flying Tiger; even that two-engine bomber Jimmy Doolittle had made famous, the B-25 Mitchell.

When JJ had his tonsils out and had to stay in bed, his folks gave him balsa-wood models to glue together. Palmer went to visit and caught him taxiing a Black Widow down his leg, the other planes scattered across his bedclothes like a miniature air force squadron. His face turned red to be caught playing with *toys*.

Palmer herself still dreamed war's-end images of the *Enola Gay* and the mushroom cloud that blossomed like time-lapse photography of a beautiful, poisonous flower. Without a word, the fluoroscope machine in Stephen's Bootery had disappeared. At school they held A-bomb drills now, crawling under desks when the alarm rang, their foreheads to the floor, hands over eyes and backs of necks. They looked like they were praying toward Mecca, to this radioactive god more fearsome than Jehovah, Allah, or Zeus.

At the La Mar, Palmer and Maggie sat through grainy images of backyard bomb shelters that looked for all the world like the playhouses they'd always coveted. Little beds and stacking cookware, jugs of water and canned goods, tiny front doors where somebody's father stood proud and defiant.

She remembered air-raid drills during the War when she'd tried to slip outside to the front porch to watch the night sky. Manhattan Beach itself had offered nothing strategic, but the refineries and oil storage tanks next door in El Segundo were feared to be targets. The drills always seemed to come at night, or anyway those were the ones she remembered. She never did see an enemy plane in those black skies, only the giant, swinging arcs of searchlights.

Daddy would put on his air-raid warden hardhat and white armband, grab his flashlight, and go door to door, making sure families remembered to draw their room-darkening shades at the siren's first bleat. Mother thought he should have stuck around to protect his own family, but that warden outfit was as close as Daddy was going to get to being a soldier, and he wasn't about to miss his chance. Mother grew pale and made Palmer come inside and sit with her beside the radio while baby Maggie slept through it all.

But Palmer's favorite part of each newsreel was the Hollywood segment—featuring that glamorous world nearly outside her own front door that had tried to cheer the country during the War—and the Depression before that—if only for a few hours at a time. Movie stars like Ingrid Bergman, Claudette Colbert, and Gary Cooper smiled and waved at the news cameras. James Cagney saluted from his sailboat, a red frigate named *The Swift*. (Daddy snorted at its name, when the boat took forever just to reach Catalina.) Victor Mature doffed his cap at photographers as he walked his fierce-looking boxer or drove his Lincoln Continental around Laguna.

For the Duration, all breakwater harbors had been closed with nets and gates. In those panicky days of submarine sightings off Santa Barbara, no one was allowed to head out to sea. Even The Strand was blacked out every night, its streetlights painted dark on the side that faced the ocean, and the Pier guarded because of the threat of sabotage, though no one ever explained the military significance of a fishing pier. Soldiers patrolled the beaches with dogs. Barbed wire was strung north and south from the Pier. Every city on the West Coast had its rumors of sightings.

But once the War was behind them, everyone who could afford it, and that mostly meant movie stars, wanted to go boating. Santa Catalina with its beautiful Avalon Harbor became a glamorous getaway once again. Daddy talked about the Wrigley chewing-gum magnate who owned the Chicago Cubs and brought them to the island for spring training, said Wrigley had built the circular casino, Catalina's oceanfront ballroom. All that money, Palmer marveled, just from chewing gum.

Humphrey Bogart sailed over in his yacht *Santana* (now there's a man, Daddy said, knows how to name a boat), and John Wayne motored across the twenty-six-mile channel in his converted minesweeper. Zane Grey owned a Pueblo-style home on the island, built where the Gabrieleno Indians once lived. The newsreel showed boars and descendants of bison, brought in long ago for old movies, still roaming the island's wild and craggy interior. Zane Grey himself eluded the newsmen, which disappointed Palmer, given her clandestine moments with him in the library.

Business surged in short-wave radios and marine direction finders—knobbed boxes with antennas on top in the shape of loops. Daddy said anybody who could work a slide rule and had a little electronic know-how could make a bundle. How unfortunate, said Grandmother Sydney, who arrived quite suddenly to spend Christmas with them, that such a group didn't include her son-in-law.

Mid-morning sun streamed into the kitchen, promising a warmth the sharp air of December was unlikely to deliver. Mother had walked down to the store, and Grandmother Sydney was drinking coffee, saying she and the girls were the only star-struck members of the family, but Maggie seemed more interested in galloping her toy horses across the kitchen table. Grandmother Sydney read Hedda Hopper and Louella Parsons religiously and accepted *any* show business rumor as gospel. The more scandalous the gossip, the more she beamed: white slavery, drug addiction, sexual *hijinks*. Errol Flynn's escapades left her weak with outrage and satisfaction. This morning she was speculating on Katharine Hepburn's affair with Spencer Tracy.

"She's insane if she thinks that man will marry her. He's Roman Catholic, for heaven's sake!"

Just as she launched into an elaborate object lesson about chastity, Claudia walked in with a sack of groceries and thumped it on the table. She pulled out milk and oranges, and molded the Wonder Bread's squished middle back into shape. She looked over at her mother. "Mama! The girl is barely thirteen!"

Sydney lifted her eyebrows and made a nimble shift from sexual temptation to *drugsandalcohol*. Palmer stirred uneasily; it didn't seem a good topic after her mother's recent "spell," as her father called it.

"It's common knowledge that Robert Mitchum was incarcerated. Serious drug charges. Not that he was the only one, of course, but I believe he *flaunted* it somewhat. Then there's that poor Robert Walker who's simply drinking himself to death."

Palmer wondered about Granddaddy Burl and *his* drinking, but this certainly wasn't the right time to mention it. Besides, hadn't Daddy already blurted out the essentials?

"Why can't more of them," Sydney said, addressing the kitchen at large, "be like this young actress Colleen Townsend? You watch, in time she'll be one of the big stars. She's quite religious and doesn't touch a drop of liquor." The praise of abstinence hung accusingly in the air.

"I suppose you get this from the lady herself?" Claudia banged a skillet onto the gas burner, quieting her mother for the moment.

The silence vibrated like waves hitting the Pier. Palmer hoped to turn the conversation toward safer waters than who did or did not drink. After her mother's spell it even seemed her father had a beer in his hand more often. "What if someone else," she asked, knowing she was distracting her grandmother, "had played Rhett Butler?" Sydney was fascinated by casting decisions. As Palmer bent over her drawing, she saw her mother's sly curve of a smile as Sydney took the bait.

"Darling, they could *not* have cast another man in that role. American women would not have allowed it! You have to consider the chemistry between stars."

Mother's knife peppered the breadboard as she sliced cheese for grilled sandwiches, and Grandmother Sydney's gaze wandered out the window. "Of course," she said after a bit, "Gable had to settle that name business first. *Sound* is critical. Until he dropped the *Billy*, you simply pictured poor white trash: Billy Clark Gable, indeed. And John Wayne? Lucky the studio made him get rid of *Marion,* even if he did play football for USC."

Maggie had wandered out to look for Floozy. Claudia slipped the buttered sandwiches into the skillet.

"Look at the young stars coming up, Claude," Sydney said to her daughter's back. She was trying to make up, but Claudia didn't answer. She turned back to her granddaughter. "I'll bet you don't even know who Roy Fitzgerald is." Palmer shrugged. "Of course not, because no roles came his way until he became"—she paused for her revelation—"*Rock Hudson.*"

Claudia patted the sandwiches impatiently with her pancake turner.

"Another example is this starlet Marilyn Monroe. *Norma Jeane*

Baker?" Sydney shook her head in sympathy. "Just not *euphonious* for a beauty like hers, though mind you, I am not condoning that business with the so-called calendar art—"

"Palmer, go find your sister," Mother said. "These sandwiches won't be any good if we keep dilly-dallying."

Now it was Grandmother Sydney's turn to look slighted, as if being a Hollywood expert was a trivial thing.

Palmer always found her grandmother's movie-name interest at odds with their own family history of naming daughters. Maggie had been named for Margaret O'Brien in one of her parents' few nods to the movies, but before Maggie was born, the names had sounded as much like boys as girls. Palmer's great-grandmother—Sydney's mother—had so wanted a baby boy that she named her firstborn daughter Leslie. That infant died, and her second and last pregnancy delivered up yet another daughter. She called that child *Sid* until the girl was old enough to demand her full name and birthright spelling of *Sydney*.

Knowing her grandmother, Palmer thought that *demand* was probably the right word. It puzzled Palmer that after three miscarriages, her grandparents had named their only child Claudia Gene Palmer and from birth on had often called her Claude.

About being given her mother's maiden name, Palmer was more or less resigned. Had she been consulted, she would have preferred Natalie. And even if Natalie Wood wasn't as big a star as Maggie's Margaret O'Brien, Palmer thought she might be someday. She wondered if her grandmother found *Palmer* in any way "euphonious."

Earlier in the week, when Sydney arrived, she tried to pass it off as a "surprise Christmas visit." But Palmer overheard her father snarl at Claudia, "You called the bitch, didn't you!"

Sydney insisted she would sleep on the lumpy couch in the living room and complained each and every morning about her sciatica, somehow managing to imply that the blame was Daniel's. In a way, it was.

When Daniel married Claudia, he owned little more than his clothes and a coffee pot. Claudia, on the other hand, had all the furniture from her first marriage, as well as a new car. Palmer remembered that furniture from Portland and from the Center Street house before that. But it was also from another kind of life.

There had been a heavy Mediterranean dining table in dark oak, the matching chairs upholstered in deep-red leather with brass upholstery studs. Palmer had loved to play her pretend-games beneath that table on the carved crossbeams that connected its big clawed feet. She remembered a long ebony library table on which had stood the statue of a black lion, its mouth open in a roar. Every Easter Palmer would find a jelly bean resting on that fierce black tongue. There were lamps and vases and pictures and two Nubian heads—a man and a turbaned woman who faced each other on the wall—the man smiling with white teeth that looked real. Her mother said they were ivory. The woman just looked sad.

At War's end, when they moved back to California after those nine months in Oregon, Lyon Van & Storage came to the Portland house to pick up all their belongings. Mother had stuffed the bureaus and the buffet with family albums, silverware, books, clothes, toys, and linens—everything they couldn't carry in the car. By the time they arrived in Los Angeles, the postwar housing shortage was full upon the whole region.

They stayed at a tiny motel out on Sepulveda while they house-hunted, but the weekly rate was eating up their money fast. From there they moved to a one-room basement rental.

"They call this an *apartment?*" Mother moaned.

Palmer and Maggie slept in a closet that just barely held metal bunk beds picked up at a navy surplus store. Palmer slept on top, but the ceiling was so low she couldn't sit up in bed. For some reason that gave her asthma.

The toilet huddled in a corner, surrounded by a curtain. Claudia and the girls bathed in a corrugated washtub. Daniel had already begun his showers at the Norquists'. When Maggie, with an adventurous tone, said it was like living in a cave, they gamely christened the place Sweet-Cave, and the tradition of naming houses had begun.

From there they found a guesthouse they could rent until the owners' married son showed up. It had no bathtub *or* toilet. Claudia hated having to go inside the main house every time she or the girls needed to use the bathroom. Daniel, of course, went on showering at the Norquists'. No one called that place anything more than the Guest House. At least the curtained-off toilet at The Cave had felt like theirs.

Next they found a huge house for rent right *on* The Strand— with a sunken dining room and five bedrooms, furnished. Claudia had thought she could take in roomers to meet the rent. The realtor told them that Gable and Lombard had honeymooned there back in '39. Because of its size, they dubbed it The Barn. Palmer immediately developed a crush on a beautiful, dark-eyed boy two houses down, but just as she had begun to think he liked her back, the family decided the big house was too much work for Claudia. Besides, the roomers, all of them single men, had come and gone too fast to count on for rent money. Finally, the McNeils had found The Shack.

By this time, all of Claudia's furniture, Palmer and Maggie's baby pictures and baptismal certificates, the Nubian heads and the lion had been in storage for months. Daniel was barely making enough money at Wahlberg's to support them. He hadn't a prayer, he said, of getting the stuff out of hock. Each month the storage bill grew larger and Claudia's hopes grew smaller. Legal-sized white envelopes with notices demanding payment arrived regularly in the mail.

Finally, Lyons threatened to auction off everything to pay the storage bill. A few months later, they did exactly that. When the official notification arrived, Claudia sat down and cried. She imagined strangers tossing her daughters' photos into the garbage, keeping the frames. Some other child would be fed from Maggie's silver baby spoon. And another family would sit down to a holiday dinner at her Irish linen tablecloth spread over the table that she and Philip had chosen together. Palmer wondered if anyone besides her mother would think to put a jelly bean in the lion's mouth at Easter, wondered if anyone else felt like Lyons had galloped across the savannah to gobble them up, library lion and all.

These days the family made do with the shabby furniture that came with The Shack. Whatever grief Claudia felt over her lost furniture and family treasures, she never mentioned a single piece after the auction. But Sydney had no such compunctions. She thought Daniel had brought her daughter down in life, and she wasn't shy about saying so.

December 1949

On the first Saturday of Christmas vacation, the girls dashed out right after breakfast to go roller-skating on The Strand, as if it were somehow a day more special than other Saturday mornings. Sydney walked down to the store to pick up more of the coffee they were constantly running out of, and Daniel had already left early to go fishing.

Claudia stood alone under the archway between the kitchen and the living room—hands on hips, one foot tapping. As if she were in the center of one of Maggie's pinwheels, she could slowly turn and see every room, including the sunporch that was the girls' bedroom. Odd thing about that sunporch. It had a door to the outside that opened onto nothing. Enough to make a person nervous.

Because the house faced a steep alley, the kitchen was level with the street while the sunporch, downhill, was built on stilts. Probably there had been stairs up to the sunporch, but once the apartment house crowded in beside it, the stairs were either torn down or left to rot away—wood decayed quickly at the ocean—and the sunporch door had been nailed shut. Eventually some inventive soul had sawed out a square in the upper half of the door, covered it with screen, and then put the wood back with hinges, so that in the summer it could be opened.

A Dutch door to nowhere, Claudia thought. Well, that seemed to fit the direction her life had taken. Week in, week out, she scoured the chipped and stained bathtub (at least it wasn't that damned washtub), and each day she made up their double bed in a room so small that the bed was pushed up tight against the wall. She had to lie across it to smooth her side.

Mornings like today, the winter sun seemed to show every crack in the linoleum, each room with a different pattern, as if a crazy person had glued the place together. A gas heater forced air up through a grate in the living room floor, and on these winter mornings Palmer and Maggie would straddle it, pulling their clothes on quickly while the hot air rushed up their goosebump-covered legs. The couch and chair sagged, their worn upholstery covered with thin brown bedspreads. At the living room windows, short, heavy curtains—black with garish flowers splashed in primary colors—hung from brass rods and were dragged shut during the hottest part of the day.

In the kitchen, behind sheer curtains, aged parchment shades glowed amber and let in cracks of light around their frayed edges. Here Claudia set up her ironing board. Sprinkled clothes filled the wicker basket at her feet: Daniel's five white shirts—starched, dampened, and rolled—his tennis clothes, khaki work pants and sport shirts, the girls' school dresses, her own housedresses and slacks, her mother's travel blouse. Claudia lit a cigarette and inhaled deeply, her ashtray perched on the wide end of the ironing board.

"Well," she thought, "look at it this way: at least you don't have any table linens left to iron." The oilcloth spread over the kitchen table was practical, even if she hated its slick, greasy feel. There was no getting away from it: she hated everything about the place, like not having a bathroom sink, so that the kitchen sink did double duty—washing vegetables and washing hands, rinsing fruit and shampooing hair. Daniel shaved in the kitchen, looking in a small mirror on the shelf over the sink.

Palmer would prop whatever book she was reading on that same shelf, sometimes so lost in her story that she washed the same plate over and over, until Claudia reminded her to get her head out of the clouds. Who could blame the girl? Sometimes the clouds had a lot going for them.

Claudia wished she had a little something to drink in the

house—just enough to take the edge off. She spit on her finger and lightly touched the iron. She was as bad as Palmer, dreaming away. She just needed to get on with it—the ironing was going to take hours, anyway, and she wanted a head start before her mother came back.

She stroked her cheek gingerly. The bruise had faded, but the deep tissue was still tender. Daniel's temper was getting worse. *And with her so sick.* She swallowed against the lump of self-pity that stuck in her throat, already more than half believing her invented version of the truth. She had probably been running a terrible fever—105 degrees was her mother's guess—to have hallucinated that way.

Claudia's memory of the threatening strangers was fuzzy, but she could still remember how danger had risen up through the linoleum, poured out of the thin-framed walls to choke the kitchen, squeezing breath out of her like some dark bellows. She had tried to protect her daughters. No more than any mother would have done. And she really hadn't touched a drop that day, not a drop. Nor in the eight days since.

"Delirium tremens," she thought scornfully. Why, he made her sound like some Bowery bum instead of the mother of his children. In front of the girls, he referred to it as her "spell," as if she were a witch. No thanks for the big pot of soup she'd made, nor any mention of his having taken off for five days.

She wished her mother would get back from Wahlberg's. Claudia could almost taste the bitter black coffee. She was just feeling—weak, that was all—after being so ill. Her hands trembled as she guided the hot iron between the buttons of the dress shirt on the ironing board. She'd called her mother the day after the so-called spell to come for Christmas, and Sydney had dropped everything and hopped on a Greyhound, probably sensing trouble from Claudia's voice.

Now, glancing down at her ankles, Claudia saw they were slightly swollen. She sighed, remembering back when she'd worked for a time in an office. Every day she'd worn high heels to work. Then later, after she and Philip were married, she'd done housework in heels and been proud of it. If Philip came home during the day or anybody came to the door, there she would be, looking good as any of the starlets at the studio. She could even run downstairs in heels by turning sideways. After *The Wizard of Oz* came out, she imagined wearing the ruby-red slippers, though it was a silly notion because by that time Philip was lost to her, and she and Daniel had already had Palmer.

Now, as she bent over the ironing board, even the idea of rubies seemed too glittering to bear. Instead the hot, clean smell of Clorox and Oxydol, rising from the shirt like antiseptic, reminded her of the free clinic. She'd had her teeth X-rayed last Thursday, the pale green snout of the instrument snuggled beneath her cheekbone, where silent, invisible beams had penetrated the inflamed tissue of her gums. The dentist was worried about pyorrhea. He hoped he'd be able to save her teeth. The memory of being nuzzled by the X-ray machine and the ordeal of future visits, not to mention the extra money, even though the visits were practically free, sent her tongue on a furtive pass across her lips.

She hung the pressed shirt on a wire hanger and pulled another from the basket. She couldn't think of high heels without remembering the dancing. How she had loved it, a way of letting care go, of feeling beautiful. A drink or two hadn't hurt, either; had made her dance even better, in her opinion. Her partners felt they could hardly make a mistake, so quick and light was her response to the male lead. She'd met both Philip and Daniel at parties.

Men had never understood the fierce concentration that let her anticipate their dance moves, no breath of hesitation between their direction and her following. Like butter brushed on roasting fowl, she melted into their arms, and she knew they stepped out on the dance floor with a newfound confidence they never ascribed to her. It had always pleased her to leave each partner a better dancer than she found him, and it had amused her, or so she'd always told herself, when they had taken the credit.

Claudia figured that had she been born as beautiful as she

wished, she might have been a poorer dancer. A talent for dancing was perhaps a compensation developed in lieu of being as she desired. Though other times she thought it wasn't so much beauty she lacked as—what? Opportunity? To do what, exactly?

She sighed and slid the iron onto its metal stand, rearranging the yoke of the shirt on the board. She had always danced on her toes, ready to shift her balance, to make up for a partner's missed beat with an invisible adjustment of her own. And once in a while, if she were very lucky, a partner came along who led in time with the music, who used his peripheral vision to keep from bumping other dancers, who supported her back instead of letting his hand slide down her hip. Then for brief periods, she permitted herself to relax. Daniel had come as close as any.

They even entered a dance contest and won. He told her that as a teenager back in Ohio, he'd had a brief job singing and dancing in a chorus at a theater where Bette Davis had appeared, and she'd been his favorite actress ever since. Claudia couldn't remember when they'd stopped dancing, but it seemed a long time ago. She wasn't even sure they'd ever gone dancing once they were married.

She finished the collar, both sides, and hung the second shirt. Where in the hell was her mother, anyway? She snapped on the radio. She didn't listen to her programs every day, but she wished they were on today. *Ma Perkins* and *Backstage Wife*, *Our Gal Sunday* ("Can a girl from a little mining town in Eastern Colorado find happiness as the wife of the wealthy and titled Lord Henry Brinthrope of Black Swan Hall?"), and even *Stella Dallas* would have helped her get through the hours of ironing that stretched ahead into the sunny day, this one so like the next, like a string of laundry hung on a line so long you couldn't see to the end.

In the morning the kitchen was already warm from the stove, where Mother was cooking oatmeal. Daddy had gone fishing again, bundled against the Pier's chill, and Grandmother Sydney was down at the Rexall buying the Sunday paper. She'd been plenty bundled up, too. The winds were unpredictable.

Palmer sat at the kitchen table and studied her mother's back. "I want to buy some Christmas cards," she said finally. Claudia stirred the cereal, its Pilgrim beaming from his red and blue cylinder.

"Oh. Well, okay, honey."

"I mean, I want to buy a few *boxes*."

Claudia held the wooden spoon above the pot and looked over at her. "How many kids are you sending to? Your whole class?"

"I want to send out cards from us, from our family."

Claudia turned back toward the stove, and Palmer couldn't see her face. "Oh, Palmer." Her mother's shoulders seemed to sag as if a blow she hadn't seen coming or hadn't recognized for what it was had just landed across her back.

Palmer waited.

Claudia took her time. "Cards are expensive, you know, and that doesn't even count the postage."

"I could help. We could use my allowance—"

"Honey, that's very sweet, but why don't we just skip it this year?"

"*This* year? We never send cards, except to Grandmother Sydney, and now she's *here*."

Claudia spooned the oatmeal into two bowls. "Maggie, come eat your breakfast." The lump of blanket in the lower bunk didn't move. Palmer got up to set out milk and brown sugar, spoons and paper napkins.

Claudia ran cold water into the pan. "Palmer—" The word was in that tone that her daughter understood meant *no*.

"We could buy them at the dime store," Palmer said quickly. "They come in packets there, not boxes, and they don't cost near as much as the ones at Anderson's."

Mrs. Stafford bought her cards at Anderson's Gift Shop, beautiful winter scenes of the ocean or funny ones like a seagull sitting on top of a piling with a Christmas wreath around his neck, the wreath the only spot of color on the pale-gray card. She had these cards printed with their names:

The Stafford Family
Ford Elinor Bonnie

And on the day after Thanksgiving, Mrs. Stafford would stack the boxes of cards on a small mahogany desk that she called a secretary, with a fold-down writing table. The desk sat in a corner of the dining room, the three drawers in the bottom full of folders for PTA, Brownies, and Sandpipers work. But when the drawers were closed and the top folded shut, then the desk beamed, serene and orderly as a well-fed cat, its claw feet and brass hardware awash in the sun that flooded that many-windowed house. Palmer was going to have a desk like that someday.

"How many cards in a packet?" her mother asked.

"Ten."

"And how much a packet?"

"Eighty-nine cents."

Claudia grimaced. "All right," she said finally. "You can buy three packets plus the stamps, but that's going to come close to five dollars, so you'll have to make do. It should be enough to send to anyone you really care about." She turned towards the sunporch. "Maggie! Your breakfast is ready, and I'm not calling you again." Gently tugging on one of Palmer's braids, she added, "But let's not bother your father with our Christmas doings, all right?"

Palmer nodded. When Mother wasn't drinking, Daddy always said she could stretch a quarter farther than anyone, and Palmer knew that was a very good thing, especially since they'd left Portland and become poor.

On Monday after lunch, Mother gave her the money, and Palmer walked to the dime store. The front door was propped open, and Palmer stepped into the cool store with its oak floors and row upon row of flat counters with their glass partitions. She took her time getting to the Christmas section, saving it for last.

First came bins with barrettes and hairnets, sewing needles and zippers, nail polish and remover, face powder, and white jars of Pond's Cleansing Cream with bright-pink lids. She examined the hairpins and bobby pins in black and brown, and even in white for waitresses and nurses. She walked past safety pins, knitting needles and yarn, ladies' underwear, penny candy, and ribbon by the yard. She ran her fingers lightly over boxes of foil stars, wooden sock darners shaped like eggs (her mother used a burned-out light bulb, laughing that it was riskier but *free*), wooden clothespins, and washboards in all sizes.

"Rooted in thrift and elbow grease," her mother said about the dime store. "A testament to the virtue of making do."

In the toy section, Palmer briefly coveted, though not, she hoped, in a sinful way, the small harmonicas, magnets, marbles, jacks, Duncan yo-yos, and red rubber balls attached to paddles. At Halloween they'd had masks and wax fangs. In the back of the store tiny turtles crawled in watery terrariums, their shells abloom with decals. Canaries and parakeets perched in wire cages beside boxes of birdseed, the air scented with Johnson's floor wax.

Because of the season, one whole side of the store was devoted to Christmas trimmings, tinsel, angel hair, ornaments. Next came candles in the shapes of Santas, reindeer, and angels; then Christmas cards, candy canes, and ribbon candy. The riches rolled on, green and red, silver and gold.

Palmer studied the cards. She wanted all three packets to be the same. She wanted the cards to look as if her mother had chosen them. Finally, she picked an impressionistic rendering in jewel-like tones of the Three Wise Men. The card read simply, "Merry Christmas and Happy New Year." She tried to imagine the cards spread out on the writing surface of the mahogany desk, Mrs. Stafford writing short notes and addressing envelopes, Palmer and Bonnie licking the stamps and smoothing them on the growing stack.

She looked up at the sound of women whispering, then quickly turned back toward the cards. She'd recognized two of

Mrs. Stafford's friends from Sandpipers. They'd been looking at her, and Palmer sensed they were talking about her, too. Or more likely, they were talking about her mother. She held herself still, studying the cards before her, and bit at her thumbnail. She could feel her face getting red, her neck hot. She wanted to yell, "You don't know anything about it!" She wanted to grab a box of cards and smash it into their faces.

One woman nudged the other.

"Remember," Mother always said, "if you misbehave, people will judge not you but your mother."

The women were buying Christmas candles. Tomorrow the Sandpipers were having a holiday art show at their clubhouse. Palmer had thought she might go. Wear her navy-blue taffeta, drink tea from china cups and eat *canapés*, as Mrs. Stafford called them, maybe ask her grandmother to come along.

As the women moved down the aisle, she gathered up her cards. She'd never set foot in their stupid art show. When she was grown up and famous, they could beg her to join their snotty club, but it wouldn't make a bit of difference. Palmer threw back her shoulders, lifted her chin, and walked toward the cash register. Only her blazing cheeks gave her away, if anyone had wanted to notice.

It took several days to hunt down the addresses she wanted. The last tenant had taken the phone book, so the McNeils just kept a few numbers written on a pad beside the phone. With the Norquists, she actually walked over to their place to see what their house number was. She couldn't ask because she didn't want her father to know she was sending cards in the first place, and she didn't want her mother to know—and perhaps resent— some of the people on her list. She sent a card to the Staffords, to her seventh-grade teacher (but not to her art teacher), to her principal and to the family who had lived next door to them in Portland, to Loretta Sprague in San Francisco, and to their doctor and even the dentist at the free clinic. She sent cards to every grown-up she could think of who had the slightest contact with her parents, and she tucked one into her grandmother's handbag.

All the cards were signed in neat blue-pen handwriting:

Daniel, Claudia, and girls

As if they'd come from the mother, which was how she imagined it was done in all those normal families in their snug houses spread clear across the wintry country like scenes from someone else's Christmas cards.

Christmas Comes Early

CHRISTMAS WAS ONLY THREE DAYS OFF, and Daddy was hunched over the funny papers in his easy chair, laughing so hard he had to pull out his handkerchief to wipe away tears. "*Pogo* again," thought Palmer with a dismissive sniff. Every year around the holidays the *Okefenokee Irregulars* would appear in the comic strip to sing at least one of the six verses of a song called "Boston Charlie." Though when Daddy invariably said, "Listen to this, kids," it sounded exactly like "Deck the Halls."

"Listen to this, kids," he said, trying to keep a straight face:

> *Deck us all with Boston Charlie*
> *Walla Walla, Wash., an' Kalamazoo!*
> *Nora's freezin' on the trolley,*
> *Swaller dollar cauliflower alley-garoo!*

Palmer wasn't even sure her church would approve of this *parody*, as her father called it. The comic seemed vaguely sacrilegious, and besides, she never had figured out what was so all-fired funny about a bland-looking possum who played the banjo. Daddy said it was a political satire. "*Grown-ups*," she thought. Still, it *was* good to hear him laughing about anything. His light baritone filled the living room:

> *Don't we know archaic barrel,*
> *Lullaby Lilla Boy, Louisville Lou?*
> *Trolley Molly don't love Harold,*

He'd come home from work in a good mood, settling down with the paper to wait for dinner. Mother was adding fresh peas to a pot of stewed chicken, and Grandmother Sydney was stirring up a batch of dumplings to drop one by one into the simmering broth. Palmer had already set the table and was waiting for her turn at the funnies.

Sometimes Daddy read them aloud to her and Maggie, if the girls *happened* to be nearby. That's why Maggie had collected her toy horses to gallop them softly along the linoleum patterns of the living room floor, pretending to be riding high mountain trails. On the couch, Palmer copied a picture of *Sheena, Queen of the Jungle*, from an old comic book.

Just then, someone pounded at their kitchen door so hard it made the house shake.

Daddy started up from his chair. "What in the Sam Hill—?" He thought it was some ill-mannered kid, and Palmer scooted into the kitchen, hoping it was no friend of hers. Maggie was right behind her.

Outside in the alley idled a sea-green Plymouth coupe, not new but still pretty—at least what could be seen of it, almost buried as it was under the heavily laced limbs of Christmas trees tied to its roof. Maggie gaped. Palmer recognized a cute college boy from church sitting behind the wheel. He waved. She'd never seen the burly man standing at their door.

"Mrs. McNeil?" Mother nodded at him as the family gathered in front of the screen door. "Donald Malcolm here, from Prairie Presbyterian. We're distributing Christmas trees. Got one with your name on it." Mother looked puzzled. "They're for folks who might—uh—need some cheering up this time of year." No one knew what to say to that.

He turned and hoisted the topmost tree off the car. With two strides, he was back. "If you could just hold that screen door, little girl?" Maggie jumped into place, and he swung a tree tall as Daddy into the kitchen. The man nodded at her father, "Mr.

McNeil." Then he looked at Mother. "Where would you like it set, ma'am?"

The tree seemed to fill the kitchen. Through its branches, Palmer could see the stove and the pot of chicken still bubbling, as if the whole room had been whisked to the treetops.

"In here," Mother said, leading the way to the living room. She smiled tentatively. "You could just lean it against the bookcase."

Mr. Malcolm must have seen the scraggly artificial tree perched right in front of him, but he gave no sign. "She won't be shedding needles anytime soon, that's for sure. We just drove down from Wrightwood, where we topped a dozen—Noble firs, all of 'em. Sorry we couldn't get hold of any cross-planks to hammer into stands. Try a bucket of sand, keep it wet." He surveyed the tree with pride as it rested against the bookcase like an oversized angel, its many wings outstretched. "You'll throw 'er out before she ever dries up on you."

"We thank you," Daddy said formally.

But the man waved him off. "If God didn't intend for us to have Christmas trees, guess he wouldn't have grown so many!"

"Would you like a cup of coffee?" Grandmother Sydney asked. "And the young man in the car?"

"Thanks, folks, but we're off to deliver the rest of this bunch. Merry Christmas now!" And he was out the door, the car coasting down the alley to turn left on Ocean Drive.

For a moment they all just stood there staring at the tree. "Well," Mother said softly, "a gift from the Magi."

Grandmother Sydney put her face practically into the branches. "I can smell mountains," she announced as the tree's fragrance filled the house. Mother handed the little artificial tree to Palmer, and Daddy moved the bookcase out from under the living room window and slid it across to the opposite wall. Pushed up close to the window, the tree's branches still brushed the arm of Daddy's easy chair.

"It really does need a couple of cross-boards nailed across the bottom," Daddy said. That was how trees came from Wahlberg's or a Christmas-tree lot. But they didn't have any wood, and what tools Daddy had were lost in storage.

From under the kitchen sink, Mother fished out the bucket she used for mopping the floors, while Daddy took the dishpan over to the sandy vacant lot across the street. No one hurried or got impatient. Daddy set the tree into the bucket, holding it steady while Mother poured sand from the dishpan all around it and Palmer gurgled in water from an old milk bottle. Maggie stirred the mixture with a wooden spoon so the water would wet the sand through. Finally, Mother swept up what spilled, and they all stood back to admire their work.

Palmer didn't know if their other trees had been this large and just looked smaller because the houses were bigger, but Daddy finally said, "Those fellows got carried away. Probably hard to tell how much tree you've got when you're topping them." His voice held a grudging admiration, as if he wished he'd been along, maybe a note that he would have judged the trees better. But nobody really cared. Daddy even snapped on the radio and turned the dial to a station playing carols.

Palmer and Maggie carefully lifted the foil disks from the artificial tree and scattered them among the fir branches, so alive with scent that Palmer thought of frankincense and myrrh, though she wasn't quite sure what either one was. The star from the top of the other tree was too small for a topper now, so Maggie hung it in the lush green sky of branches.

Mother quietly put the artificial tree in a paper bag to store under the bed. Who knew what next Christmas might hold for them? "We can string popcorn and cranberries," she said. "That will help."

Grandmother Sydney was on her knees, wrapping a sheet around the bucket and making it look as if the tree grew out of snow-covered ground. She touched the needles lightly, blessing the magic that had found its way to their house just three days before Christmas. Or perhaps she was merely breathing in the spell of limbs once restless as waves in their windy mountain home.

Palmer glanced over her shoulder just as Mother touched

Daddy's arm and his hand covered hers. Like a comet, joy skimmed through Palmer, stinging her eyes. When she looked back at the tree, she caught moist flashes of silver starlight. For just a moment the dark green looked like the night sea with phosphorescence flashing in the waves, reminding her of that night almost a year ago now when she'd looked down from the snowy cliffs of Palos Verdes.

Breathless

Palmer hurried home from the Saturday matinee. Christmas had come and gone. New Year's, too, and school would begin again on Monday. It felt important somehow to be in a new decade. The Fifties. She buttoned her red jacket close around her neck. During the movie, January fog had poured in, and now it floated about her, so milky she had to look sharply before crossing streets. A car could loom out of the mist before you had time to react. Daddy said fog turned driving into a game of blindman's bluff. Mother warned about the dangers of intersections.

As she walked along, Palmer mentally ran her tongue over memories of Christmas, like worrying a loose tooth: no pain to it, just something you couldn't quite wrench your mind from. On Christmas morning she'd unwrapped a Brownie box camera with a roll of Kodak film, amazed at her parents' extravagance. Maggie shrieked over a tin barn and corral with two miniature palominos.

They had feasted on halibut steaks from a twenty-pounder Daddy caught off the Pier (no one was ready for another turkey), along with artichokes and fresh-baked yams and Grandmother Sydney's apple pie.

But Palmer always felt that Christmas really happened when their tree arrived. That mutual touch between her parents was the holiday memory she replayed as she walked back and forth from school or fell asleep at night.

Now as she rushed along, condensation clung to her bangs and flattened them against her forehead. Fog pressed from all sides, making it hard to breathe, though perhaps she'd been trying to catch her breath ever since the newsreel.

Pathé News had featured Rancho Los Amigos, located in the heart of the Valley. The camera panned across the sunlit grounds of the stucco-and-tile sanatorium, bordered with gleaming oleander, while hibiscus and bougainvillea waved like flames in the foreground. It looked like a resort.

So Palmer was not prepared for the sudden view inside, the row upon row of iron lungs, long tubes lined up like torpedoes in submarine movies, with each cylinder holding its prisoner—a victim of the dreaded infantile paralysis. The newscaster said these patients were among the lucky ones: children and adults who had lived through polio. But they could never breathe outside their metal chambers. Palmer felt their entrapment, heads curiously flattened from months and even years of lying on their backs, faces melting into necks and tears.

Before he'd died, one man held the record for number of years in a lung. After five years, he was moved next to a window because of *seniority*. After seven years, his wife divorced him to keep the County from confiscating their home to pay for his care, the home in which she still lived with their children. After the divorce, she had visited him twice each week for the rest of those record-breaking ten years.

The pitiless camera panned over the ward and settled on a patient with a fly crawling across her forehead. No wonder her own mother was obsessed with contaminated water and infectious crowds.

Palmer wondered if any of the patients suffered from *claustrophobia*, a condition whose name had been on her last spelling list. And what could they do about it, anyway? There in the theater, she had heard her own first squeaky wheeze. She knew she was being suggestible. Mother had explained all about the mind's power over the body. In matters of healing, her mother mostly gave credit to the mind, while people at church gave credit to God.

Anyway, mind or God, nothing had worked for Jerry Paulsen,

a seventh-grader who had come down with polio last September and died. The story was that his folks were Christian Scientists. If someone had put him in an iron lung, it would have been better than dying, wouldn't it?

In the newsreel, the bellows of the respirators squeezed out eerie music, an ocean song like that of sirens luring sailors across the waters. She shivered at those haunted patients, entombed in metal shrouds.

On the screen Eddie Cantor asked people to give to The March of Dimes. Other afternoons Palmer had watched *pitches* (that's what Daddy called them) by Judy Garland and Mickey Rooney, another by Greer Garson. During intermission the theater took up a collection, like a church offering, and she and JJ dropped in what little change they had between them.

At school, kids were given March of Dimes cards with slots into which to slip dimes. No one ever forgot that President Roosevelt was in a wheelchair. Children were pictured on posters with withered legs encased in metal braces. The whole nation gave to the National Foundation for Infantile Paralysis in The Fight to Stamp Out Polio. Slogans swam in Palmer's head along with the deep currents of her mother's fears.

Mother said poliomyelitis came with progress, that homes these days were cleaner (though *her* family, she was quick to add, had always kept a clean house). Children encountered germs *later* in life, after they'd lost their immunity from mother's milk, so more of them were vulnerable. That was Mother's theory.

But now with the sound of the respirators still laboring in Palmer's ears, the rhythm echoing her own wheezing, her heart seemed to flutter like a tern trapped in her chest. Was it this sudden glimpse of human fragility that was sending her home on the run?

Theoretically she knew everybody died eventually and that she was a part of that great, bulky *everybody*. But Rancho Los Amigos seemed to have lifted the theoretical right off the screen to paralyze her lungs, which now in her imagination seemed turned to stone.

With death pressing close as fog, Palmer suddenly understood the urgency behind Pastor McManus's message that without Jesus her loved ones were doomed to an eternity in Hell. He would probably say she was having a revelation. Grandmother Sydney would call it an *epiphany*.

When Palmer dashed into the warm little house after the movies, her grandmother was sitting alone at the kitchen table reading *Silver Screen*. Palmer tried to calm her heart. It was racing even faster now that she'd decided to give her *personal testimony* after seeing the iron-lung images. As she caught her breath, she didn't even sit down before words tumbled out of her about the Youth for Christ Rally: the altar call, Original Sin, and the Devil's own spawn.

"I see," Sydney said thoughtfully, drawing the words out like a doctor making a diagnosis. "A conversion experience."

Palmer felt a little let down. She had expected—well, what? At least a toss of her grandmother's hair, the artfully drawn brows arching in surprise. Instead Palmer seemed to be delivering old news. She pulled a chair up to the table.

"They call it *born again* or being *saved.*" Palmer wanted to be absolutely sure her grandmother understood.

"It's all one and the same, darling."

Palmer was afraid to leave anything out, this being her first time witnessing. The way they put it at church, you just told the story of how you came to accept Jesus Christ as your Personal Savior. That seemed straightforward enough.

"Yes! Washed in the Blood of the Lamb." Sydney sang it out so suddenly that she scared the bejesus, as her father would have said, out of Palmer, who realized too late that *bejesus* was actually taking the Lord's name in vain. She glanced sharply at her grandmother. It was not beyond her to be making fun, and with her eyes squeezed shut behind her glasses, it was hard to tell.

Suddenly Sydney's bright eyes flew open, and she glared at Palmer. "This isn't some new teenage fad?"

"Oh, no—"

"Then I'll buy you a white Bible with your initials embossed in gold in the lower right-hand corner."

"A white Bible?"

"Every proper Christian lady should have a white leather Bible." That matter settled to her satisfaction, Sydney picked up her magazine again.

"Well—" Palmer thought it a nice idea, but she wondered how to move off accessorizing and get down to witnessing. It was hard to take charge of *any* conversation with her grandmother, but this one concerned her immortal soul, and there wasn't much time, since she was going home to Seattle next week. She said a month's visit was long enough. Palmer was glad her father wasn't around to mutter "too long."

At her Christian Endeavor youth group last week, they'd been urged to testify to their unsaved families. "Are you—um—have you ever been—"

"Oh, my dear! I was saved at a tent meeting put on by the Reverend Billy Sunday, who, in my opinion, puts this newcomer Billy whatever-his-name-is to shame."

"Billy Graham," said Palmer.

"When they gave the altar call, I glided down that aisle as if I were caught up by doves, tears just streaming down my face." Telling it now, Grandmother Sydney seemed to shine with sacred memory. "And that was just the first time!"

"I thought—I mean, isn't one time all you need?"

"Darling, I know what they say: 'Once saved—always saved.' But can you really be too sure about eternity? About anything metaphysical, for that matter?" She looked searchingly at Palmer.

"I guess not," Palmer said hesitantly. And yet—wasn't being *sure* the point? Or as sure as belief could ever be? The word *salvation* had, she thought, a pretty definite ring to it.

Sydney seemed struck by a thought. "Palmer, are you *witnessing* to me? Making sure your dear grandmother has accepted the Lord?" Palmer's face flushed, and Sydney reached across the table to pat her cheek gently. "My baby, there is *nothing new under the sun*—and you may quote me. Or anyway quote Ecclesiastes."

She frowned. "Or maybe it's Proverbs."

"Anyway," she said, waving the specifics to a kitchen corner, "you're not the first in this family to come to God. I myself have had extensive spiritual travels. An odyssey of the soul, you might say, even setting aside, for the moment, my *manifestations*. Let's see, I've been a Christian Scientist, a Mormon, a Seventh-day Adventist"—she ticked them off—"but you know most of this. Oh, yes, I might have given the Catholics a whirl if it didn't take so long to get in with them."

Grandmother Sydney's fingers brushed back and forth across the oilcloth. She was always searching out errant sand in the beach house. "I also spent some time with Four Square Gospel," she added, "but really, for sheer rapture, it's hard to surpass the Pentecostals."

Palmer didn't know what to say. With all this religious experience, maybe she really was saved and Palmer didn't have to worry, could take her grandmother off her Salvation Prayer List, where she'd also carefully printed the names of her mother, her father, her sister, and Bonnie. She worried that this witnessing could turn into a long, tiring business. Not that immortal souls weren't worth every effort.

Sydney poured herself a cup of coffee from the pot stationed over the ring of tiny blue flames on the stove. "You must understand that the Mormons don't permit stimulants, not even Coca-Cola, and certainly no coffee or tea, so that might have created something of a stumbling block if I had chosen to stay with *them*. Of course, where tea is concerned, I only brew it in order to read the future."

"Grandma?" Mother called these tangents "going around your elbow to get to your nose."

"It was your grandfather who decided my eventual path in religion."

"Grandpa was saved?"

"Well, I'd be heartbroken if not, his dying so young—"

Dances on moonlit ferries floated into Palmer's mind.

"We lost him in the flu epidemic after the Great War, but you know that, too. Of course"—her smile trembled, then brightened—"your grandfather was always a trifle more conservative than I."

Well, who wasn't? Then suddenly, from some history book or other, Palmer saw in her mind the dates of that long-ago war and realized with a sad flutter that her father was right about the *Kalakala*. But the flutter was brief. She seemed to have known all along. What was one more tall tale in a family like hers? Sometimes, though, she just wished her father didn't need to "set the record straight."

"He was Congregational. And that's where I came by my own white Bible—a wedding gift from the ladies of the church."

Palmer could hear one of her grandmother's long stories coming. Sometimes they *were* elbows. ("Off on a tear again," her father would say.) But Palmer had started this church talk in the first place, so she had only herself to blame. Still, she began to wonder what Bonnie was doing about now.

"Your grandfather didn't hold with any of my Powers, but then I didn't think it appropriate to make an issue of them, either. Hearts beat to different rhythms."

Christian Endeavor hadn't covered Powers, but Palmer had a pretty good idea what her church would think of fortune-telling and tea leaves—or worse yet, the occasional *vision*. Still, she found it hard not to be intrigued by her grandmother's special ways. And, anyway, hadn't St. Paul himself had a vision on the road to Damascus?

Sydney nodded toward the stove to indicate Palmer should pour her yet another cup of coffee. Her grandmother didn't smoke, but she sure could put away the coffee, any time of day or night. "It has never once kept me awake," she'd say serenely. "To me, a cup of hot coffee is better than a sleeping potion." Though Daddy said she was skinny as a hairpin and twice as bent.

"Did I ever tell you about the time the ace of spades kept coming up over and over again?"

"Well—" Palmer had heard that story a million times, how the man had died a week later and her grandmother had given up fortune-telling for a whole year because of it.

"Of course, I did. See how psychic I am?" Sydney smiled slyly and sipped from her china cup. "How about the Dixie Ball?" She saw the light in Palmer's eyes and cleared her throat as a kind of overture.

"When I was just a young lady," she began, "one of my best girlfriends was Berenice Simpson, and this college boy Berenice knew invited her to their annual Dixie Ball, an antebellum dance, with the men gorgeous in Confederate uniforms—all rented, of course. The women wore long dresses with gloves above the elbow. Some even managed to get hold of hoop skirts. It was always perfectly elegant." Satisfied that her granddaughter was paying attention, she took another sip of coffee.

"So Berenice's mother made her this beautiful dress, just the color of her eyes. Berenice had wonderful coloring. You know how everyone has a best feature—"

Palmer didn't know, and wondered what her own best feature was. To her knowledge, no one had ever said. It would be just her luck to have it turn out to be an eyebrow.

"So the dress was nearly finished, and her parents were planning to have the young man over for lemonade and open-face sandwiches before the dance. It wasn't proper to go out with a man your parents hadn't met.

"Nowadays," she said, "there's just the honk of a horn, and the girl flies right out of her house." She looked sternly at Palmer. "I always want you to wait for a boy to knock at your front door."

Palmer nodded. She'd heard this lecture from Mother, too. In any case, going out in cars seemed centuries off.

"So one afternoon at her house—she lived in a lovely neighborhood—a beautiful package arrived addressed to Berenice, all wrapped up with a white satin bow. And what do you suppose was in it?"

"Flowers?"

"Her mother would have known to open a box of flowers and put them in water right away."

"What was it then?" Palmer knew how to be the audience when needed. "Jewelry?"

"Too large for jewelry." Grandmother Sydney paused dramatically. "No, it was a doll!"

"A doll?"

"About six inches high, dressed in a little *antebellum* dress, snow-white, I recall, with ruby-red slippers on her feet—"

Palmer cocked her head. Ruby-red slippers? Snow White? Could her grandmother be getting her stories mixed up?

"—and she had long, dark hair, almost as dark as Berenice's. Tied around the doll's waist with golden cord was a tiny red program that read, 'Dixie Ball, 1902.' It was like a party favor."

Palmer thought wistfully of Bonnie's Storybook Dolls. "I'll bet Berenice was happy," she said.

"Well, yes and no," said Sydney. "She was pleased at first, but when she handed me the doll and saw my reaction, she didn't know what to think."

"You didn't like the doll?"

"That wasn't it, exactly. I held that doll between my palms, and I had a vision so frightening that I don't really know if I should tell you about it."

"Grandma—"

Sydney lowered her voice, as if they were not alone in the house. "It was a vision of a bloody and mangled body." In spite of herself, Palmer sucked in her breath.

"I said, 'Berenice, you just *can't* go to this dance, because something terrible will happen.'" Sydney's fingers searched again for invisible sand, her eyes focused on that earlier time.

"So did she stay home?"

"Hmm? Oh, her mother had the nerve to say, 'Sydney, could it be that you're a little jealous?' And Berenice looked at me with those deep-blue eyes of hers, and I could see that she thought maybe her mother was right. That poor little me was just being mean because no college boy had asked *me* to the Dixie Ball, and, frankly, I was always a much better dancer than Berenice."

"What happened?"

"Well, I handed her back that little doll, and I said, 'Berenice, I've never been anything but a good friend to you, and that's my sole aim and purpose now. If you go to that dance, you'll regret it!'"

"And—?"

"She went to the dance," Sydney said matter-of-factly.

"But did something happen to her?"

"Well, yes and no."

"Grandma—"

"She went to the dance, had a fight with the boy because he was drinking, and asked one of the chaperone couples to take her home. Later that night, the boy's carriage tipped over on his way home, and he broke his ankle."

"Broke his ankle?" Palmer felt let down, then ashamed that nothing short of bloody and mangled would have satisfied her. "But Berenice didn't get hurt."

Grandmother Sydney looked slightly exasperated. "But if she'd been with the boy, heaven only knows how she might have been injured, and that was exactly what I saw in my vision."

Something was missing, but Palmer couldn't put her finger on it. Maybe these sixth-sense stories had a logic of their own. Or had the magic in some way slid out the side of this one? Anyway, it didn't seem a good idea to press her grandmother, who was starting to look cross.

But how had their talk gotten so far off track? Palmer just wanted to testify to her grandmother because she was one of her Most Important Loved Ones. But now she'd gone and annoyed her, and if there was anything the McNeil house didn't need, it was someone else getting mad.

Palmer felt her chest tighten with guilt and hoped the asthma wasn't going to start back up. The kitchen seemed to press in on her, and she swallowed hard, trying not to remember how she had started down this path in the first place today. But like the elephant you try not to think about, those wheezing iron lungs rose up in her mind. She saw again the vacant faces gone slack in that hospital of gray visitors, that ward of silver tears and artificial breath.

Thou Shalt Not Covet

Perhaps it was just the dark days of early January, but Palmer was praying hard not to be envious. Even so, the Staffords' piano was getting the better of her. When it came right down to it, Palmer envied a lot of things about her friend, and the list was growing. She supposed she should be praying about all her character flaws—another list that scrolled out in her mind toward eternity.

That lucky pup Bonnie took lessons once a week from Mrs. Prouty and then spent the rest of the week complaining about having to practice on her beautiful piano in her beautiful living room. They'd been back at school in January only two days, and perhaps because her grandmother was going home the next morning, Palmer confided in her, not expecting anything to come of it but simply because Sydney was always interested. A few years back when Palmer had been elected treasurer of her fifth-grade class, her grandmother had refrained from pointing out that arithmetic was Palmer's weakest subject, though Claudia had been known to say, "Oh, she's just like me—great at spelling and terrible with numbers!"

But as the world entered this new year of a new decade, Palmer knew one thing for sure: she was destined for greatness as a piano prodigy. Her only drawback, and she was ready to admit that it wasn't a small one, was that she didn't know how to play the piano. But with all her soul she could feel the music, especially piano music, when her heart rode high and her fingers tingled as if waking from sleep. And no matter how her art teacher had criticized her use of color, Palmer saw in her mind the sweet, bright hues of piano music: notes of lemon-drop purity, crescendos like green waves, nocturnes in deepest navy. Beyond any doubt, she could play if given half a chance.

Imagine having your very own piano right there in your living room, a room that looked out onto the ocean, with a view that stretched from Santa Monica to Palos Verdes, a view that included the daily comings and goings on the Pier. If the day was clear, you could walk up to that bank of windows and sight Catalina like a thumb smudge off toward the southwestern horizon. When you slid your bottom across the polished mahogany piano bench, light would be streaming into the room, even on overcast days.

You'd open the piano—lift that cunning shelf that disappeared into the piano itself—and place your hands on the keys. Oh, she'd seen all sorts of famous pianists in the movies: Oscar Levant and José Iturbi, their delicate yet powerful hands playing "Flight of the Bumblebee" or "Scheherazade," heads bent forward like dreaming swans. Surely she was destined to play like that.

Bonnie had rehearsed her recital piece—"March of the Toy Drums"—for Palmer, and though Palmer had been polite, it was obvious Bonnie herself was no prodigy. Given the opportunity, Palmer would make that piano croon. Hadn't she learned almost everything she needed to know from watching prodigies in newsreels, those girls in their frilly white dresses, their shiny Mary Janes, seated at gleaming grand pianos three times their size?

But that night at dinner, maybe because she was leaving the next day, Sydney passed along Palmer's musical ambitions to Claudia, hoping perhaps to shame Daniel into finding a secondhand upright for his daughters. Really, Sydney said, piano was the *most* cultivated of instruments for young ladies to play. But Daniel wasn't shamed, didn't even register it as any kind of possibility. Hadn't he wanted to take trumpet lessons as a boy, mostly from admiring parade buglers? That dream had been well beyond the reach of his railroading family. So Daniel ate in silence while Sydney rattled on. He didn't even think about hunting up a piano in a secondhand store. There was no money, plain and simple.

But after Sydney had taken the bus safely back to Seattle, Claudia whirled into action. Perhaps the plan was born with the help of a few nips from the bottle, but the next thing Palmer knew, she was taking piano lessons once a week from Mrs. Prouty at the Staffords', right after Bonnie's lesson. What Palmer didn't know, and what later pricked Daniel's pride, was that Mrs. Stafford was paying for the lessons herself. A small price, Elinor had rightly figured, for the companionship for Bonnie; and maybe Palmer would be a good influence on her daughter's practicing.

Claudia also arranged with the Community Church for Palmer to practice three afternoons a week in the church basement on their old ebony upright. When it came to her girls, Claudia could get things done.

So the lessons began, and Palmer paid attention to her teacher's clipped instructions. She found middle C and learned her scales. The bass and treble clefs. Half and quarter notes, eighths and sixteenths—more like math than music, which didn't strike her as a good sign.

She practiced childish songs over and over, though whatever she did was never enough for Mrs. Prouty, who pressed at her cap of tight dark curls, as if daring one to bounce free. Palmer pictured her teacher at bedtime, her scalp a whirl of pin curls and porcupine bobby pins—a prickly creature in an old flannel gown. Every week she asked Palmer if she'd been practicing. Waiting her turn through Bonnie's lesson, sitting before those windows lighted by the western sky, Palmer never once heard the teacher ask her friend that question, though she knew Bonnie practiced only fitfully.

And pride, or shame, kept Palmer from explaining how the church piano was available for only an hour three days out of the week. How sometimes it was a little less than that because even though she rode her bike, by the time she bumped it down the basement stairs and leaned it on its kickstand beside the piano, she might have already lost six of the sixty minutes for that day. How going to the basement restroom or getting a drink of water forfeited more time. And then there were the moments lost clawing at her itchy legs.

She tried to tell Mrs. Prouty about this last one.

"Mostly my calves and shins."

"No," Mrs. Prouty said, "pianists don't have—that problem." Her voice implied a disease of the unwashed.

"But sometimes I can hardly stand it—"

"No," the teacher repeated. "Only violin students, when they're beginners. It has something to do with standing still for practice sessions, a lack of circulation perhaps."

"Maybe the piano bench presses on the backs of my legs? It doesn't happen until almost the end."

Mrs. Prouty waved her into silence. "I myself have always considered it a stalling tactic. Something boys might do but certainly not girls. And I've *never* heard a pianist complain." The teacher looked at her with something like distaste.

Palmer blushed and bit the inside of her cheek.

"Now, if we can continue? I was about to explain that the piano is more than a mechanical device. Once mastered—" She stopped, and Palmer could tell Mrs. Prouty considered mastery forever beyond her itchy pupil. "Sometimes, piano can express the most exquisite and sensitive of human emotions."

Looking down at her hands, Palmer nodded.

"—and so a piano is not usually regarded as a member of any section of an orchestra."

That made sense, though Palmer couldn't say exactly why. She had thought the solo performances of those dressed-up girls to be glamorous, like the performances of any celebrities in the spotlight. But now she saw the piano was not so much the center of attention as just another outsider.

After that lesson, when she tried to talk to her teacher and failed, the colors of music began to fade for her; even the adagio lost its crimson hue. On practice days at the church, she arrived late and left early. Though Mrs. Prouty grew no more impatient than usual, Palmer's fingers felt clumsy during her lessons and especially during practice. The church basement was chilly.

Winter passed into mid-March. Palmer had been taking lessons for eight weeks. One afternoon when she'd ridden through yet another afternoon fog, her fingers seemed especially cold. She blew on them, but they hit the keys stiff as twigs, and she scattered wrong notes like birdseed. Doggedly, she kept at her piece, an English folk tune called "The Morris Dance."

"It's supposed to sound sprightly," Mrs. Prouty had told her.

Sprightly. Palmer took a deep breath and wedged her hands beneath the warmth of her jeans-clad bottom and the piano bench, determined to pick up the pace. Why did it feel as if so much depended on this? Was it because everyone—her grandmother, Mrs. Stafford, her mother—had tried to make her dream come true? "We've gone to great lengths," her grandmother had written to her, probably meaning to encourage. But Palmer could no longer remember what this dingy piano and smelly basement had to do with white dresses and dainty curtseys. And once again her legs were starting to itch.

"Don't get yourself done up in a knot," Bonnie said about the lessons. Was that what she was doing?

Once more she fastened her eyes on her music book, and her barely warmed fingers pecked at the keys. She played four crystalline notes, but before she could even register their fine, quick tempo, her index finger slid sideways onto a flat. In frustration she banged the key she'd meant to strike, then hit it again harder for emphasis, as if to drive it—where? Into her stupid brain?

Then all at once heat exploded like a crown fire in the treetops of her head and shoulders, running down her arms, and she was hitting the key over and over again. Someone was making a funny sound like rough hiccups, and with both hands she banged at the keys—any keys now—the song forgotten. Pain flashed up her wrist, so she struck at the keyboard with the heels of her hands, then pounded with both fists. All the while, she was conscious of that roaring in her ears like wildfire and the harsh noises she was making, sounds she'd never made in her whole, well-behaved life. She scraped the bench back, gripped its edge, and with legs splayed, knowing she was in a dark place and beyond ridiculous, threw the heels of her feet onto the keyboard, drumming with all her strength.

But even the frenzied beat of tennis shoes was too muffled to satisfy her. She slammed the piano shut and with one jagged tear ripped "The Morris Dance" out of her music book, then all the pages she could claw together—notes and lyrics, staffs and treble clefs—more and more pages, like those ads in which musclemen tore phone books in half, the crumpled sheets flying onto the floor.

Panting, she slid off the bench onto her knees and swept the pages into her arms. Murderous now, she stamped toward the bathroom, shoving the door with her shoulder and stuffing sheets of broken music into the toilet, which she flushed again and again, not waiting for the tank to fill, her nose running, the swipes of her hand carrying snot and tears across her cheeks.

But the music stopped disappearing down the rabbit hole, and the water in the bowl was rising fast. It burbled over the edge like a fountain, and though she kept on flushing, the lever turned useless in her hand. Her tennis shoes went slippery beneath her, and she watched with horror as the water poured across the floor, washing under the door as if a wave had broken on a linoleum shore.

Panicky, she plunged her hands into the soggy mass in the toilet bowl, trading rage for revulsion. Scooping up all the pages she could see—though more must be clogged in the plumbing because the water just kept coming—and grabbing up all that had fallen onto the wet floor, she pushed them deep into the wastepaper bin beneath crumpled paper towels, candy wrappers and orange peels, and God only knew what other trash.

She jerked open the bathroom door and rushed toward her bike that leaned forlornly at the piano. Her shoes slapped wetly across the floor, but her eyes were fear-dried now, her mouth as parched as a day at the beach without water. Her throat hurt, probably from those sounds she'd tried to stuff back down. Her arms trembled as she wrestled her bike up the stairs. A Brownie troop was scheduled to use the basement in the next hour. She could only hope their leader knew something about toilets.

She thought of Noah and the Flood—her rage now drowned in the floodwaters below. Of plagues upon pharaohs, of Job and his miseries. And something about that patriarch's dour old face summoned the image of Mrs. Prouty. How would the teacher even describe such behavior? Palmer pictured the woman's curls unscrewing, spiraling out from her head like the snakes of the Gorgon she'd seen in a comic book. A small thrill of wickedness splashed over Palmer, and she realized that in the deep pool of her tantrum—what else to call it?—her legs had completely stopped itching.

Tonight she would pray for forgiveness. What *had* she been so furious at? Surely not a crummy little song? And now she was running, like any coward, from the scene of her crime. She'd tell Mother she was too busy with school to take piano lessons, and she'd never have to see Mrs. Prouty again. Her heart lifted. But as she jumped on her bike and fled the church, she shuddered at this strange and sinful penchant of hers for destroying the holy temple of God— from floors to ceilings.

Love, On-Screen and Off

MAGGIE WOKE WITH A START, KNOWING something was not right. She could hear Palmer's breathing in the top bunk, see the slight bulge of her sister's rump bowing the mattress with its blue-ticking. Floozy was a softly curled shadow at the end of the bed in the early-morning April light. The house was quiet, and with weary disappointment, Maggie shifted slightly and felt the dampness beneath her, her pajamas sticking to her bottom.

It didn't seem to matter what efforts she made the night before—drinking nothing after dinner, going potty before bed. Some nights she dreamed she was climbing out of her bunk and walking into the bathroom, but when she sat on the toilet and peed, she'd suddenly wake and find herself lying in bed, her pajamas and sheet sopping. She didn't know which was worse— that soggy dampness or the betrayal of the dream.

It was barely light outside, too early for Mother or Daddy to be up. She threw back her covers and padded barefoot through the living room, past the draped doorway of her parents' bedroom, through the kitchen, and into the bathroom, where she pulled her bath towel off the rung. Retracing her steps, she stopped outside the bedroom doorway with its flowered black curtains that her mother hated so much. Maggie liked them. Sometimes she'd pretend she was a bee and travel the brushstroke petals from flower to flower. Or she might be Tarzan swinging through the fabric jungle. But not Jane. She'd rather be the hero than the girlfriend. And in her opinion, Tarzan had too much tummy for his loincloth. Even Flash Gordon seemed a little fat. Her father said they were champion swimmers and had to carry some extra meat to protect them during cold hours spent in the water.

She put her eye up to the crack between the curtains. In the dawn light her parents looked different asleep—smaller somehow. Mother was turned to the wall, her hair mussed in a pretty sort of way. They weren't cuddled up like the times Maggie crawled into their bed and they threatened to squash her between them with bear hugs. Her father lay on his back, one arm shielding his eyes, the other flung over her mother's hip. His hair stood straight up on one side, as if he'd slept most of the night facing away from her.

Maggie remembered she wanted to ask them something, but her wet pajamas were chilly, and she thought it might not be such a good idea to wake them just now. She'd ask later.

Back to her bunk. She knew the routine. So did Floozy, and the cat barely woke as Maggie shifted her to strip off the sheet and mattress pad. She kicked the linens under the bed and placed the folded bath towel over the damp mattress. Pulling off her pajama bottoms, she tugged on yesterday's underpants and hooked an arm under Floozy, who opened one blue eye, and the two of them snuggled back under the covers.

Later, Mother would purse her lips and hang the bedding out to dry in the sun until wash day, but she never scolded. She seemed to know how bad Maggie felt to still be doing a baby thing. Once Mother had even asked the doctor about the bed-wetting, but when he said something about nervous tension, Mother looked the same as that time the doctor had said Palmer might not have so much asthma if she weren't "overstrung."

Maggie didn't *feel* tense. Now that she was warm and dry, she rubbed her face into Floozy's fur and fell back asleep.

That night Mother was frying corned-beef hash for dinner, Maggie's favorite. She'd helped Palmer set the table so her sister could run down to The Strand to watch the sunset before they ate. Palmer really liked sunsets these days, dreaming over them in a mushy sort of way. Maggie thought they were pretty enough, but a glance or two was all she needed.

Daddy sat at the table, finishing his newspaper, Maggie across from him, cutting out her Margaret O'Brien paper dolls, a present mailed by her grandmother. Suddenly she remembered what she had wanted to ask her parents early that morning.

"What does *fuck* mean?" she asked conversationally.

Daddy's head snapped up. "What did you say?"

"*Fuck*. I don't know what it means." The family often discussed words at the dinner table. "Vocabulary building," her parents called it.

Daddy very deliberately took a sip of his after-work coffee. "Where did you hear that word?"

"Somebody wrote it outside the girls' lavatory, and the boys were laughing. Mrs. Dye made the janitor scrub it off. I asked her what it meant."

Mother was spooning stewed tomatoes over buttered cubes of Wonder Bread. "What did she tell you?"

"She said I should ask my parents." Maggie cut carefully around a blue-satin party dress.

Daddy glanced at Mother. "It's a vulgar expression." He searched for the clearest way to express the least information that would satisfy his daughter. "It means," he said, pausing and then giving up on various euphemisms, "sexual intercourse." Mother rolled her eyes at the ceiling—that wasn't likely to get the job done.

"What's sexual intercourse?" Maggie asked as Palmer walked in the door, the sunset fading behind her. Palmer did a double take.

Mother said quickly, "Put your paper dolls away, Maggie. And Palmer, you forgot to mix the Delrich again." After sliding a serving of hash onto each of the four plates, she eyed the plates critically. "A crusty-rusty dinner, for sure." She handed Palmer the plastic bag of white margarine, its orange pellet of dye like a daisy in snow. "Set it on the drainboard for after dinner. We still have a dab left."

After setting the margarine out, Palmer sat down at the table, waiting to hear who was going to say what next.

"Intercourse," Mother said, passing the broccoli to Daddy, "happens when a husband and wife love each other very much. It's beautiful and natural, and you want to kiss and hold on to each other." Her eyes, flirtatious with silent laughter, slid to Daddy.

"But," he added, "we do not use that other word in this house. It's just not ladylike." He patted his daughter's arm, not meeting his wife's bright glance.

"What other word?" Palmer asked.

"*Fuck*," Maggie said, and Palmer's mouth flopped open.

"Magpie!" Daddy put his finger to his lips.

Mother smiled slightly. "Right now I think two young ladies need to wash their hands." She turned to Palmer and with the barest hint of yearning, asked, "How was the sunset tonight?"

While she preferred romantic movies, Palmer saw practically everything that came to the La Mar: *Body and Soul* with John Garfield and Lilli Palmer; *Calcutta* with Gail Russell, who got slapped around plenty by Alan Ladd; *Gentleman's Agreement* with Gregory Peck; and the terrifying *Snake Pit* with Olivia de Havilland.

The newsreels called Darryl F. Zanuck the producer to watch, while the House Un-American Activities Committee hunted communists. Daddy said writers like William Faulkner and Ray Chandler were too good for Hollywood; same with Scott Fitzgerald, who'd burned out too young. Meanwhile, Prairie Pres condemned Rita Hayworth's striptease in *Gilda*.

Something called *film noir* was popular, shadowy movies with stars like Humphrey Bogart and Lauren Bacall, Veronica Lake and Zachary Scott, Barbara Stanwyck and Edward G. Robinson. Everything seemed to happen at night. Palmer liked Technicolor better.

Daddy told her the violence and paranoia of these movies were probably the result of a lot of postwar guilt. Mother said, "You talk to her like she's thirty, Daniel."

What even a girl could notice was that the women in these

films were locked up, tied down, beaten, or murdered. Maybe, thought Palmer, that was why they looked sullen.

Bette Davis, Gloria Grahame, Shelley Winters, and Lizabeth Scott—sulky and pale-faced, with lipstick that looked hard and black in the chiaroscuro images of those shadowy films—bruised women all.

As for men in these movies, Palmer was drawn to the strong, masterful types like Glenn Ford and Dana Andrews, Robert Mitchum and William Holden, but she wished they could be masterful without being so mean. She liked the dashing Paul Henreid, sweeping Maureen O'Hara up into his arms in *The Spanish Main*, her nightgown a swirl of lace as beautiful as any of Maggie's paper-doll gowns. But that was back to Technicolor again.

And back to pirates, too. Palmer had not quite recovered from Gene Kelly, even after learning in social studies that most seventeenth-century pirates had been afraid of water. What courage to go to sea in a wooden ship when you couldn't swim if you fell overboard. No wonder walking the plank was such horrific punishment, the sea opaque as a blind eye, with leviathans— she'd read the word in her Bible—lurking beneath the surface. Palmer couldn't help but think of sharks and sewage and tar, of possible land mines and unexploded torpedoes: old monsters and modern terrors hidden together in the dark, glassy sea, while overhead flashed the innocent, kicking feet of swimmers.

It might have seemed as if movies jump-started Palmer's explorations of sex, but while picture shows fueled her daydreams, it was JJ's family television that launched her into the realities of *necking*. To most kids this meant anything above the waist, but there were a few purists—she and JJ included—who reserved the term for above the neck. Petting included the more mysterious lower regions, but you were never sure, no matter what kids said, exactly how far anyone went, though few claimed to have gone all the way. Only the tough boys talked about getting to home base, and they were probably lying.

Palmer saw the whole business of making out as a sort of

quadrant system, the body neatly divided by dotted lines like those charts of butchered animals in her mother's cookbook that showed roasts, chops, hams, and ribs.

JJ's family bought one of the earliest TVs in all of Manhattan Beach. Once the novelty wore off and his parents fell into a routine of programs, JJ started asking Palmer to his house on Saturday nights. He would walk down to pick her up, and together they would trudge back over the dunes to his place.

With his mother and father lounging in easy chairs, JJ and Palmer would sit together on the couch, their erect shoulders barely touching in the dark living room. They watched Spade Cooley's Western variety show on the twelve-inch screen, its glow the only light in the whole house. Bluish shadows flickered across their faces from the black-and-white picture.

Because the family rose early on Sundays to get ready for church, JJ's father could be counted on to stand and stretch before long. "Well, it's 'bout time to call it a night."

"You kids don't stay up too late now," his mother would say, folding the newspaper and pushing the bowl of jelly beans and sugared orange slices closer to them.

Palmer and JJ stared fixedly at the screen—it didn't matter what was on—until the sounds of his parents' shuffling back and forth down the hall between the bathroom and the bedroom gradually quieted, and their bedroom door closed for the last time. JJ always waited through one more commercial to be sure his folks were settled before he stroked the back of Palmer's hand, which she had helpfully placed between them. It was their prelude to weekly, ritualized necking, because after the first time JJ never varied. (Down the hall behind the bedroom door, another Saturday-night ritual probably took place with little more variety, though they had no way of knowing that.)

Next would come the arm around the shoulders, the heat from JJ's surprisingly muscled arm penetrating her white blouse, its broadcloth puckering in the dampness that rose between them. JJ waited patiently until she looked up, the signal for him to bend forward as they kissed and breathed—proud to have mastered both at once.

But tonight Palmer pulled her knees up onto the couch and turned to face JJ, half lying across his lap, enjoying the sturdiness of his chest. With his arm cradling her head, he kissed her and then kissed her again, the pauses where once they'd stared fixedly at the TV disappearing.

Made bold by Palmer's innovation, JJ, in a burst of daring, toyed with the top button of her blouse. He was not particularly ambidextrous, but maybe in the long run that merely prolonged the pleasure. His goal was not, after all, to remove any clothing, but simply to enjoy this tentative exploration. At this he turned out to be better than his taut kissing might have predicted.

Perhaps it was the nature of forbidden fruit that made so little seem so exciting. Prairie Pres had strict rules against premarital sex, not to mention those various temptations known to lead to it, temptations which JJ and Palmer often wished someone would elucidate so they could gauge what to avoid or, more importantly, what they might be missing.

It was a curious double standard of a spiritual sort. They didn't play cards, drink, or smoke. JJ was still thinking about giving up movies, a bit of a thorn between them presently, since it would disrupt their practice of meeting Saturday and Sunday afternoons in the center row directly in front of the loges.

Palmer herself had foresworn makeup, namely her recent experimentation with a Tangee shade called *Natural* from the dime store. But religious convictions aside, they had worked out a mutually agreed-upon but never actually articulated boundary, restricting themselves to necking only. And this they did relatively guilt-free.

Palmer felt JJ's gentle lips grow more insistent somehow. Then he surprised them both by unfastening that top button.

Technically, the move fell within the province of the usual definition of necking, and truthfully Palmer liked it, but even so she gently brushed his hand away. He understood it as the appropriate response of a Good Christian Girl, reluctant though he was to leave the soft shadow in the open neck of her blouse.

As far as the Good Christian Girl was concerned, she had simply not yet been able to talk Mother into buying her a training bra. Bonnie, who was no more than a double-A, already had several. Palmer was not going to have JJ encounter her babyish cotton undershirt. For his part, JJ knew perfectly well there was no bra under the broadcloth and certainly didn't consider that a problem.

But he accepted her rebuff good-naturedly. Wrapping their arms around each other, they kissed until the ten o'clock news, which was JJ's signal to walk Palmer home. Hand in hand, they headed back along the dark trail over the dunes, then down the hill toward the ocean and The Shack, where Maggie was probably asleep, Mother and Daddy reading in bed.

They stood in the shadows, reluctant as they always were to say goodnight, when JJ suddenly stepped forward and pressed Palmer against the house's rough siding. With her pinned beneath him, he covered her mouth with his and darted his tongue between her lips. Like a fledgling, she opened to this delicious departure from tradition—one of several in the space of just one evening.

Finally drawing away, Palmer opened the screen door and waved at JJ. He waited to see her safely inside, his shoulders thrown back in the salty night air.

As she shut the door behind her and turned into the dim kitchen, she caught a glimpse of her parents through the crack in the black curtains. Daddy's reading light was on. Mother wore her best nightgown, the ivory satin. Hearing Palmer, Mother quickly smoothed her hair. Daddy reached out to slide her lace strap back onto her shoulder.

"Good night, Palmer," Mother called out. "Come give us a kiss on your way to bed."

Seismic Regions

WHEN IT WAS OVER AND DONE with, neither Palmer nor Maggie could remember which parent had hit the other first, or what either sister had said or done. Maggie had cried, but Palmer couldn't picture her sister in any particular room of the house. And Maggie swore she had seen Mother weaving her way toward the bedroom where Daddy lay asleep in the chilly April night, a wine bottle raised over her shoulder like a weapon, but Palmer didn't remember a bottle or broken glass or anyone sweeping it up. Could that have been a dream? Why would Maggie, who slept as if she were hibernating, be up just past midnight, anyway—too early even to have wet her bed?

Worse than their other fights, this violence in the kitchen seemed to shatter in memory like shrapnel, a reality that fractured like paintings by Picasso in Palmer's *Learning to Draw* book. Depending on where you stood to look at the whole scene, events shifted with every teller, the blame mounting as each angry and hurtful act was recalled over and over again.

Their late-night battle flickered like film noir, the villain seeming to hide in shadows to jump out as the least likely culprit, or the one too obvious to be suspected. Palmer saw first one and then the other parent as guilty, then all of them together because in some mysterious way she couldn't quite unravel (never mind that she had been sound asleep when it had begun), Palmer felt she should have prevented that terrible night, should have saved her mother from one assault after another—her father, the police, even the Snake Pit.

While movies reached The End, family life rolled on with endless, bitter scenes. Sometimes Palmer thought of God as an all-knowing movie director, an omniscient Cecil B. DeMille who worked from His eternal script to bring flawed or raging humans toward a predestined plot. At Prairie Presbyterian they said God worked in mysterious ways, so surely Someone was in control, or at least that was Palmer's prayer.

But when Mother was released from Camarillo and came home with her left hand wrapped in an ACE bandage the color of a dingy girdle, Palmer had trouble seeing the Hand of God in any part of her mother's ordeal.

They had fought, that much was certain, and Palmer remembered hearing noises and waking to climb out of her bunk and look towards the kitchen, where Mother and Daddy were struggling. Then Mother went down hard on her knees, grabbing at the front of Daddy's pants.

"Why, you dirty—" he spit the words, and Palmer saw the strange light that played on Daddy's face. But as fast as she dashed for the kitchen, Mother was already crumpled on the floor, with Daddy standing over her.

Palmer never forgot that part of the scene: the struggle, her mother's body so still, the unfathomable expression on her father's face, whether of triumph or false bravado or despair, she never knew. And where had Maggie been? In her bunk? In the kitchen?

Palmer remembered only fragments, like her father's going to the phone, ordering her back to bed, and Lars Norquist's walking into their kitchen wearing his uniform. Together the men dragged Mother outside to the squad car, and suddenly Daddy was back inside the house. Had he soothed them, told them Claudia was "only passed out," told them not to worry? Later he said it had been the only way he'd known to try to get help for her. Did Palmer believe him when he looked into her face, his hazel eyes so earnest? Could she not?

Many days later, Mother told a different tale, and with each retelling it became more vivid in Palmer's mind. How Lars and another cop had thrown her, literally flung her, into a cell where her hand had been broken, twisted beneath her body. It was a miracle she hadn't broken her neck or fractured her skull. She may have had a concussion as it was—you can't do anything for a concussion, you know; healing just takes time.

How she had begged and moaned in pain, but no one came to her cell until morning, and by the time they'd gotten a doctor to look at her hand, it was too late to set it properly. It had already begun to knit at a raw, awkward angle, and at this point she always held the injury up like a wounded paw, and sure enough, there was her pretty hand with the thumb frozen like that of a pitiful hitchhiker.

"Falling-down drunk," Daddy said. "Out of control and hostile as hell. What was I supposed to do?"

"They shipped me off," Mother said, "right off to Camarillo State Mental Hospital, saying I was crazy as a bedbug, an unfit mother and a danger to my children."

To her husband, thought Palmer. To herself.

Mother spoke of how they threw her into the Snake Pit with all its lunatics—no supervision, no protection. It was filthy dirty, the food inedible. Unbelievable neglect. She'd had to listen to the loonies scream. Why, they'd probably even lost track of some of those patients. It was a miracle she hadn't been beaten up or even killed.

In Palmer's mind, the terrified, dark-circled eyes of Olivia de Havilland were superimposed on the bruised vision of her mother. Projected on the twin screens of her imagination and the La Mar, the black-and-white roiling of the insane became both Camarillo and the Snake Pit of the movie—melded into a single, great holding pen of an institution, a literal pit of vipers that whirled like a vortex. And Palmer, watching all of it at once, tasted pity and grief like bitter medicine forced down her throat.

It had taken three days before Mother had was interviewed by the staff psychiatrists whose job had been to certify her insane and commit her involuntarily—or judge her competent and release her to home and family. "Of course," Mother said, "it took them less than five minutes to see I was not only perfectly sane but quite intelligent. They could tell my daughters were such good girls I couldn't possibly be a bad mother, and they let me out of that place in a flash."

"Too bad they gave her time to sober up," Daddy said. "Too bad you can't commit an alcoholic."

Mother came home *nervous* (sober, Daddy muttered) but looking beautiful. Before the hearing, they had let her shower, even lending her bobby pins to set her hair and makeup to do her face.

"Those nurses could see right away what kind of a person they were dealing with," Mother said. "They didn't treat me like some common mental patient. Do you know, they won't even give you an aspirin in that place unless a doctor prescribes it? You can't imagine how I suffered." And several times over the next few weeks, she sent Palmer to the Rexall for Empirin tablets, which she took in double doses when her hand throbbed.

"It will never be right again," she said over and over. And Palmer wondered if she were talking only about her hand. As frightful as the on-screen images were, it was easier for Palmer to think about the movie hospital than about what had happened in her own family. She wondered if Mother herself had actually seen *The Snake Pit*. Her parents went out so seldom that Palmer figured her mother had only read about the movie, seen the ads, heard about it on the radio—knew just enough to meld the two.

But weeks before her mother had been committed for those three long days, Palmer had watched the shadowed horror on the screen, the bars and catwalks, the women caged like animals in a zoo. She remembered that vague but dangerous condition—nervous breakdown—and treatments that ranged from a new "truth serum" called sodium pentothal to straitjackets that bound a woman's arms to herself. When Olivia de Havilland raged at such treatment, they knocked her out with a shot and she awoke trapped in a canvas-covered tub of water with only her head showing. Hydrotherapy, they called it, and if women screamed, they were labeled claustrophobic.

When all else failed, there lurked the unthinkable lobotomy.

In a scene set in something like a courtroom, Olivia de Havilland failed her first staff examination because of a mean psychiatrist. What if Mother had come before such a doctor?

Palmer dreamed about Ward 33—the movie's Bedlam—with women dancing to their own screams, wild laughter echoing around them. There was the patient who called herself First Lady of the Land, long hair flung forward to hide her face, and the Bell Ringer, who swept an imaginary bell through the air and made impassioned speeches. Like the refrains from her Saturday-morning radio programs, Palmer remembered word for word the heroine's description of the "deep hole and the people down in it like strange animals, like snakes."

But nothing was as horrifying as the gel on the temples, the paddle stuck in the mouth to prevent biting of the tongue, the patient who believed she was being electrocuted for misbehaving. And Palmer remembered the treatment's justification: that if a sane person could be shocked into insanity, then perhaps the reverse would also work.

So much cruelty in the name of healing. Palmer lay in bed replaying the movie as if it might blot out her mother's stories. The character was a novelist, and as she got better, a kindly doctor prescribed one hour of writing each day. A sadistic nurse stood over her, waiting for the words to be written down. "I can't write when I'm being watched," the heroine said, and the nurse told her being a writer was nothing special. "It doesn't set you above the other ladies, you know." The nurse looked down at the empty page and smiled thinly.

What if someone had tormented her mother like that?

"Your father sent me to the Snake Pit." How many times would Mother say it? And Daniel still didn't want her back with them; unlike the husband in the movie, he would never say tenderly, "Come on, darling, we're going home."

But when Palmer finally worked up enough courage to ask her father about it, he painted a completely different hospital than the Snake Pit her mother kept describing.

"It's a bunch of vineyards, princess, an old Spanish land grant. Orange groves all over the place. Patients can see clear to the Channel Islands. There's even a seminary up there—St. John's. I've driven by when I've been working in Ventura."

Like Rancho Los Amigos? Palmer wondered. As nice as a resort on the outside, polio on the inside?

"A prison," Mother said. "Just a concrete fortress to hold women helpless."

He said he'd driven by? Had he planned before that awful night to commit Mother? Had he waited for a time he knew would come?

In the end Palmer had to believe that Daddy believed her mother could have been helped at Camarillo in some way none of them understood. If husband and family were helpless, surely doctors would know some way to cure her mother. Vaccinated, splinted, or purged of whatever demons made her clutch a bottle. Inoculated, poulticed, or transfused—miraculously healed in a Snake Pit that held no charming, all-wise doctors, the sort of men Palmer suspected existed only on that glistening movie screen.

Later Palmer would wonder how her parents made it through such a damaging time. She didn't think her father apologized. She didn't think her mother forgave him. But just as you figure you've reached a movie's climax and then find out there's really more to come, Palmer was afraid that bad times waited around corners she hadn't yet rounded.

Sometimes she seemed to be listening so hard that she thought the sand and water and even the salt air sent hints about her family, if only she could read the signs, the way Grandmother Sydney listened to her Powers. Maybe pelicans sang clues, and scudding clouds rained information into rough waters.

In these fancies, she pictured Maggie an onshore wind, full of fresh, wild energy. Her mother? Maybe an undertow—quieter but able to knock you off your feet when you least expected it. And Daddy would have to be a Santana, always on the move, hot and edgy. She couldn't even begin to figure out her own place in this restless seascape.

Mostly she thought about her parents' marriage. If they divorced, a judge would give Maggie to Mother; young children always went with the mother. But after you turned twelve, you had something called *volition*. She'd overheard a girl whispering about it in the school cafeteria. Palmer would have to tell the judge which parent she wanted to live with. It would be like cutting off one hand because somebody decided you couldn't keep two, even when most people did.

"A broken home." Palmer tried the phrase on her tongue, said it aloud sometimes, riding her bike, letting the air whip the words out of her mouth, throwing them back over her shoulder like those word-filled bubbles above heads in the funnies. She was practicing, so that if the time came, she wouldn't be caught off guard. Rent asunder, the Bible said. God could do that sort of thing. So could grown-ups.

She imagined a simple, square house like the kind she had drawn in kindergarten—rectangular door in the center, chimney on top with smoke spiraling out, stick figures for Mommy and Daddy, one corner filled by a huge orange sun, the rays aimed straight at the house like flaming arrows.

Once when she'd been on the floor drawing just such a picture, Donnie Broussard rode his tricycle over it, the tear widening like a fissure, a paper earthquake breaking that little house in two, with a parent planted on either side.

The idea of choosing between Mother and Daddy made her feel like those animals who sensed earthquakes before they happened. Her teacher said they might have a sensitivity to barometric pressure. Sometimes Palmer almost wished there might really be an earthquake: fault lines, overlapping plates, a terrible rupture beyond anyone's control that could stop her family in their tracks.

And, she told herself, hovering between hope and fear, there was always that chance. Just last month the *Weekly Reader* reported that most earthquakes took place beneath the Pacific Ocean, their energy traveling away from the fault in seismic waves.

Invisible waves, marveled Palmer—no ink-blue water and white froth, but waves invisible as thoughts. Based on that article, she'd written a school essay on earthquakes that occur in deep-sea trenches, sometimes beneath underwater volcanoes.

"Keep your main point specific," her teacher said, "your focus narrow."

Don't let them get divorced; don't make me choose. Was that narrow enough? A focus specific as prayer?

"A seismic region like California," she wrote in her careful cursive, "may expect a catastrophic earthquake"— (excellent word choice, her teacher said) "once every fifty to one hundred years. The last big quake happened in San Francisco in 1906, leaving seven hundred people dead, mostly from being unfortunately burned up in a fire." She got an A.

She didn't really want people burned up, of course. Maybe just a slight earthquake that could be mistaken for the rumbling of a truck. Over the years Palmer had felt lots of small quakes, like that one in the La Mar when she'd just felt carsick, a small temblor in which dishes tinkled and knickknacks stuttered on shelves.

Or maybe one strong enough to shock everyone into helping, like in those newsreel shots of hurricanes in Florida or earthquakes in Mexico, with Red Cross workers handing out blankets and powdered milk. That was what was needed at home these days—some humanitarian aid.

An earthquake rumbling along for her benefit? Not very likely. But deep down in that shifting bedrock that was her intuition, Palmer nevertheless imagined Mother and Daddy poised on the earth's crust and wondered how much pressure she could expect them to take.

One Day at a Time

AT THE MOVIES, THE BIG WEDDING had been the marriage of Rita Hayworth to Prince Aly Khan. In the comics, Joe Palooka married his long-time love, cheese heiress Ann Howe. Even the nation's capital celebrated nuptials when Alben Barkley became the first vice president to marry while in office. But at home romance was on the scarce side. The bandage came off Mother's hand. And for the most part, she and Daddy were polite to each other, walking around carefully, like Palmer when she was trying not to track sand into the house.

And each night, the relentless April fog slid into town.

"Three days," Daddy mumbled, finishing off his third beer since dinner. His chair scraped the linoleum as he got up from the kitchen table to toss his can into the trash. "She was up there just three days. Christ."

Palmer's head snapped around. Daddy looked startled, as if he'd forgotten about her and Maggie eating their bedtime snack of "Poor Man's Soup," as her mother called it. Maggie sliced off a hunk of margarine and watched it melt into the warm milk, a yellow river meandering through the crumbled graham crackers. She acted as if she weren't listening. Both of them had been quiet around the house ever since Mother had come home from Camarillo. When Mrs. Stafford asked Palmer how her mother was doing, Palmer continued to answer shortly, "She's fine."

Daddy opened another beer with the metal opener that hung from a nail above the drainboard. "Sorry, girls. Just thinking out loud." He turned back toward them. "Judas Priest, Maggie! Use your napkin, will you?"

"The oilcloth wipes right up," Palmer said, shoving a paper napkin at her sister. Maggie blotted up the milk that had slopped over the sides of her full bowl.

"Don't correct me, Palmer. She can't drool all over the place. Manners still count for something around here." Palmer's face was hot, and Maggie looked pale. She hadn't drooled, just spilled. Daddy jerked his head at them. "Finish up and wash the dishes. I don't want your mother to say I don't take care of things while she's off gallivanting."

After Mother came home from Camarillo, she went back to her AA meetings. She didn't talk about what they did there, just said it was meant to help people with social-adjustment problems, and Palmer couldn't tell if her tone was sarcastic or not. The minister had a master's degree in sociology from USC, and the church sponsored a lot of community programs. JJ frowned and reminded Palmer it was a modernist church that didn't hold to the literal interpretation of the Bible. Still, she couldn't help wishing that Prairie Pres held AA meetings, too. It didn't seem a bad thing to her.

Mother usually came home late from AA. She said that since they met only one night a week, they had a lot to talk about, especially afterwards over coffee and cigarettes. Chitchat, she said, but Palmer could tell she liked going. Her night out, Daddy called it. The chapter was new and hoped to meet more often before long. Mother had the phone number of someone she called a "sponsor," but Palmer didn't know if she ever called the woman. The church ladies provided brownies or sometimes day-old cake from Weber's Bakery. Maggie always asked about the "refreshments," as if they were party snacks like those that room mothers prepared for school.

Since Mother had rarely gone out at night by herself, it was unusual for the girls to stay home with Daddy. They might have enjoyed it except that lately nothing seemed much fun for any of them. He had even begun skipping the bedtime-story ritual, telling them they were too old, that it was pointless to read aloud to girls who could read perfectly well for themselves. Maggie cried, and even Palmer missed story time.

But what Palmer couldn't get her mind around was that ever since Mother had stopped drinking, and even before that, her father seemed to be drinking more. He'd always had his beers at the Knothole or over at the Norquists', but now he was drinking at home, and Palmer felt uneasy—like those lonesome times when Mother would drink while Daddy was on the road.

One Saturday when he was washing his car, Palmer went out to call him for dinner. She saw him slip a half-pint of whiskey into his glove compartment. And later that night when he kissed her at bedtime, Maggie long since asleep, the aromatic scent of whiskey had mingled with his Mennen aftershave and Camels.

Tonight, with the three of them in the kitchen, he again smelled of whiskey, though Palmer had seen him drinking only the beers. She'd started noticing his drinking about the time Loretta Sprague had moved to San Francisco. Palmer remembered only because Mrs. Stafford had thrown a November bon voyage party for Loretta one Sunday before Thanksgiving. Mother and Daddy didn't go, but when Palmer got home, full of chicken-salad sandwiches with their crusts cut off and tiny cream puffs, neither of her parents had even been listening to the Sunday-night radio programs. Daddy had that whiskey smell and was snoring in his easy chair, though it couldn't have been much past seven. At the kitchen table, Mother smoked one cigarette after another.

Tonight he was so grouchy that Palmer and Maggie hardly minded going off to bed without stories. Maggie played with her horses under the covers, while Palmer screwed in her radio earplug and listened to *Inner Sanctum*. By the time the program was over, Maggie was breathing softly and regularly.

From her bunk Palmer watched through the slit in the curtain as Daddy settled down in his easy chair to read the paper, beside him a jelly glass filled with liquid the same color as her asthma medicine. Soon he was snoring. Palmer heard Maggie's sleep-murmur, and finally she must have drifted off to sleep herself.

A strange sound woke her, like rain against the window, and an acrid, familiar scent rose in the room. Confused, she thought Maggie had wet the bed, half feared she might have done so herself, but the sound kept pattering at the foot of her bunk. In the dim light reflected from the living room, she realized Daddy was standing at the entrance to the sleeping porch, one shoulder toward her as he faced their closet. He was peeing, and the arc of it was hitting against their sandals.

"Daddy?"

"Just be quiet, Palmer."

"What are you doing?" Palmer didn't dare name it. Her father was a modest man. He always closed the bathroom door; she never even saw him in his underwear. Her stomach twisted with fear. Was her whole family going crazy?

He was huffy, indignant, as if she'd intruded upon him. "Go to sleep," he slurred. "Why are you in here, anyway? Can't a man have a little privacy?" He pulled up his zipper and staggered off toward bed.

She stayed as she was, half propped on her elbows. "Please, let it be a dream," she thought, but the fumes of urine filled the tiny room. Maggie was still asleep beneath her. Palmer turned and pressed her face hard into her pillow, wishing for her mother but at the same time relieved she wasn't home. Mother always said that Daddy was more fastidious than was good for him. He buffed his shoes daily, polished them with two coats of wax polish each Sunday night. "Natty," she called him.

In the dark, Palmer pulled at her sheet, heavy now with the scent of shame.

The next morning, Maggie couldn't find her sandals.

"Oh, for heaven's sake," Mother said, "don't tell me you left them outside again!"

"I didn't!" Maggie cried, twisting the hem of her nightgown.

"C'mon, Mags," Palmer said quickly, "let's go look." Maggie followed her out the door into the cool morning air, Mother watching suspiciously before she turned back to the stove.

"I didn't leave 'em out last night, Palmer."

"Maybe not. You try the vacant lot, and I'll check around by the house."

"Okay," Maggie said, not happy but preferring to be outside looking for vanished shoes to being indoors with Mother's exasperation.

As soon as her sister was out of sight, Palmer beat it over to the apartment-house yard, and there beneath their bedroom window was a tumble of shoes, right where Palmer had tossed them the night before. She had sopped up the floor of the closet with toilet paper, flushing it down the toilet in batches, afraid it would stop up the plumbing. She'd had her fill of overflowing toilets. Now the shoes were soaked from the night's fog. Palmer banged them together at the soles to shake away the sand.

"I found them!" she called to Maggie, who came running and skidded to a stop, amazement on her face. Palmer's arms were filled with all six pairs of their shoes: sandals, tennis shoes, and a dress pair apiece. How had they gotten outside?

That's what Claudia wanted to know, too.

"Phew," she said, screwing up her face. "Some dog's peed all over them. I wish you girls would be less careless. It's not as if we can afford to trot right down to the shoe store any time we want!" She shooed Palmer back outside. "Set them by the front door. The sun can bake some of that stink out of them. And here"—she shoved newspaper at Maggie —"wad this up and stuff it in the toes of every pair; otherwise they'll warp. I'll wash the tennis shoes, but the others are just going to have to air out. I never did see such a thing!"

Claudia turned away angrily. She shut the door on her daughters and poured herself another cup of coffee. What a morning. First Daniel was as hung-over as she'd seen him in years, crabby as all get-out, and now the girls' shoes were practically ruined. She was in recovery, goddammit—you'd think somebody would give her a hand. No wonder she was nervous these days.

Distances

On the concrete curb that hugged the ocean side of The Strand, lovers touched shoulders in the May warmth, children walked the curb like a tightrope, and skaters sat to tighten the metal clamps that gripped the toes of their shoes. Skate keys hung from necks on heavy string or chains, but all kids learned to tuck the keys into their shirtfronts. More than one tooth had been cracked by a sudden spill and a flying skate key. Kids also learned to be vigilant about keeping their skates on tight. Nothing sent you sprawling quicker than a skate's coming loose. Bare knees were no match for concrete, and sometimes a scab got knocked off three or four times before it had a chance to heal. Palmer's knees were already well scarred, with Maggie's close behind. Now even Mother would bear a roller-skating scar.

Daddy had come home a little early Friday night. With dinner finished and the early-May evening still light, he thought it would be fun if he and Mother borrowed the girls' skates. Maggie couldn't remember when the four of them had ever sat along The Strand, their backs to the onshore breeze. Beneath them, the cement wall fell away to low cliffs blooming dark pink with ice plant, then giving way to white sand stretching toward the surf. Daddy leaned over to use Maggie's skate key to make the skates fit his grown-up feet. Things had been nicer lately, Maggie thought, except Mother was nervous a lot.

She was laughing a little nervously now. "I haven't been on skates in such a long time, Daniel! Is this really a good idea?"

"You'll be fine. It's like riding a bicycle—nobody really forgets how." Mother looked doubtful, but Daddy knelt down to put on her skates. "Oh," Palmer laughed, "Cinderella and the glass slipper!"

Daddy got that look, like when they crowded against him at story time. Mother saw his face change, and she stopped laughing. For a moment there was no sound except the pounding of the surf as the tide swept in. Daddy tightened her skates and put the key in his pocket.

"It's the gloaming," Mother said softly to him. She turned to Maggie, anticipating the question. "The dusk at sunset and the hour after," she explained. They all glanced at the darkening horizon, the sky a charcoal blue, shot with silver and pale gold.

"Here," Daddy said, holding out his hand to Mother but glancing at Palmer, who kept her mouth shut.

Mother stood, tentatively at first, trying out her balance, the sense of slippery feet coming back to her, not really so different from dancing, she said, except with skates you were pretty much on your own. He waited until she was steady, and then they skated holding hands, with Maggie laughing and running behind. Mother pursed her lips in concentration, her eyes focused on her skates, only looking up from time to time to see where she was going. After a bit he dropped her hand, and they skated side by side.

Suddenly, Daddy pulled away to go faster, with Palmer laughing and running to keep up with him. Maggie stayed back with Mother, who was not as good a skater as Palmer, but she was doing okay and even knew how to stop by turning her feet out like a ballerina and spinning around. Maggie was proud of her and of Daddy, who was skating hard, already several blocks down The Strand. Even Palmer couldn't keep up with him.

That's when Mother fell, and neither Maggie nor Palmer knew how, because at that very moment they were both watching Daddy get smaller and smaller ahead of them. Mother gave a sharp little cry as her skates stuttered before she plunged headlong onto the sidewalk. She threw her hands out to break her fall, saving her face from the punishing grit of concrete. Maggie was closest and reached her first, kneeling beside her, small hands hovering over Mother like little birds, too startled to know where to light.

Palmer ran back to them. "Mama? Are you okay?"

Claudia rolled over carefully, using her fingertips to push herself gingerly into a sitting position. As they helped sort her out, blood welled from abrasions on both palms as well as one elbow. She pulled up the right pant leg of her torn slacks. Blood ran down from her knee, a scrape big around as a silver dollar, as if someone had taken a carpenter's tool and planed off a layer of flesh.

Palmer started to yell for Daddy, but by then he was just a dot far down The Strand. The girls watched helplessly as Claudia sat herself up on the curb. She gave a trembling laugh. "What was I thinking?" she said, shaking her head slowly. Her daughters flanked her. The wind blew Claudia's hair across her face, where it clung like dark feathers to her wet cheeks.

Finally, she reached down and loosened her skates with Palmer's skate key, the one belonging to Maggie so far away now in Daniel's pocket. She might as well head home and clean herself up, she said. Iodine was probably what she needed, but that was going to sting like hell. Maybe hydrogen peroxide would do the trick—boil those germs right out.

"You girls stay down here." She handed Palmer the skates. "Wait for your father." She stood up and grimaced. Then she smiled slightly, but Maggie thought it was an odd smile. "Don't worry. I'm old enough to have known better. Funny how you can tell sometimes, and still you go ahead."

Deep Tremors

THE EARTHQUAKE STRUCK ON THE THIRD SUNDAY morning in May, unexpected as a January snowfall, though afterwards many said they had sensed a gathering of forces. The dawn light had a greenish cast, like a beetle's wing; the air tasted metallic as new nails. But earthquakes always made people say these kinds of things; no one ever seemed to warn you beforehand.

Sometimes earthquakes barreled down the tracks like locomotives; other times they rumbled like trucks over gravel roadbeds, creating deep vibrations of metal and rock. But that morning at 5:00 a.m. the McNeils were deaf in their sleep—Claudia's knee a healing scab from her fall two weeks before—when their bed frames banged against the walls like drunkards pounding to be let in, the pots and dishes crazed with noise. Floozy woke up spitting, as surprised as the rest of them even though some said animals could sense earthquakes before they hit.

With their bunks stuttering on the floor, Palmer hauled Maggie, who was trying to corral Floozy, to the doorframe of their bedroom. They crouched down, facing away from the windows of the sunporch. It was a familiar drill. By the time Mother reached them, the violent shaking had stopped. Not a window had shattered. Palmer saw a small crack in one pane but couldn't remember if it had been there all along. Daddy had his air-raid warden flashlight out and was making sure the pilot lights were still waving blue in the stove and the floor heater.

"Let's just take our time here," he said. "Likely to be an aftershock. You girls stay with your mother. I'll check around outside." He started for the door, then hastily hugged all three together, mashing Palmer's face into his warm shoulder. When he let them go, he rubbed his neck in that way he had when something bothered him.

"See if you can catch the news," he said to Mother. "Find out how strong this baby was. Give a yell if I'm still outside."

According to the radio, the quake had registered a five-point-nine on the Richter scale, its epicenter near Barstow. No loss of life or major damage reported so far. Daddy called Lars, who told him not to worry, that aside from a few bumps and scrapes from toppling bric-a-brac and bedside lamps, the area had gotten off pretty easy this time. Palmer watched her father on the phone, noticed how he seemed to know what questions to ask. Morning sun crept around the dark curtains, backlighting him like a movie star. He rubbed his neck again, but there was only one tiny aftershock around noon that none of them even felt.

The next morning, when her father was *stricken*—that's the word her mother used forever after—Palmer was so deeply asleep that she incorporated the sound of his fall into a dream not about an earthquake, which would have made sense, but about Maggie's pulling the silverware drawer out too far again. That balky drawer, always sticking on its wooden glides, probably swollen from the early-morning dampness, suddenly giving way so that knives, forks, spoons—mismatched silver that was always tossed into the drawer, not separated into tidy sections the way it was at Bonnie's—all of it, drawer and silverware, crashed to the floor as noisily as if it were a quake. Palmer sighed and dreamed Mother would make her and Maggie pick it all up, hoping they wouldn't have to wash everything. You could never tell when Mother would want to go the whole way.

Then suddenly Mother's voice was screaming, "*Daniel!*," then yelling for Palmer, her cries so piercing that Palmer's eyes snapped open and she knew it was no dream. She wrenched the bedside curtains apart to see her father crumpled on the floor.

It hadn't been the silverware drawer at all, but the whole kitchen table—dishes and silver, spilled coffee and scattered toast. The table lay on top of her father, who looked helpless as a doll thrown down in play. Later Mother would tell how he had pulled it over on himself when he toppled backward, one hand clutching his head. But now she was lifting the table off him, her screams dimmed to murmurs—"Oh, Daniel"—while Palmer ran to grab the other end to help set it right.

"Call Lars!" Mother's voice was tight against panic. "Get him over here now! Tell him Daniel has passed out, maybe had a heart attack!" She fell on her knees, her ear at Daddy's mouth, listening, hoping for sounds of breath.

Afterwards, Palmer remembered the Norquists' number darkly penciled into the pad by their phone in her father's careful printing. She remembered her mouth gone dry, like when she'd had her appendix out. Maggie's pale face. Lars bursting through their kitchen door without knocking, not looking at her—just gathering her father up in his arms and taking him out to the patrol car. Mother's cheeks stained with mascara.

Palmer and Maggie were sent to spend the day at the Staffords', school not even mentioned, until Mother finally called for them to come home.

Now Daddy lay in the hospital. Mother told them only what she thought Maggie should know and then privately told Palmer everything about the cerebral hemorrhage, until Palmer thought she might have an asthma attack from holding her own breath. Especially over the spinal tap: a huge orderly holding Daddy in his arms, folded like a tent, the ridge of his spine bared to a needle that was longer than Palmer's forearm. A lumbar puncture, the doctors called it.

He had to have a complicated operation, like brain surgery, to tie off the carotid artery, an operation so delicate it had five possible outcomes; and every time Mother repeated the story, she held up her hand with the fingers splayed to match her hitchhiking thumb. She ticked off the possibilities: Loss of Memory. Paralysis. Full Recovery. Coma. And finally Death—the most unimaginable. But always in that order, so that Full Recovery stayed buried in the middle—the least accessible of all.

When Maggie asked what a coma was, Mother said, more brusquely than she meant to, "He could be a vegetable forever."

Claudia didn't want to talk about the details with her younger daughter. She was too distracted herself to realize that Maggie was pondering Brussels sprouts and okra, trying to connect her father's last job in the produce section of Wahlberg's with this sickness that made no sense. Where was the thermometer? The bottle of sticky red medicine? Why wasn't Daddy tucked into bed like she had been that time with chicken pox?

But Palmer understood too much, and possibilities haunted her. She tried to tell JJ some of it on the phone.

"We won't know right away," she said. "Well, unless—" Palmer thought she wanted the comfort of putting her father's illness into words, but she was suddenly fearful that giving voice to what could happen might make the nightmare more real than it already was, like she was violating one of her grandmother's many superstitions. As if not spilling salt, or tiptoeing around ladders, her mother had said after the earthquake, could keep them safe in a world that trembled beneath their feet.

"Sure," JJ said quietly. "My dad was in the hospital for a hernia." When Palmer didn't reply, he added, "That probably wasn't as serious, though."

"Maggie cries at night." Palmer didn't say that she cried, too.

"Sure."

"I need to stick around here for a while, so, you know, I might not be coming to the beach too much."

"No—"

JJ seemed on the verge of saying more. She hoped he could be a little more comforting, wished she could feel his hard arm around her shoulders. She heard his intake of breath.

"Are you—" He paused, either from shyness or to lend emphasis. "Are you praying for him? God can heal the sick, you know, and if God wants your father to be healed, He can make it happen if you pray."

She felt condemned already, armpits turning sticky. The truth was that everything had happened so fast and they'd all been so busy that Palmer hadn't spent any time at all praying for her father, unless you counted the *pleasepleaseplease* that echoed through her heart every time she thought of him.

Now she wondered if her father's recovery might rest on the *number* of prayers delivered up. Were short prayers as good as long ones? What if she under-prayed by a minute? Or fifteen seconds? How would she ever know what was enough? Did God add up *everyone's* prayers? Did the prayers of the *saved* count extra? Didn't the Bible say to *pray without ceasing*? Should she give up sleeping and eating?

Her breath was coming hard; she heard a wheeze. How much prayer time had she already wasted? This whole business of healing had turned topsy-turvy. Only moments before it had seemed up to the doctors.

Then another question occurred to her. Almost to herself she said, "If God can make him better, why'd He make him sick in the first place?"

Not for a second did JJ hesitate. "God works in un-fath-om-able ways," he intoned and seemed to think she would find that answer satisfactory. Unfathomable. She heard Daddy's voice when she showed him her weekly spelling list: "Now there's a showstopper of a word."

A vaporous cloud slid into Palmer's chest. "I gotta go help my mom," she said.

Claudia was really still at the hospital, but Palmer didn't think she could talk to JJ a minute more. And especially not about God's role in the cerebral hemorrhage. Palmer suddenly pictured that famous painting on a ceiling, with God's heavenly finger pointing at her father—a thought that did nothing to open the cold fist that had closed around her heart.

The morning of Daniel's surgery was brilliant but cold. A wind swept in from the north, and the swells were running high. Claudia gathered her daughters at the breakfast table.

"I'll be at the hospital all day," she said, trying for the right tone: serious but not frightening, though her own heart seemed stuck in high gear. "You'll be with Mrs. Stafford." She looked into their faces. Maggie didn't understand everything, but she knew her daddy was very sick. Palmer had the dark half-moons under her eyes that often signaled an asthma attack.

Claudia took a deep drag of her cigarette and placed it back in the ashtray. God only knew how this day was going to turn out. The moment called for some sort of—what? Jesus, could she ever use a drink. She thought about calling her sponsor, but she felt too rushed, facing the early drive to the hospital, planning for what the girls might need while she was gone. Tonight, when she got home, when for all she knew—please, God, no--she might need to place such a phone call even more.

"Why don't we hold hands and say a prayer for your father?"

Palmer's eyes widened. Maybe, thought Claudia, her daughter considered herself the expert on religion since that conversion business on the Pier. Well, there couldn't be too much of a good thing. Claudia stretched out a hand to each girl, waiting until they bowed their heads, their hands cold as her own.

For a moment she was silent. "Oh, God," she thought, looking sideways at her daughters, "don't let everything blow up. How in heaven's name am I supposed to get us through this? If Daniel had stuck it out in Portland, there'd be sick pay, but now—"

She felt Maggie's hand wiggle in hers. "Dear Heavenly Father," Claudia said softly, "please protect our father and husband. Bring him safely through this operation and home to all of us who love him." She paused. "Help us do our jobs while he is gone."

A sudden wave, hot as outrage, washed over her. *Don't You dare let him die. And while You're at it, somehow keep me the hell sober.* "In Jesus' name," she finished more loudly than she intended, "amen." She gave the girls' hands a quick squeeze.

"Amen," her daughters echoed. They squeezed back—but too gently somehow. Like a moth, the thought fluttered in Claudia's mind: they were overly careful, as if their young hands could bruise her.

Recovery

AFTER THE SURGERY AND THE TUBES, the drugs and the nurses like white ghosts padding through his dreams, after endless cups of untouched Jell-O trembling in rainbow squares, Daniel came home from the hospital. Listless days limped by in the cramped bedroom, its one window nailed shut years ago to keep out blowing sand or dark figures in the night—no one knew which—the air smelling softly damp, like wood grown pulpy.

Then early June surprised with hot, clear days, and he lay in the double bed, sweating and fidgeting. He wished his pillows were cooler or the sheets less rough, knowing he was cranky as all get-out, his milkshake half finished on the bedside table. Every afternoon Claudia sent Palmer down to the soda fountain at the Rexall for a milkshake with a raw egg beaten into it. Trying to fatten him up, he thought, looking ruefully at his scrawny arms lying on the covers.

"No more tennis," the doctors said. "Enjoy the fishing, be glad you've got *that*."

He breathed deeply against the emptiness in his belly that no milkshakes were ever going to fill. A cerebral hemorrhage at his age. And they couldn't even say why. The best answer so far seemed to be: *Why not?* Or Why *not* you?

Well, there was little danger of his not toeing the line. He felt too weak to lift a sinker, let alone a racket. Just the thought of running across a court, even playing a point in his imagination, exhausted him. Though in sleep he dreamed of perfect backhands and precision serves—tossing the ball high and straight, white as a small moon against the daytime sky.

"Be grateful you're alive," they said, "that you made it through in one piece."

After he'd come home from the hospital, Claudia told him what he had faced when she signed the consent forms. Even now it was hard to think about, and he reached over to take a gulp of the shake, pushing aside the straw that he couldn't seem to convince Claudia he hated, reminding him as it did of the hospital.

Terrible possibilities that *all of them* had faced, he conceded. The girls hadn't squabbled once since he'd come home. It made his chest hurt the way Maggie crept around like a little mouse, Floozy draped in her arms. The way shadows bruised Palmer's eyes. Even Sydney, who'd arrived once again to help out, was being considerate. Well, in her way. She'd at least spared him any psychic predictions about his projected lifespan. To give the old gal credit, she *was* Johnny-on-the-spot when they needed her.

He glanced at the tiny bedside table. Something else about that milkshake rankled him, as if it carried false promises of youth and desire, of kids knowing no better than to play around on a Saturday afternoon. Why that should tick him off, he couldn't imagine. He just knew he didn't want its cold, sweet sludge. He missed the satisfying sharpness of a good beer. He could go for a smoke, too.

Watch for seizures—a possible side effect. No more smoking or drinking.

Watch for seizures? Not something you were likely to miss, he'd guess. Every time he turned around, people were telling him how lucky he was, but all he felt was somehow responsible for this terrible betrayal of the body. And guilty for being so crabby, though the doctors told Claudia his irritability was normal after surgery.

Lord, the cooking that was going on, all for one skinny man: stews with dumplings, split pea soup and pumpkin pies, homemade noodles and pot roast, biscuits and creamed chipped beef. He knew he should be grateful, but his bed was practically next to the stove right there on the other side of the curtain, and the bustle was driving him crazy. They tried to be quiet, but as soon as he would doze off, he'd hear whispering louder than any shout. A lid being clamped onto a pot sounded like a cannon shot. Besides, he had no appetite. Choking down half the damned milkshake was as much as he could handle some days.

The doctors said this was normal, too. After all, they had fixed an artery that was bleeding into his brain. But it annoyed him when Claudia reminded him, as though *anything* that got his goat was just some medical aberration.

And that was hardly the case, especially where his wife was concerned. She'd made a mess this time, and he didn't know if he'd be able to patch things up at work. He didn't even know when he'd be back on his feet.

Each day they got him up out of bed for a little bit longer. The first time Claudia helped him get dressed had nearly done him in. He'd eased back onto the bed in a cold sweat, "pale as death," according to Sydney—a comment he could have done without. But at least from the beginning he'd been able to manage the john on his own, saving himself the embarrassment, sparing Claudia the chambermaid work.

But what if his job were gone? As if things weren't bad enough already. Thank god the County was picking up the tab for some of his bills; the ones he'd seen were doozies. It made his head hurt, adding up what might lie ahead.

What 'n the Sam Hill had Claudia been thinking? Well, she wasn't thinking; that was the trouble. Once she started swigging booze, her smarts took off down the boulevard. Near as he could tell she'd grabbed a couple of buses and waltzed into the Smart & Final office, pulling Maggie behind her, demanding to see his manager. And, oh, god, he knew how belligerent she could get when she'd had a snootful. She had reamed Smitty up one side and down the other over lost commissions and sick pay and God knew what else, determined her husband would get his due as their *premier salesman*. That's what she had said, according to Smitty when he'd called with get-well wishes. And Daniel had been on the job only a few months.

Confidentially, Smitty told him, the big boss was worried, said a man who couldn't handle his wife might not be able to handle a territory, either. Jesus. At least she'd had enough sense not to drive the car.

The curtain across the doorway trembled. "What is it?" he asked, trying not to sound cross.

"I brought you today's paper," Palmer said. "Plane crash on the front page." She said it hopefully, as if other misfortunes might weigh against his own.

"Thanks, princess."

Palmer set the paper down on the bed too carefully. She must have read some annoyance on his face, because she backed quickly out of the bedroom. What was the matter with her, anyway? He wasn't going to bite her head off.

Daniel glanced at the headline and then picked up the paper. A Northrop jet, a Scorpion F-89, had crashed into the oil refinery just down the road in El Segundo. Killed the pilot, poor bastard, and started a bitch of a fire. They were still trying to pinpoint the cause. "Well, good luck and God bless," he thought. "Hope you fellas have more luck with answers than I've had."

Another week passed before he was able to sit in his easy chair reading, the curtains drawn against the afternoon heat, June usually a disappointing month of overcast days. Evenings he listened to the radio. The doctors were concerned about his frequent headaches and prescribed short walks, only a couple of blocks to start with in the morning and evening cool. Finally he made it all the way to the drugstore and back. He began taking a longer route each night, buying the evening paper on his way back. Soon he was able to walk the round trip to the Pier. When his headaches persisted, the doctors suggested he must be under some sort of strain. They thought he should be gaining weight, too. Now the girls were out of school for summer vacation, and even though they spent a lot of time at the beach, he felt crowded. Claudia and Sydney, Palmer and Maggie, even Floozy—their concern seemed to press from all sides. Finally he took things into his own hands, talked to Lars, and made his announcement at breakfast.

Claudia was stunned. "I just don't see how something as strenuous as *camping* is going to be good for you, Daniel—this soon, anyway."

Palmer sat at the kitchen table, finishing her scrambled eggs while Daddy pushed his around on his plate and gulped the one cup of coffee he was allowed each morning. Mother turned her back to him, washing out the milkshake glass.

"I won't be doing any work. Lars will take care of all that, and Allie will do the cooking."

For a moment Mother was still.

Daddy glanced at Palmer. "Why don't you run along, princess? See if you can catch up with your sister and grandmother on their walk."

"I'm almost through," Palmer said, but she had no intention of budging, that old fear of leaving them alone strong in her chest, though she'd never known how she'd helped yet. Let Maggie have her time with Grandmother Sydney. With Daddy leaving for Yosemite tomorrow, she needed to be here, whether any of them knew why or not.

"You don't think we've been taking care of you, is that it?"

"Claudia, you've knocked yourself out. I know how hard you've worked. The doctors just think I need to relax more—"

"I don't see why you can't relax here with every single one of us waiting on you hand and foot."

Maggie had whined, "Why can't we all go?" before Grandmother Sydney had whisked her out of the house. Palmer wondered, too. They'd never been to Yosemite, never been camping anywhere, in fact, and she'd always wanted to see El Capitan and Half Dome. But especially the Firefall—pictures of it alive in her mind from newsreels. That long wait in the valley for the night to swallow the last trace of dusk. Stars shining in the eyes of campers as they watched the darkening sky from campsites and meadows. Finally, gasps and cheers as the bonfire erupted on the mountainside. Sparks pouring like lava off the cliff as the rangers levered the bonfire over the edge, a river of fire plunging into blackness.

Now Mother was twisting a tea towel round and round inside the milkshake glass. Palmer wondered if *she* wanted to go along, too, the whole family on vacation.

"You've all taken very good care of me," Daddy said carefully. "For God's sake, Claudia—sorry, princess—this is no reflection on your nursing. It's just a chance to tag along with the Norquists and soak up some mountain air and sunshine. Don't louse it up."

"You're obviously more comfortable with *them* than with your own family." Mother's cheeks were blazing. She turned and slammed the thick glass down on the table in front of Palmer. "Take this back to the drugstore. Now," she added, as Palmer started to protest, "and don't bother ordering another. Your father won't be here to drink it. *Our* sunshine isn't good enough for him."

Daddy started to say something, then took a deep breath and leaned back in his chair. "Palmer, what did your mother just tell you to do?"

Palmer pushed away from the table, picked up the milkshake glass, and banged through the door into the morning brightness. She couldn't stay with them, but she could make the trip as fast as she knew how. She started to run.

Except for that foray into his office when Daddy had been in the hospital, Mother had stayed sober and busy. The next morning, when Lars showed up in blue jeans and flannel shirt to load Daniel's duffle bag into the Norquists' car, Mother kissed Daddy goodbye and then disappeared into the bathroom. The two men drove off to pick up Allie, the food, and the remaining gear.

When Claudia emerged, her eyes were red, but she'd applied fresh lipstick and brushed back her hair. Grandmother Sydney had a pot of coffee perking. Mother seemed determined to keep things running, but Palmer had trouble shaking that old, scared feeling. These days Mother had her meetings and her sponsor, but she'd stumbled before when Daddy had made just ordinary business trips. Those hadn't hurt her feelings like this Yosemite trip.

Palmer knew she should be glad for her father's sake, for his health. She had been standing outside when he left, ready to give a final wave. So when he climbed into the car, she overheard him mutter to Lars, "Let's get the hell out of here." He slammed the car door shut, then had looked over and seen her. His smile through the car window felt automatic as a flashbulb accomplishing its job.

She wondered if he'd felt smothered the way she sometimes did when she had asthma. People thought the difficulty was breathing in, but they were wrong. The doctor had explained it to her: "Think of your body as an airtight compartment, like a submarine underwater. It's the trapped carbon dioxide—all that air inside trying to get out."

On Monday she stopped by the library to look up *Yosemite* in the encyclopedia. Mark Twain said the national park had "air the angels breathe." She looked at pictures of granite cliffs carved long ago by glaciers, blanketed now with lichen and moss, a few struggling whitebark pines. And the valley itself where visitors camped was lush with meadow grass, ponderosa pine, and incense cedar. She wondered if Daddy felt free in that wilderness. She wondered if he missed them.

After a week he sent a postcard of a huge sequoia named the Grizzly Giant. He wrote that a Douglas squirrel had "barked" at him. Mother propped the card on the kitchen shelf so they could read it whenever they wanted.

The next week Daddy received what looked like a get-well note from Loretta Sprague. Palmer brought the mail in and set it on the kitchen table, admiring the soft-gray envelope, the San Francisco postmark. That night, when Mother reminded Palmer to empty the trash from under the sink—"I don't know why you can't just do it without being asked every time!"—bits of gray paper fluttered into the garbage along with bread wrappers, tin cans, and orange peels. Palmer read the word *sorry* on one scrap, but everywhere else the spidery, feminine script was damp and blurred.

In the morning Mother bought a bottle. She stumbled off to bed by the middle of the afternoon, and Grandmother Sydney slammed pots and pans around the kitchen. But after that one incident, Mother stayed sober, even when Daddy sent a second postcard, saying they'd decided to stay an extra week.

Palmer wished he'd come home. How often had he said, "C'mon, kids, give your ol' man some breathing room"? Now she felt to blame that he needed air from mountain passes. Did he feel better in that other sunny place?

Then, just when they most needed to think of something else, the organ-grinder showed up with his little trained monkey down where The Strand met the Pier. Maggie was excited when the stocky man in his old brown suit metamorphosed, his musical organ strung diagonally across his chest. As soon as a child stopped by, the organ-grinder began the rhythmic tugs and jerks on the tethered monkey that signaled commands for somersaults or backflips. Sometimes the monkey tipped his green hat over and over; it was round-brimmed like a miniature vaquero's, its ball fringe always atremble. When children held out pennies, he would scamper over and snatch the coins with his hard-scrabble fingers that felt like tiny bones, stuffing the money into a pouch he wore around his furry waist in the style of a newsboy.

The organ-grinder was a silent man. His job was to fade against the storefronts; the monkey was the show. Sometimes, the circle of kids and parents would be four or five deep. Neither Palmer nor Maggie ever saw him arrive, and they never saw him leave. He was simply an apparition of the summer, usually arriving, as he did this year, in early July. He said, "Please no feed" when some kid held out candy or peanuts. Just silver coins, please, or pennies—new, shiny copper or old ones brown as the monkey's stringy arm. Mother said it didn't seem like much of a life at the end of a leash.

Palmer found the monkey sad, too, still doing the same tricks in the same old costume. In summers past, she'd enjoyed the show as much as Maggie. Just this morning, she'd felt an oddly sympathetic twinge looking at a June bug trapped in a glistening spiderweb. She didn't even like them, especially when they batted against her bare legs in the evenings. Lately snares just seemed to be everywhere.

The day before Daddy was due home, Palmer's back began to ache.

"Well, I shouldn't wonder," Grandmother Sydney said. "The goings-on around this place are enough to give anyone a pain."

By the next morning Palmer's backache had migrated around to her stomach, and when she crawled out of bed, she saw that the crotch of her pajamas had bloomed with blood. She was surprised but not shocked. Mother had told her about menstruation ages ago.

Now it had actually happened. It would be a story to tell Bonnie, but she herself wasn't much impressed. She had to soak her pajama bottoms in a pan of cold water, wash herself off, and then throw the stained washcloth in the cold water, too. So this was what women got to look forward to every month.

Daddy got home that afternoon, looking tan and stronger, hugging them all except Grandmother Sydney. He kissed Mother, and she kissed him back. Everyone helped to put his gear away. Mother waited until Maggie was out of earshot before announcing to him, "Our Palmer has grown up today."

He caught on to her tone and kissed Palmer on top of her head. "That's what we call a real sea change, princess."

Grandmother Sydney looked miffed, as if she'd been left out of something. Maybe her Powers had failed to notify her of the Big Event. Palmer was oddly out of sorts herself without really knowing why.

Mother's powers were on the job, though, because when Palmer had gone to her, she rummaged in a dresser drawer and brought out a new sanitary belt she'd purchased months back; it was a narrow piece of elastic that circled Palmer's hips with tabs front and back to grab the ends of a sanitary napkin. Over this bulky arrangement Palmer pulled on her jeans, then an old white shirt of her father's that hung long and covered her bottom.

She felt something important had settled over her as surely as a fishing net, but she was uneasy, too, as if she were about to be hauled in with the catch. Not even a trip to Yosemite would get her out of this one—every twenty-eight days. Most of what she understood about getting married and having babies seemed so far in the future that she couldn't quite tell how she felt about "leaving childhood behind," as her grandmother kept saying once she learned the news.

When Palmer felt grouchy for no apparent reason, her mother nodded knowingly, as though that explained anything, and handed her a couple of Empirin tablets. From what Palmer had seen of grown-up life, she was in no particular hurry to move on.

From Yosemite, Daddy had brought Maggie a little horse carved out of redwood. He gave Palmer a nugget of fool's gold on a genuine-gold-plated chain. "Pyrite," he called it. A common-enough mineral, her grandmother sniffed, emphasizing the *common*. "The word is from the Greek," Daddy said. "It means 'fire.'" That took some of the wind out of Grandmother Sydney's sails.

"That chain is delicate," Mother said, touching it gently. "Be careful not to let it tangle."

Palmer wished Daddy had brought Mother a present. She fingered her lump of pyrite, glad those days of climbing into the church attic were behind her, because oddly she could feel the temptation to strike a wooden match against the glittering nugget. Just to see what would happen. Maybe the necklace itself would burst into one pure flame. She smiled at such *whimsy*— her grandmother's term for these notions. Palmer was too old to play with matches now.

She liked to think the necklace was meant to console her for the missed Firefall, though of course she'd never mentioned that to anyone. The clasp scratched against her skin, and with no particular thought, she slowly rubbed the back of her neck.

Small Steps

By August Daddy was back to work full time. He'd started with half days, buffing his shoes the night before, calling on grocery stores in territories closest to home, taking orders for new products like Nestea and old standbys like Morton Salt.

Things would have seemed almost normal except that Mother came home one day with a full-time job at the Metlox Pottery factory. When she announced it at dinner, her face looked tight, like those movie stars who tried to stay young and almost succeeded. But Daddy looked relieved.

From then on, Monday through Friday mornings throughout the remaining days of summer vacation, the girls walked Mother to the plant's side door, where assembly workers punched in. Her daughters kissed her goodbye before she shooed them back home, where Grandmother Sydney had their breakfast ready. Palmer turned to watch her mother wait in line with the others, her lunch in the brown paper bag that she brought home each night, smoothed and folded to use again the next day.

Mother wore slacks with a neatly tucked-in blouse, her hair tied back in a snood made from a silk bandana. Because of the conveyor belts, unbound hair was not allowed. Palmer noticed how slender her mother was. Maybe she'd lost weight while they'd been paying attention to Daddy. Newsreel shots of Rosie the Riveter flitted through Palmer's mind, but those wartime factory women, waving to the cameras, had always acted so plucky. Her mother seemed a frail reed.

Mother glanced back and gave the girls a jaunty wave before

disappearing inside the building.

At night her hands were swollen from the piecework. She'd pull off the scarf, her hair aged by white dust from the unfired clay pieces, the workers painting roosters or apples or ivy, one design over and over until an order was filled.

Palmer was used to watching over Maggie at the beach, but now she had to help out Grandmother Sydney, who stayed on while they all got used to this new arrangement. If Palmer went to Bonnie's, Maggie had to come. But at least they were comfortable, Grandmother Sydney reminded them, while Mother was stuck inside that horrid shell of a plant.

From blackouts during the War, the windows at Metlox were still painted over a dull tan. Old-time workers said that all summer the corrugated aluminum building heated up like a sweatbox, even though the metal was supposed to reflect the sun. In winter, the factory was drafty, and they worked in sweaters and jackets, their hands chafed red with cold and the dry dust. No one could paint wearing gloves.

Palmer hadn't even known her mother *could* paint, her brush following the raised patterns of each cup, saucer, and plate, the bowls and pitchers, the serving platters. One night when Mother was rubbing Vicks into her crooked thumb, crooning under her breath at the lingering ache, Palmer asked, "Does it get in your way? When you paint, I mean?" As soon as she spoke, she felt as if she'd stared at a person on crutches—a rudeness forbidden. She'd meant only to be sympathetic.

"Oh, you just learn to compensate," Mother said airily, not seeming to take offense. But her mouth turned bitter. "That's what we do with anything that's hurt beyond repair."

After she'd worked a couple of weeks, Mother began to bring home a few of the unfired rejects—mostly small figurines that were missing details like buttons on a dress. Mother said some of the rejects had no noses or hands, but she brought home only the best ones. Before long these plaster statues lined the windowsills of the sunporch like white corpses. At the dime store Maggie and Palmer bought a set of poster paints in primary colors to paint the figures, mixing yellow and blue to get green, red and blue to make purple. But without the glaze of firing, the little statues were dull. After the paint dried, it rubbed off on their hands like chalk.

One day Mother brought home a glazed cup and saucer. Not rejects this time but seconds—fired pieces with minuscule imperfections, pieces the employees could buy dirt cheap before they were sold to secondhand shops. Mother had taken to the ivy pattern. "I can't imagine eating off those disgusting roosters," she said, "especially after painting them all day."

Before long the family had service for two, then four, and finally six. Their old dishes, chipped and mismatched, picked up at rummage sales, were donated back to the Community Church for resale.

One night before dinner Mother proudly unveiled a creamer and a covered sugar bowl from her lunch bag. They were gleaming and seemed perfect. Palmer was surprised and shamed to find herself wondering if they might not be seconds after all.

Maybe it was Mother's satisfied laugh. "I dare you to find the flaws," she said. "Just try."

"How much did these cost?" Palmer asked, though money was not a topic of polite conversation in their family.

"Don't be impertinent," Mother snapped. "It's little enough to have something extra for working in that blast furnace!" She snatched at her cigarette pack and pulled out one before she remembered she'd given up smoking inside the house. Nowadays she walked up the alley so she wouldn't tempt Daniel by smoking in front of him or even by leaving the smell of smoke in the air.

She coughed dramatically on her way out the door. "No telling what damage that dust is doing to my lungs. Not a breath of fresh air in that whole place from sunup to sundown." She pointed to the new dishes. "Make sure you wash those. We don't need to be eating the stuff, too."

But once the kitchen shelves were stacked with creamy pottery, the glazed ivy crawling from dish to dish (sometimes, just opening the cupboard, Palmer felt slightly carsick), Mother seemed to lose interest. She was tired in the morning and tired at night. By now the chalky rejects they'd painted had been tossed out, and every windowsill and tabletop sported seconds— dogs and coy kittens, curved statuettes of women holding urns on their shoulders, a lighthouse with a painted-on beacon. Maggie thought they made the house beautiful. Palmer wasn't sure.

But maybe she was just annoyed because of the time it took to dust them. These late- summer days she had more housework to do, but she was still glad her mother was working at Metlox. The wages weren't much, but her mother's paycheck *was* helping. Money was tight, but at least with two jobs in the family, they'd finally gone off County Relief. Best not to think of the dismal factory that squatted next to the railroad tracks, yet hard to keep from it.

When school started after Labor Day, both girls had new shoes from Stephen's Bootery, penny loafers like the ones Bonnie wore, buttery brown leather that Palmer adored. She felt what popularity she had was precarious at best, especially with no money for clothes. There'd been stretches when Mother couldn't even afford to shop the rummage sales. Last year Palmer had seen other girls eyeing her plain clothes supplied by the County. Bonnie had kept a tactful silence. Daddy tried for cheer. "Neat but not gaudy," he said.

But clothes didn't seem to matter so much to boys, at least not yet. She toyed with JJ's ring hanging from a chain around her neck. Having that emblem gave her a certain status, along with being a ninth-grader—"top dogs," Daddy said—so she wondered at her recent tugs of restlessness, deep as undertows. Back when JJ had asked her to go steady, she'd been flattered and excited.

But for some reason, ever since Daddy had taken sick, other boys could seem more fun than JJ, a shift of current she couldn't explain. As if once the bedrock that was Daddy had shifted, she felt unsteady. Sometimes she even wished that Grandfather Burl were alive and sober, that Granddad McNeil and Lars Norquist were men who could be trusted.

Worst of all, she even wished sometimes for *auxiliary* boy-friends—that's what she called them in her mind—as if other boys could be backups in some way. But she was ashamed to want boys around like spare tires in case of a slow leak. Certainly *she* wouldn't want to be thought of that way—as extra change in some boy's pocket.

She didn't understand her dissatisfaction. On anybody's scale, JJ was the best catch in their class. Someone else would snatch him up for sure, and that would be the end of that. So far as she could tell, this business of breaking up and getting back together in some Technicolor glory only happened in the movies. It made her tired to try to figure it out. It made her think about Mother and Daddy.

Sticking it out was always best. Wasn't that what the church taught? Though the church didn't have a whole lot to say about boyfriends.

She sighed. Her grandmother said she was sensitive, and it was not a compliment. "Thin-skinned," she called it. Too bad you couldn't toughen a heart the way you toughened feet, a summer project for every kid when the shoes came off. Their feet were already scarred from broken glass or tin-can lids—lethal jetsam that worked its way in and out of the shifting sands. Eventually a layer of callus built up from playing barefoot basketball or just walking over concrete, and thick skin was a big help when a kid stepped on a smoldering cigarette butt, a burn that for a fraction of a second felt icy, then like boiling grease. First aid lay right at hand—ocean water—but mothers still slathered butter on burns. Most kids kept their injuries to themselves and endured. Otherwise they had to battle the order to "wear your sandals."

Palmer wondered if she thought too much about shoes—how they looked—and about feet—where to put them. She'd read of something called a foot fetish and worried she might have caught one, the way you catch scarlet fever. "Watch your step," her grandmother told her. "Look before you leap." Boys snick-ered and pointed at girls' patent-leather shoes, though Palmer could never see anything when she looked down at the shine on her own Sunday shoes. Mothers told daughters to cross their ankles and keep their knees together when they wore dresses.

She recalled watching Bonnie's ballet class one afternoon. The teacher had carried out a box of faded pink toe shoes from the back-room storage. The girls stuffed the too-big shoes with their rolled-up socks, then took a few teetering steps on their toes, their legs magically elongated like those of women in high heels. "That's enough," the teacher had said too soon. "No more until your muscles are stronger."

Still, Palmer *was* light on her feet; there was that. Grandmother Sydney said it was because of her asthma. Since she had to breathe extra hard, she took in more air than the ordinary girl. It was a wonder, she said, that Palmer didn't levitate right off the ground like a balloon that slipped its tether.

But when they bought the penny loafers, the shoe salesman at Stephen's Bootery told Mother that Palmer was developing bunions. Could she really have bunions before she was even fourteen? The malady sounded so elderly. She thought of the bound feet of Chinese girls, tortured by every mincing step.

Crooked little feet? Though not so little, really, and she probably hadn't helped matters months ago when she told Mother that the cute pair of black flats at the rummage sale was just the right size. Even with the shoes pressing hard against her toes, Palmer had worn them until finally the leather had split at the instep.

"Didn't your feet hurt?" Mother scolded when she discovered the ruined shoes in the trash. "Look at these—so short they're torn apart!"

They'd hurt plenty, but she'd figured it a small price to pay to avoid those ugly oxfords from the County. Besides, every time Mother wanted to give her a Toni home permanent, she'd blithely tell a scowling Palmer, "Beauty must suffer!"

But now, with school starting, these brand-new loafers fit right as Dorothy's ruby slippers. Palmer felt selfish when she considered what it had taken to earn them, but she knew she wanted her mother to keep on working. So she rationalized a benefit in addition to satisfying her own greed: Didn't people have to stay *sober* to hold down jobs?

Mother hadn't been going to her meetings. She was too tired after dinner to do more than press her slacks for the next day and take a hot bath. Because of the dust, she washed her hair every other night, brushed it long and hard the nights between. Maggie missed the leftover treats that Mother sometimes brought home from AA and asked if she'd given up going forever.

"I'm making atonement in my own way," Mother said. Palmer wondered if atonement was really the point.

On weekends Claudia shopped, washed and ironed, cleaned the bathroom. Maggie damp-dusted, Palmer swept. The girls did all the dishes. Grandmother Sydney helped wherever she could. Daniel steered clear of the tennis courts; he couldn't bear to sit on the sidelines and watch the players he used to beat handily. He washed his car, then told the girls to hold down the fort while he headed out to fish the weekend away on the Pier. Whatever he caught and cleaned, Mother cooked. They ate fillets, usually halibut, at least twice a week.. The girls still went to weekend matinees, but the grown-ups stayed home every night. They all read and listened to the radio. Claudia muttered that she might as well be back in the Snake Pit.

One day when Maggie was outside playing, Grandmother Sydney handed Palmer a small white box. "A bit of magic for you," she said, "to mark your entry into womanhood."

Palmer knew she was talking about menstruation, but she'd never heard of celebrating it with presents. The box looked old, with the name of a jewelry store in Seattle stamped in dark blue. Mother always said good things came in small packages. *Please, be something pretty*, Palmer wished. Lifting the lid and poking through the small wad of cotton balls, she pulled out one of her grandmother's beloved opal earrings. Thrilled, she began to search for its mate.

Her grandmother touched her lightly on the wrist. "It's only the one, darling." She cocked her head apologetically. "They're my sole legacy from your grandfather, and I have to save the other for Maggie. But since you're the oldest, I wanted you to have the box they came in."

"Oh," Palmer said, glancing up. Sure enough, for the first time she could remember, her grandmother's ears were bare of the beautiful opals. She felt like crying, for more reasons than she could name. "Thank you, Grandma." But what could you really do with one earring? What kind of magic could this ever be?

"Besides," her grandmother hurried on, "your ears aren't pierced. It's not really considered proper these days, is it? When you're older, I thought you could have the opal made into a necklace or perhaps a ring."

Palmer nodded. That seemed about as likely right now as going to college, as flying in a blimp, as jumping off the Pier.

"It's a valuable stone, Palmer. It has power. Don't be disappointed by just getting the one. When your womanly time came, I always planned to have something special for you, but there never seemed to be any extra money, or what there was got spent on bus tickets. And I wouldn't begrudge a cent of those."

Palmer felt ashamed for being greedy. It was just that she was so tired of ugly houses and furniture and clothes. For a few shining seconds, it had seemed she might be wearing rainbows in her own ears.

And she felt a little sad to think she might be outgrowing her grandmother's magic. Yet for all that, she *was* holding her own sliver of fire in her palm.

Her grandmother had called it a stone for change, a talisman of womanhood. Carefully, Palmer tucked the earring back among the balls of cotton in its box, like a secret power to be hidden in clouds and saved for another, older time.

Glory Road

Grandmother Sydney's vision impressed even Palmer, who was trying not to honor the occult, as they warned at church. It wasn't every night that her grandmother claimed to have looked up from her bed on the living room couch to see a turquoise-blue light in the darkness, big as a beach ball, perched on the end of the curtain rod.

"It woke me from a perfectly sound sleep." Sydney sipped her coffee and glanced across the kitchen table at Maggie and Palmer to judge her story's effect. Late-afternoon sun shivered across the oilcloth, reflecting on their faces, pale as candle's light. "Why, the apparition might as well have reached out and given me a shake—"

"So it had arms," Palmer marveled.

Sydney gave her the eye. "Are you being sassy? It's a figure of speech. The power was that focused, almost as if it could speak. 'Sydney, get yourself awake and pay attention.' And, no, it didn't actually talk out loud, so don't even ask, but somehow I could hear these words in my head. It glowed at me like it had a pulse, like an artery swelling until I was afraid it would burst!"

But with those words, the memory of Daniel's illness clouded over them. Sydney wished she could reach into the air and in a heartbeat snatch back words never meant to link her apparition to that arterial terror in her son-in-law's neck.

"I didn't get to *see* it," Maggie sulked, as if she hadn't been invited to a birthday party.

"Oh, darling, it was meant for me alone. You know that. Because of my Powers."

"Here, Mags." Palmer spread margarine and brown sugar on a slice of bread. It was Maggie's favorite after-school snack. Sydney poured herself more coffee. She'd need to make another pot before Daniel got home, since he no longer seemed to be curtailing his caffeine these days. And on Fridays he was sometimes early if store managers themselves had cut their workday short.

"So what happened next?" Even to herself Palmer sounded too peppy. She was working overtime, as her father said of anyone who was trying too hard. But sitting around the kitchen table there seemed a lot to take care of all at once—banishing the sudden spectre of his illness, pleasing her grandmother, and diverting Maggie, who'd been pouting ever since she found out about the opal, snooping through Palmer's stuff. Things needed smoothing over, especially since her grandmother was going home to Seattle on the bus next Monday. She'd outstayed her welcome, she kept saying, had been there ever since mid-June, maybe wanting Mother to say again how much she'd helped out. Even so, Palmer wasn't sure she should be encouraging her grandmother's Powers.

Sydney cleared her throat for effect. "'Go to the water,' it said."

"Out loud?" Maggie asked.

"Oh, my, will you pay attention?" Sydney sighed. "These messages don't come in words. You just *know* things. You listen with an *inner* ear."

Maggie chewed her sandwich and ran a bare toe along Floozy's flank as the cat lay on the cool floor beneath the table.

"Well," Palmer said brightly, "Maggie and I go to the water almost every day." She smiled at her sister as if to say they were already doing magic. She wanted the three of them to feel easy together. Peaceful times were rare enough.

"Can I have a peach?" Maggie asked.

"Wash it first," Palmer said automatically.

Sydney sighed again and waited for Maggie to get the peach out of the crockery bowl on the drainboard. The little girl washed it under the tap, trying to wipe off all the fuzz. She dried it with the dish towel hanging by the sink.

"Are you finally ready to listen, little sister?" Sydney asked.

Maggie scowled.

"The blue light," Palmer said helpfully.

"Well, as I said some time back—" Sydney glanced at Maggie, who slurped her peach. Palmer handed her a paper napkin. "It was a message, a directive really, to go to the water—"

"Grandma—," Palmer began gently.

"Not just any water," Sydney said quickly. "'Go to the canals,' it said. 'Let the family experience a time of renaissance.'"

Palmer knew this word from schoolbooks, something about old and dark paintings.

"Transformation," Sydney said firmly. "It's what this family needs. A little trip to the Old World might straighten us out."

"What old word?" Maggie swiped the napkin across her face.

Sydney scowled at her. "Listen here, young lady—"

"Old *world*, Mags." Palmer suspected her sister had understood the first time. Still, what could this blue light have in mind? Their family didn't travel anywhere except that one time back and forth to Portland, and of course her father's trip to Yosemite. "What do you mean, Grandma?"

Sydney raised her chin. "This message emerged in color. Think about *that* for a second. A red light might have meant danger: put on the brakes, whatever you're doing. Green would signify going straight ahead with any plans. But a glowing blue orb?" A shiver danced over her shoulders. "And no robin's-egg blue, either. More aquamarine, like the sea." Her eyes shone with the memory. "That color stands for rebirth, pure and simple. It's a sign. Like a spiritual quest where you have to follow hints and clues. Unwind the ball of string 'til you come to the end." She paused dramatically. "Girls, the Spirits do not equivocate."

It seemed to Palmer that was exactly what spirits did best. At times even the Holy Spirit seemed to be hedging bets, probably a blasphemous thought, but for now she brushed it aside and looked expectantly at her grandmother. "So what do we do?"

Sydney barely paused before proclaiming, "We must travel to Venice!"

Maybe it was not a miracle equal to loaves and fishes, but it certainly seemed like a small one when two days later, on the first Sunday after Labor Day, the whole family found itself packed into the Plymouth and headed up the highway to Venice Beach.

Wedged between Playa del Rey to the south and Santa Monica to the north, the tiny town of Venice boasted man-made canals and a stretch of beach-hugging asphalt they called the Boardwalk. Two square miles of worthless swampland had been bought up by a cigarette baron who wanted an American replica of Italy's famous city.

First chewing gum, thought Palmer, remembering Catalina and Mr. Wrigley, then cigarettes. Amazing, the ways fortunes could be made, like pirates' chests dug up to spill out emeralds and rubies. She'd seen the parchment maps in movies—*X* always marked the spot. Crazed fingers running through gold doubloons and necklaces of real pearls, not fake like those beads at the dime store painted over with opalescence.

She wished her family could find a treasure, but didn't the Bible warn that "where your treasure is, there will your heart be also"? So maybe if they were to promise to give half to the church, it would make the wish more spiritual, though she knew full well you shouldn't bargain with God. "Silver linings," her grandmother liked to say, "are treasures enough." Okay, today she'd settle for one of those.

To Palmer's surprise, it was Mother who knew all about Venice. Daddy said something about "rich stiffs and show-biz types" and then grew quiet behind the wheel as they drove north along Sepulveda Boulevard.

"El Camino Real!" Grandmother Sydney gestured grandly from the back seat, where she sat squeezed between Maggie and Palmer. "The royal road from Mexico." She beamed at Palmer. "Young gentlemen on horseback."

"Caballeros," Daddy muttered, his eyes meeting Sydney's in the rearview mirror.

Daddy read the papers, listened to the news, kept up on politics and world events, but Mother was the one who'd lived in Brentwood, who worked for a while as a movie extra—her stage name *Claudia Palmer,* though by then she was married to Philip. She didn't talk about those days often, but Palmer guessed her mother remembered things from a world her father scorned—or maybe one that scared him a little.

Palmer knew by heart every story her mother told about those olden times: how Philip had painted the insignia on the Lindbergh airplane, *The Spirit of St. Louis,* how they had big parties in the house on Butterfield Lane for famous people like Lucky Lindy and Ramon Navarro. Her mother served buffet dinners on china and crystal, and everyone had drunk dry martinis from stemmed glasses.

Back then Philip had bought a baby grand piano for the Brentwood house just because her mother played a little. "There was nothing he wouldn't do for me," Claudia had tearfully confided once, when she'd been drinking. And Palmer knew that buried under clothes in a bureau drawer, her mother had a brown-tinted picture of Philip in his military uniform, smiling with the perfect teeth and clear eyes of a young pilot who planned to live forever.

So that Sunday afternoon it was Claudia who spun the history of the city. "C'mon, Daniel," she had said earlier when Grandmother Sydney, wisely not mentioning the blue light, suggested a drive up to Venice, "we hardly ever do anything all together."

Palmer figured her father really wanted to go fishing. No one talked anymore about tennis. Mostly he just disappeared down the alley, headed out to fish the Redondo breakwater or the Pier, his tackle box in one hand and his fishing rod over his shoulder. He no longer asked if either girl wanted to go along.

It had taken all morning to get ready for the outing. Maggie's good playsuit was in the ironing, so it had to be sprinkled and rolled, while Mother set up the ironing board. As long as the iron was already hot, Grandmother Sydney said, would Mother mind just giving her black slacks the merest touch-up? Mother suggested Grandmother Sydney mix tuna salad for sandwiches, because if they didn't pack a lunch, eating out would take about two minutes flat for the five of them to use up a week's worth of grocery money. Even after so brief a consideration, Maggie and Palmer had hungered after restaurant hamburgers and French fries.

Palmer brushed her hair an extra fifty strokes, then searched everywhere for her favorite hair ribbon, a thin yellow satin, to tie around her ponytail. Daniel washed the car more carefully than usual, though he claimed he just couldn't face having to do the job once they got home at god-knew-what hour. Worse than getting up to last night's dishes, he said, though when that had happened, Palmer couldn't remember.

But they all did their jobs without squabbling, and now as they drove along with the Plymouth's windows rolled down, Palmer felt as though it really was a true family outing. The breeze was fresh and salt-scented, with Mother in a good mood, talkative, not thinking about Metlox. She passed around the sandwiches wrapped in wax paper. "Finish them in the car," she said, "because we're not risking ptomaine with leftovers!" It was a warning they'd heard before.

Claudia told them construction of Venice Beach had begun in 1904, with a large lagoon dug in the center of town. Palmer was surprised her mother knew the exact year and then felt guilty for underestimating her. Ocean water had flowed right into canals that radiated from the central lagoon. Gondoliers plied the waters with their slender gondolas. Though that had been a long time ago now, Claudia added a little wistfully. The city had even sported camel rides and a miniature railway. Artists and movie stars flocked to the beachfront community, some of them building beautiful cottages on the tiny lots that faced the ocean. Claudia's face softened with memory.

"Well, why not?" Daniel said. "That type could afford whatever they took a shine to."

Claudia looked out her open window, then closed her eyes against the wind.

Sydney prompted, "Well, what happened then?"

But Claudia's face had folded in on itself somehow. Offhand-edly, she said, "Oh, it just became one more part of L.A. years ago."

"And the cigarette financier?" Sydney asked.

"Long gone."

They were driving past the oil fields of El Segundo—land owned by Standard Oil. Claudia's voice was flat. "Once oil oozed into the canals, they got smelly. Most were paved over. I've heard it's pretty run-down now."

"Well, Judas Priest, what's the point of driving all this way just to see a slum?"

"It's still an artists' colony, Daniel." She didn't look at him.

"*Bums* is more like it."

"Old buildings mean cheap rent." She paused and then added, "As we've learned."

His hands tightened on the steering wheel. "We're damned lucky to have a place, and you know it."

That fast, the ghost crowded into their car. Palmer took a deep breath, trying to muffle a wheeze. Grandmother Sydney looked at her sharply and nudged her toward the window. "Have some fresh air, darling."

At least the Boardwalk still endured. As soon as they parked, Maggie pulled on her skates and tightened the clamps with her skate key. Almost before Claudia could tell her to be careful and to stay in sight, she was gliding down the long stretch of asphalt that bordered the sand like a whip of dark kelp.

Guarding the beach side of the Boardwalk were umbrella-shaded kiosks where readers of palms and tarot cards would unfold your life for a fee. Palmer would have liked to hear that a prince awaited her—the mysterious stranger who was supposed to be in every girl's future. But even if she'd had the money, she was afraid her grandmother's feelings might be hurt if she paid a stranger to peer into that realm already claimed by her grandmother's Powers. Still, unless somebody promising strode around a corner pretty soon, it would be obvious that this blue light wasn't much interested in romance.

Beach artists offered to sketch their portraits in pastels or charcoal while they waited. But the family just bought ice-cream cones, Maggie skating back in time for a double-decker pistachio before she took off again.

They dodged a self-styled evangelist, also on roller skates, his purple choir robe billowing. As he swept by them, his reedy voice soared into melody: "Out of the ivory palaces, into a world of woe…" Ferociously waltzing to his own hymn, he nearly collided with a group of high school students handing out religious tracts, one young man playing a saxophone. Like Pastor McManus, Palmer recalled. Could something about that instrument be especially Christian, she wondered, maybe sanctified by the church? Then she realized she was staring, and the boy was smiling back at her. Daddy moved them along smartly.

Maybe *she* should consider handing out tracts, but the idea embarrassed her, especially when others passing by avoided eye contact with the young Christians. The boy started to play again and closed his eyes to all of them. Apparently *he* didn't figure romantically in her future.

They passed booths with hawkers selling snow cones and hot dogs, popcorn and cotton candy. It was like a carnival. But Daniel couldn't help looking beyond, into seasons of the future.

"Bet this place is nothing but dismal and damp come December. Boarded up, vendors gone, and the canals smelling worse than today." Damn it to hell and gone, he wished they'd never come.

Maggie skated back to them once more. They headed up one of the streets towards the canals, crossed a curved bridge, and looked over the edge into the water below. Oil oozed into the dark canals, floating in rainbows that twisted like iridescent snakes.

The purple-robed preacher suddenly skated over the bridge, weaving towards them at an alarming speed, and as he veered off, all of them saw he clutched a bottle in a brown paper bag. Unshaven, unkempt. No one believed for a second, least of all himself probably, that he could be a harbinger of wisdom or hope. Daniel wondered if the skinny man would even last through winter.

Palmer leaned against the railing and peered into the stagnant water. There were no signs warning swimmers of contamination or infantile paralysis. But why bother? You'd have to be crazy even to wade, let alone swim. Like the skating evangelist, first glimpses seemed to offer promise that second ones swept away. Was this what was meant by *second sight*? Had they driven all this way for no more than an ice-cream cone?

She caught her grandmother's eye. Where was that stupid blue light now? Palmer tasted something bitter and wished she were back on the beach in Manhattan.

Claudia sighed. "Disintegrated pretty badly, hasn't it."

"Some hangout for your old Hollywood crowd," Daniel said. "Talk about a false-front, movie-set town."

But Grandmother Sydney was staring out at the horizon. Her eyes seemed unfocused, their color aquamarine though Palmer knew perfectly well her grandmother's eyes were hazel. Maybe it was just the reflection of the ocean.

"Californians are careless about sunshine," Sydney said softly. "They let whole days of it slip through their fingers as easily as sand from their beaches. They're careless because like the rich anywhere"—she glanced at Daniel and smiled almost kindly— "they think they can afford to be."

Palmer watched her grandmother closely. It wasn't like her to hold center stage with Daddy around. She looked different, her lips stained as if she'd been eating blueberries, though surely that was Palmer's imagination.

"Californians just expect sunlight," Sydney said. "They let it spill from one day to the next." She raised a hand to shade her eyes from the glare off the canal, then looked northward, as if she could see all the way to Washington state. "When the sun comes out in Seattle, people rush outdoors. Up there, we're careful how we spend a sunlit hour. Californians may be called sun worshippers, but people don't value what they take for granted." Despite the words' edge, her face was soft with reverie. "Weather or jobs or even family."

Daniel and Claudia exchanged a look. Sydney told long-winded stories with little encouragement, but she never made *speeches*, dithering on about the weather or—the suspicion just nibbled—talking about them.

Daniel hoped the old lady hadn't had some kind of stroke. Just as well she'd be leaving in the morning. For him this trip was pretty much a gas-guzzling bust.

Claudia wished her memories had stayed untouched, even though she'd cajoled Daniel into the outing. Palmer wondered how transformation had flopped and died like a hooked fish.

Maggie skated up to the railing and leaned against her grandmother. The little girl finished her ice cream and wiped sticky fingers against her rompers, surprised that no one bothered to scold her.

As the family headed to the car, clouds began to build over the horizon. For just a second or two, they all saw the same optical illusion, as if the fog held steady while the water raced backwards toward the mist, as if the haze would swallow the whole blue ocean.

Perhaps, Grandmother Sydney said briskly, feeling responsible now for their somber moods, they'd just seen a California version of the Northern Lights, dancing out there just for them. A harbinger of hope, she said. But Maggie was the only one who smiled.

The Light Fantastic

PALMER QUICKLY SETTLED INTO BACK-TO-SCHOOL RHYTHMS: a new homeroom with new subjects, JJ's election as ninth-grade treasurer, the weather more like summer than summer, producing warm mornings and brilliant days. Now when the sisters said goodbye to Mother at Metlox, they walked on up the hill to school, and each day Palmer had to come straight home to stay with Maggie. No chance to linger with JJ. And no hope, either, of running into the new boy in her class who'd transferred to Las Olitas that first week.

This year they studied U.S. history, social studies, algebra, English, and ballroom dancing. One day each week, they pushed desks tight against walls, the hardwood floor pooling with afternoon sun, its years of varnish glowing like thickened honey. The dance teacher, Miss Cascales, who ran the Oceanside Dance Studio at the foot of Marine View Drive, would open the classroom door and sidle in, as if not wanting to draw attention to herself. Palmer could never quite square the woman's shy entrance with her flamboyant blue-black hair and false eyelashes.

Miss Cascales wore more makeup than any other woman Palmer knew, including Allie Norquist; she wore it all the time, too, not just on stage for tap and ballroom recitals. Her hair was swept into a chignon so tight her penciled eyebrows perched like taut wings. Scarlet lips slashed a face pale as a vampire's. Behind her back they called her Sunless Cascales.

Each Friday Miss Cascales divided the class into four lines that stretched across the classroom. She had them hold their arms out to make sure they didn't touch their neighbors. On the blackboard she drew squares and arrows and little feet, showing the movements for boys and for girls. "This is home position for the gentlemen," she would say in her breathy voice, "and home position for the ladies."

Donnie Broussard snickered. *Ladies and gentlemen*? Who was she kidding? But he eyed her black costume with interest—the tight leotard, the silky wraparound skirt, her soft ballet slippers.

After the class practiced the box step, Miss Cascales had them pair off. With more girls than boys (Palmer was sorry JJ wasn't in her homeroom this year), one girl often danced with Miss Cascales. Since Palmer could follow the diagrams on the board and even do it in time to the slightly scratchy recording of "In the Mood," she was often chosen.

Palmer wasn't unhappy about being singled out this way, but she would also have liked being paired with Donnie. He showed a modest flair for dancing, and he liked Palmer in a boyfriend-girlfriend sort of way, though he took elaborate pains not to show it because of JJ, sometimes teasing her roughly.

Even more, she hoped to be paired with the new boy, the one Miss Cascales had begun demonstrating steps with, even when there *were* extra girls. But so far that hadn't happened.

Palmer had been dancing with Daddy since she was little. Before she was ten, she knew how to transform the basic box step into the polka, the fox-trot, and even a half-decent waltz. Out on the playground in seventh grade, she invented Polka-Tag. Girls paired off, singing "Bye, Bye, Blackbird" at the top of their lungs, galloping around in the polka step Palmer had taught them. If the couple who were *It* broke step too badly and began running, they were disqualified for one round. The boys watched and hooted, but mostly they were envious because they had no idea how to manage the quick-footed step these girls took to so naturally.

At junior high dances Palmer had often danced with fathers who were chaperoning. They told her she was light on her feet, which she took to be good, though she still didn't think much of her grandmother's theory of levitation.

Maybe she'd inherited her lightness from Mother and Daddy, who'd won a first-place dance trophy back before they married. Palmer had never known them to go dancing, but once in awhile Daddy might catch Mother up around the waist while she was cooking, especially if one of his favorite Frank Sinatra songs was playing on the radio. They'd dance around the kitchen until Mother's cheeks turned bright. Sometimes she'd break it off—"This food is going to burn, Daniel!"—but most of the time the song just came to an end and Daddy dipped Mother backwards before pulling her up and kissing her quickly on the neck.

Dance didn't fix anything, Palmer supposed, just as a matinee didn't really change anybody's life, but both of them made you feel better when you floated back into your regular day. Now that she thought about it, her folks hadn't sashayed around the kitchen for some time.

So boys had a last chance before high school to learn the dance positions, how to move their feet, and where to put their hands, though LeRoy Larson still let his right hand sag below the small of Palmer's back so that it rode the swell of her bottom. It was hard to get mad at him when he kind of sagged everywhere, maybe because he was so tall and bony and generally in a daze. Palmer would just reach around and pull his wrist up, and he'd grin at her, embarrassed, holding her waist until he forgot again.

Like many athletic boys, JJ was a good dancer; he just didn't believe he was. Palmer suspected he was secretly relieved a few weeks ago when, in the middle of Sunday Worship service, he'd experienced a *conviction* that Christ wanted him to give up dancing, as a witness and a testimony to others. He hoped Palmer would be similarly moved, though such decisions, he assured her, were always between a Christian and her Savior.

His self-denial being a spiritual matter, she could hardly criticize him. But if kids wanted to get out of the house on a weekend evening, especially during the school year, there wasn't all that much to do besides school dances. Sometimes they went miniature golfing or bowling, but those both cost too much to do often. JJ confided that his conscience was still struggling over matinees at the La Mar, since Prairie Pres disapproved of movie-going, along with drinking, smoking, playing cards, swimming on Sundays, wearing makeup, and especially dancing—the latter well known to lead to *going all the way*. Now that they had both turned thirteen and movie tickets cost a half-dollar, his religious convictions might kick in with a vengeance. At least school dances were free.

But the truth of it was that Palmer loved to dance. She was used to dancing with Daddy, not to mention with a boyfriend who could manage his feet in time with the music, as well as chaperones who complimented her with a charm noticeably lacking in schoolboys. She had no intention of abandoning something that was so much fun. Grandmother Sydney called ballroom dancing a social grace. And how sinful could it be if a public school taught the box step?

But what Palmer's "*modernist leanings*"—as JJ called them, his efforts not to condemn her both obvious and annoying (*Judgment belongeth to me, saith the Lord*)—might mean between the two of them now, she wasn't sure.

Lately, she'd even been eyeing the makeup counter at the dime store, coveting a fuchsia lipstick that was definitely out of bounds at Prairie Pres. Maybe JJ would want a girlfriend with stricter religious convictions. She waited to feel panicky or sad, but oddly the thought did not trouble her as much as she expected.

At least there were still the occasional Saturday-night parties. And so far JJ hadn't given them up, or even talked about it, which was good because Palmer was looking forward to their first fall party this Saturday at Frida Yarborough's.

The parties had started simply enough in seventh grade: soda pop, snacks, and dancing to records. Parents were out of sight, sometimes even out of the house. Daddy said they fled the premises for good reason.

Last year they had started playing spin the bottle. It didn't take long to hit on the idea of privacy, of course, so that the two who were going to kiss simply stepped into a dark pantry or hall closet while everyone else goofed around, waiting for the next spin.

Frida's house was a rambling stucco behind Live Oak Park. Her folks had gone to the La Mar for the evening, and Frida had already dimmed the living room lights for spin the bottle. Bonnie's spin had landed on LeRoy, who returned glowing from the unlighted sunporch they'd commandeered for the kissing part of the game. LeRoy spun the empty Coke bottle, which pointed back to Bonnie. Kissing the same person was against the rules, so he spun again. It stopped on Palmer, who was holding hands with JJ. LeRoy was no bargain, but the tacit agreement was never to hurt anyone's feelings. She followed him out to the sunporch, where he kissed her three times and was diving in for the fourth when she suggested they give the others a chance. He didn't seem as saggy about kissing, she noticed.

Back in the circle, she gave the bottle a hard spin. JJ was always her first choice and Donnie usually her second. And even if the bottle were by some chance to land on Campbell Reyes, Palmer wouldn't dream of carrying on like Frida, following the new boy out to the sunporch, giggling nonstop and leaning all over him. Even now Frida was slapping playfully at his shoulder.

The bottle swiveled to a stop and pointed at Donnie. He rolled his eyes as if greatly put upon, which no one believed, but it was his way of acknowledging that Palmer was JJ's girlfriend. Out of sight, it was a different matter. Somewhat regretfully she pulled away at last out of a sense of loyalty. Even so, they were gone long enough that JJ looked at her quizzically when they came back to the circle.

Frida suddenly scrambled to her feet and pulled Campbell up beside her. "Dance time," she sang out, turning off yet another lamp on her way to the record player. Palmer looked at JJ, and he shrugged. This was their first party since he had given up dancing, but it was understood that *she* could dance if she wanted to. Right off Donnie asked her, and when, after two songs, she came back to JJ, he was looking slightly wistful about the whole arrangement. They sat on the couch, his arm around her, watching the other couples.

Count Basie's "One O'Clock Jump" split the air, and Palmer's toes beat a secret jitterbug inside her shoes. Sitting out dances wasn't easy. Her eyes slid over to Frida, who was picking out a second stack of records, laughing too loudly, her arm brushing Cam's.

He was a transfer student from Redondo Beach, and when he'd started school, she'd seen his name on his room-assignment slip: Campbell Allende Reyes. She watched him from that first day when he walked into their classroom a few minutes late, his shirt starched and freshly ironed, its cuffs neatly turned halfway up his forearms. At recess he pulled on a leather jacket, the first one to show up at Las Olitas. One of the boys said it was only vinyl, but he didn't say it to Cam, who already had a look about him. Not wild exactly, though Palmer wondered what Daddy might think of this tall, wiry boy. Not that her father was all that fond of JJ.

Frida and Cam began to dance. Palmer tried not to stare, though all the other kids were watching, too. Frida couldn't quite keep up with him, but somehow he still made her look good, twirling her out, then snapping her back into his arms. Palmer didn't take her eyes off him, and she didn't care if JJ noticed. Though maybe later she'd find out that *watching* was another sin in that growing list of his.

At the end of the record, Frida reluctantly left Cam's side to set out more snacks, her blouse damp and sticking to her back. A slow song, "The Nearness of You," started. LeRoy asked Bonnie to dance, and JJ got up to go to the bathroom.

When Cam turned toward Palmer, his hand was already outstretched toward hers. He knew she'd been watching.

Palmer was her mother's daughter. She stood and walked into the circle of Cam's arms with every nerve alert to his first move. Most of the boys were shy and kept inches away, but Cam lightly pulled her to him with an air that said this was how it was done; he led with his torso as well as his arms, the way grown-ups danced.

His dark hair swooped into a perfect ducktail, the edges meticulous and gleaming, and his hair cream smelled like pecans. When the next record slid down the automatic changer, it seemed natural to keep dancing. She found out he had three sisters, and the oldest, Virgie, had taught him to dance when he was only seven. Palmer did the math in her head: he was a year older than most of them.

He swung her out and twirled her twice under his arm. Briefly, she thought of Mother and Daddy in the kitchen. Cam didn't try to dance cheek to cheek, but every so often he looked at her with those Hershey Bar eyes. Then suddenly he made up a few of his own steps to "Mairzy Doats," their third dance, and she collided against him. They were laughing when JJ, seated again on the couch—though Palmer hadn't noticed when he'd come back from the bathroom—cleared his throat loudly. Frida sulked beside him.

By silent agreement, Palmer and Cam stopped dancing and walked toward the brooding couple. He still held her hand, casually. Kids were watching. JJ looked pointedly at their hands, stood up, and stalked out of the living room.

"Thank you," Cam said formally, just the way Miss Cascales instructed all the boys, but most of them did it only in dance class. Palmer wanted to believe his eyes lingered on hers, but it was really too dark to be sure. He held out a hand to Frida.

Their hostess brightened and bounced off the couch.

When the party was over, JJ was nowhere around. It was obvious he'd left Palmer on her own.

"Your father picking you up?" Cam asked. She shook her head. Most of the kids walked everywhere. He jammed his hands into his jeans pockets. "Want me to see you home?"

She hesitated. "Are you headed down by The Strand anyway?" He nodded. "Okay," she said. "Thanks." Manhattan Beach had little crime, but it *was* after ten and the streets were dark. Palmer thought of their walking together up to her door. She was glad Mother had been sober for a while now.

The night air was cool and salty after the indoor stuffiness of dancing and laughing and making out. She pulled on her cardigan, and Cam shrugged into his jacket. They walked a full block in silence before he broke off a hibiscus blossom, flicked the yellow stamen a couple of times to make the pollen fly, handed the flower casually over to her. "Didn't mean to start anything with your boyfriend."

"It's okay." Not that it was, but how to put her finger on the problem exactly?

"He doesn't know how to dance?"

She shook her head. "He thinks it's wrong." *Sinful* sounded too dramatic, even insulting, to say to someone who'd been dancing since he was little. "His religion," she added and wondered how long the flower would last if she floated it in one of their Metlox bowls.

"Not yours?"

"We go to the same church—"

"But you keep on dancing." He half smiled. "Maybe you're rebellious?"

She knew he was teasing, but for a moment rebellious seemed a fine way to be.

"A *quiet* rebel?" he asked when she didn't answer.

"I don't know. The church does have a lot of rules …"

He nodded as if he knew something about that, and they walked on. As the soft and quiet night stretched between them, she felt responsibility settle like a cloak over her shoulders, as if she should keep the conversation going, get to know him better. After all, he was new at school, and he was being polite to walk her home. Mother said boys liked to be asked about their interests. She knew she didn't want to talk about church anymore, even to ask about his, if he had one.

"You like sports?" she asked. Of course he liked sports; what a dumb question.

But he answered quickly, "Baseball and track. The high jump especially."

The high jump was JJ's event, too, but Cam was taller. Almost

Daddy's height already. She was used to being eye to eye with most of the boys she knew.

"I like to draw," he offered suddenly. "Art's my favorite subject." He grinned and took the hibiscus back, held it toward the shadows. "I'd do this in charcoal, maybe a silhouette. People expect flowers to be in color, but sometimes a surprise can make us see better." When Palmer didn't answer, he added ruefully, "Art's usually my best grade, too."

She laughed. "I'll bet Miss Cascales gives you an A."

He seemed neither modest nor proud, but he did change the subject, asking her about Donnie and LeRoy, some of the other boys, as well. She wanted to know what he thought of Frida but couldn't figure out how to ask the question without showing too much interest.

He was curious about Howie Stoute, a boy from their class who had not been at the party. "He doesn't usually get invited," she said, as if that explained something. They headed downhill from the City Hall. At Manhattan Avenue, she gestured toward the alley. "We turn here."

Approaching her house with Cam, she saw its shabbiness afresh, imagining it through his eyes. She never apologized for the best her parents could do, and no one ever said anything, at least not to her face. JJ and Bonnie were the only ones who came over, anyway. Mother's condition was always unpredictable, though that was better now that she was working. But kids who gave parties had nice, regular houses.

Campbell was quiet for a moment, considering the shabby cottage lighted by its single-bulb porch light. "We had trouble finding a place to live after the war, too."

She liked that he didn't pretend about the house. "Where do you live now?"

He gestured vaguely with his head. "Oh, east of Sepulveda."

The other side of town. He'd walked the opposite direction toward the beach just to bring her home and probably added a couple of miles to his own trek. They called the east side of the highway "the backcountry," and people considered it the other side of the tracks. Maybe his family was poor, too. Though he dressed better than most of the boys. Vinyl or not, that jacket didn't come from County Relief.

"You told me The Strand was on your way home."

"Well, I decided it was."

Just then the porch light flickered as Daddy banged out of the kitchen door to empty the trash.

"Whoa! You kids gave me a start." He took his time shaking out the container over the garbage can, giving this boy who obviously wasn't JJ the once-over. He clamped the lid back on, and Palmer introduced them. "Campbell," said her father. "That's a distinguished-sounding first name."

"My mother's family is Scotch."

Daddy smiled. "Ever think they might be shirttail relations to the canned-soup Campbells?"

Cam seemed at a loss for words, but Palmer could tell her father already half liked this boy.

"Maybe we're in the same business, son, in a shirttail sort of way."

"Daddy sells to grocery stores," Palmer explained. Cam just nodded.

"Guess you don't favor your mom's side." Daddy settled the lid more firmly to keep out night-wandering animals.

"No, sir, I take after my dad." The same matter-of-fact tone he used to talk about dancing and drawing.

"Hm-hm. Reyes," Daddy said. "Means *king*—"

Just then a shadow detached itself from the dark side of the house, startling them all.

"Jesus, JJ!" Daddy didn't even apologize for his language. "What the hell are you doing, lurking back there?" He glanced at Palmer and must have seen something on her face. "Well," he said. "Anyway. Looks like the gang's all here." He started toward the door. "Nice meeting you, Campbell. Don't stay out here too long, princess." He ignored JJ, who was studying the ground, and let the screen door slam behind him.

No one spoke. With the porch light shining on Cam's face,

Palmer could see the shadow of a fledgling mustache on his upper lip, a small blemish starting on his temple. At a distance his skin had looked smooth as taffy. She also saw he was at least three inches taller than JJ.

Cam moved first. "Well," he said, "I'll see you."

"Thanks again." She tried to smile.

Cam nodded to them both, then walked up the alley, one fist jamming the blossom into his pocket, leaving her to mend or settle or do something with her boyfriend.

Surely, Palmer thought, watching Cam disappear, she was relieved JJ had shown up. So why did she feel like she'd swallowed her opal earring, the lump small and hard somewhere below her collarbone?

"I went back to Frida's," JJ said, "but you'd already left."

She sat down on the porch step. He lowered himself beside her. When he didn't say anything further, Palmer began, "He was just showing me how he dances with his sister."

"Sure," JJ said.

"We've always danced with other kids. Only now it's just me."

JJ hesitated. "You don't usually look like it's that much fun."

Palmer tried to keep her face neutral. Fun? It had—*oh, God*—been fantastic, and now she'd used the Lord's name in vain and what was the matter with her, anyway? She suddenly felt guilty and confused, so she leaned over and kissed JJ on the cheek, a gesture too sisterly. And they both knew it.

She could sense JJ struggling. Was he as mixed up as she was, or did he know deep down how he felt? Maybe the Lord was revealing it to him at that very moment. He always seemed surer than Palmer about everything.

He leaned over and kissed her quickly on the mouth. It wasn't romantic exactly, but it was better than cheek-kissing. It was a make-up kiss with a promise of better to come, another time, another night. An insurance kiss. And for now that seemed enough.

Later, as Palmer lay in her bunk with Maggie softly asleep

beneath her, JJ's word traveled the tired valleys of her mind. *Fun* still seemed incredibly understated. She felt herself afloat in Cam's arms, the other kids falling away in her imagination to give them room. It had been Gene Kelly, Tyrone Power, Fred Astaire—all rolled into one beautiful, lithe boy. And she became Ginger, trailing feathers, an angel in high heels that flashed silver while movie cameras rolled on into her dream-filled night.

Fleeting Shadows, Startled Birds

The buildings of Las Olitas Junior High School connected in a stucco square like a giant hacienda. At its courtyard—a hard-packed dirt playground—the children were shielded from traffic and Santa Ana winds. With its red tile roofs, Spanish arches, and porticos, the school looked like a peaceful California mission once the students were quietly shuttered inside their classrooms. Along the Center Street border, clumps of white oleander grew, stately and poisonous. Benign and more flamboyant, bougainvillea climbed the creamy school walls like dark flame. Only the track and the football field across Pacific Avenue to the west were ringed with practical wire fencing.

That morning, when Mrs. Cline let them out for first recess, Palmer and the other ninth-graders spilled noisily into the slanted sunlight. The seventh- and eighth-graders had already been out and gone back inside. In those first aimless moments before they figured out what to do with their freedom, a few boys started in teasing Campbell about his name, calling him "Pork and Beans" and making farting noises with their armpits. The girls looked disgusted. Only a week and a half into the school year, they knew the boys were still a little wary of this newcomer. Cam just laughed—maybe he'd heard it all before—but his eyes darkened as if he'd stepped into the shade.

Palmer lingered nearby, glad for some reason that JJ's class hadn't let out yet. She and Bonnie drew idly with sticks in the dust, keeping an eye on the boys. When Cam wouldn't rise to the bait, the boys shrugged. Donnie and LeRoy began to organize a game of kickball. And in that quicksilver way of boys, the players on each side now wanted Cam to play for them.

Howard Stoute had been standing alone by the tetherball post. Suddenly, the heavy-set boy catapulted toward them and elbowed his way through the pack. "Hey, Chicken Noodle," he sneered, trying to enlist the boys who'd been ragging Cam, not realizing he was already late and they'd moved on to their game. "Chicken-Chicken Noodle!" He sang it like a nursery rhyme. "Haircut like a poodle!" Howie strutted in a circle with his hands in his armpits, flapping his elbows in imitation of a barnyard fowl.

What was it with boys and their underarms? Palmer wondered. Cam just studied the ground, but she sensed a kind of electricity from him, as if his body were humming like the music teacher's tuning fork. He slowly took his hands out of his pockets. A few boys drifted over to catch what was going on.

Howie had a growing audience, but he still wasn't getting a rise out of his victim. Deliberately he lowered his gaze to stare bug-eyed at Cam's fly. "I'll bet even your noodle's a chicken," he guffawed, "a skinny, little, scrawny—" Cam's forearm caught him across the throat, and the crowd of boys erupted. Howie was no one's favorite, mean to anyone handy except JJ, who'd already had it out with him last year. Now this new guy was taking him on. It was almost too much to hope for on a day that had started with little promise other than that of the endless sun.

Howie's face flamed, and with a gurgle he windmilled into Cam, his bulk formidable against the taller boy. One fist slammed against Cam's forehead; the other caught him in the chest, knocking him backward.

Somebody yelled, "Fight! Fight!" and boys and girls came running, leaving monkey bars empty, abandoning their games of dodgeball. "Howie's fighting!"

Blood trickled from Cam's eyebrow. He swiped the back of his hand across his eye, and Howie caught him in a bear hug. They tumbled onto the dirt, arms and legs churning the dust. Clutching furiously at each other's shirt, they struggled to their feet.

"Sonofabitch," Cam grunted and aimed a punch at Howie's head, catching him full on the ear. The boys cheered, partly for Cam, since they'd all been taken down by Howie or feared they would be. But mostly they cheered for the fight itself—the swearing and sweating—the thrilling sight of some *other* boy's blood. They wanted this brief glory to last as long as possible.

Cam landed another blow just off-center on Howie's nose, and the kids exploded at the red trickle that Howie smeared across his upper lip. *Watching* a fight was the absolute best, especially for the boys, like seeing George Raft or John Wayne kick the stuffing out of some bully. Retribution and Justice. The stuff of Westerns—and all the better when it was some other boy's fight, with no need to explain to Dad, or worse, to Mom.

This time Palmer was right in among the crowd as Howie lunged at Cam and the two rolled again through the dirt. She was scared that Cam would get hurt, but excited, too, in some strange way that prickled down through her fingertips.

Too soon for most of them, the principal elbowed his way through the pack of kids. "Break it up right now!" Mr. Eberhard yelled. "I mean it! Get off him, Reyes." The principal hauled both boys to their feet. "Now, who started this?" Always the same question. Cam spat dust and glared at Howie, who wiped his bloody nose, stunned that the blood on his hands was his own.

"All right," said Mr. Eberhard, "that's the way it is then. Ten laps around the playground, Stoute. And Reyes"—he jerked his head in the direction of the street—"you take ten laps around the football field. That'll keep you two separated *and* busy." The boys in the crowd exchanged glances.

"But the football field is bigger—," Donnie blurted out.

"You want to join 'em, Broussard?" Donnie studied his shoes, and the principal turned back to the brawlers. "Take off. We'll put some of that energy to better use. As for the rest of you, this recess is over—right now."

Later, during Art, everyone looked up when Cam walked in, face flushed, shirt tucked in, ducktail damp and freshly combed, his eyebrow sporting a Band-Aid. He picked up a sheet of art paper and a stick of charcoal, and carried them to his desk. The kids whispered, checking his time per lap, giving him extra minutes to get across Pacific to the track and then back again and to make stops in the lavatory and at the nurse's office for that Band-Aid. Cam's eyes met Palmer's just before he bent over and started drawing.

Mrs. Cline gave the class one of her looks, and they settled down to work but mostly to wait for Howie, timing him in turn on the big wall clock. Rarely had they been so quiet. Twelve and a half minutes later, he banged through the door, dripping with sweat, his hair stuck crazily to his forehead, his nose swollen and red. Palmer and Donnie exchanged a glance. Some of the boys snickered. Cam didn't look up.

Later that afternoon, while the kids worked arithmetic problems, Mrs. Cline took down the previous week's artwork and taped up the day's pictures. Palmer's pastel of a woman in flight off a diving board, birdlike above turquoise water, drew approving looks, but Cam's charcoal drawing of a towering eucalyptus caused the biggest stir. Trees were hard to draw, and his shaggy giant seemed to shake the wind itself.

Kids wrote their names in the lower right-hand corner of their artwork, but Cam with dark charcoal signed only his initials: *C.A.R.* Not surprisingly, he earned his nickname that day, the boys dubbing him "The Car," after that coveted emblem of speed, power, and freedom, of that day far into the future of being sixteen and grown up.

Palmer daydreamed about Cam when she was walking to and from school, washing the dinner dishes, doing her homework. She imagined his father as a vanquished *ranchero* whose land had been confiscated by unscrupulous government agents, forcing him to forfeit foam-green alfalfa fields, brown-velvet hills. She saw the family's adobe hacienda, its patio swept smooth. She built them a fountain of mosaic tiles, planted hibiscus beside a giant saguaro, imagined hummingbirds iridescent as opals drawn to the water and the lipstick-red flowers. Her fantasy bloomed wild as poppies.

One day at school while she was mentally furnishing their cool, dark interior with Navajo rugs and Mexican paintings, she overheard a boy say Cam had been born in Wyoming. The family had moved to California after the War so his dad could work for Lockheed. Glad to have some facts about his life, her nimble imagination quickly seated a windburned Cam on a buckskin horse that rode high Wyoming trails. She knotted a bandana dark as hibiscus around his neck, tipped his cowboy hat low over shadowed eyes, and wrapped his lean legs in fringed chaps. She memorized the lyrics to "Cielito Lindo."

But daydreams were a small part of living, as unreal as movies, whereas real life swirled like currents inside a breakwater—unpredictable and unforeseen. Take Bonnie's folks. They were talking about selling their big house next summer and moving to Santa Maria. Palmer couldn't imagine being without her best friend. The girls made a pact not to think about it for now.

On the other hand, Lars Norquist had moved to a police department up north in Vallejo, and never having to run into him again would be a big relief. Mother told Grandmother Sydney that he'd gotten off too easy, plain and simple, but she stopped talking when Palmer walked into the living room. The word *secretary* hung in the sudden silence.

When Daddy found out the Staffords might move, he tried to reassure Palmer that she'd find a new buddy. She wondered if he felt the same about his own friend's move. Losing people in this way made her think of a song's coming to an end on the radio, how the music grew thinner and thinner until it finally disappeared into the air.

The last days of September hung warm and golden, still promising everlasting summer, but soon the subtle alchemy of fall would transform sunlight into shades of silver-gold. On the last Friday of September, Las Olitas held Field Day, its annual homage to the sun, and next to Christmas, it was everyone's favorite school celebration.

Girls were allowed to wear rolled-up jeans or pedal pushers, and anyone who wanted could come to school barefoot. A few eighth-grade boys unbuttoned their shirts to bare young chests tanned like those of the surfboarders at the beach but less muscled. Mr. Eberhard, policing the playfields, put a stop to that, telling them it was as bad as if the girls wore shorts. The boys' eyes gleamed at that vision.

After taking attendance and giving special instructions for the day, teachers hauled equipment out to the playground and organized gunnysack races, egg tosses, three-legged races, work-up baseball, and half-court basketball. Under the burnished sun, noses turned red, and kids formed steady lines at the porcelain drinking fountains—long troughs that caught the overflow from bubbling spigots. The cafeteria ladies had the day off, so everyone brought sack lunches, and at noontime, room mothers handed out half-pint bottles of milk, along with homemade cookies wrapped in wax paper.

In the early afternoon the girls' races were held, and Palmer was disappointed to come in third. Last year she'd won first place. But lately her body with its slowly emerging shape seemed less swift—she'd noticed it roller-skating, too. More filly than colt, her grandmother had said.

At two o'clock, sweaty and excited, everyone poured across Pacific for the boys' exhibition track meet. Washtubs with melting ice chilled bottles of Dr. Pepper and orange and grape Nehi.

The exhibition allowed the track coach to look over the field of talent for the upcoming spring season, so the competition was serious. Kids and teachers swarmed onto the wooden bleachers, grateful to sit down and press icy drinks against foreheads. Palmer and Bonnie crowded together four rows up in the center, the benches burning through the seats of their pedal pushers, their bare feet hot and sore.

When the two dozen or so boys came trotting onto the field wearing their blue and gold shorts and jerseys, the stands roared a welcome. Mostly ninth-graders, these were the best athletes in the school, with JJ among them, already captain of the football team. He played second base on the varsity softball team and held the school record in the high jump.

Palmer loved the pace of track, the suspense and tension between events and between boys, the bursts of drama. She loved running herself, dreamed of doing it sometimes with her feet barely touching ground, as if she were flying into the salty wind.

She wished girls ran track, but except for these special days, they played only intramural sports like girls' basketball, the half-court play frustrating for those who wanted to race the full length. Last year the girls had gathered signatures on a petition to play touch football and presented it to Mr. Eberhard, but he'd turned them down. Playing football might cause problems for them later when they wanted to have babies. Palmer didn't see how, though she knew a blow to the breast could lead to cancer, a warning most mothers, including her own, dutifully delivered. Daddy had been going to teach her tennis, but that would probably never happen now that he'd stopped playing. *She* certainly wasn't going to bring it up.

Daddy followed track in the newspapers, favoring UCLA. He liked to say the high-jump bar represented real intimidation. How even brushing it lightly could cause it to fall. College jumpers, he said, were known to clear bars in their dreams. But on the field in the open air, the bar was unpredictable, with a will of its own. Sometimes it might get hit and not fall, or it could jump up a full foot and fall miraculously back into place. Palmer thought JJ would see the hand of God in a hopping bar—a celestial moment above the sawdust.

By three thirty she was nearly hoarse from cheering the four-man relay, the broad jump, and the mile. JJ had taken second in the fifty-yard dash, letting his eyes dart toward her as he paced afterwards, hands on hips, catching his breath.

The sun dazzled them all, and they squinted against the glare. At last they came to the final event—the high jump—and everyone buzzed about whether JJ would make it to the highest mark by throwing himself headfirst over the bar, a move more reckless than the usual scissors jump. He'd done it before to win in track meets with other schools. Incredibly brave, this business they called *the dive*. He would never do it unless it was the only way to place first. She felt afraid for him, but excited, too, like she'd felt that day on the playfield a few weeks back when Cam had fought Howie.

The competition was finally down to three boys: a sturdy eighth-grader named Stanley Chance (who'd taken the hundred-yard dash), JJ, and Cam. She remembered Cam's telling her it was his event, and now she could see what an advantage his height and long legs gave him. He was matching the other two jump for jump with each raise of the bar.

But JJ's muscled speed could make him the winner. At each new level, he chose the long-running approach, the first six strides straight ahead, then curving slightly to the side, his body lowered in a gathering motion as he thrust his arms harder, his speed transforming to power at the height of his jump. It was beautiful—the leap so close to the flying of dreams.

Each boy took his time getting ready with elaborate stretching and shaking out of tension in arms and legs; it seemed to go on forever. But as soon as a jumper cleared the bar, he scurried from the pit, sawdust curls clinging to his uniform. Once he was safely out, even if the bar fell, the jump would still count. Palmer knew the jumpers played invisible games against each other, that focus counted for everything and even a sound or movement could cause a loss of concentration.

She bit at the inside of her cheek. Bonnie nibbled a hangnail. Suddenly Frida Yarborough's scream cut through the crowd: "CAR! CAR!" And even though a few others joined in, Frida's yell sounded proprietary, her hair bouncing in rhythm to her chant, her arms waving overhead. When Frida's enthusiasm nearly toppled her off the bleacher, Palmer smiled. There was a time to cheer and a time to shut up.

The event moved slowly, as always. Finally, Stanley knocked the bar down at five feet, a height JJ and Cam had already cleared. That gave him third place, and they all applauded him wildly, yelling and whistling. The bar was raised another two inches.

She was surprised to hear LeRoy and Donnie rooting for Cam. Maybe JJ's intensity and his often-voiced belief that God helped him win events had put them off. In his heart JJ was a good sport. He got mad only at himself, but when he was stomping around, muttering under his breath, it was hard to tell.

At each jump, JJ approached the bar from the more common right side, Cam from the left. Palmer analyzed every detail. When the event had started, JJ bypassed the starting height, hoping to intimidate the others with his confidence. Cam used it as a warm-up.

JJ had the speed, Cam the height. If JJ dived, would he tuck and roll without getting hurt? And what about Cam—did he even know how to dive? Not many had practiced that total commitment to air, hurling the body into a future with no guarantees. JJ was the only one at Las Olitas who'd done it successfully. And a failed dive could look so absurd, the chest or knees banging hard and clumsy against the bar.

Bonnie's hands were pressed tightly together. Palmer wondered if JJ considered the high jump a leap of faith. As he readied himself to go first, his lips were moving, whether in prayer or pep talk, she didn't know.

She tipped her head back to drain her Dr. Pepper, relishing its sweet burn. Did she even know which one she wanted to win? Did an event like this really matter, compared, say, to losing a job or taking one drink too many? She thought how the high jump was the opposite of treading water: the plunge over the bar like Technicolor compared to the black-and-white of just keeping your chin above water, though no swimmer would deny the need for the latter. In some way she couldn't explain, she felt the high jump was symbolic, though it must certainly feel real to the jumpers. All she knew for sure was that she admired these brave boys.

JJ began his long approach from the right, the almost-silent running steps, the turn, the gathering power in his bunching muscles. Then at the last possible moment, he did it, launching himself headfirst into the air. Rising like a bird, he curved over the bar, his arms stretched straight in front of his body like Superman soaring above skyscrapers. He landed with a tumbler's somersault through the wood shavings. The bar trembled but held as he scrambled out of the pit.

The stands erupted, and Palmer jumped to her feet along with them. He had tied his own record. Surely no one could touch him now.

As the cheering finally quieted, it was Cam's turn. Almost casually, he shook each limb, each ankle, the joints loose and easy, but he blew out breath like a spooked horse. Digging in his toes as if he wore the cleated shoes of high school or college, he settled into himself, eyes dark behind lowered lids. He gulped air until Palmer imagined that his lungs must be inflated like blimps. If this wasn't invoking levitation, she didn't know what was.

Would he dive? It seemed an impossible height for the scissors.

Cam grew still. He bent at the waist, facing the bar not so much like an opponent as what—a conspirator? What was it about his body that suggested an attitude less pugnacious than JJ's? An intuitive feel for flight? Some sense of exchanging air the way a tree breathes? Palmer thought of those little arrows in her science book showing osmosis, or was it aspiration? A whole orchard of pecan trees sprouted in her mind, and she wondered where such fancies came from.

She couldn't tell who began the chant. It wasn't Frida, though she could hear her squeal above the grunts from the boys: "CAR! CAR! CAR!" The sound itself was like an engine set loose into the still sky. She didn't know if it helped or bothered Cam. She half wished he would look up at her, but how could she encourage her boyfriend's opponent? JJ sat on the players' bench, gripping a towel. She saw him glance at the coach. The chant became a steady bark, the kids hoping for a dive, a miracle, a Field Day finale like Fourth of July fireworks when the last is always filled with yet more wonder and glory.

Cam dug in. The crowd settled down. He gasped one last time, as if it might really be his final breath. Then he hurled his body forward from the left, his approach numbering fewer steps than JJ's but his stride longer. Palmer held her own breath along with everyone else on that playing field under the blue tent of sky, beneath that full, full sun.

In one mesmerizing movement that no one could fully describe afterwards, Cam launched himself high into the air, rolled his trunk as if he were attached to invisible guide wires, and rocketed headfirst and *backward* over that bar, the sky flashing down into his wide, black eyes as his back arched and his hips rose, an upside-down leap that no one had ever seen before, that no one could even name. And though nobody saw him touch the bar, it, too, did the miraculous, hopping a good four inches into the air, only to land back in place, all as Cam hit the sawdust on his shoulders, rolled quickly, and started for the side of the pit.

But not quite in time. Some said the bar trembled before it fell. Others claimed it was the wind, though there was little that day. Later JJ would confide it might have been the very hand of God. But everyone agreed the bar had been in place the moment before it fell, as if in slow motion, nearly striking the one foot Cam had not yet pulled from the pit. The crowd was too stunned even to groan, their sighs like the softness of air.

Cam brushed the shavings from his shoulders and started back toward the players' bench, his hand already outstretched toward JJ. Then the bleachers erupted. Kids screamed and stomped and took up the *CAR* chant once again. The boys on the bench swarmed over the two contenders. Frida was already on her feet, and Palmer clapped until her palms were on fire.

Cam nodded at JJ. First place was first place, no two ways about it, but the crowd was cheering Cam. Who had ever heard of a backward dive in the high jump? Cam waved in acknowledgment, then quickly grabbed JJ's wrist to raise both their arms toward the crowd like boxers in the ring.

The cheering and yells and hoots carried across Pacific Avenue, over the playground, and halfway down Center Street, eventually to disappear at last into the cloudless September sky.

The next day was Saturday, with the temperature cooler by several degrees, and JJ didn't show up at the beach. Donnie and LeRoy couldn't stop talking about Field Day, but Cam seemed restless. Finally he got up and waded into the surf, diving under waves, then swimming long and hard. Palmer kept watch, her eyes half closed against the blaze off the water. He stayed in for nearly forty-five minutes, bodysurfing towards the end. Finally he whipped his hair out of his eyes one last time and walked back up to the dry sand before dropping onto his towel. With a shiver, he seemed to fall into an exhausted sleep.

The other kids began to drift on home. Bonnie waved a silent goodbye to Palmer. Maggie played close to the water's edge, building a drip castle and dredging a moat to protect it from the incoming tide. Finally she gave up, rinsed herself in the shallows, and stomped back to her towel. She whined about losing the castle, not wanting to hear the obvious, that she should have built it further from the water.

"You have to have *drippy* mud," she argued to no one in particular, "and it *has* to be close by the water, or the dribbles won't look like a castle."

Cam lifted his head and grinned at her. Maggie smiled back, almost coquettishly, and dropped her head on her towel. He rolled over and sat up, stretching as if warming up for some new event. "His skin," thought Palmer, "is tan year-round." It was a shade she could only dream about between sunburns and peeling and more recently her nightly applications of medicated Noxzema. If only she could melt her freckles into one smooth color, the way Mother spread caramel frosting over applesauce cake, the knife dipping into hot water.

Cam's glance grazed Palmer. "Maybe I'll walk on out to the Roundhouse," he said, so lightly she had to steel herself not to look around, as if in she were in some comic take in a movie, to see who else he might be talking to. He brushed invisible sand from his navy-blue trunks. Undertows tugged at her legs. She hoped her silence and dry mouth could be mistaken for poise.

"You coming?" He held out a hand to pull her up from the towel, the gesture so like that first time he'd asked her to dance. Suddenly she seemed to have swallowed a flock of tiny gulls. She nodded.

The late-afternoon glare on the silvery horizon was fierce as a searchlight, the sunset yet to come. He scooped up both their towels, stepped away from Maggie to shake out the sand.

"We can roll these up and put them on my bike," he said. "Then you won't have to walk back down here afterwards." He looked at Maggie. "Hey, Schnickle-Fritz. Okay if she just gives you a yell when it's time to head home?"

Maggie nodded sleepily. She liked Cam, the way he called her funny nicknames. "But leave me her towel," she said. Cam gave it a final snap, then spread it ceremoniously over the little girl from her toes to her head. She grinned up at him from under the terry-cloth tent.

Cam and Palmer walked across the cooling sand, up the concrete steps, Palmer breathless enough to briefly consider asthma. He dumped his towel in the wire basket on the back of his bike. Her peach-colored suit shimmered in the slanted rays as she slipped into her sleeveless blouse.

Palmer thought back to that stormy day when she and Bonnie had walked the length of the Pier, twitterpated over *The Pirate*. It seemed a hundred years ago. How many times in her life had she walked out to the Roundhouse? All those days when Daddy went fishing and would take her along. A million or more times with Bonnie, and the night of the Youth for Christ rally with JJ, when she had been saved.

And beside her now, this boy more darkly handsome than Gene Kelly.

Cam narrowed his eyes against the sun. He shortened his stride to match hers, and she thought about JJ's ring at home on its chain, the going-steady ring that she never wore to the beach—a place more dangerous for jewelry than even a kitchen drain.

How could she be any kind of Christian girl and like two boys at once? And yet Grandmother Sydney said that in her day nobody ever went steady, didn't even want to. A girl's popularity was determined by how many suitors she had. Only an engagement put a stop to dating. But that was back when people had used words like *beau* and *courting*, not modern times.

Cam pointed across the water to a pelican dive-bombing for a fish. The Pier was clearing out for suppertime, only a few of the old guard stubbornly fishing on. Two little boys toyed with a dead sand shark someone had left behind. Eventually a fisherman would throw it over the railing to the gulls.

Again she thought she should start a conversation, though Cam seemed content to walk in silence. "At the track meet," she said finally, "you were really good."

"Thanks." He didn't seem any more eager to discuss it with her than with the boys down on the beach. Was he just modest? Was he disappointed not to have come in first?

She moved toward the rail and leaned against it. A floating patch of kelp prickled the nickel-blue water, its trailing forest underneath, amber and succulent. Kids were careful to stay away when kelp washed in closer, partly because it felt like swimming through snakes, but mostly because it could be a treacherous net. One more danger that entangled. A plant as complicated as life, as her family. Another hazard that was easy to see from a distance, but hard to spot when you were already in the swim.

He looked warily over the edge, his shoulder close to hers.

"Would you ever jump off?" she asked.

He swallowed. "The signs say *no jumping*."

She waved her hand dismissively. "Mostly high school guys do it. Nobody our age except LeRoy, but he's half crazy, anyhow. I think he wants to be a surfer. Then it's like an initiation. Mostly kids just talk. The guards get really mad."

Cam dragged his eyes from the water. She was pleased to see he was feeling what they called *the pull*, that odd compulsion to jump that came over people, especially at night when the black water beckoned softly, the Pier's lights floating like stars on the dark swells.

"How about you?" he finally asked.

"I've never known a girl to do it. But I'll show you something." Palmer glanced toward the lifeguard tower, then slipped under the pitted steel railing. Cam looked alarmed. "It's a way to get closer, to pretend to jump. I call it *yearning*."

He frowned. "Learning?"

She laughed. "It's the urge to jump. Everybody feels it. Look, you just stand outside the rail, holding on behind. Brace your feet, and then lean out over the water." Palmer demonstrated, never fearing her hands might slip and drop her face-forward into the spray-filled air, belly-flopping painfully onto the water's surface that grew harder in proportion to the height of a fall. Daddy said planes falling into the ocean might as well smash into concrete.

"Then you imagine letting go," she explained. "It's wanting to jump but being too scared." She grinned. "Just don't let a guard see you. Or my dad."

Cam wiped his sweaty hands on his trunks. Gingerly he ducked under the railing to join her, looking both ways as if for a speeding train.

"That's right," she coached. "Your arms are so long you can lean out really far. It's the next best thing to an actual jump, probably nothing for you."

"How do you mean?" Cam said stiffly through his teeth.

"Well, I guess anybody who could throw himself headfirst and backwards over a high-jump bar could go off the Pier!" He was sweating. "If he wanted to," she added, suddenly remembering he hadn't grown up at the beach.

"I guess," he muttered.

"Well, anyway," she said. They ducked back inside the railing. "That's about it."

Cam looked relieved to be away from the Pier's edge and the swell of waves below.

"There might be a difference," he said evenly, "between high-jumping and walking off a damned pier."

He was scared, and she should have seen it. Wanting to cover her blunder and make him feel better, Palmer started talking, grabbing at the first thing that popped into her mind. "My father says the beach is growing wider. That the dredging is changing currents, so new sand is washing up." She ran her fingers through her hair to smooth the wind's tangles. "He says someday the Pier will be high and dry. Anybody tries to jump then, he'll break a leg!"

Cam didn't smile. "Oh, stupid, stupid," she thought. Why couldn't she keep her mouth shut? "The fishing has already changed," she rattled on, desperate now, "but it might be contamination from the Hyperion." She saw his puzzled look. "You know, the sewage plant." Oh, yuck, why even mention *sewage*? She rushed ahead, not knowing where she was going. "Did you know someone made up the word *smog,* for smoke and fog mixed together?"

He reached for her then. In that split second of gratitude that he was stopping her endless babble, Palmer also sensed he wanted her to think his kiss was impulsive. But that was really why they'd walked on the Pier, and she'd held the moment at bay without quite meaning to—all that nonsense about jumping off the Pier. Or maybe she'd just been too scared, not wanting it but wanting it, too.

Then the jumble of thought ceased altogether as she sank into this new sea and slid her arms around his neck as the breeze or something like it took her breath, and who cared if fishermen watched or little boys giggled?

Cam's mouth held a spell she'd never known in Saturday night kisses or Spin the Bottle. She wished the sun would set, the wind fall silent, the world tip off the very edge of the sea. She wished this magic could be endless as pin-prick stars.

His hand moved slowly up the bare skin of her back inside her billowing blouse, along the tender-sturdy ridge of her spine. She felt the pads of callus on his palm. He eased his fingers underneath the knot at the back of her bathing suit halter, and there he stopped—a warmth pressing just below the wings of her shoulder blades, not trying to do more, just taking that one liberty.

But it was enough to propel her like a diver shooting to the surface for air. She blinked her eyes open and in that half second caught a softness on his face before he opened his own eyes and dropped his cool look into place like a changeling. Without speaking, they turned and walked back. He held her hand. He was not sweating now.

Cam left her at The Strand, swinging onto his bike. Before she called down to Maggie, she watched him ride off. He looked back over his shoulder, and she waved. He hesitated a fraction of a second, then waved back, and Palmer had the odd impression his wave was less familiar to him than the kiss. Like an updraft sweeping a thought before it, her hunch that Cam was experienced with such kisses was not, she realized, particularly disturbing.

At school the hubbub over Cam's unorthodox jump buzzed on for most of the week. By Thursday it was embedded in school lore, especially after LeRoy dubbed it "The Car's Caroom." By Friday kids had begun to move on to other interests, the boys to football and the girls to trading cards, always watching for favorites like Lawrence's *Pinkie* and Gainsborough's *Blue Boy,* or any picture of any horse.

On Saturday, JJ met Palmer at the matinee. Afterward he offered to walk her home, unusual in itself since they lived in opposite directions, and it had never been a problem for her to scoot the few blocks home from the La Mar in the late afternoon.

He suggested they walk down Center towards the Pier, then along The Strand, and up to Palmer's house—the long way round. She figured he wanted to talk and hoped it wasn't about another of her spiritual shortcomings.

So she was startled when JJ suddenly turned and spat at her, "He's a *pachuco*!"

Palmer wasn't sure about the word, but she knew the tone, and JJ wasn't much given to insults. "Judge not, that ye be not judged," he'd said more than once. She also knew immediately who he was talking about. "What do you mean?"

He shrugged. "They're all gang members."

"His whole family?" she asked, only a shade ingenuously.

"You know what I mean."

Palmer thought of those early California lovers Ramona and Alessandro, of Joey Gutierrez who'd gone to school with her and JJ since kindergarten, of Cam himself. "You're wrong," she said flatly.

JJ glanced sideways at her. "So what are you suddenly, some kind of expert?"

She felt heat rush through her. "Are you?"

Except for their short-lived fight after Frida's party—and even then only JJ had been mad—they'd never fought, never worked through those stages of getting friends to serve as intermediaries, of passing notes and making up like other couples.

"Frida Yarborough calls Campbell the *gaucho*," she said, surprised at her sharp pleasure in telling him. It had stung when she had heard Frida scream it from the bleachers. Palmer wished she'd thought of it herself.

JJ absorbed that blow and changed tactics. "Well, he's Catholic."

"So?"

"They worship the Pope, Palmer, they pray to the Virgin Mary."

"You don't know anything about it," she said.

"Ask anyone at church. And Christians aren't supposed to marry Catholics, either."

"Well, who's getting married? Besides, Catholics *are* Christians."

"I mean *real* Christians—*born again* Christians."

They turned up 13th Street and headed the block over to her alley. "So," she said, "you think Christians ought to be prejudiced."

JJ was stopped only for a moment. "Well, he's not saved," he said, as if that summed it all up, "so he's going to Hell."

Old fear fluttered in her stomach, not just for Cam but for all the people she loved. And just that fast she felt the old weight of responsibility. She hadn't witnessed to anyone since her talk with Grandmother Sydney. Hated even the thought. How was it she could give a report or even act in a play with the whole school watching, but the idea of talking to people about their *personal relationships with Christ*—it was just embarrassing.

They reached her house. "I have to go in," she said, mad that he'd gotten the last word. But something had shifted. A new doubt pricked at her, a small but steady irritation like a weedy foxtail snagged in her sock. Religion for JJ was getting too small somehow, a stingy little box he kept tightly sealed, a treasure that belonged to too few. Distaste brushed her mind, subtle as an eyelash.

He mistook the tone of her goodbye and stepped forward, his face gentle with victory and anticipation. But when he leaned over to kiss her, even though it would have been a casual, daylight kiss right in front of her house, Palmer turned away and opened the screen door. It banged against his chest.

"See you later," she said, without apology for the door. They looked at each other through the screen. In the late sunlight, his hair shone chestnut, and the muscles in his arm danced when he caught at the door. She saw his face flush from temper or embarrassment. She didn't really care which. JJ was going to be just fine without her. She undid the clasp of her necklace, slid the ring off, and handed it to him. Another girl would wear it soon enough.

Palmer walked inside and shut the door firmly behind her. No one seemed to be home. She grabbed the jelly glass sitting on the drainboard and filled it to the brim with cold tap water. Had she ever been thirstier, even after popcorn or a day at the beach? She took a long swallow before realizing the water tasted funny. She leaned against the sink, suddenly very tired, and poured the water from the twice-used glass down the drain. The taste had been familiar too—like that of juice gone bad, like the faint taste of stale wine.

Half-Light

MOTHER HAD BEEN TO THE DOCTOR. Every time Palmer asked—"What's the matter?" "Are you sick?" "What's wrong?"— her mother shushed her and said they'd talk about it later. More alarming yet, Grandmother Sydney showed up.

"Bounces on down here like a paddleball," Daddy said, though he didn't sound particularly cross, and that seemed worrisome, too. Her grandmother had been in Seattle no more than a month, and this time Palmer found her black outfits more ominous than stylish. (In school they were reading a poem about a raven.) Like a telegram or a long-distance phone call, her grandmother's sudden arrival seemed to signal bad news in a way Palmer couldn't quite explain.

During dinner—biscuits in bacon gravy, Swiss chard with crumbled bacon, and sliced tomatoes—nobody talked much. The Santa Ana winds blew against the side of the house. Palmer and Maggie cleared the table, and Mother poured hot coffee into three mugs. Her eyes were slightly bloodshot. Passing her in the warm kitchen, Palmer caught that whiff of overripe fruit.

"Run outside and play," Mother said, handing each girl an orange. "The grown-ups need a little time to themselves." But later when she called them back in, her face was so pale her rouge looked clownish. Daddy was frowning into his empty mug, gripping it with both hands, and Grandmother Sydney had started washing dishes—Palmer's job.

"Sit down, girls," Mother said. "We have something to tell you."

Palmer felt her chest closing, the kitchen air being sucked out through every crevice and open window.

"I saw the doctor today." Soft as feather down, the hint of doom breathed in Mother's voice. "Well?" she said too quickly. "Aren't you going to ask what he said?"

"C'mon, Claudia, they're on the edge of their seats. Give 'em a break."

So her father already knew. Palmer searched his face but saw only annoyance. She'd overheard him earlier when she'd come into the kitchen to set the table: "Belted back a few, have we?"

"What did he say?" Maggie asked.

Fear like a night mist chilled Palmer. Daddy reached into the cupboard behind him for a toothpick. "Let's not make a production out of this," he said. The same words as when Palmer and Maggie would ask to walk down to the drugstore with him.

Mother's eyes darted toward Daniel. "I think I have a right to take my time," she said. "After all, *cancer* is no joke." Grandmother Sydney's hand fluttered to her ear, as if to stop sound itself.

"Sweet Louise, what kind of stunt—?" Daddy jumped up, his chair nearly toppling over. He flung the dregs of his coffee into the sink.

"They have to take out my uterus—it's called a hysterectomy—just as soon as the doctors can schedule it."

Palmer's tongue thickened. Her father's reaction meant Mother hadn't told about the cancer until just now. And the only illness worse than what her father had been through was this awful disease whose name people hesitated to say aloud.

"The doctor says I'm absolutely full of tumors." Claudia's voice was flat, as if parroting the doctor's diagnosis. But Palmer could hear that same familiar tremor of belligerence as when her mother was drinking.

Maggie squirmed in her chair. "Does this mean you're real sick?"

"Oh, sweetheart." Claudia's eyes glimmered with tears. "Mother has to have an operation like when Daddy had surgery."

She paused. "Except … I'll never be the same again."

"Claudia, it's not as if you wanted more kids—"

"But this is just the excuse you've been waiting for, isn't it?"

"Oh, Jesus, here we go."

Palmer flinched, more because he was too mad to beg his daughters' pardon than because he had used the Lord's name in vain. The Lord seemed conspicuously absent at the moment.

"Let's not stage a full-fledged melodrama," Daddy snapped. "We can talk more about this later."

"When would that be exactly, Daniel? After you've moved out?"

Palmer gasped.

Daddy took a step toward Mother, his body coiled, each hand already a fist. A plate slipped out of Grandmother Sydney's grasp, hit the edge of the drainboard, and shattered on the linoleum. Daddy jammed his hands into his pants pockets.

"It's no more than the truth," Claudia said. "And a terrible time to desert us." Like a tossed lariat, her pronoun looped through the air to circle both girls.

Daddy glanced at Grandmother Sydney, almost as if for help, but she was picking up the broken plate, her new sapphire-colored earrings dull under the kitchen light.

"Okay, that's about enough." He grabbed for his briefcase, still propped beside the door. "There's no talking to you in this condition. You're not even fit—"

"Don't you accuse me of being an unfit mother! Look at these children and tell me I haven't slaved to raise these girls. No one can say they aren't well brought up."

"Daddy—," Palmer began.

"This is between your mother and me," he said curtly

"Then why not keep it that way?" Grandmother Sydney said softly. Maggie slipped out of her chair and squatted to help with the broken pottery, its ivy pattern severed as if by crazed pruning. Her grandmother motioned her back to the table.

Daniel's face reddened. "There's precious little choice here, Syd, so best keep your nose out of it."

Her lips tightened, and she busied herself with the broom and dustpan.

Mother rallied. "There's always the choice not to abandon your family—"

"You've got a rotten sense of timing when you're drunk, you know that?" He ignored the look of outrage on her face. "One thing at a time here. Nobody's putting this show on the road—"

"If you're going to leave, don't expect me to be the one to tell them," Mother said.

"Christ, could you just rein it in for one second?"

Maggie started to cry, and Mother clumsily pulled her onto her lap. Grandmother Sydney noisily emptied the dustpan into the trash. Daddy backed toward the door.

"No child who gets Palmer's grades could have an unfit mother," Claudia said, as if someone had claimed otherwise.

Feeling as if a coat were falling heavily on her shoulders, Palmer thought of that picture at school of Hercules bent by the earth's mass.

"You're gone all the time, anyhow. First tennis, now fishing"—her voice faltered—"or finding someone else to keep you company."

"There's no point—"

Mother sputtered, "You throw your weight around like a banty rooster, strut for all you're worth, but when it comes right down to it—"

"Just shut up, Claudia. You are such a lousy drunk." Daniel edged away, eyeing his wife.

"Don't!" Palmer yelped, not sure what she meant exactly.

Then he was out the door, heading up the hill, his car keys in hand, the screen door slamming behind him. Maggie was wailing. Even Claudia looked startled.

Palmer leaped up, her legs electrified, and ran out the door. She only half heard her mother scream, "Daniel!"

He was already around the corner, heading for his car, and Palmer tore up the alley after him.

"Daddy!"

He started the Plymouth; then he saw her and leaned across to open the passenger door. His forehead gleamed with sweat. "What happened to your tan?" he asked her, managing a tired smile.

"What?"

"Get in, princess. You're so pale your freckles are standing at attention."

She took a shuddering breath, tried to match his tone. "You used to call them fairy kisses," she said. He nodded. She pressed her hands together, as if in prayer, whether to a father in heaven or on earth she had no idea. "Don't leave—" Her voice broke in mid-sentence.

He squeezed her knee, put the car in gear, and drove along Manhattan Avenue. He turned right at Center and parked downhill near the Pier. They sat quietly, watching the twilight sky, bloodshot with coral clouds.

Could it really have come to this, her worst nightmare of all? But surely her father wouldn't really pick now to leave. And she really meant, leave her mother, didn't she? Because he couldn't leave his daughters. He couldn't leave *her*, could he?

Above the horizon, dark was bleeding into the sunset, turning it muddy. She thought she saw a prick of light, wished for a meteor, a nova—some sign of hope more powerful than even the first star of night.

"I'm just headed into the Knothole." He jerked his head toward the tavern. "Get my bookwork done with some peace and quiet."

Would he have a drink, she wondered, even though he wasn't supposed to? Finally she said, "Mother really needs you"—she squeezed it out—"now that she has *cancer*."

Daddy rubbed his face with both hands, his eyebrows wild over tired eyes. "She doesn't have cancer, Palmer."

"But—"

"You know how your mother tends to"—he paused—"exaggerate."

"The operation—"

"For fibroid tumors. I know the words are scary, but fibroids are benign. She has to have surgery, but she's not dying."

Palmer's world was so busy righting itself she could hardly move for fear of disturbing some cosmic gyroscope. Could this be one of her mother's stories? She *was* drinking, and that was always when the tales got told. But maybe Mother was just scared the doctors weren't telling her everything. Maybe she was brave or tipsy enough to give a name to her deepest fear.

But if the cancer was made up, then maybe other things weren't true, either. Palmer turned to her father. "And you aren't leaving?"

He rolled down his window, reached across to roll down hers. The last of the Santa Anas blew hot and strong through the car. He cleared his throat. "Sometimes—that is, if parents do divorce, a judge decides young children like Maggie will stay with their mothers. Older kids choose."

Her eyes stung, but no tears came. The hot wind had sucked her dry. Even her lips seemed suddenly chapped. She knew what he was saying. The age of accountability, of volition. Her thirteen years loomed before her. Daddy seemed to be waiting, as if he'd asked her a question.

"I promised I'd stay with Maggie," she said finally, remembering her mother's lying on the couch, those deathbed vows, "if Mother ever—" She couldn't make herself say words that had seemed real minutes before.

"Nothing's going to happen to her, kiddo."

A sudden gust shook the car, then the winds died down in their unpredictable way, the quiet too loud between the two of them. "It's just that she really needs me."

"Maggie?"

She held her breath. "Mother," she whispered.

He stared through the windshield at the darkening water, his shirt wrinkled, his shoulders slumped. Without looking at her, he rolled up his window. "Hop out and run on home, honey. I'm not going anywhere tonight. Just across the street." She leaned over and kissed his cheek, smelled his faint Mennen's aftershave, the scent of him that had always been reassuring in their houseful of women.

Heading home along The Strand, she wrapped her arms around herself, trying to put the pieces together, taking deep breaths of dampening air. A fog bank was moving in, the twilight deepening. He'd said the tumors were fibrous or something like that, and she pictured an old tree having to be yanked out by its gnarled roots. Growing like crazy. Wasn't that what cancer was? But Mother's tumors were *benign*—a gentle word without the serpent's hiss of disease.

Yet also echoing loudly was that silent moment before Daddy had rolled his window back up, before he said he was only going across the street—tonight. And before she'd closed the car door, she had seen the pale envelope, small and gray as a dove, lying on the back seat, his name in that feathery handwriting, nearly hidden under his briefcase in the half light.

Late that night after everyone else was asleep, her father finally home from the Knothole, her mother long since passed out, her grandmother softly snoring in the living room, Palmer tried to ease the fist tightening in her chest by reading in bed. Her goal was to eventually read all the way through her *New Testament*, though at church they urged them to read the whole *Bible,* said it could be finished in a year.

But she couldn't imagine where she might be in a year or what parts of her family would even hold together that long. So though it felt like cheating, she skipped ahead to I Corinthians, looking for a verse on love. Something more comforting tonight than plodding through Acts.

She was definitely wheezy, and sometimes sitting up and reading could help. If she could just manage to stop thinking about her mother's drinking, about her father's leaving, about Loretta Sprague's trying to take her mother's place—though why she should think that from a single pale envelope, she didn't know, but who could understand what grown-ups might do next, anyway?

If she'd been paying attention, she might have felt that kernel of anger, hard as the nugget of fool's gold, burning in the center of her chest, its red ember sucking at the very air in her lungs.

She finally fell asleep still propped up by pillows, the white imitation-leather Bible from her grandmother splayed across her lap, mouth-breathing heavily into the deep hours of dreaming. And into that dream walked her parents, turned to stick figures like drawings she and Maggie had made in kindergarten.

She scooped them up, one in each fist, knocking their heads together until they turned into a game of pick-up-sticks—blue, green, red, and yellow—sticks she threw down onto The Strand, their spiky arms and legs tangled across the concrete where she stomped them into broken pieces. She pummeled them like she had those balky piano keys in the church basement, rage now thick as snow packing her nose and mouth, like the deep drifts on that night in Palos Verdes, and she knew she should pull her face out of this snowbank to breathe.

She fought in a panic, even though her mother told her you never die in a dream, and it was a dream, wasn't it? She heard her breath, a ragged thing like cloth torn to make rags, like prophets rending their robes in rage and lamentation.

Her eyes snapped open to thin morning light with Mother holding the glass medicine dropper of adrenaline above her lips, pinching Palmer's cheeks to make her open her mouth, birdlike. Daddy was pressed in close beside Mother.

"For God's sake, watch the teeth! You'll cut her if it breaks."

Mother was trembling. "Just hold her hands, Daniel. I've done this a hundred times."

Grandmother Sydney hovered behind them. Palmer gasped, and a drop of amber grease slid along the back of her tongue, almost choking her.

"I'll put the kettle on," Grandmother Sydney said. "Some steam will open up those lungs."

"Once more, princess. Let your mother get that dropper in your mouth."

With their heads bent over her in the bunk, Palmer couldn't

remember why she'd been so mad at them in her dream. She heard Maggie's voice below her, querulous with sleep.

You don't die in dreams, her mother had said, and no one ever dies from asthma. That must be true if her mother had said it. Except her mother told stories. Panic wedged into Palmer's chest.

She hadn't really beaten on them; that was just a crazy quilt of a dream, but now they both looked so scared. Even with the second drop of adrenaline and maybe a third—she couldn't count—her breath rolled out of reach, elusive as a pick-up-stick blown, rolling, down The Strand.

They bundled her up and raced through sparse early-morning traffic to the Torrance hospital, leaving Maggie with Grandmother Sydney. Palmer battled for each breath. She slipped deeper into that doctor's image of her body as a submarine, all hatches battened down with air struggling to get out, not in.

Because she hated shots, that's what she remembered most from staying all that day and the following night in the hospital, except for a breakfast of watery poached eggs. They brought her home with dark circles under her eyes and an ache across her upper back, with instructions not to go to school for a week. It was finally Daddy who decided after a few days to get her out into the sunshine.

"C'mon, princess, we can't have you looking so peaked." He grabbed his fishing gear. "Get a sweater in case it's windy." She didn't argue that the day was warm. It was nearly two in the afternoon, and he'd come home early, a surprise in itself, helping himself to a quick mug of reheated coffee. Maggie was still at school, Mother at work.

"Do you really think—?" Grandmother Sydney began, looking doubtful about this outing, but a glance from Daniel cut her off.

"A little fishing never hurt anybody," he said and whisked Palmer out the door, herself startled to have been invited by her father, who seemed to hoard the places he could go alone these days.

Out on the Pier the afternoon breeze softly brushed against

the day's heat. Palmer knotted her sweater around her waist. Her father picked a spot about two-thirds of the way out and settled her on a bench with his tackle box before he headed toward the live bait shop. "You want a snack or anything?" he asked. She shook her head, and alone for a moment, she opened her mouth and pulled at the salt air—test breaths really—making sure the hiss of air and water came only from the surf, her own breath sliding free.

Daddy came back with a small bucket of anchovies. Meticulously he baited his hook. Then with his rod pointed toward the water, he began that graceful sweeping back and forth before he cast the line out into its long arc. He stared toward the Santa Monica mountains, reeling in slowly, occasionally lifting the tip of his rod.

He looked down at her. "You gave us quite a scare. Remember much?"

"Mostly the shots. Awful eggs."

He smiled, nodded. "They pumped you full of adrenaline, then had to sedate you back down. Put you on oxygen. You don't remember?"

Palmer shook her head. "No," she said when he turned to look at her.

"Your mother and I went around to that little chapel on Olvera Street. Same one as when you were a sick little tyke years back." He reeled his line in and cast again, taking his time. "Guess it didn't do any harm."

They were quiet together. He didn't offer to let her take the rod, and she didn't ask. A couple of pelicans dove into the water just past his line. The breeze picked up a notch, just the slightest fanning of a bird's wing.

"The doctor wanted to know what had you wound up tighter than a toy. Said kids can outgrow asthma, but if we wanted you to live out—" Abruptly he cleared his throat.

The breeze chilled slightly. Could her mother's reassurances down the years have been wrong? She remembered her own icy doubt during the asthma attack. "Could I have died?" she asked softly.

"Where'd you get that idea?" His voice held an edge.

"You said if you wanted me to live out—"

Daddy hardly hesitated. "If we want you to spend time *outdoors,* in the sun, not be some sickly kid, then—well, I guess things need to change."

"What things?"

He rummaged in his tackle box, patted his shirt pockets as if from habit, the cigarettes still a memory. In that pause, Palmer's imagination flared, and she pictured her parents leaning close together, as they had that day when the church had delivered their beautiful Christmas tree and it filled their house with air that smelled like mountains. She would be able to breathe in a house like that.

Suddenly Daddy's rod jerked toward the water. The muscles in his jaw bunched as he bent his energy to landing the fish. How many times had he done this over the years—let the drag out, tire the running fish, tighten the drag, reel in slowly?

"Could be a fourteen-, maybe fifteen-pounder. Halibut, f'sure," he said softly. The fishermen on either side moved their lines out of the way. A couple walking by drew closer behind them. A young man ran to get the net kept at the bait house.

Palmer leaned as far over the railing as she could, her fingers white as they gripped the rail. She'd seen this often enough to know he had a big strike. Always she believed that if she looked hard enough into the green depths, she would see the dark shape of the flat halibut rousted from the sandy bottom, not a wild fighter like the sand sharks or stingrays that sometimes got hooked, but a stubborn fish, unwilling to give up to the large hook that had sunk deep onto the ocean floor.

"Easy does it," counseled a fisherman to their right. Daddy didn't seem to hear, his attention focused on battling the fish. He forgot his daughter beside him, leaning too far out over the railing, forgot his wife working the day away, his annoying mother-in-law, forgot even the pale-gray envelopes that now and then arrived for him at work.

The man with the net was thudding down the concrete towards them when the line suddenly went limp and Daddy muttered a soft curse.

"Looks like you lost him," drawled the fisherman. "Too much tension, maybe. Those babies sure want to dive."

Daddy reeled in his line, which seemed to take forever. Finally it cleared the surface, and there, clinging to the hook, was the severed head of a good-sized halibut, maybe close to an eighteen-pounder. Shredded flesh hung from the hooked jaw.

"I'll be," the fisherman said. "Looks like something sure enough took off with your fish."

"Barracuda," Daddy said grimly, hoisting the little that remained up and over the railing.

"Don't see *that* every day," said the guy with the net, but already he was turning back toward the bait house. The crowd that had gathered began to move along, the excitement of a big one being landed dissipating like morning fog.

Palmer peered into the water. Shifting shapes seemed to dart everywhere. "Is it a whole school?" she asked, remembering surfer tales of barracuda slicing up swimmers.

Daddy wrested the mess off the end of his hook, tossed it over the rail. They watched the bloody chunk waver underwater before it disappeared, gone before either the gulls or pelicans could rally.

"No," he said, "but *some* sucker sure robbed us of dinner."

Together, elbows on the railing, alone now as even the fisherman pulled up his line to try another spot, they gazed into the water. A stirring of wind riffled the surface, its fractured light reflecting off their faces, the ocean's dark silhouettes and razor teeth hidden below.

"Well," Daddy said at last. "Some things can't be helped. Everybody down there"—he nodded towards the green water—"needs to eat."

Palmer undid her sweater from around her waist and pulled it over her shoulders.

"You getting cold, princess? We should probably head back."

The afternoon angle of the sun had sharpened, and the September sky seemed a long way from the Christmas she'd been picturing before Daddy had gotten his strike. He'd been talking about things being different, and though she was afraid, she needed to ask. "You said something—before the fish—about change."

He looked startled, then seemed to pick up the thread, maybe even remembering some earlier purpose to their outing, something that had slipped away like the lost catch. He gathered his fishing gear, offered the unused bait to an old man fishing nearby.

"You need some peace, honey, that's all. Everybody does, I guess." From the horizon a late-afternoon wind swept shoreward. "Now put your arms in that sweater," he said, before glancing away from her. She followed his eyes toward the hills that marched up and away from the beach.

It wasn't enough, but she didn't know how to ask more. Together they turned their backs on the sun and headed in off the Pier, the day's sunlight filtered by disappointment, their shadows running ahead of them.

Beachwalker

Startled from ocean's
mirrored edge, seabirds
dart at sky's blue pulse,
nature's arrowheads.
Tiny wings and bodies veer,
a snap of blinds, the dark
flickering birdcloud
swerves invisible, a disappearing
heartbeat that flashes black,
then back—sunspots shot
against the far horizon.
A thousand skyprints,
beckoning.

Seaborne

"MOONS AND TIDES," HER GRANDMOTHER SAID, delicately sweeping a few grains of sugar off the table into her palm, "the pull of gravity." She dropped the sugar into Claudia's ashtray and patted Palmer's arm. Noonday sun poured through the kitchen window, bright as paint. It was Friday, Palmer's last day of her weeklong "excused absence" following her asthma attack. She felt fine, her breathing deep and natural, except now, wouldn't you know, her period had started early.

"Heavenly and earthly rhythms. Women's cycles, just one more part of the celestial plan. Perfectly natural, all of it." Sydney lowered her voice, though Maggie was still at school and Daniel was at work. "Of course, a hot-water bottle does wonders. Just remember not to soak in the tub or jump around too much. And never go swimming."

"Oh, Mama," Claudia said, "those are old wives' tales. A long walk and a couple of Empirin will do the trick." She glanced at Palmer's sandwich. "You might try avoiding those pickles if you're puffy."

Claudia came home for lunch more often these days. She could drink coffee with her mother and smoke a few cigarettes in *some peace and quiet*. Afterward, she aired the kitchen out. Daniel didn't seem to notice the dusky scent, or if he did, he didn't say anything.

They were discussing Palmer like a medical specimen. She guessed the word *menstruation* would never appear on one of her spelling tests, but she listened closely, hoping to learn something.

At the same time she stayed alert to the language of sighs and gestures between her mother and grandmother, but the women kept to easy talk. No one mentioned cancer or asthma or what plans her father might or might not have.

Claudia massaged her temple and helped herself to the Empirin. Since Palmer's asthma attack, she had already been to two meetings that week. It was a start, at least. Once again.

"Eventually, she's going to be regular just like me," Claudia said. "Exactly twenty-eight days. Some girls take a year or more to settle down." She nodded at Palmer. "You'll feel better before you know it."

Mother finished the last of her coffee and stretched her arms toward the ceiling. Her loose blouse hardly pulled across her breasts. She *had* lost weight, Palmer thought. "Oh, hell, I've got to get back." Mother ignored Grandmother Sydney's frown at her language. "Much as I hate to. It's a scorcher over there. October had better cool off, or we'll all melt by Halloween."

She stood up to look for her pocketbook, kissed Palmer on top of her head, and glanced at her mother. "I'll have to give notice. The recuperation takes a full six weeks."

Only a few blocks away, the world of Metlox still seemed as foreign to Palmer as the Land of Oz. She imagined the Wicked Witch of the West melting into a hot puddle of sweat on the factory floor. Her stomach felt queasy. With the last of her milk, she gulped down a couple of tablets from the squat green bottle.

After Mother walked back to work, Palmer changed out of her pajamas. It had been settled that Grandmother Sydney would stay until Claudia was on her feet again. Pulling a blouse over her bathing suit, Palmer checked herself in her mother's dresser mirror to make sure the Modess pad didn't show. After lengthy consultations about shape and absorbency, she and Bonnie had decided to switch from the Kotex brand each of their mothers used. Maybe it was no more than the word itself, echoing *modest* or *model*, or even the name of the Mode O'Day dress shop. More womanly somehow with its feminine ending, like *actress* or *tigress* or *temptress*. Palmer frowned at her reflection and pressed her tender belly. It looked poochy.

"Nothing but colored brassieres and girdles," her grandmother huffed about modern swimsuits. "Girls cavorting and showing themselves off on the beach." Looking at her peach-colored suit, Palmer thought it a half-fair description.

While Palmer was dressing, Sydney quickly washed up the lunch dishes. Truth to tell, she'd been looking forward to autumn in Seattle, and she wouldn't have minded some relief from this heat, either. Give her the rain any day over this godforsaken sand they were all so wild for.

Daniel's health seemed stable for the moment, but now it was Claudia with her operation. Last night Sydney had awakened thinking she heard voices, fervent somehow, even the word *divorce* whispering back on itself through walls and dark windows, but when she'd opened her eyes, the only whisper was the night surf. In the morning it had seemed a dream—not, she hoped, one of her premonitions. But it didn't take psychic abilities to see how things were going—Daniel and Claudia were too careful around each other. How much Maggie understood, she couldn't tell, but that Palmer kept her ear to the ground, that was for sure.

She put the last plate in the cupboard, smoothed the tea towel, and hung it up beside the sink. Lots of women had the hysterectomy these days. Claudia would surely do fine, especially with her there to help out. After that—well, don't borrow trouble. She reached for the coffeepot before she remembered they'd finished it off. Think about it tomorrow: about the operation and her daughter's lost income, about this family on the verge of the poorhouse, about the parents trying to mend their lives, about a girl with asthma and her baby sister. It was Scarlett O'Hara's philosophy, and in her mind she pictured the perfect, heart-shaped face of Vivien Leigh, a face that had always reminded her of Claudia.

Palmer pushed past the screen door into the sunshine. Already her goodbye with JJ only a few days back seemed to have happened *eons* ago—another spelling word. She felt oddly buoyant, just a little, the way it was easier to float in salt water than in a swimming pool, nothing you'd even notice all that much unless you swam often in both.

Well, her grandmother was right about one thing: life never stood still, and with Cam in mind, and her parents, too, she supposed it was a good thing, but a person sure needed to stay on her toes. Surprises—good and bad—came like waves, one hidden behind another so you never knew if you were going to get a breathless ride over the top, a wet smack in the face, or a mean pounding into the bottom.

She would try to put her parents behind her. Just for the afternoon, she amended, feeling the guilt threaten for what nameless sin she couldn't imagine. But what if she were overlooking the one good thing still hidden like invisible writing that needed only lemon juice to be deciphered, that one clue she might use to keep them drawn to each other? She felt irritable and restless now and wondered if this was how Mother felt when she said she was nervous.

She knew Grandmother Sydney had shooed her out, wanting the house to herself. And why not? Sometimes she felt a little protective of her grandmother. Take those new earrings.

"No one would ever suspect they came from the dime store," her grandmother had said, cocking her head before the bathroom mirror. "Why, I believe this blue is more flattering to my complexion. Maybe those opals washed me out just a bit." How brave she could be. And so what if she had the occasional vision?

Barely past noon and already a scorcher. Mother was right about this heat. Palmer wandered down the alley, across Ocean Drive, toward The Strand. She needed wind in her face. Her cheeks felt too hot even for sunburn, as if a furnace smoldered inside her brain. Maybe this was caused by her period, too. Wouldn't it be nice for once to fix blame on a single thing?

She wished she'd brought a book, but she certainly wasn't going back. Her grandmother could change her mind in an instant, want Palmer to iron something or run to the drugstore. She felt too lazy for any of it. But it felt odd not to have a plan. She could have ridden her bike, but her grandmother would have claimed it was too much exertion, too soon. And truthfully just the idea sounded hot, made her thirsty.

At least there was a drinking fountain at the Pier. At home she'd just be underfoot. Better to wait until her grandmother got lost in soap operas. Then if Palmer decided to go swimming against her advice, there'd be time to walk back for her cap and towel.

The Pier was already crowded with fishermen. And despite the heat, the early-afternoon sunlight was aslant, autumn-clear and thinner somehow, as if offering less loft for the birds than in summer. A silly notion, she thought, as if anything worked against gravity in the first place.

At the lifeguard tower, she stopped to drink at the fountain, letting the water run cold, glancing up at the *No Jumping from the Pier* sign. Its black letters seemed to bark their command, reminding her of the redheaded lifeguard that day in the surf. But instead of embarrassment, she felt another lift in her chest, like an expansion of heart.

What a strange day it was turning out to be. Nothing at all like a Friday but not a weekend day, either. A *no-name* day, a pure gift of time. She hadn't seen who was on duty in the tower, but she hoped it might be the redhead. She imagined herself reflected in his sunglasses: a girl to be reckoned with. "Keep your eye on that one," he'd say. "Could be a troublemaker." She liked that vision of herself. But she guessed such an image had to be cultivated, like the Victory gardens during the War, when everybody had to work backcountry soil into the sand. Breaking rules just didn't seem to come naturally, at least not to her.

By the time she reached the middle of the Pier, most of the fishermen were knotted by the bait house. Others clustered around the Pier's end. She drifted over to the railing. To the north, the foothills of Santa Monica tumbled golden brown as ripe figs, while the Pier's shadow rode the waves and shaded part of the beach. The other side was livelier with people.

She glanced furtively back at the guard's station and slipped under the rail. Planting her feet as always and gripping behind her, she *yearned* her body out over the water. Below, the tide was so high the green water seemed swollen and deep. She smiled that Cam with all his courage was unnerved by this drop before her now. And a Wyoming boy knew nothing of the other risks that she had known for as long as she could remember.

Like the submerged pilings from the original structure—the Old Iron Pier. Nine hundred feet long before storms had knocked it down way back when Mother was about her age. She tried to imagine the fury of waves that could smash an iron pier to pieces. Folks still wondered how many shattered pilings remained beneath the water's surface. At the library, she'd seen the old photo display showing how lengths of railroad ties had been fastened together, then driven into the ocean floor.

Her folks told of suicide jumps during the Depression—"a few years back," they'd say. Good reason for these signs against jumping. No wonder the boys leaped out as far from the Pier as possible. Most of the dangers were hidden.

She ducked back inside the rail, walked further out, then drifted to the other side of the Pier with the sun full in her face and the air so clear she could see the wild grasses green on the Palos Verdes' cliffs. Out to the southwest, she spotted Catalina, as if the sky itself had cast its shadow on the horizon.

Her ritual was always to do both sides, so she slipped under, not even bothering to check this time for guards. A fisherman glanced at her as she leaned out over the water with her arms stretched behind. She hoped she looked like the prow of an old-time ship, face lifted to the sun, hair carved back by wind. Her body had changed this year. She was showing off and knew it.

But she never needed an audience to slip into her private illusion of flight over the smooth water, pretending to be a gull. All sense of trouble evaporated as she leaned into that crystalline moment of sweet salt air and surf. Later in the afternoon when the onshore wind picked up, there'd be whitecaps, but for now she imagined how she'd fly away, a snowy tern with her wings spread over silk water that glittered green with coins of sunlight.

So for no particular reason that she was ever able to name, on this odd but ordinary Friday, it seemed to take little thought and even less planning to take the leap she'd imagined on so many sun-dazzled days.

With no one to stop her now, not even herself, she flexed her knees, the muscles in her thighs bunching as she vaulted out into that blue space above the gleaming, dangerous water. Almost like walking on air, she leaped with one foot ahead of the other, hurling herself as far from the Pier and the fishing hooks and the barnacle-covered pilings as possible, trying in one moment to avoid all the dangers she'd heard about her whole life.

Torn away by the leap, her hands scraped the pitted railing, as if different parts of her body had their own flight plan, feet first with the hands more cautious by just a fraction, trying to feel their way into the next second, the next decade.

Her feet said, *why not oh why not if Christ walked on water and Peter too then why not her?* Why not this last daring of childhood? Or was it something grown-up? Maybe one in the same. She wished the jump were slow motion like a movie, but in fact she sailed out like a tossed shell, barely glimpsing the pure line of the horizon. She held her breath and pulled her arms in tight, riveting her eyes downward as her feet pointed like a ballerina's toward water that rushed at her.

But somewhere in the free fall, slow motion did take over. With eyes wide, she saw her toes slice the water, herself swallowed, bubbles rushing past her legs and shoulders, half blinding her for the moment it took to plunge to the soft bottom. She registered gratitude that nothing seemed broken, though the impact had smacked her harder than she'd ever imagined. Then for just the barest hesitation before she could raise her arms above her head and push off with strong feet and ankles, she remembered the blood-soaked pad between her legs.

As a darkness loomed to her left, she saw all the sharks ever caught from the Pier, how they thrashed against fishing lines, their rows of teeth deadly. She was moving toward the shadow, but somehow the shape itself was still. The current had swept her toward a different kind of danger beneath the Pier—the concrete pilings blanketed with barnacles sharp as sharks' teeth. With all her strength she pivoted in the sand and angled upward to the green light that gleamed at the surface.

She burst out of the water, gasping, then twisted to see how close to the blue-black mussels she'd been swept, their razor shells gripping the pilings. She looked for fishing lines, too, with their shiny bites of hook, but the surprised fishermen above her had separated, moving their lines up and down the Pier to keep the water clear for her. She wanted to laugh at how amazed they must have been to see a half-dressed girl throw herself off the Pier. The blouse was plastered to her shoulders like a filmy remnant of parachute. She shrugged free and watched it drift away, a shedding snake's skin. The truthful lie she'd have to tell her mother appeared without even trying: *A wave took it.* And best of all, she hadn't seen any broken pilings from Old Iron.

She knew what to do and struck out away from the Pier, parallel to the beach, as if she were swimming out of a rip, except there were no rips today. But she needed to compensate for the current: probably she should have jumped from the other side. She might not have calculated perfectly, but she *had* jumped. Elation flooded her, powering her stroke.

"Keep your chin up," her father would say—his favorite phrase for courage and one that had never made so much sense as now. Nothing on her body hurt, and her breath was sliding clear and easy. No sign of asthma. She wondered if she had clenched her rump when she jumped. Boys often cackled about jumpers getting "high-water enemas."

She also wondered if she were trailing blood. Her period seemed a dangerous time to be in deep water. But wasn't that what her mother was always telling her—there were dangers whether you leaped or not? Her mind skittered like a stone skipped across water. Time to rely on herself, and in many ways she always had.

She thought how she would tell Mags about this adventure. Only a few more yards now before she could catch the first swell that would lift her toward the shore. But what if that very moment an earthquake should hit? There'd be a tidal wave, so the trick would be to ride out the surge without being tossed on shore. Could any swimmer really handle it? It felt like those days in the Redondo Theater when she had been sure she could ride out a quake. Already the place had been condemned and demolished. Her mother had been right about that one.

Was she trying to scare herself more than she already had? Yet right now the thought of riding out an earthquake seemed no harder than this past year of trying to hold her family together. She couldn't imagine being parted from her sister. Some waves could form perfect tunnels, and if one broke over you, you might see blue sky at the tunnel's end. Loving Maggie felt like reaching for that bit of sky.

So why was she still bobbing around out here? Why not swim right in? Somehow the jump had not been as hard as she'd expected, that is, if she didn't count the years getting up her nerve. Maybe that was often the way. You took the plunge and then breathed a sigh of relief that it hadn't been as bad as you'd imagined. But how could she want more when she'd just done something she never believed she'd do, something hardly any kid ever did? Disappointment dragged at her like an anchor.

Abruptly, Palmer turned her back on the shore and started swimming straight at the horizon. She thought she could see startled looks on the fishermen's faces, saw some of them nudge a neighbor, point to the crazy girl in the water. But she had a plan. She was going to swim all the way around the Pier. Now there was a rite of passage for you. Not even the surfers took their boards across that broad sweep of water, and for good reason—obvious risks like fatigue and cramps (though at lunch she hadn't eaten all of her sandwich). But once she pulled even with the Roundhouse, she'd be entering that other fabled area of danger, worse than Old Iron.

To swim around, she'd have to pass through the territory of an old wooden extension. Who knew how many of its wooden pilings hid underwater or how high their jagged ends still reached? Before the War, that extension had stretched two hundred feet beyond the Roundhouse; then it was swept away by storms. Riding now over swells, Palmer wasn't sure she could even estimate two hundred feet.

Suddenly she felt like laughing, and in the same instant broke out in goose bumps. How many wooden piers would a woodchuck build if a woodchuck would build wooden piers? She flipped over and did a few backstrokes. What was the matter with her, anyway?

Even the bait boat approached from the side, never directly from the end. And now a girl was going to thread among those ruins, swimming blind and hoping for the best. She felt brave and terrified and a little dumb.

The fishermen had bunched together and followed along the rail to stay with her. At any moment she half expected a lifeguard to explode out of the water and grab a fistful of her hair. Perhaps one of the fishermen had already gone running the length of the Pier to the station. Maybe the guard had her sighted in his binoculars. She didn't think of being rescued so much as getting in trouble. Right now that coveted bad-girl image seemed pale as a tomcod's belly.

Gradually she pulled even with the end of the Pier, but she knew she'd have to give it a wide berth, not only because of the submerged pilings but also because once she began to round it, the swells would push her toward the Pier. It was another compensation she was just now calculating. As she swam, still breathing with every other stroke, she could see how acting on impulse was exciting, but never before had she thought seriously about drowning.

Into the turn, she forced herself to keep her eyes open underwater to patrol for shadows that could be broken pilings. The high tide kept more leeway between her and anything submerged, but it also made the beach look miles away, so much farther than even that day when she had taken Maggie over her head. Wings of panic fluttered in her chest.

Be calm. With half her mind, the pun registered, but she couldn't imagine a windless sea. Right now her whole world was motion. A prayer to herself—*be calm*—in rhythm with each stroke. Oddly, it didn't cross her mind to ask for Heavenly help, perhaps because she'd so clearly brought this on herself. Schools of fish darted beneath her. Once, facedown, she thought she saw a barracuda and almost gasped. Instead, she blew out breath and felt every inch of the sea's enormity. The bottom itself was invisible, swathed in dark layers of green fabric, and she wondered about the depth. Thirty feet? Forty? How many fathoms—the deepest-sounding word she knew—swirled beneath her kicking feet? Somewhere out here did the bottom fall off into an underwater canyon?

Finally reaching the dead center of the Pier, she turned to face the mammoth structure and caught her breath. How many people had ever seen it head-on? Daddy said the round end was designed to keep killer waves from breaking against all the pilings at the same time. Now its mass seemed to bear down on her like a huge oil tanker. As the waves moved her closer, she had the illusion that the structure was steaming right at her, an ocean liner run amuck.

But treading water, she realized with a start, was a luxury—the swells had already pushed her toward the Pier. She had to angle away toward the horizon again, and this heading out to sea scared her. She needed to think about something else, but all that came to mind were those people who committed suicide by swimming toward the horizon to the ends of their endurance. She imagined a swimmer's wide-eyed face, pale as her white blouse when it had slipped beneath the surface. Did they change their minds too late and struggle to live? If you were already exhausted, how long could you hold your breath underwater? A minute? More? Did the first gasp smother you or did you keep choking, the swallowed water a heavy weight pulling you down? She fought the urge to splash toward shore.

One stroke after another, slower now, arms burning. She could rest once she reached the north side, safe from submerged pilings. There the current would keep her from being swept against the Pier itself. All these years in her daydreams, she'd imagined she'd emerge tired but victorious on the sunny side, her friends swarming around her. But now with the sun in the southern sky, she'd swim in the Pier's shadow. And none of her friends would see her, anyway, because they were all in school. Maybe that was just as well, though she couldn't say why.

Strong legs, a Girl Scout leader had told her, can take over when the arms give out; just keep your head. Palmer gave her kick all she had.

At last she rounded the Pier's end, and now she could take a moment to tread water again, to catch her breath and rest her arms because, as she'd known, the swells were gently moving her toward shore. She was losing body heat, and she remembered how Maggie had shivered and chattered that day in the riptide.

She looked up at the people on the Pier. The men were waving her in, and it seemed to Palmer they might be cheering. A couple of women pushing baby buggies had joined the crowd, because when had they ever seen a *girl* jump, let alone *circumnavigate* the Pier? She waved her arm slowly back and forth. That night at Bonnie's beach party, how lovingly her mother had kept track of her moonlit face.

The calm on her sea was beautiful, the water turquoise now. She must have been out here longer than she realized for the light to have changed so. Some mornings before the crowds showed up, Mrs. Stafford and her friends floated on their backs—though not this far out—over navy-blue swells, arms outstretched, fingers almost touching. Palmer hadn't known it could be this tranquil with the surf still so far away.

So far away. She felt sleepy. Strangely, softly, her mother's voice echoed the old refrain over the water: "Palmer, you've no business with your head in the clouds." Half reluctantly, she began to swim through this blue serenity toward the surf that was running higher now. The seas were gathering to push her toward shore.

All things work together for good to them that love God, to them who are the called according to His purpose.

Provided, she thought, you could swim in the first place, and she began to giggle, rolling onto her back, trying not to swallow water. And floating there, she watched her laughter take flight into the sky, hysteria circling overhead, riding thermals with the gulls. In the underside of their wings, the sun sparked opalescence, and she felt herself lifted toward the seabirds. Her eyes closed, and opal earrings flashed in the darkness of her lids.

As if she'd been given a shake, she knew she couldn't afford to get any colder and turned back into a breaststroke. The day was hot, but cool currents snaked around her legs, their temperatures fluctuating. Far ahead a wave rushed the beach and peaked so high she couldn't see over it, couldn't see the houses lining The Strand or people sunning on the beach or little kids digging in the shallows. Behind her another swell was gathering force; in seconds it was high enough to block the horizon from view, and for one moment in the trough between the two, Palmer's whole world was water, rising up behind and before, washing everything else away.

And then she saw the blue lights like tennis balls bouncing along the lip of the wave, smaller than the notorious beach ball of her grandmother's vision, and Palmer felt the odd laughter bubble up again. Sunspots danced on the swells, and her field of vision narrowed to one blue circle pirouetting over the water. It beckoned her toward shore.

Grandma had been right. "Go to the water," she had said. Where was the world any older, and where had they all come from, anyway? JJ didn't believe in evolution, but who cared? And look where Palmer found herself now. "In the soup," her father would say.

Suddenly, a shore-bound wave flattened in its forward rush, and she saw the shimmering beach like a mirage. If people lying on the sand knew she had jumped off the Pier, they gave no sign. A whitecap smacked her in the face. Water ran down the back of her nose, and she tasted brine, stronger than tears, more like pickles shared in the bathtub with Mags. Her head cleared. Once again she'd treaded water long enough.

"Slow and steady," she told herself, and then struck out for the shore that even now seemed on its way to meet her. At last her feet touched bottom. Folks on the Pier had lost interest, and like a starlet with a single scene, her fling with fame was over. On the other side between the pilings, she spied the redheaded lifeguard talking to a slender brunette, his torpedo buoy propped casually against one hip. For a second she felt insulted, as if her terrifying, amazing jump were not even worth a bawling-out. Then she was relieved and finally indignant that with a high tide running, the guard would stand around flirting. Feelings, deep as swells, nearly swamped her.

She was trembling and couldn't remember ever being so cold, even that day over two years ago when she and Maggie had been caught in the riptide, or the night they had played in the snowstorm. Watching that frozen miracle of weather from beside their bunk beds, Mother had stood apart from Daddy at the open window.

Even that night Palmer had not been this tired. The leap had not been safe, had not been smart, but against all reason, she had never felt so content. As she pulled out of the surf, a thin line of blood marked her thigh. Well, what could she expect from a waterlogged pad? But when she swiped at it, she saw it was a long scratch, deep enough to mark her but nothing she wouldn't recover from. Which danger had snagged her after all?

She waded the last few yards through shallows to where the waves had left behind a scant inch of water up to the watermark, a magic mirror blazing with reflected sky. She could never tell her parents. Not even her grandmother. Maggie, of course, and Cam and Bonnie. The word would spread, and there'd be time enough for stories later on.

Heading home, she walked across this liquid sky, leaving footprints in the perfect arc of sun that bordered her beach, that trimmed her sea.

ACKNOWLEDGEMENTS

With love and thanks, I am grateful to my gifted fellow writers Ann Putnam, Beth Kalikoff, and Courtney Putnam, who shepherded my many drafts over these years; to my sister Bobbi St. Lazare, who sends me magic; to my daughter Carin Conner, a light unto herself; to my son Marc Conner, who carries the Irish love of language, my daughter-in-law Barbara Reyes-Conner, and my grandsons Matthew, Noah, and Isaac—the five bright waters of my life; and to Christopher Putnam, who brought this book, at last, into the light. And finally I thank my husband, Terry, for our shared sense of family and love across beaches near and far.

My appreciation also goes to Pat Mallinson, copyeditor extraordinaire, and to the Manhattan Beach Historical Society.

ABOUT THE AUTHOR

Beverly Conner's work has appeared in the collections *Private Voices, Public Lives: Women Writing on the Literary Life; Colors of a Different Horse;* and *Nine by Three: Stories.* She has published short fiction in *Puget Soundings* and was awarded two fellowships at the Hedgebrook Writers Colony. Currently she is at work on her second novel. She teaches creative writing, rhetoric, and literature at the University of Puget Sound.

Made in the USA
San Bernardino, CA
27 March 2014